Cover Story

Cover Story

Gerry Boyle

BERKLEY PRIME CRIME, NEW YORK

COVER STORY

A Berkley Prime Crime Book
Published by the Berkley Publishing Group,
a division of Penguin Putnam Inc.,
375 Hudson Street
New York, New York 10014

The Penguin Putnam Inc. World Wide Web site address is
http://www.penguinputnam.com

First edition: January 2000

Library of Congress Cataloging-in-Publication Data

Boyle, Gerry, 1956–
Cover story / by Gerry Boyle.
p.   cm.
ISBN 0-425-16893-X
I. Title.
PS3552.0925C68   2000
813'.54—dc21   99-27295
CIP

Printed in the United States of America

10   9   8   7   6   5   4   3   2   1

For Vic

Acknowledgments

Cover Story could not have been written without the generous assistance of Jeanne Boyle, a truly intrepid city planner; and of Joy and Willie Rodriguez, who graciously showed me their piece of Brooklyn. Very special thanks go to my literary agent, Helen Brann, who provided steadfast support and invaluable guidance.

There is no odor so bad as that which arises from goodness tainted. It is human, it is divine, carrion.

—Henry David Thoreau

New York City, September 1968

It was the year he was ten, a new boy in a new school who had taken to long walks home, enjoying the solitude after a long day with his blue-blazered tormenters.

That September afternoon, he poked along. Into the park, out of the park, found an umbrella in a trash can and pretended a stiletto popped out of the end. He was still carrying the umbrella, twirling it like Fred Astaire, when he decided to continue past his street and visit his father at work.

It was five more blocks uptown, then up the steps, through the lobby and past the Tyrannosaurus rex. *As always, he flitted through the museum like a bird through a familiar thicket, skipping up the marble stairs, darting around corners, giving a brief wave when his father's colleagues passed.*

But on this day there was something odd about the place. An emptiness, an ominous echo to his footsteps. A gray-haired woman he'd seen many times before turned as he hurried past. She didn't say hi, didn't call his name, just looked at him like she felt sorry for him. Had his father told her about the big kids at the new school?

He wondered as he trotted down the last long corridor.

Why would his father tell her? Had he told the whole place that his son was being picked on? The boy frowned at the thought, and then he rounded the corner and there was another woman, the younger one who worked with his father on the beetles and looked sort of like one with her big nose.

She walked toward him, with that same weird expression, and he stopped and she touched his shoulder and looked at him like he was sick. And he said, "What?" but before she could answer, Butch came from behind her and put an arm around his shoulder and hurried him away, back down the corridor the way he had come.

Butch was his museum friend, two years older, a freckle-faced public-school kid who was allowed to wear dungarees with the knees ripped out. It had always been just the two of them, waiting for their fathers, the beetle man and the security guard. And Butch always led the way into some sort of adventure, filching food from the cafeteria, shadowing pretty girls through the darkened exhibits.

Jack was Tom; Butch was Huck.

But this day Butch was different, too. Serious. Intent. Leading Jack down the hall, his broken umbrella no longer twirling, until they turned in to an alcove behind a marble bust of some long-dead explorer. And Butch looked down at Jack, keeping one hand on the younger boy's shoulder.

"They're gonna try to keep you in the dark, Jackie," he said. " 'Cause that's what grownups do. That's what they did to me with my ma. They treat you like you're an idiot."

"What?" Jack said. "What's the matter?"

"It's your dad, Jackie. He had a heart attack. A real bad one. They took him to the hospital. They think he might make it, but he might not."

"My dad?" Jack whispered, his own heart nearly stopping.

His dad could die? No, he couldn't. He mustn't. No, they couldn't let him.

"No," he said.

His eyes welled with tears. His lower lip started to tremble. His legs began to buckle, and he felt like he was going to be sick. He let go of the umbrella and it clattered on the floor.

Butch, who had lost his mother at seven, put both hands on Jack's shoulders.

"Yeah, it's tough, Jackie," he said. *"But that just means you're gonna have to be tougher. This is just one of those things that happens, you know? You can't give up. You just suck it in and keep going. You got that? I'll help you out, buddy. I'll be there for you. Now let's go."*

So they headed for the hospital, two boys on the subway. And when they got to the waiting room, they found Jack's mother. The floor around her chair was littered with tissues, like petals fallen from a flowering tree. She sat on one side of Jack and Butch sat on the other. Butch offered M&Ms. Jack's mother offered Kleenex. But Jack didn't need the tissues because on the way up in the elevator, Butch had given him more advice: Guys don't cry in public.

So Jack didn't. And his father lived, with a fragile heart the doctors said had been damaged by some jungle parasite contracted during a collecting trip. And when the older boys at school said Jack's father had heartworm from kissing a dog, he fought them until he was exhausted and bloody, the playground gravel ground into his face. When Jack told Butch, he waited outside Jack's school with his public-school friends.

The prep-school kids never bothered Jack again.

"You can always count on me, Jackie," Butch said. *"And I can count on you. Sometimes there'll be things you can do for me. We're gonna stick together, 'cause we're buds. Like brothers. You remember that."*

Many years later, Jack McMorrow did.

One.

It was late afternoon, sultry and sooty with an occasional drip from an air conditioner falling on the sidewalk like the first drop of summer rain.

Times Square was overrun, not by the hustlers and hookers of my time, but by tourists. Hand-holding couples, families with children, all stared into the shop windows, gathered in clumps to eye the menus outside the restaurants. And when they ventured in, they kept their bags from F.A.O. Schwarz and Planet Hollywood close to them. They ordered in loud voices as though the waiters, because their accents were unfamiliar, must be hard of hearing.

I walked with them, from 57th Street down Eighth Avenue. Like kids on a field trip, we gazed up at the walls of the glittering canyon: the streaking lights, flashing Vegas billboards, strobes that blipped from rooftops like muzzle flashes. The colors were brighter, gone digital in my absence. The streets were clean, the people were smiling and laughing, and even the one or two remaining topless places seemed shiny and wholesome as supermarkets.

At the corner of 45th Street, I paused and looked down the street as the crowd swept by. In the old days, the roaring 1980s, I would have been accosted by men selling women, by women selling themselves, by people who presumed that because I was male and apparently alone, I wanted to go to a place where people wore flea collars and beat each other with rubber hoses.

Sometimes I'd gone along.

I'd had coffee with runny-nosed, crack-addicted prostitutes. Interviewed doormen at clandestine backstreet clubs. And those excursions I turned into stories for the *Times*, where I was a metro reporter. I covered some city politics, education for a time, but I was most at home on my forays into the jungle of humanity. I'd drop by the precincts, ride with the detectives, venture into the world where there were two types of people: those who were pursued and those who did the pursuing.

And I'd listen to them all and scribble in my notebook, then hurry back to the newsroom by subway, by cab, but always walking the last blocks through Times Square so that I could feel the city before I sat down to write.

That night I walked the same route, down to 43rd Street, across Eighth Avenue, and halfway down the block. I paused in front of the glass doors, stepped aside as a photographer burst outside and trotted up the street, his camera bag bouncing on his hip. I didn't know him, but I felt the urge to call out: Where are you going? I'll come along.

But then I took a deep breath and pushed inside. The door swung shut behind me and the dissonant symphony of New York was replaced by a marble-walled hush.

One of the security guards looked up. He nudged the other one. They stood with their hands on their holstered hips and looked me up and down.

"Well, look what the cat dragged in," the first guard said.

"Mr. McMorrow himself," the other guard said.

"Holy Toledo," the first guard said. "Where you been, buddy?"

"He went to New Hampshire and joined a commune," the second guard said.

"It was Maine," I said, smiling as I approached the counter. "And I didn't join anything."

"Well," the first guard said, "you always was a little antisocial."

He grinned and we shook hands. His name was Gerard. His partner's name was Dominic. They wore blue uniforms and silver hair.

"How's it going, guys?" I asked.

"Same old, same old," Gerard said. "You know, it's the *Times*."

"Changes course about as fast as an oil tanker," Dominic said.

I remembered Dominic saying that before.

"You guys look good."

"You, too, McMorrow," Dominic said. "All that fresh air and pine needles must agree with you. What's it been? Three, four years?"

"Seven. The first four you didn't notice I was gone."

"Sure we did," Dominic said, coming around the counter. "Then the next three we forgot all about you. So whatcha been doing? You find something to write about up there in Maine?"

"Only when I can't find honest work."

"You coming back?"

"Maybe some stringing in northern New England."

"Gonna interview a few moose or what?" Gerard said.

"I could. Had a cow moose and a calf in my backyard most of the summer."

"Whatcha got?" Dominic said. "A goddamn estate?"

"No, just woods. Where I live, the woods sort of go on forever."

"I'd like that," Gerard said.

"I wouldn't. Gives me the heebie-jeebies," Dominic said. "You seen that movie *Deliverance*, haven't you?"

We grinned.

"At least in the city, they *shoot* you in the backside. No, you can have that country stuff. I like the sound of a goddamn siren every little while, you know? Tells you everything is under control. Up there in the woods, in the goddamn dark, bugs and noises . . .''

Dominic shuddered. Gerard put his pen to the clipboard on the counter.

"Who you seeing, Jack? We gotta fill this in, 'cause technically you're a visitor."

"Technically and otherwise," I said. "Ellen Jones. National desk. Newsroom still on the third floor?"

"Yessir."

I walked past them to the brass-doored elevators and punched the button. The doors slid open.

"Good seeing you, boys," I said. "Keep those psychos at bay."

"Just don't write nothing to get 'em riled up," Dominic said. "Write nice stories."

"What's that?" I called.

And the doors slid shut.

I never had been very good at nice stories, I thought, as the elevator moved upward. Not at the *Times*. Not at any of the other papers where I'd worked over the years. I'd been drawn to the stories that had a serrated edge, stories that tore away pretensions and comfortable misconceptions. My instincts had served me well in the early years when my eagerness to tackle the toughest subjects had separated me from the pack. Most reporters, like me, wanted to move up the ladder as far and fast as possible. I moved faster than most, farther than almost all. I was hired by the *Times* from the *Providence Journal* after I crossed paths with the *Times'* organized-crime specialist. We both were doing stories on an aging mobster and the chaos caused by his infirmity.

Back in New York, the *Times* reporter mentioned me. She said she thought I was pretty good. The *Times* metro editors read my stuff and agreed. They invited me to apply. I did and I was hired. But as they say, be careful what you wish for.

As the elevator moved to the third floor, the clip

whirred yet again. By Jack McMorrow. My byline in the *Times*. Thrilled to be there, pinching myself to make sure it wasn't a dream. Working nights and weekends for the metro desk. And soon finding my stories edited back, their volume turned down. Hints here and there. A metro backfield editor who reminded me that the *Times* wasn't the *Post*. A night metro editor who objected to the "breathless quality" in my prose.

And then my story proposals seemed to get knocked down more and more. The veracity and motives of my sources were questioned more closely. And then the first glimmer of death: a memo from on high in which the editor had underlined phrases in one of my stories that he said betrayed bias. And when I was called before my inquisitors, I was accused of worse. For my future at the *Times*, it was a kiss of death, square on the mouth.

I shook my head at the memory, and then the elevator door opened and I was back.

TWO.

I'd known it was going to be strange. You define yourself by what you do, pretend to have sought what actually was plopped in your lap by circumstances. Was I Jack McMorrow, *Times* metro reporter, or Jack McMorrow, freelancer from the Maine woods? Had I run from my life at the *Times* or had I walked away?

In Prosperity, Maine, I didn't have to ask that question. Or if I did, I could invent an answer. In New York that wouldn't be so easy.

For that reason, when the *Times* had called, I'd first decided to stay home. But Roxanne, my voice of reason, had told me I should give it a try. Tom Wellington, my former editor at the *Boston Globe*, had moved to the *Times* national desk and issued the first invitation. And then, on the phone, Ellen, my former *Times* editor and stalwart supporter, had told me the newsroom atmosphere had changed, that my nemesis had retired to devote himself to writing an editorial-page column and going to parties with rich people.

The coast was clear.

As was the newsroom on a Sunday night.

I walked through, past the blowups of historic *Times*

photos of Times Square full of buggies, into the vast, sprawling newsroom, and once again felt that tingle that came from the thrill of being part of this newspaper.

The newsroom had changed. They'd taken out the false ceilings, replaced the dim lights with industrial-looking fixtures that bathed the place in a white, surgical glow. The room was brighter, the carpets a pale gray, the partitions lowered. But still it was the *Times*, an institution, a newspaper with a tradition of excellence like no other. I took a paper out of the rack on my way in and continued on.

I was Ebenezer Scrooge. This was Christmas Past.

It was a skeleton crew on Sunday nights, and the few reporters and editors on duty were staring intently at their monitors. They didn't look up. They hadn't gotten to the *Times* by engaging in newsroom banter.

I recognized a few. A photo editor called the Bird Man because his passion was bird watching in Central Park. A national backfield editor named Stanley, a pedigreed, cardigan-garbed Upper West Sider. A reporter from Biz Day named Nadine, who walked by me, then stopped and turned.

"Hello, Jack McMorrow," she said. "How nice to see you. How have you been?"

Nadine was carefully groomed, big-boned and attractive with prematurely gray hair and soft, fine skin. She was married to the sort of industry giant she wrote about. I remembered her once telling me her $70,000 *Times* salary was travel money.

"Hello, Nadine," I said. "I've been fine. How are you?"

"Well," she said. "Are you back?"

"In a manner of speaking. Freelancing."

"Didn't you go to live in Maine?"

"That's right. I still live there."

"How nice," Nadine said, twiddling the gold chain around her neck. "We had the boat in Northeast Harbor for a month last summer. Had friends over from France. It was positively gorgeous sailing. Do you sail?"

"No," I said. "Mostly I cut wood."

Nadine laughed, then realized I was serious. She looked vaguely alarmed.

We parted with the usual phony niceties, and I moved on. From the next cluster of cubicles a head rose like a target in a carnival game.

"McMorrow!" D. Robert Sanders exclaimed.

"D. Robert," I said.

I stopped. He came around, a reporter's notebook in his hand. He switched it to his left, shook mine with his right. He gazed into my eyes with his customary look. Intense. Humorless. Furiously ambitious. My rival from our first days at the *Times* hadn't changed.

He dropped my hand, stuck his in his pocket. Enough touchy-feely.

"What, pray tell, has brought you in from the cold?"

I told him about the stringer job.

"Well, great," he said, relieved that I would still be out to pasture. "I'll be looking forward to more of that compelling McMorrow prose. Guy we had up there the last couple of years wrote like a lost tourist."

He attempted a smile, but came up short. D. Robert's smiles were reserved for professional purposes. Relaxing a reluctant source. Easing his way into a gathering closed to the press. Back in the newsroom, he was all business, a passable writer but a tireless reporter, unfailingly accurate. The joke in the newsroom had been that before D. Robert made love with his dour currency-trader wife, he asked if she would spell her name for the record.

"What do you think of the city?" Sanders asked.

"Sanitized," I said. "But I suppose it's an improvement if you live here."

"Comes at a price. We have to see Johnny Fiore on the news every night. His honor the mayor takes credit for the sun coming up."

"I don't know. He must be doing something right."

Sanders looked at me.

"Well, that's high praise, McMorrow. Coming from you. I mean, after what happened."

I felt the barb in the comment, the pick at my past. And

then a tremor of misgiving about coming here at all. A pull toward the elevator and the exit. But it passed and I set off deeper into the newsroom, wondering just where I'd crossed it.

The point of no return.

She'd jettisoned her black dancer's bun and was blonde now, and the first sight of her, swiveling toward me in her chair, was strange, almost unnerving.

"I turned fifty," Ellen Jones said, giving me a hug. "What can I say?"

"I turned forty," I said. "But I couldn't settle on a color."

"You're getting a little gray, McMorrow."

"I worry too much."

"In Maine?"

"You'd be surprised," I said.

"And you got muscles, McMorrow," she said.

I glanced down at my forearms, rerolled my sleeves.

"It's all those lobster traps I've been hauling."

"Really?"

"Just kidding. I live twenty miles from the coast."

"What about the scar on your cheekbone there?"

"It's a long story," I said.

"It's very sexy. Very Zorro."

"They throw the scar in when you get your buns lifted."

"With liposuction you get two?"

"And an eye patch," I said.

"We laugh," Ellen said. "It could catch on in New York. The right celeb gets slashed and the rest is fashion history, as they say."

She smiled, brushed at her blonde hair and stretched her legs. She was wearing khakis, a blue Oxford cloth blouse and heeled sandals. It was a New York look I'd forgotten. Ellen's manner—vaguely playful, probingly flirtatious—I remembered well.

"Well, Jack. So is there life after New York? Tom

Wellington tells me you live at the absolute edge of no-where.''

"I don't know. Some of us think it's the center of the universe.''

"Like the *New Yorker* cover of Manhattan?''

"Except the center of our world is the general store.''

"That's it?''

"And farms. And woods. Mostly woods.''

"Does the store have the *Times*?''

It was her instant gauge of civilization.

"Uh-uh.''

"Not even on Sunday? Do you get the *Times*?''

"You can get it in Belfast. That's twenty miles away. Or you can get it in the mail, but it's two or three days late.''

"Ick,'' Ellen said. "Don't you feel, I don't know, iso-lated and primitive?''

I laughed.

"I like it. Last week a bear crossed the road when I was coming home.''

"A wild bear?''

"With two cubs. That's when the sows are dangerous. You don't want to surprise one.''

"Right near your house?''

"A couple of hundred yards away. It was great.''

"Oh, great. Go for a walk and come home mauled.''

"See,'' I said, grinning, "just like New York.''

"I'll take my chances in Manhattan, thank you very much. Now, McMorrow, how long are you staying? Are you here alone?''

Ellen Jones. Getting right to the nitty-gritty.

"I'd planned to come down with a friend.''

"A friend?'' she said.

"Yes, a good friend.''

"A close friend?''

I smiled. "Yes, Ellen. A very close friend.''

"What's her name?''

"Roxanne. But she had an emergency. She works for the state in Maine. Child Protective, they call it up there.''

"And she had to go protect a child?"

"Yeah. I came anyway."

"Interesting. Any kids of your own, McMorrow?"

"No," I said.

"Longtime friend?"

"Years. Several years."

"Well, oh, my goodness," Ellen said, leaning back in her chair. "He's finally been landed. Speaking of which, guess who I saw just last week."

"I don't know. Who?"

"Christina."

"Really."

"She had a show. Right around the corner from me, actually. Very nice blurbs. It looks like she might actually break out."

"Good for her," I said.

Ellen swung her long legs around and looked at me slyly.

"I told her you were coming to town."

She waited for my reaction. I tried not to show any, but her grin meant I'd let something slip through.

"She said she'd love to hear from you. She looks gorgeous, I might add. Even modest success becomes her. Of course, Christina looked smashing when she was a struggling artist."

I wound back the years and agreed.

"We had a nice chat. Talked about what rats men are."

She smiled.

"Thanks," I said.

"We didn't mean you, McMorrow. Well, I didn't, anyway. We talked about other men. Christina was with this fellow named Christophe. Several years."

"Lived together?"

"That was an issue. He didn't like the 'willywacks' of Brooklyn."

"What happened to SoHo?"

"Christina finally got bounced. Did you know we have Vuitton on Greene Street now? It's turning very high-end.

Real estate is through the roof. So Christina went to Dumbo.''

It took me a moment.

"Down under the Manhattan Bridge?''

"Still frontier artsy. Gave Christophe the absolute willies.''

"So he left?''

"He directs commercials. He went to do something on location in Saint Kitts and pulled a Gauguin.''

"What, a native woman?''

"Well, actually she's Australian.''

"So he didn't come back?''

"Nope. Took his son, for whom Christina had been attempting to be some sort of mother figure.''

"How old?''

"Fifteen. Sixteen. I guess he was hell on wheels.''

"And Christina as his surrogate mom? Good luck to him.''

"She was quite good at it, in an odd way,'' Ellen said, giving me the smile again. "Sit down, McMorrow, now that I know you're a married man and it's safe and proper.''

"You still with . . .''

"Robert?'' Ellen looked at me and smirked thinly.

"No,'' she said.

I didn't press and Ellen didn't offer. There was an awkward moment and then she gathered herself together and switched gears, from flirtation to business. She talked about the job, that it wasn't full-time, that it would be a mix of assignments and my own enterprise. The money was good but it was sporadic.

"A perfect match,'' I said.

"Now Jack, you haven't turned into a hermit on me, have you?''

"Hell, no. I get out every day. Shoot at passing airliners.''

"Glad to hear it. Tom said you did some good work for the *Globe*, Jack. I saw a few of your pieces. I wasn't surprised. You did good reporting for us, too.''

"That's one school of thought."

"Some of us here thought you got a bit of a raw deal back then."

And there it was. My retreat, revived and well.

I looked up at the TV on the stanchion over the national desk sign. CNN was on but the sound was off. A correspondent was reporting amid generic rubble. I often thought they had just one tape.

"Well, some of it was deserved," I said.

"But not all."

"No, not all."

"If you'd stayed, you probably could have ridden it out."

I shrugged.

"I know. Not your style, McMorrow, letting things ride. Or keeping your mouth shut."

I looked at her.

"I suppose."

"What was it you called him? A sycophant to celebrities? A Ken doll of a journalist? If I'd been suicidal, I would have applauded."

She leaned toward me. "He is a pompous ass."

I shifted in my chair, tried to ward off memories of that tirade.

"I don't remember any of that fondly," I said.

"Of course you don't, McMorrow. And now you've gone to Maine to forget it all."

I looked at her and almost winced.

"Sorry," she said. "That was just always my theory."

Ellen stood up. She said she had to prepare for the 5 o'clock meeting. She looked at the national budget on the computer screen.

"Clinton trying to show he no longer has a libido and the White House is now a monastery. A fourteen-year-old boy who killed his parents and two sisters in Idaho. The dad was trying to get the boy into counseling the day before it happened."

"Sad."

"Yes. The world is going to hell, as usual. Let's see. And also for outside, a piece on migrant workers and how their housing situation is getting worse. Very strong art."

She handed me a color printout. A man was asleep in his car. His cowboy hat was on the rear shelf.

"Nice," I said.

Ellen turned to me. "So, McMorrow. Still have the fire?"

I thought it over. "Yeah, I do."

"We'll be looking for news features. Stories on big news events. But also anything you unearth that's small but sublime."

I nodded. Got up from my chair and rolled it over to its place at the next desk. Ellen got up, too, uncoiling herself in her languid dancer's way and taking my hand briefly in hers.

"So McMorrow," Ellen said, "a pleasure to make your reacquaintance. How 'bout lunch tomorrow?"

"It would have to be breakfast. I'm leaving early."

"That might work. I'll call."

"The Meridien."

"Fine. And now that we've got you back at the *Times*, maybe we'll get you back to New York."

I shook my head.

"I don't think so. I like it where I am."

Ellen smiled knowingly.

"I don't know. I had a friend tell me once that New York is like malaria. Once you catch the bug, it never quite goes away."

She raised an eyebrow.

"And you did have the bug, McMorrow."

Ellen turned back to her desk and picked up a legal pad and a printout of a story list. I could see headings for Los Angeles and Detroit. She whirled back to me, stood close.

"You know what you told me once, McMorrow? You told me you wanted to be the Ernie Pyle of New York

City, telling the story of the war through the guys on the battlefield.''

I didn't remember that, but it was the eighties. How many hours had I wasted waxing on in some smoky saloon?

"How presumptuous," I said.

I said goodbye and turned toward the aisle that led between the cubicles to the elevators. I had gone just a few feet when I felt Ellen touch my arm.

"Jack, I do have to run," she said. "But I was wondering, what ever happened to that detective."

I hesitated before I answered. Ellen's eyes were alive, her mind working something over, spinning as it considered all the angles. Ellen Jones wasn't "just wondering" anything.

"Butch Casey? Nothing, really," I said. "He went out on stress disability."

"So you've stayed in touch?"

There was an implication in her voice.

"Not constantly," I said. "But, yeah. I mean, we've known each other for so long. He sent me a postcard a few weeks ago. Said he had a story for me."

"What about?"

"I don't know. He just said it could be big, like they always do. But it's probably nothing. I'm meeting him for a drink tonight."

"Have you considered a follow?"

I stopped and looked at her. The elevators were to the left, the executive wall to the right.

"A follow?" I said.

"I wouldn't ask you to write it, obviously."

"No."

"And it would be a metro story, of course. So technically I couldn't even assign it. But is there an anniversary or anything?"

"His wife's murder was ten years ago last week."

"So that's the hook. And don't you think there's a story

there? The long-term consequences of a random street crime. It ended a detective's career, and—''

Ellen paused.

''And mine?'' I said.

I smiled.

''I wasn't going to say that.''

''But you were thinking it.''

''Yes,'' Ellen said. ''I was.''

Three.

I replayed it in snippets all the way back to the hotel, where I opened a bottle of ale and the drapes and, sitting in the armchair, stared out the window. I got up. Wandered about the room. Tried Roxanne on the phone but got no answer.

Sat down and lived it all again.

Butch's wife, Leslie, an English-born emergency-room nurse, killed on the street outside Columbia-Presbyterian. Not just killed, but shot point-blank in the face by a guy who wanted her car. It was a big gun; it was gruesome and terribly sad.

So there was numbing grief for Butch, vain sympathy from me. And all the while, a relentless hunt for the piece of shit who killed a cop's wife.

I wrote the stories. The murder. The pursuit. The arrest.

The guy's name was Muriqi, but that was an alias and his real name turned out to be Ortiz. He was a small-time thug who, by inadvertently targeting the wife of a New York homicide detective, had made the leap to notorious criminal.

I reported his arrest in the *Times*. And I wrote the story when the case was dropped, when Fiore, then Manhattan district attorney, said a witness had been coached by the cops, by Butch himself.

Sitting there in the hotel room, I sipped the ale and shook my head.

I still could picture her: Annie Scott, a tiny, stoop-shouldered woman in her fifties who lived with her brother in East Tremont in the Bronx. Worked in dietary at the hospital and saw Muriqi when her brother pulled out of the hospital entrance after picking her up that night. Afraid, she didn't call until a month later. She said she could place the suspect at the crime scene. She was a miracle, a witness sent by God. But then she backed out, rattled by the cops, caving in to a brother who didn't want her to get involved. But leaving the station house, Annie Scott and her brother ran into Butch.

He bought them coffee. They talked about Leslie. After a half-hour, Annie Scott had changed her mind. They had Muriqi nailed, and they went up to the Bronx and picked him up and made sure TV got a good long look at his face, that the newspapers had printouts of his police record. And then Fiore, Manhattan DA, found out that Butch had made contact with the key witness. Annie Scott was out; Muriqi, too. Butch soon followed.

And when I still pursued it—repeatedly contacting Annie Scott, trying to convince her to talk—I was gone, too.

Fiore got me yanked from the story for not divulging my longtime friendship, since childhood, with Detective Casey. I still could remember my dressing down, staring into the editor's angry red face and saying, "Yeah, we grew up together. Our fathers knew each other at the Museum of Natural History. But show me bias in my stories, show me where the reporting isn't balanced. Show me one word. . . ."

I shook myself loose. Finished the last swallow of ale and, hoisting myself from the chair, went to the bathroom. When I came back, I sat down heavily on the edge of the king-sized bed.

It had been turned down and a mint had been left by my pillow and by the pillow that would have been Roxanne's. I ate both of them, then got up and opened another bottle of India pale ale, one of two I'd brought in my bag. I took a swallow, then went to the eighth-floor window and took in the view of the building next door. Its brick wall was pocked with office windows behind which people moved like ants in an ant farm. I watched them for a minute, then turned back to the phone.

It was quarter to nine and I'd called Roxanne three times, leaving messages at her office in Portland and at her condo, across the harbor. I'd considered calling the house in Prosperity but couldn't think of any reason why she would drive way up there, not with work to do, not alone.

Roxanne probably was working, trying to find placements for—what had it been? A boy and two girls? Two boys and a girl? I couldn't remember, but I did know the emergency-room people had found scars and scabs, broken and healed bones. Roxanne had stepped in.

Her phone had rung while we were packing late Saturday night. With the shrill ring went our plan for a couple of days in Manhattan, our first trip to the city together. There was a worker on call, but these kids were close to Roxanne. She'd go to the hospital. She'd go find a judge to sign a petition to take the children.

"I'm sorry, Jack," she'd said, grabbing her briefcase, her suitcase still on the bed.

"I'm sorry, too," I'd said.

But I hadn't been, not entirely.

Like someone reluctant to bring a date to a family reunion, I hadn't relished the idea of bringing Roxanne on a tour of my old haunts. I'd left the old Jack McMorrow behind. We'd lost touch. He didn't call. I didn't write. We didn't hash over old times.

Hey, what was the name of that place on Seventh Avenue? You were there with that blonde who looked like Debbie

Harry. She worked for some magazine. Yeah, right.
Vogue. *Little Miss Name Dropper. Telling us she'd just been at a party with Ron Wood. You don't remember? Well, I do. You went home with her and we didn't see you for a week.*

No, part of me wanted to keep that life in the past. McMorrow the highflier. McMorrow the *Times* reporter who drummed himself out before others got the chance. I didn't talk about it. Roxanne didn't ask.

Some things you carried alone.

I looked at the phone. Turned and looked out at the office workers, each framed like a painting. I stood and watched and drank the ale, leaning forward to look down. A guy came to one of the windows and looked up. The phone rang and I grabbed it.

"Hello."

"Jack."

"Hey there, darlin'."

"I got your message. I just got home."

"Long day?"

"On top of a long night. I was at the foster home. The oldest one wouldn't let go of me."

"She liked you."

"She didn't have much to compare me with."

"She would've liked you anyway."

"I don't know about that," Roxanne said.

"I do."

"You like me?"

"I love you."

"Well, thanks. I love you, too."

She sounded a bit startled, a little perplexed.

"Jack, you okay?"

"Yeah," I said.

"How is everything? How's the room?"

"Very nice. You'd love it. I think it's taupe but I'm not sure."

"Taupe is sort of a dull gray with a tinge of yellow."

"It's not taupe. It's beige with a tinge of purple."

"That's mauve."

"Okay. It's mauve. But very soft and soothing. It would have been—"

"Fun," Roxanne said.

"Sorry," I said.

"Oh, well. Did you get to the *Times*?"

"Oh, yeah."

"How was that?"

"Fine."

"Fine?"

"Well, a little strange," I said. "Like going back to your high school or something."

"Did you see anybody you knew?"

I told her about Ellen and D. Robert and Nadine.

"Were they glad to see you?"

"Sure. I mean, they weren't jumping up and down or anything. But it was all very cordial. I guess you'd call it cordial."

I took a swallow of ale. Then another.

"Jack, what's the matter?"

"Nothing, Rox. I'm fine."

"You sound a little sad or something."

"I miss you."

"I miss you, too. But it's only been a day."

"It's not that. It's just different. Being back here."

"You'd rather I were with you?"

"Of course."

"Well, next time," Roxanne said. "It couldn't be helped."

"I know," I said.

I paused again.

"What is it, Jack?"

I sat down on the bed. The people across the way still were at their desks. They worked late in New York. It was a rat race and the other rats were always nipping at your tail.

"Jack, you there?"

"Yeah."

"What are you going to do now? I don't want you to

sit around the hotel just because I'm not there.''

I told her my plan for the evening. A drink for old times' sake with Butch Casey.

"The police detective?"

"He called a couple of weeks ago. Did I tell you that?"

"No."

She paused.

"But that will be nice. Catching up with your old friend."

My oldest, I thought. From when we were kids and his father was doing museum security and mine was doing beetles. His dad had a red nose. This big jolly retired cop who always smelled like beer.

I sipped my ale, turned the bottle in my hands, the phone propped against my ear. From Roxanne's end, I heard a cork pop.

"Well, enjoy yourself."

"I will," I said, but I was thinking of Ellen, how quick she was to bring the Casey thing back up.

"You all right, Jack?" Roxanne said.

"Fine. Just a little tired. I'll have a quick beer and get back here and get some sleep. See you tomorrow night."

"You sound like you don't want to see him. Is he okay? I mean with his wife and all."

"As okay as you could be if that had happened to your wife."

The woman he loved, shot in the face. A hole in the back of her head the size of a fist. How okay could he ever be?

"It's horrible," Roxanne said.

"Very sad. She was really nice and he just loved her. For a cop, he was kind of shy. At least around women. You know how some cops use their job to get to women? He used the job to hide from them, in a way. Then he finally connects with someone and bang—she's gone."

Roxanne didn't say anything.

"And then the guy gets off," I said. "So Butch didn't have even that much solace."

"And that was the end of it?"

"Except for Butch's long slide."

"Well, maybe seeing you will be a help."

"Maybe."

"So drive safely tomorrow."

"You drive safely down here, you get rear-ended."

"Well, just do whatever it takes to come back to me, safe and sound."

"I will. I always do, don't I?"

Roxanne didn't answer.

"Most of the time?" I said.

June 1986

It was ten-thirty and still no Jack. Butch and Leslie waited, at this little restaurant on East Thirty-eighth, a nondescript sort of place that Butch had found the week before while hunting down a witness.

"So I order the roast chicken," Butch was saying, "and I say, 'But don't do anything to it. Nothing weird.' Everybody's gotta be more bizarre than the next guy. You order chicken and it comes garnished with eye of newt. Just cook the chicken, you know what I'm saying? There's a reason why you're the first guy to think of stuffing chicken with weasel brains. It's 'cause it isn't edible, pal. Some things humans just aren't meant to eat."

"So how was it?" Leslie asked.

"What?"

"The chicken."

"Very good. It was just chicken. They give you some canned cranberry sauce, you want to get garnishy."

Leslie looked at the menu doubtfully.

"Oh, and they have Spaghetti-Os," she said.

"Really? Haven't had those in years. Maybe I'll—"

"Butch," Leslie interrupted, "I was joking."

"Oh. Got my hopes up. Last time I had Spaghetti-O's I was probably twelve. Me and Jack coulda had 'em for old times' sake."

He looked at his watch.

"Guy's always late," Butch said. "I add at least a half-hour to everything. Probably writing on deadline. You been reading his stuff?"

"I've been looking for his name. I saw the one about that man who was killed on the subway. The man who played the saxophone and they killed him for the money in his saxophone case."

"We got a lead on that one," Butch said. "Commissioner wants a collar. Mayor leans on him. He leans on the commander. Down the line it goes."

"It was a good story. I liked the way he went to the man's hometown in—"

"Orange County."

"And talked to his music teacher in grade school and all. It was quite well done."

"Oh, yeah," Butch said. "Jack always goes the extra mile."

"You helped him with that one?"

"Just gave him a few names. He does his own legwork."

"The boyhood chums," Leslie said.

She smiled.

"You're proud of him, aren't you?"

"Proud? Sure. I guess I'm pretty proud of Jackie. But mostly I'm proud of you."

"You're proud of me? What are you proud about?"

Butch leaned toward her, his wineglass in his hand.

"I'm proud about how good-looking you are. I mean, you are hot. And you're smart. And you're tough."

"Thanks, I think."

"You're the best."

"There's lots of good nurses."

"That's not what I meant."

He leaned over and whispered something and Leslie blushed.

"God, I've fallen in with a sex maniac," she said. "Do you think of anything else?"

"No. You want me to?"

"No," Leslie said. At that moment, Jack McMorrow walked in.

Butch got up and beamed. His jacket was open and his gun showed and people looked. Leslie started to stand but Jack, taking her hand, told her to sit. Still standing, Butch poured wine into Jack's glass.

"Drink up, Jackie," he said. "Good stuff. You can tell by the fancy label. Last time Jack had wine, it was on a bench in the park and he had to share it with three other guys. Hey, you're lucky we're not half in the bag here, waiting for you. I told Leslie you were always late."

"Late?" McMorrow said. "Forty-five minutes? I'm early."

"Be late for his own autopsy," Butch said.

"Butch. Yuck," Leslie said, but she smiled and McMorrow saw that it was a broad, easy smile, the kind backed with self-assurance.

She was tall, even sitting, with short, dark hair, pale skin and rosy cheeks. She wasn't beautiful, perhaps not even pretty. But there was something warm and welcoming about her, something solid and stable.

Jack watched and listened that night, over seafood and more wine, and saw Butch more happy, more relaxed than he could remember him. The homicide cop watched every move his new love made. He smiled when she smiled, leaned toward her to hang on every word she uttered, in an accent that was almost Irish but really was Liverpool.

They told war stories, the three of them veterans of the front lines. The saxophone player. The kids Butch was hunting for his murder. A cocaine-addicted prostitute Leslie had treated that morning. The woman had overdosed, Leslie said. And she was pregnant.

"She really was quite nice," Leslie said. "But one misstep leads to another. They're all small steps but they take you so far off track. And then you come in contact with people like us."

Jack smiled. He did like Leslie Moore.

And they talked about England and the English sense of order versus the American need for change and chaos.

Butch said he'd never been east of Montauk, and now he and Leslie were planning a trip to England, Scotland and Wales.

"We're going Wales watching," he said, and Leslie rolled her eyes.

And then she excused herself to go to the ladies' room. Butch watched her sturdy stride with an almost dreamy pride. He turned to his old friend.

"Isn't she something?"

Jack was seeing a woman named Christina who was much more beautiful and much more glamorous than Leslie. But he smiled and nodded.

"Yeah, Butch. She is. I like her."

"I love her."

He said it without embarrassment, this rough, tough homicide cop.

"You might think that's goofy."

Over ten years, he could think of Butch with only two other women. Sputtering relationships, all over in a matter of weeks. They ended with Butch fleeing back to his job, his homicide haven.

"I don't think it's goofy at all," Jack said.

"I mean, she's smart. She's tough. She's beautiful."

McMorrow smiled. It was in the eye of the beholder.

"She's English. Lived in Australia. Before Columbia-Presbyterian she was in some Peace Corps kind of thing in West Africa or some goddamn place, treating the native kids for dysentery and whatever the hell else they get over there. She's just a good person. And she goes for me."

The words trailed off and Butch shook his head.

"That's why, when I don't have this stupid smile on my face, I'm kinda worried," he said. "It's the Irish in me. When things are going good, that's when you start looking over your shoulder. I go around all the time knocking on wood."

He lifted the tablecloth and knocked once more.

Four.

The bar was the Bull and Thistle, one of those faux Irish places around Times Square.

I eased my way along the aisle between the bar and the tables, squeezing by a knot of young white guys who were crowding to see the television. When I popped out on the other side of the scrum, Butch Casey looked up from a table along the wall and grinned.

I smiled as I walked toward him, and he stood and gripped my hand, patted me on the upper arm.

"Jackie," Butch said, "you're looking great."

"You, too, Butch," I said.

"Yeah, right." Butch started looking over my shoulder for the waitress. I turned as he caught her eye and held up two fingers.

"No, Butch. That's okay. I'll just—"

"No, it's on me, Jack. A coupla Jamesons for old times' sake. Just like the old days, huh? After this, we'll go up to the museum and prowl the halls. Remember that time we grabbed all those lobsters, let 'em loose in the ladies' room? I was thinking about that the other day. Jeez, Jackie, it's good to see you."

He gave my arm another tap and we sat, and he picked up his nearly empty glass. I looked at him.

His reddish hair was streaked with gray. His forehead was flecked with brown spots. His taffy-pull features— ears that stuck out, a hook nose with a bump—had been exaggerated by age. But his arms were long and his hands were big and he still had a boyish look to him, like somebody's big brother. He reached out and squeezed my arm again and said, "Hey, you been working out, you pencil-neck reporter."

And then the waitress came and banged two whiskeys on the table, like in a western saloon except for the gold ring through her left eyebrow. Butch picked up the fresh drink, raised it in a toast.

"To Jack and Butch," he said. "Back on their turf in Midtown."

He took a small sip, just a touch.

"I gotta be careful now," he said. "I got into it kinda heavy, after Leslie . . . after she died."

He looked away for a moment, then back at me.

"Stuff can get hold of you, you know? Now I try to just have one or two, like my old man did. He liked his beer but he wasn't a drunk. Funny, how you're a grown man, you still look to your dad as some sort of model. Eighty-five, in a rocking chair, and still saying, 'What would dad have done?' "

He shook his head. I smiled. A minute into the conversation and Butch already was pondering some twist of human nature.

It was our common ground, all those years. I listened to people and wrote their stories. Butch studied their aberrations and put them in jail. We compared notes, swapped tales. Butch envied my ability to put life into words; I envied his opportunity to see so much firsthand. Neither of us lost our sense of wonder at what people did and why.

I sipped the whiskey and grimaced.

"Quit drinking?" Butch asked.

"I tend to just have a beer with dinner now, leave it at

that. There's this small brewery up in Maine and their India pale ale is pretty good.''

"Yeah, they got 'em all over the place now, these little places,'' Butch said. "I remember when you either had a Bud or a Miller. Sometimes we had a few of each, remember?"

I nodded. He glanced toward the bar. The bartender was a thin man, with graying hair pulled back in a ponytail. He looked at Butch and their eyes met, then the man turned away.

"Don't tell me. You arrested him at some point."

Butch looked at me, startled.

"Who? Oh, him, naah. But I do see them sometimes, even in New York. Like being a teacher, you know what I'm saying? Everywhere you go, you see your old students. The other day, I get in a cab. The driver's this guy I got for shooting this other guy after he found the guy in bed with his wife. Just emptied the gun into the son of a bitch. Guy lived for, like, three days with all these holes in him. But they were small holes. They thought he might make it. Anyway, there he is—the shooter, I mean. Musta done twelve out of twenty. He's out and he's driving the cab. I say, 'Hey, how's it going?' He says, 'Pretty good. How 'bout you?' ''

"Like soldiers meeting the enemy after the war."

"Right. But hey, you don't want to hear that, buddy. Tell me, Jackie, how you been?"

"Good. Great. But how are you doing? Really."

Butch paused, turned his glass around in his hand. He looked impaled by the question, but then he shook loose.

"Good. I mean, fine. Hey, I'm getting paid to sit on my duff now. And living back in the city, there's lots to do. Things to see."

"Yeah?"

"I'm doing all the things I never did in New York when I was on the job. Christ, first ten years I never went to a show or a concert. I don't think I'd been to a museum since we were kids. I mean, Leslie dragged me a few places, but being a cop, you get so you don't know anybody else. Just cops and bad guys. And snitches, of course.''

He stared into his drink, then looked up again.

''Get this. I've been to a poetry reading, for Christ's sake.''

''You're kidding.''

''No, really. I'm a man of letters. I read a lot. I'm doing Melville right now.''

I smiled.

''Hey, you laugh. But I didn't get to do all this stuff in some fancy-pants college like you, Jackie. I was taking 'Modes of Death' while you were reading goddamn Walter Whitman. So I'm catching up.''

''Still working on your book?''

Butch looked away.

''Aaah, I guess it's on hold. Kinda lost momentum.''

''I liked the idea, Butch. All the people you arrested in twenty years.''

''Except I got as far as year two.''

''It was a good title. *Mugshots: A Memoir.*''

''I thought so, too. I mean, this wasn't gonna be just war stories. It was gonna be a study. Try to come up with some conclusions, you know? I mean, if it was just about locking up bad guys, so what? I want it to be more than that.''

''I'd buy it,'' I said.

''Yeah, well. Maybe one of these days.''

His smile was gone. His eyes were far away. And then he came back.

''So, I got my routine. There's a place down the street from me, I pop down for my drink. Lady runs the place, Linda, is a friend of mine.''

My eyebrows twitched.

''Nothing like that. She's gay. Lesbian. Whatever you want to call it. I go in the place one day and it's empty and I sit at the bar. In an hour it's me and twenty-five women.''

He snorted.

''Linda still tells that story. Hey, but she's a helluva

good kid. We give it to each other, going back and forth, you know? She cracked up when I told her my name was Butch. Calls me her token Irish cop.''

"So you're doing okay.''

"Oh, yeah. Fine. Now, what are you gonna do? Cover the boonies for the *Times*?''

"Stringer, they call it. Paid by the story.''

"You still live in—''

"Prosperity.''

"Oh, yeah.''

"What the hell they call it that for, anyway?''

"I don't know,'' I said. "Maybe it was wishful thinking.''

"Like Greenland,'' Butch said.

"Right. Prosperity is right alongside towns named Freedom and Liberty.''

"Jeez. Sounds like some kind of right-wing theme park. You got cans of peas buried in the backyard? Ammo stockpiled?''

I smiled.

"No, but we're well-armed.''

"Just like here.''

"But where I live they tend to shoot deer, not people.''

"Well, that's 'cause you got more deer than people. If we had deer in New York, we'd shoot 'em, too, especially if they were carrying money.''

He caught himself and seemed to wince inwardly. I looked away this time. Mercifully, the waitress came by.

"Oh, I guess we could have two more,'' Butch said, looking up at her. "For old times' sake.''

"Is this a reunion?'' the waitress said.

"Yeah. This is my old friend Jack McMorrow. Reporter for the *New York Times*, so watch what you say.''

"Hi, there,'' the waitress said, and smiled and left.

"You think she dyes her hair blonde or her eyebrows black?'' Butch said.

He grinned again, but it seemed forced.

"So Jackie, I've been wanting to come visit you up there. One time I even got out the map. But you know, you draw a line, you're north of Montreal? This was December or something and I said, 'Jesus, Butchie. Why not just go to Siberia for vacation?' "

"Maybe in the summer."

"That would have been nice."

"What do you mean 'would have been?' You still could do it, right?"

"Sure. Some summer."

"Anytime. I'll introduce you to people who've lived on the same road for five generations."

"Hey, in the Bronx, you had five generations in one apartment. You'd arrest three generations the same night. Junior, dad and gramps, all lined up against the wall. Babies crawling around the floor. A kilo on the kitchen table."

I smiled.

"So I gotta meet this buddy of yours, the one with the girl's name," Butch said.

"Clair?"

"Yeah. What'd you say he was? Some goddamn Green Beret type?"

I sipped, put down my glass.

"He was a Force Recon Marine."

"What's he do, live in a tree house with trip wires in the bushes?"

"No, he's got a nice house. Big place with a barn and tractors. He lives with his wife, Mary. We cut wood together. Me and Clair, not Mary."

Butch sipped and swallowed. His whiskey was two-thirds gone.

"She musta put up with shit, huh? Married to some goddamn commando. Sitting home worrying while he's out crawling around in the jungle. Kind of like—"

He paused, catching himself. His red face darkened as he slipped inside himself, sinking before my eyes.

"Like my wife," Butch said, with a rueful smile. "Except she wasn't sitting around worrying. She was waiting for me and I was late."

He paused and then snapped back with a smile.

"Never put your job first, Jackie. Remember that."

"Butch, that's not why she was killed. She was killed because some psycho picked her out. Some animal."

"Picked her because she was alone. And she was alone 'cause I didn't show up. And I didn't show up 'cause—. Did I ever tell you about that, Jackie?"

I shook my head slowly. He gave a brief, unfunny laugh and shook his head, too.

"Yeah, well. Maybe a few more drinks. You know, I wanted to try to make sense of it, all this killing. I don't want to think it's just—"

"Chaos?"

"Yeah. I mean what's wrong with these people, anyway? I mean, she gave him the car. So drive away. I mean, you don't get in the car and then shoot the person right there on the curb. For no reason."

I didn't answer.

"And then that bastard Fiore lets the guy walk. We coached the witness. Yeah, right. Didn't have to coach anybody. The lady saw that scuzbag there. She was scared to talk and I told her not to be, that the other cops were good people. End of story."

"Butch."

"And you go to bat for me and that little City Hall prick Dave Conroy gets you practically canned. I'm flushed down the toilet. And now they're talking about Fiore for Senate. Running for president, the son of a bitch. You know what I should have done? I shoulda just taken care of that mutt myself, screw Fiore. No arrest. No trial. Just give me the name. They find Ortiz in the trunk of a car down by the docks someplace. I shoulda just . . ."

His voice trailed off.

"Sorry."

"It's okay," I said, but it wasn't really. It had been a long time. Why was this wound in him still so raw and open?

"Jack, we gotta talk," Butch said, leaning closer.

"I thought we were talking."

"No, I mean really talk. Jack, I've been looking into all of this."

Butch glanced down at his watch. Then looked around the room.

"Let's talk outside."

He stood, flipped a bill onto the table and started for the door. I followed.

Outside, the air was moist and warm and smelled of grease and garlic, smoke and exhaust. We stood on the sidewalk for a moment, and I glanced up the block, where Times Square glowed and crowds flowed. When I looked back, Butch had moved close.

He leaned forward, and in the sidewalk light, his eyes were unblinking, afire, the look of someone obsessed.

Five.

"I'll give you the *Reader's Digest* version," Butch said, his voice low. "You know I still got friends."

"Uh-huh."

"Friends on the job, I mean."

"Right."

"Well, I ran into this guy I used to work with. Young guy. I mean, he was young when I first started working with him. Whatever."

"Whatever," I said.

"We're in the bar at this Mexican place on the Upper East Side. I mean, I like hearing what's going on in the department. So anyway, we get talking and I'm saying, 'Am I the only person in all of goddamn New York who hates Johnny Fiore's guts? I mean, me and the shitbums who are in jail 'cause the mayor knows putting people away is good politics?' And this guy says, 'You'd be surprised, Butchie.' I say, 'Whaddaya mean?' He says, 'You just don't hear about it.' ''

Butch paused.

"Hear about what?" I said.

"Hear about the people who hate his guts. This cop says he was just given a case where some nut calls up

City Hall and starts screaming about the mayor. 'He's a bastard. He'll burn in hell. He killed my brother.' "

"So? This is New York."

"Hey, you'd be surprised, but New Yorkers, they like their mayors. I mean, sometimes they hate 'em but they like hating them. It's like the Mets in the old days. I mean, look at Fiore. He goes around the city with nobody around him. Just him and maybe a uniform cop, but no security. Not like the president or something."

Butch's eyes narrowed knowingly. It gave me an odd feeling.

"So?" I said.

He smiled and leaned away, then back to me.

"So he looks into it. This guy I'm talking to. He looks into this threatening thing."

"Yeah?"

"For about twenty minutes. And then he gets the word, from way up high. Forget it."

"Guy says, 'Why? This is a threat to the mayor. Lemme at least make some calls, stop by, maybe make this mutt piss his pants.' Except it's a lady."

"Who made the threats?"

"Yeah. And they don't want anything said about it. No arrest. No report. No nothing."

"Huh," I said.

"And you know what else?"

"What?"

"I'm not the only one," he said.

"Only one what?"

"Who this guy burned. Listen to this, Jack. There's lots of us. This Johnny-Fiore-we-love-you shit is a scam, Jack. The Hispanics love Johnny Fiore. The blacks love Johnny Fiore. The Jews and the West Side Wasps love Johnny Fiore. The East Side Yuppies love Johnny Fiore. The second coming of Jesus H. Christ."

He paused. I waited.

"Bullshit," Butch said.

"Yeah?"

"The cops. The press. They're all in on it, Jack. They

were all in on it when you were here. It started way back when, back when fuckhead Muriqi-Ortiz, whatever the hell he called himself, he murdered my wife. Fiore used my wife. He used these other victims, too. And when he couldn't milk 'em anymore, he tossed 'em out.''

I looked at Butch. The sidewalk was full of people and voices and noise, but for a moment it seemed to go still. And I felt a shudder of déjà vu that brought me back to every other conspiracist nut I'd listened to over the years. Interviews where I'd suddenly stopped taking notes.

"I got facts, Jack,'' Butch said.

"Yeah, I know, Butch, but these kinds of stories are hard to—''

"I got names. I got dates.''

"Okay,'' I said. "We'll talk about it.''

"You could take the lid off this city, Jackie. There's a pattern of abuse of the criminal justice system. Not now. Back then. I'll get you the stuff.''

He started to ease away.

"Well, maybe, Butch. But I don't really even cover New York anymore. Not for the *Times*.''

"You could sell this story anywhere. *The Voice*. Right up their alley.''

I didn't answer.

"I'll get you those names, Jack. I got documents.''

"Okay. We'll talk about it some more.''

I stepped aside as three women passed, dressed for the theater.

Butch stepped, too, staying with me.

"This could be the story of your career, Jackie.''

"I suppose it could be, Butch, but it would take a lot of work.''

"I'll help you. I mean, you don't have to pay me or anything. But this story is huge. Really, really huge.''

"We'll see.''

"When are you going back to Maine?''

"Tomorrow,'' I said.

"I'll get it to you.''

"What?''

"The stuff."

"Oh," I said. "Okay."

"The Meridien, right?"

"That's right. But I'm checking out in the morning."

"It'll be at the desk. It's a hard story to explain. You gotta see it for yourself."

"Okay," I said, and I stepped off the curb and held up my arm. A taxi swerved toward me and stopped.

"You want to take it?" I said.

"No, you can have it," Butch said, backing away.

"I'm only going twelve blocks."

"Yeah, but that's okay. I gotta find a men's room," he said.

I looked at him.

"You okay?"

"Yeah. Fine. I just got a stomach that sometimes gets even with me for all the bad things I put in it."

"Yeah, well, where are you going to go?"

"I don't know. I'll figure it out. I'm a big boy."

"You want taxi?" the driver called.

"Yeah," I said. "Butch, you're sure you're okay?"

"Great seeing you, Jackie. You call me after you read the stuff."

"I will."

"Promise?"

"Yeah, sure," I said, and opened the taxi door. Butch stepped off the curb and came toward me.

"Thanks, Jack," he said, and he gave my shoulders a squeeze. "You're a good friend, you know that? You've been a good friend for a long time. Since we were kids."

I looked at him, wondered at the ring of finality in his farewell.

"Buds, right?"

"Right," I said. "I'll be in touch."

"You bet," Butch said as I got in the cab. He stepped back to the curb, and gave a little wave.

"Where you wanna go?" the driver said.

I told him. He punched the meter and the cab pulled away. I turned in the seat and looked back, and saw Butch hurrying away, not back into the pub but down the street. I almost told the driver to stop, but he'd run the light, squealed onto Sixth Avenue, and was weaving through traffic, heading Uptown, the taxi bucking like a porpoise.

It was too late, I told myself. And by that time, it was.

Six.

In ten minutes I was in the room, where the message light was glowing red.

Roxanne had called, saying she loved me, she'd call in the morning, see me in the afternoon, make love with me that night. Message two: Christina. She said she had to talk to me before I left New York.

"You just have to make it happen, McMorrow. I know you can if you want to. Call me, Jack. Any hour, day or night. I sleep lightly, but you know that. Just kidding. Hey, McMorrow, things are in a bit of a shambles. I could use a friend from the old days."

She reeled off the number. Hung up.

I didn't call. Wresting myself away from the phone like a sailor from the Sirens, I went to the window and looked out at the lights. Why the hell did they think I'd left? I wasn't a New Yorker, I was a Mainer. This was over, wasn't it?

I walked back to the bed and sat down, took off my shoes and my smoky shirt. Butch, Ellen, and now Christina, with her ice-blue eyes, tousled blonde hair. What color was it now?

Tossing my shirt away from my bed, I picked up the

remote. Flicked the TV on. It welcomed me to New York, then offered movies, first run and adult. There was a sit-com in Spanish; a Manhattan tour in Japanese. I flipped through the channels, but in my mind I scanned images of the past.

I remembered that Christina had slept like a nervous bird, taking flight at all hours, moving through the loft like a wraith. I'd hear her sketching. Talking to herself. And then back into the bed she'd climb, lithe and vora-cious. How many times had we made love through the sunrise?

"Oh, jeez," I said, and shook her off.

And Butch. I shook my head. He'd always been so savvy, knowing a story, predicting how and where it would be played. What was this story? Was he just rav-ing? Fiore was spin-doctored. They were all in on it. The mayor—

And there he was.

It was WNYC, all New York news. Fiore was on the scene of a cop shooting in the Bronx. The cop, an under-cover detective making a drug buy, was in critical con-dition, the bush-jacketed reporter told the camera. There was a shot of a Mac-11 machine pistol, the gun the shooter had used. Then there was Fiore again. He looked past the bouquet of microphones and said the criminals would be brought to justice, that the detective's heroism would not be in vain.

His eyes were unblinking, his stare unwavering. His finger pointed at the lens.

"We have taken this city back. And now we will de-fend it at all costs," Fiore said.

New Yorkers believed him. They believed in him. Watching the mayor on the screen, I believed him, too.

Butch was wrong. Fiore had become larger than life, dwarfing the man I'd met years before. His accomplish-ments had accumulated month by month, year by year. Cleaning up Times Square. Running the panhandlers out of the subways. Sweeping the homeless away like so many bags of trash. Making the schools safer, chasing drug dealers out of their safe houses. And when the few critics dared speak, they were drowned out. By the working poor. The idle rich. The middle class, who saw Fiore as their friend at City Hall.

I watched as the news moved on, to a water-main break in the West Village. Johnny Fiore was there, too. And then he was at a press conference at City Hall, unveiling his administration's new anti-drug policy. In another segment, his appointment of a Latina to head the city's welfare system was applauded. The entertainment report included a review of a Mel Gibson movie set in New York; it had the mayor's endorsement.

Of course.

I shook my head and turned off the television, then went to the phone. I set the answering machine. Turned off the lamp. Sitting on the edge of the bed, I pulled off my khakis, pulled down the covers and stretched out on my back on the cool sheets. I looked at the ceiling. In Prosperity, the house often was washed in blue-gray, lighted by the moon. Here the room was lighted by the city's hazy golden glow. For a long time, I'd told myself that the moon was the more beautiful of the two. Now I wasn't so sure.

I was sure I wanted the *Times* job. And yet I felt like a day in New York had rattled the foundation of the life I'd built in the woods. In a way, I felt like I'd betrayed Roxanne by just being here, by being an accomplice to my own past. Butch wanted my help. Christina wanted my time. Ellen wanted me to help with a story on my own demise.

I sighed and closed my eyes, and I must have slept, because when the phone rang, it was morning.

I groped for it. Tried to speak but my throat and mouth were dry. Tried again.

"Yes," I said.

"Is this Mr. McMorrow?" a woman's voice said.

The desk, I thought. I'd slept through checkout.

"Yes," I said again.

"Mr. McMorrow, this is Stephanie Cooper. I'm a reporter with WNYC television."

"Oh."

Still muddled, I began to say that I'd never done TV.

"No, Mr. McMorrow. It's Jack, isn't it?"

"Yes."

"And you are a former reporter with the *Times*?"

"Yeah. But it was a few years ago."

I swung my legs over the side of the bed and sat up.

"Mr. McMorrow," the woman said, hesitating just slightly, "do you know a former police officer named Patrick 'Butch' Casey?"

Oh, God, I thought. He's taken his crazy theory to TV and given them my name.

"Listen, I don't mean to be rude, but I really don't think I can help you with—"

"Just a couple of questions. Just one minute."

"How'd you get my name?"

"We got a tip. You know how that works."

"Yeah, but I don't see—"

"Mr. McMorrow, I understand you were with Mr. Casey last night. Is that correct, Jack? May I call you Jack?"

I paused. Stood.

"Yeah."

"You both were at a bar in Midtown, Jack? The Bull and Thistle?"

"Yeah. What, did something happen to Butch?"

"Jack, are you aware that—"

"What?"

"That the mayor's been killed."

"Oh, God," I said.

"And Casey has been arrested."

"Oh, my God."

I sat.

"Now, are you saying you didn't know that, Jack?"

Seven.

Still reeling, I started to say no. But something in her voice stopped me.

"I've got no comment at this time," I said.

"Well, could I call you later, when you've gotten your thoughts—"

I hung up. Grabbed the remote and turned on the TV. It asked me if I wanted to watch a movie. I hit no. It told me about the video checkout. I pressed the buttons furiously.

And there it was.

The Algonquin, roped off with police tape. The reporter saying, "We'll continue to update you on the murder of John Fiore, mayor of New York, here late last night. As we've reported, a former New York police officer, Patrick 'Butch' Casey, has been arrested for the crime and is in custody. Casey was arrested at his West Village apartment at a little after 9 A.M. As the investigation continues, Public Advocate Judith Golden, now running the city, has pledged to continue Fiore's initiatives for making New York a better place, a goal which Mayor Fiore strived for until he was so brutally struck down."

The tag at the top of the screen said "Breaking News."

The reporter, a striking black woman, looked like she'd been crying.

I stood and whirled through the channels, my stomach sick, my breath coming in shallow gulps. A reporter on Fifth Avenue said the city was numb. The camera showed people walking, dabbing their eyes. The governor said he would call for the death penalty for this heinous, brutal murder.

"This is the man . . ." Dan Rather said, and there was Butch, younger, slimmer, with more hair.

A file shot.

". . . police have charged with this unprecedented crime. Casey is a former New York homicide detective. CBS News has learned that his wife, Leslie Moore, was killed in a carjacking in 1988. Casey at the time was critical of the Manhattan district attorney's handling of the case, in which a suspect was released after charges that the police—and Casey himself—manipulated witnesses in order to get a conviction."

Rather paused for dramatic effect.

"The district attorney at that time was John Fiore. And now we go to the Algonquin, where police . . ."

I went to the phone, where the message light was on. How had that TV reporter gotten through? Probably called the desk, said it was urgent. I didn't bother with the messages. Just dialed the operator and said, "Give me the police." A police dispatcher answered, and when I said the name Butch Casey, patched me through to a sergeant. The sergeant patched me through to a woman who answered the phone, "Ramirez."

I told her my name, that I'd been with Butch Casey.

"When?" she said.

"Last night. Until 11:30 or so. I just heard about it."

She covered the phone, then came back on.

"Where are you now?" she asked.

"The Parker-Meridien. Room 821."

"Can you stay there until an officer can get there?"

"I can," I said. "And I will."

I hung up and, still in my shorts, dialed again. Asked

for Ellen Jones in the newsroom. A man answered "Copy desk," and I asked for Jones again.

"She's in a meeting," he said brusquely.

"This is important," I said.

"Yeah, well, we've got a lot going on right now, and I think she's going to be tied up. Could you call back another time?"

"I could, but I'm sure she's been trying to reach me."

"Is that right?" he said, like he'd heard that before.

"Yeah. I think you'd better get her right now."

I heard him sigh. I was his cross to bear.

"Who is this?"

"Jack McMorrow."

"Hey," he said over the newsroom hubbub. "Could you tell Ellen that some guy named McMorrow is on the phone."

There was a pause, and then I heard a man say, "McMorrow? Holy shit. No, don't transfer it. She'll take it right there."

The phone clattered. I waited. Ellen came on.

"Jack," she said breathlessly.

"What, you run up the stairs?"

"Across the room. I've been trying to reach you. I was about to send Sanders over to pound on your door."

"TV reporter woke me."

"We got a machine."

"She must have said it was urgent."

"I said that. I got this line about hotel policy."

"She must have sounded urgenter."

"I don't know how she could have. God, we've got to talk. Were you there?"

"At the bar? No. I was with him just before. At another place."

"Late? I mean, how close to the time that—"

"That he was killed? I don't know. When was it?"

"Around midnight."

"How?"

"We're still working on that. All we've got now is that he was stabbed in the men's room."

"Oh, God. "

"So you think it really was—"

"Butch? I don't know. I can't imagine it. When I left him, he was in good spirits. We were going to talk some more."

"What time was that?"

I paused.

"Are you taking notes?"

"Well, yes," Ellen said. "For the meeting. For planning. I've got to know what we're dealing with. How we're going to handle it. I want you to talk to Sanders, for starters. We want to get something on-line. I also have this idea of a first-person. An account of your night. You know. A chronology. Background on Casey and your long relationship with him. Friendship. Whatever you want to call it. I mean—"

"Ellen, slow down."

"Jack, this is the biggest story in New York City history."

I thought for a moment. She was right. It was.

"Ellen, I just need to think for a minute. The TV reporter woke me up. I'm still in my shorts. I had no idea—"

"Did you talk to them? Who was it?"

"WNYC. I just said a couple of things before I realized what was going on. She had to tell me. I didn't even know Fiore had been killed. And I haven't talked to the cops yet. They're on their way and I've got to get ready—"

"Oh, damn," Ellen said. "They're going with it right now."

I turned to the TV. A young woman was standing in front of the Meridien. Pointing up. She must have called from a cell phone outside.

"In an exclusive report, WNYC has learned that Casey spent part of the evening with Jack McMorrow, a one-time reporter for the *New York Times*. McMorrow is staying at this Midtown hotel, where I spoke to him just minutes ago. McMorrow confirmed that he was with Casey at a Midtown pub. In a telephone interview from his eighth-floor room, McMorrow professed to have no knowledge of the mayor's murder. Told that his friend had been charged with the crime, McMorrow's only comment was, 'Oh, my God.' This is Stephanie Cooper, reporting for WNYC."

"Thanks, Stephanie. We'll have more on the Mc-Morrow connection later."

"They'll be swarming," Ellen said. "Can you get over here now?"

"What about the police?"

"Oh, yeah. Well, can I put Sanders on the phone now?"

"I'm in my underwear and I've got cops on the way. I'll talk to them and then I'll talk to you. I'll call you as soon as I'm done."

"When?"

"I don't know, Ellen. How long could it take? An hour? Two?"

"Where are you going to be?"

"I don't know. Here?"

"You won't be able to stay there, Jack," she said. "They'll be all over that hotel."

I considered it.

"How bad do you think it'll get?"

"For now, you're all anybody's got. You're the best source on Casey. I mean, there's his cop buddies, but they'll clam up and he's been out for a while. There's no parents, no siblings, from what we can find out."

"Only child. Parents dead. No kids."

"And the guy lived alone, right? Jack, you were with him until right before he did it."

"Allegedly."

"Right."

"So we're talking the tabs, TV?" I said

"Will you please talk to us only?" Ellen said. "At least for today?"

"Sure," I said.

"You know you'll be offered money. Dinner. Drinks."

"I remember how it's played."

"It's worse now. No limits. But the *Times*'ll do the story thoroughly, fairly, and accurately. That's worth its weight in gold."

"You don't have to sell me on the *Times*, Ellen."

She covered the phone, came back on.

"We're getting calls here right now. They want to know about you."

"My fifteen minutes?"

"Oh, Christ, McMorrow," Ellen said. "If only it were to be that brief."

Eight.

My hair still wet, feet scuffed into loafers, I opened the door and let the cops in. The detective from the phone, Ramirez, was a woman in her forties. Nordic-looking and stocky with white blonde hair. Behind her was a chunky guy named Donatelli.

"Like the sculptor but with an *i*, " he said, shaking my hand.

They looked me over, sized me up. I did the same with them. Ramirez had piercing blue eyes that stared at me and didn't blink. Her makeup was streaked and her pink button-down shirt was rumpled. There was a damp spot on the front of her blue blazer, like she'd spilled something and tried to wipe it off.

Probably coffee. Probably up all night.

Donatelli had a bouncer's biceps that stretched the sleeves of his Lacoste shirt. A gun on his hip. He was restless, eyes darting around the room. At first I thought he was smiling, but then I realized he really wasn't. He just had one of those mouths that lapse into a smile when at rest.

Ramirez looked around the hotel room. Donatelli glanced toward the bathroom.

"You here alone, Mr. McMorrow?"

"Yes," I said.

He glanced at the bathroom again.

"Go ahead," I said.

He did, walking into the bathroom with a bouncy, muscular stride.

I smiled ruefully at Ramirez. She looked at me wearily and didn't smile at all. I heard the shower door slide and then Donatelli was back.

"Well, we have to talk and it may take a little while. And also—now don't take this wrong—but we'd like to take your prints, sir. For differentiation purposes. Let me explain what that means. You got all these prints at a crime scene and you have to sort them out, put names on them, rule people out. To do that—"

"I know what it means," I said.

"And do you have a vehicle here at the hotel?"

"Yeah."

"Could we take a look at it?"

"Butch was never even near it. But be my guest. It's a Toyota truck with a wooden bed and Maine plates."

They looked at me with a hint of new suspicion.

"So where to?" I said.

"We could go to Midtown South, but there's no privacy there and the brass, they want this one done by the book and then some."

"I'm sure."

"Could we ask you to come to Police Headquarters Downtown, Mr. McMorrow?" Ramirez said. "That doesn't mean you did anything wrong."

"No, fine," I said. "Whatever you need. Should I take my bag? Because checkout is at eleven and—"

"You can leave it," Ramirez said. "They aren't gonna be cleaning this room, or renting it. Not for a while."

I looked at her for a moment before I got it.

"But you will?"

"We may want to have a look around. If you don't mind."

"You mean you need my permission?"

"No," Ramirez said.

So down the hall we went, me and Donatelli first, Ramirez bringing up the rear. Donatelli asked me where in Maine I lived and I told him. He said he'd never heard of Prosperity or Waldo County or Belfast, but he had been to Portland once to visit a buddy from school who had joined the Portland P.D.

"Kinda quiet," he said. "But this musta been fifteen years ago."

"Has gangs and heroin now," I said.

"No kidding?" Donatelli said. "Well, I guess that's progress."

We rode in silence in the elevator, the three of us and an expensively dressed couple who eyed Donatelli's gun and whispered to one another in French. Ramirez rubbed her forehead wearily, closed her eyes and opened them. Donatelli was whistling silently to himself.

And then the doors opened. The women behind the registration desk, the friendly French-speaking women, stared at me. The concierge, a smiling, professionally gracious man, stood stone-faced, his arms held out to keep guests out of our path.

The knot of us moved toward the 57th Street doors, and I could see them through the amber glass.

TV crews, some with cameras pointed, some kneeling, still assembling equipment. We started for the revolving door but a doorman held the swinging door to the right open.

"Would you like something to cover your face?" Ramirez asked.

"Why?" I said, as we swept toward the door.

And then we were out, and the heat of the morning hit me and then a swarm of cameras, giant eyes, microphones waving like batons, all of them jostling, shoving, shouting.

"Can you tell us why he did it?"

"Get back now, guys."

"How long had he planned this?"

"Did you have any indication that something was going to happen?"

"Out of the way, now. Move."

"Hey, asshole, look over here."

"Hey, Jack."

"This way, Jack. Over here."

"I'm Kate Moynihan. Call me at the *Post*. Here's a card."

"Detective, is Mr. McMorrow in custody?"

"Why'd he do it? Was it revenge?"

"Is he under arrest?"

"How long have you known Casey?"

"You help your friend kill the mayor, you bastard? Hey, you."

And then there was a car, it was white, and Donatelli held the door for me, and a camera bumped my forehead and I shoved it back, and the cameraman said, "Fuck off!" and I started to shove him, too, but the cops moved me toward the car. Hands held my shoulders, and I stooped and got in. Ramirez got behind the wheel and Donatelli sat in front beside her. The cameras knocked against the glass, the faces pressed close, all of them baying, like hounds under a treed raccoon.

"Mr. McMorrow, look over here . . . Hey, McMorrow, look at this."

And they followed, running alongside the unmarked car as it moved down the street. The shouts were muted, and then they faded and we were passing Carnegie Hall.

"They're like bugs, swarming all over you," Donatelli said. "You gotta keep wiping 'em off."

At One Police Plaza, flags were at half mast. I could see them out the window of the interview room, where I sat at a big table and sipped orange juice from a can. The table top was veneer. One window in the wall was gray and one-way. There was a small wooden plaque that said NYPD 1845–1975. It was painted blue and looked cheesy.

I told my story to Ramirez and Donatelli, an older detective sergeant named Donovan, and a red-faced broken-nosed boxer of a guy who came in late and wasn't introduced. Ramirez just said he worked for the Manhattan DA, whom I knew to be a buddy of Fiore's named Ralph Baldwin.

The cops didn't talk to the Boxer. He didn't talk to them.

There were a couple of tape recorders on the table as I talked. I started at the beginning, in Maine, a lifetime ago, and ended at the end, back at the hotel. They looked at me most of the time, once in a while at each other. For the third time, Ramirez asked me to go over exactly what Butch had said about the mayor. I did.

"And he was angry at Fiore?"

"He wasn't happy with him."

"Did he make any reference to the mayor's whereabouts?"

"No."

"But his theory centered around the mayor hiding his critics?"

"No, more like there being a lot of people who felt they'd been shafted by Fiore. And some sort of manipulation of the system. 'A pattern of abuse,' he called it."

"And Mayor Fiore was at the center of this?"

I considered the question.

"Yes."

It sounded damning. It was.

And then we talked about Butch's demeanor. His need for a bathroom, whether he had seemed to be feeling ill anytime earlier in the night. They asked if Butch mentioned the Algonquin and I said no. They asked if he was carrying a weapon, to my knowledge. I said no, not that I could see. They asked if he had threatened the mayor that night, and I said no, just called him names. They asked if he'd threatened the mayor ever, and I said no, not that I'd ever heard. They asked if I felt an obligation to protect Butch Casey and I said no, but he was my friend.

They looked at me skeptically. The red lights on the

tape recorders flickered like votive candles. It had been more than two hours, and I figured we were done, but I waited for them to say so. Donatelli started to get up, but then there was another question.

"This conspiracy stuff," the Boxer said. "Did he bring you anything? Papers? Documents? Diaries? Anything that might have said something about what he was thinking?"

It was the first time the Boxer had spoken.

"No," I said. "But he said he had some stuff he wanted to show me."

"But he didn't?"

"No, he didn't bring it to the bar."

"Didn't send stuff to Maine?"

I shook my head.

"So you've never seen any of this supposed material Casey was talking about?"

"No," I said.

"And you don't know where it might be located?"

"No idea," I said.

"He ever mention a locker? A post office box? House in the country?"

I shook my head. He stared at me as though he could bore through my skull and hear my thoughts.

"Hey, I'm sorry," I said. "I just can't help you. If I could, I would."

"I'm sure," the Boxer said, in a tone so flat it couldn't be read at all.

Nine.

Standing in the foyer of Police Headquarters, Ramirez and Donatelli offered me a ride back to the hotel. I said no, that if they'd drop me, I'd walk a while and clear my head. They said this was just the initial interview, and asked where they could reach me.

"Dump Road, Prosperity, Maine."

"Better off in Manhattan," Donatelli said. " 'Cause you aren't gonna be doing any hiding in Maine, Jack. Your little town up there in the woods just got put on the map."

I looked out at the mall, where TV reporters were doing spots, their backs to us. Reporters and photographers were standing and waiting.

For the cops. For the DA. For me.

I was the guy who gave James Earl Ray a ride to the motel. I was the guy who went drinking with his buddy Lee Harvey Oswald. I didn't know if Butch was guilty or innocent, but I knew what he was supposed to have done. And it had rubbed off on me and on everyone around me. They'd come to Prosperity. They'd come to Portland. They'd come after Roxanne and Clair. They'd be all over the *Times*.

"Shit," I said.

"Hey," Donatelli said, "that's the understatement of the year."

So we went out the back door of the police garage, this time in a blue Crown Victoria. I slumped in the back seat, and sat up on Canal Street. I asked them to pull over and they did, into an alley, with trash cans on one side and stacks of wooden vegetable crates on the other. Both cops gave me their cards with their pager numbers scrawled on the back.

"We'll be in touch," Ramirez said.

"Likewise," I said, "I'm sure."

"How 'bout we buy you a meal, give you a ride back to the Meridien," Donatelli said. "We'll set up another place for you to stay."

"I like it there. The service is impeccable."

"It's gonna be surrounded, I'm telling you."

"I'll be okay."

"Watch yourself," he said.

"And if I don't, you'll do it for me?"

They didn't answer. I walked.

It was 12:35, and the sidewalks were packed with New Yorkers in a hurry, tourists in their way. The throng absorbed me like a fish into a school, and I walked down Canal, past tables of silk scarves, hats, postcards, CDs. Glancing behind me, I saw the Ford double-parked, the cops watching and waiting. I turned away and kept walking, then stopped.

Tucked behind the tables, between a restaurant and a Chinese grocery, was a place that sold electronics. It was long and narrow as an alley, but inside I could see the aisle was full. I went to the door and eased my way in, along the wall of CD players, boom boxes, cellular phones, all ignored.

The crowd was facing a television. Even the clerk had come around the counter to watch.

It was Dan Rather again. This time he was outside the Algonquin, gazing at the camera, his expression thin-lipped and grim. The hotel looked almost festive, festooned with more police tape.

"Again," Dan intoned, "CBS News has learned of new developments in the murder of Johnny Fiore, the beloved mayor of New York, who single-handedly, his supporters say, took this city from the criminal elements that had plagued it, and handed it back to the law-abiding residents. As he so often put it, 'the real New Yorkers.' "

The crowd was silent. The woman in front of me shook her head and listened.

"As you probably know by now, Mayor Fiore, in one of history's more astounding ironies, has become a crime victim himself."

Rather turned and held his arm out toward the facade of the Algonquin. The camera zoomed in on a somber cop, then back to Rather.

"To cap this historic and tragic and so very discouraging story, the mayor of New York City was killed here sometime around midnight last night, stabbed to death in the restroom of this famous New York landmark, authorities say. One man is in custody, former New York City Police Detective Patrick 'Butch' Casey. Casey was arrested at his Greenwich Village apartment this morning."

"They oughta just kill him," a man murmured.

"But now CBS News has learned the identity of a second man also questioned today. This man—"

An inset showed a crowd, a cop, and then there I was. Donatelli was beside me.

I looked into the camera, scowled, then lunged.

In the store, the crowd gave a perceptible jerk. Rather looked down at a notebook.

"—was picked up by police at a Midtown hotel. Sources have identified the second man as Jack McMorrow, a former reporter for the *New York Times*. We're still working on this startling new angle, but CBS News has learned that McMorrow no longer works for the *Times*, that he left the newspaper after a dispute with management there several years ago."

"Kill him, too," the same man said.

"Kill 'em both," someone else said.

They ran the clip again, and there I was. Walking, scowling, lunging.

"He looks like a killer," the first man said. "You see that scar?"

"And the eyes," a woman said. "You can tell by the eyes."

"Now, we continue to work to bring you more information about both men. Back to you, Jane."

The crowd fell back. People started to leave the store. I turned toward the CD players and froze.

"I've felt sick all day," a woman said behind me.

"Half the people in my office went home."

"That's because it's the city, right?" another woman said. "City employees must be just devastated."

"Oh, they are. Big time."

I waited. My chest felt tight and I was sweating, the perspiration running down my temples.

"You want to buy?" a man said behind me.

I turned away from him. As I shook my head, I kept it turned and eased my way toward the door.

"Two of them," a man behind me was saying. "I didn't think one guy could pull that off himself."

"No way," another man said. "They got security."

"He was too quick to go to the crowds," a woman said, in Chinese-accented English. "He walk with the people and that's not good."

I was outside, my head down.

"Got him right on the pot," I heard the man say.

"That's low."

"Death penalty's too good for these guys."

"Oughta let 'em loose, see how long they last," the second man said.

I was on the sidewalk again, the people passing by me on both sides. I ran my hand across my forehead, let it linger in front of my face.

A woman walked toward me and our eyes met. I turned away, toward a shop full of souvenirs. An old woman was sitting on a metal chair toward the rear of the store, watching a television. She said something in Chinese and a boy hurried in from the sidewalk. She pointed at the screen. The boy, in baggy shorts and big sneakers, stared at the TV.

The woman spoke in Chinese again and the boy replied in Chinese. The woman nodded and the boy turned back toward me. I picked up a pair of mirrored aviator sunglasses. He was behind me.

"Those are ten bucks," he said.

I nodded, still turned from him, and thumbed a stack of T-shirts. I picked a gray one that said, "The Big Apple" on the left breast and had a softball-sized apple with a bite out of it on the right.

"That's sixteen, with tax," the boy said.

I moved to the caps, grabbed a blue one with a red Statue of Liberty on the front.

"Fifteen, but I give it to you for eight. On sale, today only."

"Fine."

Looking away, I took bills from my pocket and handed the boy two twenties and a five. He counted off the change quickly.

"You want a bag?"

"That's okay."

"How do you like those Yanks?" the boy said mechanically. "This is the year."

"Right," I said, and I started for the door, head down.

"It's two now," the boy said behind me. "They got another guy."

I looked up and down the street, spotted the Crown Victoria. In front of a vegetable stand, I eyed the cabbages, picked up the peppers, put on my hat and glasses. As I stepped slowly along, I readied the shirt, rolling it up to the neck. It went on in three movements, first the neck, then the two arms. This still was New York; nobody cared.

Hand shading my eyes, I watched the traffic, spotted

the police car. Would they follow me in the subway? Follow my cab? Was I really a suspect or was the media making a giant leap?

Picked up, Dan Rather had said. True, but I hadn't been in custody. I was being a good citizen, doing my duty by helping the police. But did they believe me? The people on the streets obviously didn't. To them I was tried and convicted, only the sentence left to be determined. That depended, I supposed, on whether I was the mastermind and Butch was the functionary, or the other way around.

I could hear the editors, the TV producers.

Find out who these guys are. Who is this cop? How long has he been out? Is he a nut? What makes him tick? What made him explode?

And who's this McMorrow? God, that name sounds familiar. Why did he leave the Times*? Where did he go? This guy has a life, and I want it on page one of this paper tomorrow. Find out where this guy is from and go there. I don't care if it's in Katmandu.*

Or Prosperity, Maine.

Ten.

My phone was listed, under Jack McMorrow. All they had to do was call all the Jack McMorrows on the Internet directories. Call until something tipped them off to the right Jack McMorrow, the one on the television. Or maybe the cops would just tell them. Maybe they already had.

I went to a pay phone and dug in my pocket for change. The booth was papered with phone-sex flyers, and the women leered lewdly as I dialed and the phone rang in Prosperity. I punched in the answering-machine code. It clicked, hissed and the robot voice said, "You have nineteen new messages."

A record. Not good.

I hit the numbers and they began, in the order in which they were received.

"Jack. Clair. Got a deal for you, buddy, assuming you want to get off your butt, which I know is a big leap. Anyway, I got an in on some stumpage over in Knox. Not bad terrain, and they want the hardwood taken out by someone with a delicate touch. I might take it and I'm gonna need somebody to get me coffee. Also I got wind of a good deal on a Stihl 066. Nice saw. So stop by when

you get back to Portland, or stop by when you get home. Hope you didn't get corrupted in the big city.''

"Jack, it's just me. If you call in for messages, call me. I love you and I miss you. A lot, this time.''

"Jack McMorrow, this is Ellen Jones. If you haven't left already, I just wanted to move our appointment up an hour. Meetings, meetings, meetings, you know. If you don't get this, that's okay. See you in New York.''

"Jackie, this is Butch. I guess I missed ya. Hope you have a safe drive down. Talk to ya, buddy.''

"Mr. McMorrow, this is Barry Lowell. I'm a reporter for the New York Daily News *and we're just trying to determine whether a man named Jack McMorrow who is involved in a case down here is the Jack McMorrow from Maine. I'd really appreciate it, sir, if you could call me. It's a toll-free number. Eight-hundred. Eight, eight, eight. Eight thousand. If you could call me either way, I'd really appreciate it. This is a very important story involving the death of Mayor Johnny Fiore here in New York. Please call either way. Thank you.''*

"Mr. McMorrow, this is Stephanie Cooper. I'm with WNYC TV in New York, and I'm trying to find the Jack McMorrow who is in New York this weekend. If this is the right Jack McMorrow, could you call me? Thanks.

She gave her number in a phone-sex voice.

The onslaught continued.

Four TV reporters, three from radio in New York. A guy from CNN's New York bureau, a producer from CNN in Atlanta. A reporter from *Newsweek*, who sounded very kind and soft-spoken. Whatever works.

The *New York Post*, where the reporter was a woman who sounded tough as the streets. Two tabloid types, each offering "sizable incentives" for anything that might lead to an exclusive interview or for unpublished photos of Butch Casey. One guy said he was talking "very major dollars."

And then David Conroy, from Fiore's office. Normally so precise and exact, he sounded desperate and distraught, but I supposed I would be, too, in his position. A right-hand man suddenly left without the man, like one of those dismembered white gloves from a magic show.

"We have to talk, Jack," Conroy said. "It's imperative. For the future of this city. Please call me. Really, I must talk to you. Your convenience. And, oh, no hard feelings I hope. It's time to bury the past."

If only it would stay buried.

There were more. Ellen Jones, sounding frantic. She'd called right after Conroy, at 11:17 that morning. She'd tried me at the hotel, was afraid she'd missed me. She said she was very worried about me, that I'd be "victimized by the media."

Or that I'd get away?

D. Robert Sanders, sounding like a confidant. He suggested I call him, as though it were for my own good. "Anytime, anyplace, Jack. Please, remember we're all thinking of you down here."

I was sure they were.

Some of them called back. One of the tabloid guys said he wanted to be more specific, that he was talking "high five figures." One woman said she was calling from Los Angeles, that she represented some very big people whose stories were potential properties. She'd just love to talk. Could I come to L.A.?

"On my nickel," she said.

And then there was Roxanne, again.

"Jack, call me. I don't know where you are now, but I saw the TV. Oh, Jack, I'm worried. I love you."

So standing there, with the garish naked women staring me in the face, I called Roxanne. Her office number connected me to the state's voice mail, which hung up. Her home number gave me an answering machine.

"I'm fine," I said. "Don't worry. I'm in New York and I'll call you tonight."

A half-truth if ever there was one.

In the subway station at Sixth Avenue, I sat on a bench, sunglasses in place, hat pulled low, face resting on my hand. A dozen people were waiting, and when the train rumbled up, they moved silently through the doors, as automatic as the trains themselves. I took the first seat inside the door. Resumed my pose. The doors hissed shut and the train began to move, the block walls, too.

A blond man moved in front of me, carrying a backpack that said NYU. He held the pole and rocked to and fro with the train. To my right, two boys, eleven or twelve, sat side by side. Across from me a thin Indian-looking woman was asleep, her head rocking back and forth like a stone balanced on a shelf. I sat and watched the people and stations come and go. At 57th Street, the doors opened and I stepped off, bounding up the stairs to the light. Rounding the corner on 56th, I slowed.

On the sidewalk across from the entrance, a blonde woman in a sleeveless red top was standing in front of a camera, with the hotel as a backdrop. Another crew was setting up next to her. It was Japanese. Across the street, I saw print photographers, camera bodies draped around their necks like giant medallions.

I pushed my glasses up. Pulled down my hat. Felt in my pocket for the key card to my room, and headed for the doors. There were people coming out, dressed for dinner, and I dodged behind them, shielding myself from the closest photographer, twenty feet to my right. The group started up the sidewalk toward Carnegie Hall and I quickly moved through the door. Darted through, then hesitated. I thought of Roxanne. She might have called the desk. I walked over, chose the young woman who looked at me most blankly, gave me a smile on reflex.

I leaned over the counter. Asked if I had any messages. Softly said my name.

"Monsieur McMorrow," the young woman said, as though it rang only a distant bell. "Oh, yes. I remember that name from this morning."

I started to scowl but she stooped and popped back up. She was holding an envelope, a fat one. Large and white. There was a receipt stamp on the front: "6:48 A.M. 23 July." In the top right corner were the words

"Jack McMorrow—Parker-Meridien Hotel."

Butch's handwriting.

I said, "Merci." She smiled and I turned away, mind spinning.

Had Butch gone back to the Village, picked up his package, come back Uptown? Six forty-eight. Had he walked all night? Had he walked all night because of what he had done?

Behind me, from the direction of the desk, I heard a voice say, "Who was that? You gave him that? Don't you know who that . . ."

I walked quickly to the elevators, punched the button and stepped in. On the ninth floor, the doors opened. The hallway was empty, except for a table with cut flowers. I waited. Listened. Stepped out and turned to the corridor, walked fifty feet to the exit sign. Started down the stairs.

It was cool in the stairwell, but the air was stultifying and dead. My footsteps made a scritching sound on the concrete steps and I tried to walk quietly. At the landing, I paused and listened again.

Nothing.

The door to the eighth floor swung open to an alcove. There was an ice machine in a tiny lighted room, and I stood beside it for a moment and listened to the machine grind out cubes. After a minute, I stepped out and went to the corridor.

It was hushed and empty, with muted rosy lighting. Like a school kid at a crossing, I looked both ways. There was no one in sight. I turned to the right and started walking, padding along on the carpet.

The room opposite was 828. I counted them down. Took the room card from my pocket. Grabbed the knob and slid the card in. The green light went on in the door, and I pulled.

It caught.

Too late.

I pulled the card out. Heard voices, then quick steps somewhere down the hall. I slid the card in again. Saw figures come around the corner from the elevator.

"Mr. McMorrow," a woman's voice called.

"Could we talk to you, sir?" a man said.

The green light went on. I turned the knob and the door opened.

The woman was trotting. She was small, wearing a pale green suit. The man was behind her and much bigger.

"Please, Mr. McMorrow. Could I just talk to you for—"

I stepped inside and slammed the door shut.

"Mr. McMorrow," the woman said, from the other side. "Please. I'm Kate Moynihan from the *New York Post*. Could I just talk to you for a moment, sir? We'd really like to give you the opportunity to give your side of the story."

I peered through the fish-eye lens. Her hair was short, her dangling earrings big as fishing lures. She was looking at the hole in the door earnestly, as though it were a camera and I were Larry King.

"Because your side of this really is missing from the coverage, and we'd like to be fair and not just rely on the police's take on things."

I didn't answer.

"Butch Casey is being portrayed as a real madman, and we know that you could tell us what he's really like. As a journalist, don't you feel a responsibility to disseminate the truth?"

I hooked the door chain.

"There's your answer," the man said, out of view. "Just wasted four hours."

"Shit," the woman hissed.

She pounded the door once and then disappeared from view. I exhaled slowly, started to turn.

"Nice hat," a voice said.

Eleven.

I jumped.

"Christina."

"The door was open. I think the cops did it. There were all these cops getting in the elevator when I was getting out."

"So —"

"So I just pushed on the door and it opened."

She was sitting in the armchair by the window, a magazine on her lap. Her feet were propped up on the end of the bed and her sandals were on the floor. Her legs were bare, her shoulders, too. There was a sweater sort of thing on the bed.

"Well," I said.

I put Butch's envelope on the desk and stood there.

"I thought you might need a friend," Christina said. "I didn't know you'd need the fashion police."

I looked down at the Big Apple shirt. Took off the mirrored glasses.

"I'm sort of trying to go incognito."

"Disguised as a dork?"

"It worked."

"Good thing," Christina said. "Your face is becoming an American icon."

"On the TV?"

"TV today. The newspapers tomorrow. You always did know how to make an entrance, McMorrow."

"I know. It's unbelievable, isn't it?' "

"Bordering on the surreal," Christina said. "Even for New York."

I walked over to her and she swung her legs off the bed and stood. She offered her cheek and I kissed it. Smelled her again and it all came back. I quickly put my hands in my pockets. She looked at me.

"Been a long time since you dropped off the face of the Earth."

"I'm not much of a letter writer," I said.

"I noticed. Where'd you get the scar? You look like Zorro."

I smiled.

"Cut myself shaving," I said. "But you look good."

And she did.

Her hair, long in our time, was cropped short. Her makeup was grayish around the eyes and plain. Pretty but odd. She'd always zigged when the rest of the world had zagged.

"So," Christina said.

"So."

"A fine mess you've gotten yourself into this time."

"Yup."

"I always liked your cop friend, the few times I met him. He was sort of shy, like a little boy. Funny, considering what he did for work."

"He was different with criminals."

"After his wife died it was all over, wasn't it?"

"Certainly could be now," I said.

"You think he did it?"

"I don't—I can't imagine. I just can't picture it."

Christina shrugged, her shoulders flexing in this little tank-top thing.

"Maybe you never can," she said.

"I like to think I know people. If you don't really know anyone, then what good is any of it?"

Christina gave a little chuckle.

"I've been thinking that myself," she said.

"I heard," I said. "You want a beer?"

"Sure. You still drink, McMorrow?"

"Only in moderation. You?"

"Same. If I have more than two, I feel very old, and I hate that feeling."

"You don't look any different."

Christina smiled at me.

"Thanks, McMorrow," she said. "I needed that."

The ale was warm, so I opened the minibar and pulled out two Carlsbergs, ice cold. We opened them, then raised them in unison.

"To . . . to an end to all of this," she said.

The cans tapped.

"And to old friends," I said.

"Is that what we are?"

Christina smiled as she sipped. I took a long, cold swallow. Someone knocked on the door and we froze.

"Mr. McMorrow," the muffled voice began, "Kate Moynihan again. Please could we talk? Even for two minutes. Whatever you're comfortable with. One minute. Just the most basic questions. Anything to cut through the innuendo."

She paused, waited, started again.

"This city needs some real information and I don't know who else can supply that but you. Even if you could give me some more names or just answer yes or no to a few questions. I have a deadline and you know what that's like, I'm sure. I hear great things about your reporting for the *Times*. Where is it you live now? And what brought you down here? They're saying some terrible things, Jack. WNYC is reporting that police are investigating whether you and Casey teamed up on this. I'd like to set the record straight."

"I'll set her straight," Christina said.

I shook my head and put my finger to my lips. She looked at the door and gave it the finger. I took her by the shoulder and guided her back toward the chair and the windows.

The windows—

I looked out at the building across the way, its lights showing in the dusky light. I could see people in offices, sitting at computers, talking on phones, peering at papers on desks. To the left were two or three apartments, pricey Midtown places. The night before I'd seen a man in boxer shorts go to the refrigerator and get a glass of milk.

Those windows were dark. I stood close to the wall and watched. Thought I saw movement. Closed the curtain.

"Wouldn't surprise me a bit," Christina said, behind me. " 'Can we have your kitchen? Here's a thousand dollars. Go stay at the Plaza.' "

I turned back to her.

"This is nuts," I said.

"You're cornered."

"I've got to get out of here."

"Come to my place. We'll go out the back and grab a taxi."

"Taxis go there?"

"Sometimes. It's becoming quite hip, you know."

"No more bodies on your front steps?"

"That was years ago. And it's not like they killed them there, not in SoHo. It's just not done. They killed them some other place and just left them there. I've never understood why that bothered you so much. You didn't come over for a week, and that was a long time for us back then. Remember?"

Christina looked at me and smiled.

"Yeah," I said.

"I remember, too," she said.

She fished for her sandals and scuffed them on. There was something intimate and unsettling about it, her feet, her bare legs. I looked over at the phone, its message light beaming red hot.

"How'd you find me, anyway, Christina?"

"Ellen called me, looking for you. I'm sure she's on your phone there."

"And a lot of other people."

I paused.

Christina smiled knowingly.

"It's okay, McMorrow. Ellen told me you'd settled down with someone. I'm glad for you. Actually, I thought I had, too. But then he unsettled."

"Happens."

"Sure does. The shoot was in February in Saint Kitts. Absolut. A big coup for Christophe. And afterward, he stayed."

"Is that really his name? Sounds like a hairdresser."

"You've been in Maine too long. You sound like a redneck. Anyway, he left me and then sent for his kid."

"I heard," I said. "A son?"

"Philippe. He's fifteen. Funny, in some ways, I miss him more than his dad. I always wanted children."

"I remember that."

"Then the whole thing just disappeared. Poof. Like I'd imagined the whole lot of 'em. But I'm doing fine now."

"Things have a way of working out," I said.

Christina looked at me, then went and sat on the end of the bed.

"Yeah," she said, her legs crossed, one foot etching circles in the air. "They do."

I had to take the messages. Christina asked if I wanted her to leave but I said no. Where would she go? The bathroom?

So I hit the button and listened again. The same cast of characters. Reporters, TV and print. The Hollywood woman. Producers at CBS and NBC, Fox and CNN. The tabloids, still offering money. Some guy who offered to handle my negotiations with the media.

"I've done work for O.J.," he said.

And then Ellen at the *Times*, still frantic, still asking me to call her. Leaving three numbers. I managed to write down one. Clair in Prosperity, saying it was bad enough having to look at my mug down the road, now he had to look at it on the television, too. Call him, he said. And then Roxanne, beyond frantic. "Please, Jack. I need to talk to you. Call as soon as you can," she said.

So I did.

Christina turned on the television, and sat on the end of one of the beds with the remote. I dialed and stretched the phone cord toward the bathroom. As I waited, I heard Fiore's voice, plucked from some network archive. *New Yorkers will no longer live in fear. Fear of violence. Fear of crime. Fear of the stranger who will take the fruits of your hard labor . . .*

"Hello," Roxanne said.

"Hi," I said.

"Oh, my God, Jack. Are you okay?"

"I'm fine. A little shell-shocked but fine."

"I saw you on the news. My God, it's horrible. Your friend, I can't believe—"

"I can't believe it, either."

"Did you tell them that? What did you tell them?"

"The truth. I told them we had a drink."

"Did they believe you? They have to believe you," Roxanne said. "You're not lying."

"Why would they think I was lying?"

"Well, my God, Jack. The TV, they're saying, 'He may not have been alone.' "

"He wasn't alone. He was having a beer with me."

"No, I mean—"

"I know what they mean. It's insane. The truth will come out."

"Oh, Jack."

"I know."

"Then how can they just say these things? I know how they can, but I don't know. They put your name right out there on CNN. CBS. They said you were being questioned by police."

"I was. That's what they do."

"Did you get a lawyer?"

"No. It was me who called them."

"But the way they said it on the news, it was like you were a suspect. Is that what they think?"

"I don't think so. They just asked a lot of questions and I answered them."

"All day?"

"Couple of hours. I'm sure I'll have to go through it again and again."

"Where are you?"

"The Meridien. There are reporters in the halls, TV on the sidewalk. I'm stuck."

"Did you know they've been calling Prosperity?"

"Calling who?"

"The store. The selectmen. Any name they can find. Sam at the store told Clair one of these guys said they were flying a film crew up."

"And land where? Route 3?"

"I don't know," Roxanne said. "Belfast, maybe. Rockland. Oh, this is just crazy. When are you coming home?"

"I don't think they want me to leave right away."

"So you just sit in that hotel room all by yourself?"

I glanced over at Christina, engrossed by the TV. Fiore was boasting that New York was the safest large city in the country, every word dripping with irony. I turned toward the bathroom, tried not to whisper.

"Well, I'm not alone at the moment."

"The police?"

"No, but they've assigned two detectives to baby-sit me, who knows how many more to follow me around."

"Did the *Times* editor come over?"

"No, she's just been calling all day."

"I wish I was with you," Roxanne said.

"I know."

"So who is it?"

"Who's what?"

"Who's with you?"

I paused. Roxanne did, too.

"Oh, it's an old friend stopped by. I guess she saw me on TV and thought I might need some, I don't know, moral support. You've seen me on there?"

"Attacking a photographer."

"I didn't attack him."

"Well, that's what it looks like," Roxanne said. "They show it over and over, so after a while it seems like there was a riot."

"I'm surprised they didn't put a gun in my hand."

"There you are," Christina blurted from the bed, then looked at me and caught herself, put a hand over her mouth. "Oh, sorry."

"Who was that?"

"That was Christina. I guess they just showed me on there again."

"Christina . . ."

"Christina Mansell. I've talked about her."

"Oh, yeah. The artist. The woman you lived with."

I grimaced.

"Briefly."

"Wasn't it like six months or something?" Roxanne pressed.

"Or something."

"Well. That's nice of her to stop. How'd she know where you were?"

"Ellen at the *Times*. They're friends."

"Oh. Small world, New York."

"But it's been on TV, I'm sure. The name of the hotel and everything."

"They don't just let people march right up to your room, do they?"

"No, but there are other people here. Other rooms. I think they rented a room down the hall. A reporter comes down and asks for an interview through the peephole in the door."

"That's creepy," Roxanne said.

"It's bizarre. I feel like I stepped from my life into a movie or something. And I can't get back."

"I'm sorry, Jack. I'm . . . I'm just so sorry. I wish I could be there."

I looked at Christina, who was playing with her hair, swinging her leg.

"Just the two of us, I mean," Roxanne said. "If I had come, at least it would be us, and not just you. And probably you wouldn't have gone out with Butch."

"It's done, Rox," I said. "You can't think of it that way."

"They're saying he stabbed him in the bathroom."

"Who's saying that?"

"The TV. CBS seems to have more about it than anybody else."

"Who do they attribute that to?"

"I don't know. Sources or something," Roxanne said. "You haven't been watching? What have you been doing?"

Was there an edge to the question, or was it me?

I reminded Roxanne about the police.

"Come to Portland," Roxanne said. "They don't know about me."

"Not yet. But they will."

"How?"

"There's nothing you can hide from them. These people—listen to me, I was one of them—they're very good at what they do. And what they do is find out things."

"Well, what if they call? You think I should talk to them?"

"That's up to you."

"I'll just tell them you're an innocent bystander."

"That's not what they want to hear."

"But they won't have any choice," Roxanne said.

"You'd be amazed."

"I wish I could just hold you, Jack," Roxanne said. "I wish I could just hold you right now."

I looked at Christina and shielded the phone.

"I know. Me too."

"I love you."

"I know," I said quietly. "I love you, too."

"Call me tomorrow. Or later tonight. Or whenever you can," Roxanne said.

"I will."

"And take care."

"You, too."

"And say hello to your friend for me."

"She's—"

I almost said that Christina wasn't my friend, that she was, what? My former lover?

"Watching the TV," I said.

Twelve.

WNYC had reactions from the city: testimonials from somber city officials, shots of city employees crying at their desks. The police commissioner, Robert Kiley, pledged to investigate the case to the utmost of the department's ability. The governor pledged state and federal assistance.

The camera switched to a blonde young woman with intense dark eyes. She was outside police headquarters at Centre Street. My friend, Stephanie Cooper.

"Steph, what's the latest?"

"Dave, investigators have been closeted here for most of the day. They've revealed some of the details. That the mayor was stabbed, though they're not saying how many times. That they have not found the murder weapon, but that evidence collected at the scene led them directly to former New York City Police Detective Butch Casey. But police remain tight-lipped about the possible involvement of this man—"

There I was. Walking. Scowling. Giving the photographer a shove.

"—Jack McMorrow, who was here earlier today. WNYC has learned McMorrow is a former *New York*

Times reporter who left the newspaper under a cloud about eight years ago.''

"A cloud?'' Christina said.

"Now sources have told me that McMorrow is a long-time friend of Casey and that Casey fed the reporter confidential information about police investigations when McMorrow was with the *Times*.''

"Fed?'' I said. "Those are called tips.''

Steph noted Leslie's murder, the arrest and release.

"McMorrow, sources say, was dismissed by the *Times* after he reportedly colluded with Casey as he covered a story for the *Times*. He has been living in Maine since then but has never worked for another newspaper.''

"What? Sure I have. Small ones.''

"She's got somebody inside the *Times*,'' Christina said.

Stephanie paused for emphasis.

"What about that night?'' Dave said. "What can you tell us about that, Steph?''

"Well, Dave, both men had drinks at a Times Square bar, the Bull and Thistle. Witnesses next saw Casey outside the Algonquin on West 44th Street, where the mayor was attending a fund-raiser. Casey reportedly went into the Algonquin, but the bar was full and he wasn't served, as far as we know. He allegedly waited outside the function room where the Fiore fund-raiser was held, apparently slipping into the men's room, where he lay in wait.''

She paused. Gathered herself up for her big finish.

"Was this the act of a single man or the culmination of a conspiracy? Police aren't saying, but WNYC has learned that McMorrow left the *Times* after a disagreement with his editors over stories he wrote that were critical of Mayor John Fiore and supported his friend, Detective Butch Casey.''

She took a breath.

"The investigation continues. From New York Police Department headquarters, this is Stephanie Cooper reporting.''

Dave thanked Stephanie. I cursed her under my breath. Dave said the continuing coverage of the death of Johnny

Fiore, "beloved mayor of New York City," would continue after a commercial break. The commercial was for Diet Coke.

"Can you sue them?" Christina asked.

"Nah, what good would that do? It's said. It's done." She patted my arm.

"Sorry," she said. "But I think your side should get out there. They can't just make this stuff up, can they?"

"They just did," I said, and I went to the phone. I went down the list of scrawled messages and found the one number I'd taken down for Ellen Jones. I dialed it. This time she answered.

"It's me," I said.

"Jack."

"I'll talk to the *Times*. To D. Robert. To anybody you want."

"Okay. Good. That's great."

I could feel the excitement in her voice, sense her mind leaping ahead to what had to be done.

"We'll send a car. Which side?"

"Fifty-sixth. Look for Christina, and then I'll come out."

And then, before I hung up, I heard Ellen Jones shout, "We got him. We got McMorrow."

I checked out via the television. The key went on the dresser. My receipt would come by mail. At 2:05, the phone rang and Christina answered it. I prayed it wasn't Roxanne and was rewarded. It was Ellen. They were coming down 56th Street, would be at the hotel in two minutes. My bag was packed, Butch's envelope was zipped inside. I wore my glasses and hat. The car would be a black Lincoln.

We stood by the door and listened. Heard nothing and opened it slowly. Christina peeked into the hallway first.

No one in sight.

"The stairs," I said, and we went out the door, to the left. Christina went first, into the stairwell and down, her sandals tapping on the treads. Leggy as a model, she took the stairs two at a time, and I followed, the duffel over my shoulder. After six flights, we went back into the hallway, down the corridor and waited at the elevator.

It opened. It was empty.

We stepped in. The door closed. We plummeted downward.

In a moment we were at the lobby.

"Out and to the right," I said. "They'll be at 56th."

"Then I'll see you later," Christina said.

"Where you going?"

"Home, I guess. We could . . . I was going to say we could grab a bite, but that might be a little tough. We could order something, maybe. From my place."

I hesitated.

"So where else can you go, McMorrow?"

"I don't know," I said. "Maybe the *Times* will put me up."

"Not like I can," Christina said.

The door opened. The lobby was bustling with elegant people. Christina gave me a half-smile as we stepped out. This time, the women behind the desk looked up and stared. We turned the corner, started through the glittering lobby. Turned left, past the coat check, and started for the doors. Christina was a step ahead of me, moving with a quick New Yorker stride.

"Mr. McMorrow?" a man's voice called.

"Keep going," I said.

"Mr. McMorrow?" the voice said, behind me, and I heard the sound of someone breaking into a trot. Christina pushed through the doors. As I reached them, a hand touched my shoulder. I shrugged it off and turned.

"No comment," I snarled.

He was small, bald, wearing a suit. I saw horn-rimmed glasses and chubby unshaven cheeks.

"I'm not a reporter," the man said.

"I don't care what you are," I said.

And he hit me.

The back of the head. Once. Twice. My face hit the door. He was kicking the back of my legs, flailing at my neck and shoulders.

"You son of a bitch. You son of a bitch," he muttered over and over.

He stood on my heels, stomped at my feet. My duffel fell off my shoulder and I turned, stumbling on it. I got him by the jacket, tried to duck his punches. Pulled him to me and whirled him around. Started to throw him backward, and he hit me in the nose. Blood. A glint of a ring on his hand.

"Son of a bitch. Son of a bitch," he panted.

Blood spattered. People stared. I took two more steps and flung the man away, and he fell and rolled on the tile floor.

"I worked for Johnny Fiore, you bastard," he screamed. "I hope you burn in hell. I hope—"

Christina came back through the door, said, "Oh, my God." Lunging for my bag, I pushed her back out onto the street. Blood was running out of my nose, down my chin, onto my shirt. I wiped it with the back of my hand, leaving dark smears. Christina grabbed my hand and pulled me along, and I saw strobes flash and then heard the pounding of feet, calling of my name.

"McMorrow. . . . McMorrow. . . ."

The door of the car was open and Christina dived in first, her knees on the seat, underpants showing. She scrabbled inside and I followed, but there was a photographer down low, shooting up at me, and then someone picked him up under the arms and spun him away.

He cursed. The car door closed. I heard myself panting, saw Ellen and D. Robert looking incredulous, a photographer digging for his gear. Gerard, the *Times* security guard, heaved himself into the driver's seat, threw the car in gear and drove.

"Hope that wasn't one of ours," he said.

My nose was still bleeding, the droplets hanging from my chin. D. Robert, in the front seat, handed me a handkerchief. Next to him was a young guy I didn't know. He lifted a camera and pointed.

"You take me like this and the deal's off," I said.

Ellen looked at the photographer and shook her head. He lowered the camera. She dug in her bag and found a package of tissues. Handed them to Christina, who took a couple and handed them to me. I jammed a wad against my nose and pinched.

"You okay?" Ellen said.

"Fine. Just got bumped."

"Scratched," Christina said, peering at me.

"Guy had a goddamn ring on."

In the front seat, D. Robert already was scribbling madly in his notebook, recording the scene.

"Who was that guy?" he said.

"Said he worked for Fiore."

"Distraught city employee?" D. Robert asked.

I shrugged.

"Did he say anything?"

"That he hopes I burn in hell."

D. Robert wrote that down, too.

On the ride, he went over background, mostly bio stuff about me. Where I grew up. Where I worked, before and after the *Times*. When he asked me where I lived, I said, "Maine." When he asked me where in Maine, I shook my head.

"We already know it's a town called Prosperity, Jack," D. Robert said. "In Waldo County, twenty miles west of Belfast."

"What else do you know?"

"That people in the town won't talk about you."

"They don't like big-city reporters snooping around."

"Have they snooped there before?"

"No, it's instinctual. They protect their own."

"And you're one of their own?"

"I guess so."

D. Robert smiled.

"So, you live alone?"

"That's off limits."

His eyebrows flickered with annoyance, and he turned toward Christina.

"And what is your name, ma'am?"

"That's off limits, too," I said.

"This is a joke," D. Robert said. "Am I writing this story or is he?"

"We'll just have to set some parameters," Ellen said.

"Or we get out right here," I said.

"No," Ellen said. "We can work out the details."

And we did, question by question, sitting in a conference room on the third floor of the Times Building. It was a replay of the police interview, with fewer interruptions and some sandwiches. My duffel bag was on the floor beside me. Around the table were Ellen Jones, D. Robert, a City Hall reporter and a national correspondent, two deputy editors, and the new editor of the *New York Times*, Roger Epstein. The photographer from the car roamed the room, shooting me as I spoke, with blood on my shirt but not on my nose. He left to get the processing under way, and shortly after that, the correspondent peeled away, too, starting the story for the on-line and national editions. The interview went on for another hour and then broke up as abruptly as it had begun.

D. Robert shook my hand and apologized for his outburst, trying to soften me up for next time. The reporters and editors huddled on their way to their desks. I picked up my bag, and Ellen Jones took me by the arm and escorted me to the waiting area, where Christina was sitting in a chair reading that day's *Times*.

"Gerard's waiting with the car," Ellen said. "Where do you want to go?"

She looked at Christina. Christina glanced up, then looked back at the paper.

"Well, how 'bout this?" Ellen said. "You can stay at my place. I've got tons of space and nobody will bother you. The phone's unlisted and the doorman's a bulldog. He'd kill for me."

She caught herself.

"In a manner of speaking."

I shrugged.

"How are you getting back to Brooklyn?" I asked Christina.

She tossed the paper aside, stood and stretched. The skirt lifted, along with Ellen's eyebrows.

"Gerard could drive Christina to Brooklyn after he drops you," Ellen said. "You two work it out. Jack, I may call with questions."

I nodded. There was method to her generosity. She had the exclusive—and the source tucked away in the guest room.

Ellen rode down with us in the elevator. When the doors opened, we stepped out, but Dominic wasn't at his post behind the security counter. As we stood, he came in from the street.

"TV," he said. "Waiting for Mr. McMorrow. And they want to talk to a ranking editor about tomorrow's story. The big interview with him and the profile. I told 'em to wait outside."

I turned to Ellen. She didn't seem at all surprised.

"You leaked it already?"

Ellen shrugged.

"It's a big story, and it's an exclusive and it's going on-line anyway and you're—"

"Tired of all this," I said.

We walked to the garage door but opened a single door beside it. Christina stepped out onto 43rd Street as the Lincoln pulled up. We walked to the car and climbed in the back, my bag safely under my arm on the seat beside me. Gerard pulled away and we bent low as we passed the *Times* entrance, where five satellite TV trucks were parked.

And then we were in Times Square, hunched together in the back seat as the car inched through the Mardi Gras crowds, bound to have a good time even without Johnny Fiore.

"Where to, Jack?" Gerard asked, looking at me in the mirror.

"Brooklyn, please, Gerard," I said. "Manhattan Bridge."

As he swung south, I thought I saw Christina smile.

Thirteen.

Gerard looked at the deserted street, the graffiti-swabbed walls, the windows halfheartedly broken.

"This is where you live?" he said.

"It's developing from the bridge out," Christina said. "Some great stuff is happening."

Gerard looked around. The street was narrow, with cobblestones showing through the asphalt and loading-dock doors facing the curb. The wall beside us was windowless brick. There was a mound of black trash bags in the gutter and something or someone had torn them open, strewing papers and cans into the street.

We stopped. Christina got out on her side, her skirt white, her legs pale against the stone and brick. She looked like a half-clad waif, the ghost of a drowned woman. I got out and shouldered my bag.

"It's a loft, Gerard," I said.

"Yeah, I know," he said. "I got kids. You give 'em a nice house with a lawn and a pool and they wanna live like your grandparents did, right off the goddamn boat."

As he spoke, he peered into the side mirror. I looked back and saw a white minivan pass slowly on the cross street at the end of the block. Gerard watched it in the side mirror as it disappeared.

"Followed us all the way down," he said.

"Cops," I said.

"I'll wait," Gerard said.

Christina fumbled with a padlock on a rolling overheard door, then bent and took hold of the handle and, before I could help her, pulled the door up. It made a grating rumble, then was quiet. Inside the truck bay were dim shapes of boxes and crates. There were no lights showing.

"Come on, McMorrow," Christina said, her arm raised over her head. "Going up."

I thanked Gerard. He looked at Christina again and peered at the mirror. Christina yanked on the door and it rolled down with a loud, echoing clatter. And then it was still. And blindingly dark.

"Saving on the electric bill?"

"I gave up. As fast as I put the bulbs in, the landlord takes them out. He wants everybody out."

"Apparently," I said.

"I complain to the Loft Board," she said, from somewhere to my left. "His lawyer calls my lawyer. They've become good friends."

"A silver lining."

"Hey, I'm used to it. When the elevator's off, I just count the steps."

"How many are there?"

"Eighty-two."

From the darkness, Christina chattered on. She said there were two other loft tenants: a potter on the fourth floor, and a painter and his family on the fifth, on the other side of the elevator shaft. The potter was in the hospital with cancer, and the painter was in the Adirondacks for the summer. The first floor was vacant, filled with machinery once used to make buttons for Navy uniforms.

I heard a knocking and then the sound of the lock hasp snapping shut on the inside of the overhead door.

"Here, McMorrow, take my hand."

I reached toward her, found the hand and clasped it. Christina led me as I shuffled across the pavement. I kicked something, and it rolled and bounced and shattered.

"Homeless," Christina said. "If you leave the door open, they come in here and drink. But they're okay."

We moved along a wall until Christina found the padlock for the elevator. She let go of my hand and I heard her keys jingle, and then the door slid open. A light glared overhead. I squinted. She stepped into the elevator nonchalantly. I followed. She slid the door closed, pulled a cage over and hit a button in a battered box on the wall. The elevator roared to life and we started up.

Christina, her hand on her hip, looked at me and smiled.

"This the only way in?"

"There's the fire escape but you have to climb across my bed to get to it."

She grinned. I didn't answer.

"It's great, Jack. Still raw. Dumbo, I mean. You'd like it here."

"That's what I like about my part of Maine. It's real."

"Right. This is like SoHo was before it got ruined. They're gonna have to drag us out."

The elevator stopped with a jarring bang. Christina opened the doors, then reached back to turn out the light. We were in darkness again and she brushed against me, and I could feel her breasts, her breath. She took my hand again, and led me down a hallway. The keys jingled, and a door fell open and we stepped into the white-walled expanse of the loft, hidden away like a vast room on the Underground Railroad.

Christina closed the door, fastened the locks top and bottom and then turned to me.

"You're safe now, Jack," she said.

I looked at her and our eyes met, and I saw the mischief in hers.

"I hope so," I said.

Christina led the way.

There was a cavernous main room, fifty feet across, with varnished wood floors and a ceiling strung with massive beams. On one side, there were leather couches and bookcases halfway to the ceiling and a television screen so big it made the place look like a seatless theater.

I followed Christina to the kitchen.

It was high-tech, done in her funky open-checkbook style. The doors of the double-wide refrigerator were pasted with photographs, gallery notices, arty cryptic messages and cartoons. In one of the photographs, three men and two women posed beside a rock-walled pool, with a turquoise sea behind them. The men, wearing Speedos, were handsome and in shape. The women, wearing bikini bottoms and nothing else, were in shape, too. Christina was on the right.

"San Felice Circeo, an hour outside of Rome," Christina said. "A few of us had just had it up to here with New York. So we grabbed our passports and went. Barely brought any luggage."

"I noticed," I said.

I thought of Roxanne, sitting in smoky kitchens with frightened kids and angry parents. I thought of Clair on his tractor, his wife Mary in her vegetable garden. I remembered what it was about Christina that had been so zany, so refreshing, so childlike. But so frivolous.

She opened the refrigerator and took out two bottles of beer. Corona, ice cold. She held hers against the front of her bare neck and a rivulet of condensation ran off the bottle and down her chest.

I looked away.

"Once this place heats up, it's impossible to get it cool," Christina said. "I wanted air conditioners, but they said they'd have to replace the windows and they're really old and beautiful. So I sit. And sweat."

"Feel cooped up?"

"No, I work. I get out. I have a car. A four-wheel-drive thing. I keep it up around the corner in a lot. You can't leave anything on the street."

I thought of my house in Prosperity, Maine; it didn't even have locks.

She said, "Salud," and we lifted the bottles and drank. I felt myself sigh inwardly as I gulped the cold beer, and then I was reminded of Butch in the pub, saying he'd gotten into booze too heavily. I put the bottle down.

"You okay?" Christina said.

I shrugged.

"I keep thinking I'll wake up and this will be just one of those weird nightmares that seems to go on forever. Not you. The rest of it."

"It's history, McMorrow. You're part of history. Look at it that way."

"Thanks."

"So, how 'bout a tour, McMorrow? I'll show you my piece of Brooklyn."

I saw the bathroom, with a palm tree and whirlpool tub for six. The gym, with several pieces of chrome equipment and mirrors on the wall. Christina's studio, with paint-spattered floors and floor-to-ceiling windows. Easels were grouped in a cluster like people at a cocktail party.

On the easels were small canvases, all painted a reddish ocher. I peered more closely. They were paintings of bricks, each varied slightly. Some were cracked. Some were dark with soot. Some had splotches and streaks of graffiti. A couple had bugs. There were dozens of them.

"And when you stack them up?"

"You make a wall," Christina said. "In the show, there's one panel, one painting, of a child peering out from the dark. Just the eyes and the cheeks."

"From behind the wall?"

"He's bricked up. Isolated. Like we all are, by circumstances. By our very existence as individuals. After all is said and done, we're alone."

I looked at all the bricks.

"Sad," I said. "But interesting."

"A lot of people think so. They like it. Important people. I mean, I'm getting serious attention. But you don't have to say you like it if you don't."

"But I do."

"Thanks. You know, I used to need everybody's approval but it's not an issue anymore, really."

She smiled to herself.

"It's a woman thing. We're raised to please. Once I realized that and I was able to shake it, I felt like this awful weight was lifted off my work."

"Good for you, Christina," I said.

"Thanks, Jack," she said, and with a swish of her hips, she led the way out the door and on to the bedroom where I would stay. Philippe's.

It was whitewashed and spare, with my duffel bag beside the bed, stacks of CDs, a computer. There was a cordless phone, a cell phone in a charger, a telescope on a tripod near the window.

"He didn't take his stuff?"

"A bag and a carry-on. Christophe will buy him new things. You need a telescope?"

I shook my head and looked around. The phone rang and Christina went to the main room to answer it. I went to the open window and glanced up the block.

The white minivan was parked at the corner. As I watched, it pulled away slowly and moved out of sight. I waited, looked out on the empty streets, the still factories, the ash-white sky.

And there was the van again.

It crossed the intersection at the bridge end of the block. Slowed and stopped beside a razor-wire-ringed lot. I took a step back from the window and watched as the passenger window slipped down, a hand reached out and adjusted the side mirror and then withdrew.

The window closed. The van sat. I listened, heard Christina speaking quietly in the other room. And then she hung up and I heard her cross the big room, heard the bathroom door close.

I walked back to the bed, picked up my duffel and unzipped it.

Took out the envelope and tore it wide open.

Fourteen.

There was a message on a piece of yellow lined paper. It was Butch's schoolboy scrawl.

Jackie. Here's some of the stuff. You see a pattern? I do. Great seeing you. I'll call you in a couple days and we can talk. I got more. Butch.

The next page was an NYPD incident report. It was stamped Confidential, Not For Public Release. It was dated August 13, 1989.

The cop had interviewed one Lucretia Jones, a clerk in the office of the mayor. Jones had reported receiving a telephone call from a Hispanic woman who wanted to speak with the mayor. The woman had identified herself as Maria Yolimar, of 486 West 165th Street, Washington Heights. She said her husband, Julio Yolimar, had disappeared.

Subject was insistent that mayor knew husband's whereabouts. When advised to call local precinct to report him as a missing person, subject said police took husband to jail and now he cannot be located. Jones said subject insisted Fiore knew her husband Julio Yolimar because Fiore ran the courtrooms. Jones advised that Fiore is mayor and subject Maria Yolimar said he was in charge of courtrooms when husband disappeared. Asked when this occurred, Yolimar said a year ago. Became hysterical and abusive before Lucretia Jones terminated call.

Subsequent investigation showed subject Yolimar had called on prior occasions. Other City Hall staff interviewed remembered similar conversations, always in July. No actionable threat to mayor. Jones advised that if subject calls again, advise her she is liable for prosecution for telephone harassment.

To the police report, Butch had stapled newspaper clippings, printouts from microfilm. The headline on one said "Man Nabbed in Tourist Stabbing."

That story was from the *Times*, page 25, the metro cover. It said Julio Yolimar, thirty-one, an immigrant from the Dominican Republic, had been arrested in connection with the robbery and stabbing of a French tourist on Park Avenue at 86th Street.

I looked at the date. July 30, 1988. The tourist, a physician from Rouen, was reported in critical condition with a stab wound to the chest at Columbia-Presbyterian Hospital. His wife, who was with him at the time of the robbery, was not injured. The stabbing was part of a rash of similar attacks on tourists, the story said. A spokesman for the office of Manhattan District Attorney John Fiore pledged a thorough investigation and swift prosecution of the case. The French attaché in New York City, Jacques Rioux, said his government had "serious concerns" about the safety of visitors to New York.

There was a similar story from the *Daily News*. Then some sort of memo, again stamped Confidential. It was from the New York City Department of Investigation, to David Conroy, deputy mayor for operations.

Re: Vincent H. Digham III v. Mayor John Fiore and City of New York.

David: Our investigation indicates nothing that would lead to a need for quick settlement here. After all, the D.A.'s office only recommends bail conditions; the courts set them, and for that reason I think we are effectively shielded from civil liability. However, from a public-relations standpoint, I think the city would be well advised to make this case disappear quickly and quietly from the media. For reasons that are difficult to discern after all these years, it would appear that Vladimir Mihailov was offered bail opportunities far more lenient than the norm, considering the seriousness of the charges against him. Could be problematical. All best. George.

Attached to the memo were clippings:

The *New York Daily News*, August 19, 1988, page 2: "Man Injured in Assault Is Heir to Fortune."

His name was Vincent Hillary Digham IV (pronounced DIE-um), the story said. His family had made its money by inventing plywood. Now they ran the Digham Foundation and the Vincent H. Digham Trust. Digham IV was attacked, the story said, as he left a posh East Side bar called Edinburgh. Digham IV was twenty, a student at Yale University. He was struck with a club as he got into a high-performance BMW coupe. The suspect in custody was Vladimir Mihailov, thirty-one, of 1283 Brighton 4th Street, Brighton Beach. The motive, police said, was car theft. As of press time, Digham remained in a coma.

I continued on.

There were three more cases, all similar.

One included a sheaf of letters written to Fiore both when he was Manhattan district attorney and when he was mayor. The writer was one David Tilbury, who lived in the Village. Tilbury's wife, Mary, was an anthropologist who taught at New York University. On the night of July 9, 1988, she was attacked as she left the subway station at Sheridan Square, her skull fractured and her ear nearly torn off. A city teenager, Lester John, was arrested the same night, charged with felony assault and released the next day on $2,000 cash bail.

In the first letter Tilbury wrote:

You now say that you cannot locate this monster, who nearly killed a defenseless woman in order to gain possession of her purse and $28 and change. I would suggest you take the $2,000 he forfeited and use it to pay police *officers to locate the man. He is 19 years old, an eighth-grade dropout and lifelong New Yorker. I do not think he has fled to the South of France.*

The next letter was a repeat of the first. The third was a threat of a lawsuit. It was copied to the governor, a congressman and the attorney general of the United States. It was dated July 2, 1998.

Dear Mayor Fiore:

I am writing to inform you that I have located Lester John. He is living at 123 Lorraine St., Apt. 212, in the Red Hook housing project in Brooklyn. According to a private investigator whom I hired, John lives with his aunt, Lynette Stephens. It is a second-floor apartment, with the entrance at the center of the block. Stephens works as a toll taker for the New York subway system. John does not work. I expect to be informed of his prompt arrest and prosecution.

David Tilbury
26 Carmine St.
New York, N.Y.

Carmine Street. The West Village. Scrawled in the margin of the letter were two words: *Fix this.*

There was one more.

This time the headline was smaller, one column from the *Times*, probably inside the metro section. A woman had been dragged into an alley and raped on East 82nd Street, near Third Avenue. It was a little after nine o'clock at night; she'd just left a coffee bar.

She had been beaten and was hysterical, the story said, but still was able to supply a description of the man, including a distinctive dragon tattoo on his left shoulder. Police said they were not aware of any similar assaults in the area. The victim was described as a thirty-two-year-old investment banker who lived in the neighborhood. The date was August 4, 1988.

I turned the page. An arrest.

The story was from the *Post*. The headline: ''Rapist nabbed.'' His name was George Drague. He was twenty-two. Police had arrested him August 8 at 26 Manida

Street, in the Hunt's Point section of the Bronx. A detective said a tip led to the arrest. Drague did not resist. And then there was this paragraph:

The arrest of one alleged rapist was the latest in the police effort to combat what Manhattan District Attorney John Fiore has called "a Manhattan crime wave." One rapist down; many muggers, robbers, carjackers and murderers to go.

I turned the clip over. An adhesive note was attached to the back. In a rapid scrawl it said, *She keeps calling. Please resolve.* There was a phone number. The name Kim Albert.

And that was it.

Fifteen.

Sitting on the kid's bed, I flipped through the sheaf again, paused at Butch's note.

Did I see a pattern? Sure I did. They were all violent crimes. They took place in Manhattan. The victims were mainstream, the crimes the kind that struck fear in the rest of us. And they seemed to involve victims, victims' families, who would not go away. People like Butch.

What had Butch been doing? Was he recruiting other disgruntled crime victims? People who felt maltreated by the cops or the courts?

Or by Johnny Fiore?

Butch could have put his case in the stack. Somebody who sees his wife's murderer walk? He could go right to the top.

But what was Butch thinking? He was a cop. He knew that in a city like New York, crime victims outnumbered the criminals. He knew that for every crime solved, two were left wide open. He knew that no matter how much cops did, it was never enough. You got a conviction, went back to your office, and the phone would be ringing.

A support group for cop-haters and complainers? It would have to meet in Madison Square Garden.

Then it hit me.

These cases all were from the same six-week period in the summer of 1988. Butch fit that, too.

What was the date of Leslie's murder? I couldn't remember exactly, but it was late July, because in mid-August, Butch and Leslie were going to Vermont for a week. I remembered saying I couldn't picture him floating around in a lake someplace. He said the only people he saw floating were face down.

He had a way with words, Butch did. And he knew a story when he saw one. I did, too, and this one was waiting, just out of reach.

Like the van outside the window. But when I got up and looked again, it was gone.

Christina brought out sandwiches—turkey on dark bread with assorted cheeses on the side. She put the plate on the chest table in front of the television, with two more bottles of beer. I reached for the remote.

"Are you sure?" she said.

I hit the button, the screen popped and there I was. Larger than life.

It was a still shot. I looked angry, trapped in the revolving door at the Meridien.

"Questions remain," the anchor was saying, "about what role, if any, was played in the killing by this man, identified by police as Jack McMorrow, a former reporter for the *New York Times*. McMorrow was questioned for several hours by New York police today. Police sources say they are not sure whether he was an innocent bystander in the plot to assassinate New York Mayor Johnny Fiore. Or not."

I disappeared, replaced by a solemn woman in a police uniform.

"We don't have all the answers," she said. "I can assure you the investigation is continuing. Significant progress is being made."

I hit the button, playing the TV like some grim video game.

Fiore, alive and smiling. Butch, with more hair. Then me, snarling at the camera. Golden, the ashen-faced public advocate. Then Randi Fiore in mourning, dressed in black, getting out of a black limo. The wooden-faced young man was said to be John Fiore Jr., who had rushed home from graduate school in California, where he was getting his MBA. The Fiores, who were rumored to share little with the mayor other than their surname, looked more tired than devastated.

Then a blonde announcer, her eyebrows knit in a parody of concern.

"The cause of death has not been released," she said, "but sources close to the investigation say it appears the mayor died of a single stab wound. The knife appears to have entered under his left arm, and punctured his heart."

Next channel.

"Janet, it appears to have been an almost classic commando kill. Sources here say the likelihood of a layman knowing precisely where to land such a blow is very slim. But I've been told that police and military personnel, including homicide detectives like Butch Casey and Green Beret–type soldiers, would know the heart is located very close to the left underarm, approximately three to four inches inside the chest cavity. Death is almost instantaneous. The victim, one police source told me—and this is a quote, Janet—'doesn't make a sound.'"

And then my friend Stephanie.

"David, police are proceeding very carefully with this investigation, knowing full well that a misstep at this point could prove costly at the time of trial. They interviewed Casey's friend, Jack McMorrow, at length, but did not take the former reporter into custody. But WNYC News has learned that the *New York Times* also has interviewed McMorrow at length and will carry that story in tomorrow's editions, which will go on-line momentarily. Sources at the *Times* say McMorrow spoke to reporters and editors there for more than an hour in what some see as a desperate attempt to avoid prosecution. Back to you.''

"Damn,'' I said.

And still more.

"Casey remains heavily guarded at Riker's Island. McMorrow, meanwhile, left his hotel in the company of this woman, seen running for a waiting limousine outside the Parker-Meridien Hotel in Midtown today. Some city officials are demanding to know why McMorrow was released at all, though police say they know the Maine man's whereabouts and assure the public that he has not left the city.''

I stared at the screen.

"You're pretty blurry,'' I said.

"Yeah,'' Christina said. "I could be anybody.''

"They'll track you down anyway. There was a car outside,'' I said. "Probably police. They'll leak your name.''

"That's to be expected, I suppose.''

"Maybe I should go someplace else, Christina.''

She looked at me.

"Why?''

"You could get sucked into this thing.''

"But you can't just be out there all alone, Jack.''

"I can find a place.''

"It's not safe. You could be hurt. Or worse. Nobody knows you're here. And they can't get in, anyway.''

"Yeah, but the press is going to squeeze this story like nothing you've ever seen.''

"It's okay,'' Christina said.

"Why do you want to take that chance?'' I said.

She leaned toward me, her big eyes opened wide.

"Because I always—'' Christina began, and then she paused, smiled gently and touched my arm with her finger.

"Just because,'' she said.

So we sat there, the picture of marital boredom, drinking beer and watching the tube. President Clinton extended his condolences from the Rose Garden. Dan Rather narrated an hour-long retrospective on Johnny Fiore's life.

Halfway through, I got up to change my bloody shirt but stretched out on Philippe's bed.

And awakened in silence and darkness.

I panicked, then remembered Christina and all of the rest. I shuddered. Looked at my watch, the glowing hands showing 10:35.

I sat up.

And saw it.

A streak, like a shooting star. It moved in the window across the street, then vanished.

Sixteen.

I rolled out of the bed and moved quickly to the corner by the window.

Listened.

Waited.

Stood perfectly still.

The window was open and a warm breeze wafted in. It carried the sound of sirens somewhere in the distance. The rattle of traffic, the rumble of trains. The scream of a nighthawk and then —

A cough.

It was a single sound, like a smoker clearing his throat.

I watched. The window was dark and I couldn't make out anyone. And then there was a sniff.

For the next fifteen minutes, I stood there. Was it Ramirez? Donatelli? The next shift of detectives? Would they stay there all night and watch me sleep? How could they tell I was still in the room? Did they have infrared goggles for the New York police?

I moved slowly away from the window, then eased over until I was behind Philippe's telescope. I crouched and peered into the eyepiece. Saw nothing at all. Reached for the end of the scope and pried off the lens cover. Peered again. The darkness was more palpable, and after a moment I could make out the lines of a window frame. I pressed the end of the scope gently and it swiveled away. I pulled it back. Pointed it at the window and bent to the smaller sighting scope. The window was in view. I moved to the other eyepiece.

Squinted. Waited. Took a deep breath and felt my neck start to cramp. Waited some more.

The cigarette glowed.

I could see the vague outline of head and shoulders. And then the figure moved. The head bowed. The movement was familiar. A glint of glass. A round disk. Another scope.

I eased slowly to the floor.

Had he seen me? Did he know I was watching him? How long had he been there?

I thought of the police papers with their NYPD stamp. In daylight, could he read them from that distance? Could he tell what they were? Who was he?

I waited five minutes, sitting on the floor. The person in the other window sniffed three times, coughed once. I moved away from the window, put on my bloody shirt and walked to Christina's open door.

From the doorway, I could see her. She was sprawled on her back on a big wrestling mat of a bed. There was a sheet across her legs, below her knees.

I stepped into the room, to the side of the bed. Hesitating for a moment, I reached down and touched Christina's bare shoulder. She awakened, not with a start, but with a sleepy, sultry smile.

"Don't just stand there, McMorrow," she said. "Climb in. Climb right in."

She rolled toward me and took my arm in both hands and started to pull.

"I can't," I said.

"Of course you can, McMorrow. We've got condoms. Come to me, baby."

"No, I mean I can't. Not now. I need to get outside."

Christina's eyes sharpened slightly. Her tug eased.

"You want the keys?"

"No, I want to go out the fire escape."

"Why?"

"Because somebody's watching the front of the building. I don't want him to see me leave."

She rolled onto her back again, but didn't pull up the sheet.

"How long? I'll wait for you."

I smiled.

"I don't know. You'll hear me."

"And then I'll feel you," Christina said.

Her hips gave a little roll of anticipation. I looked past her to the window and swallowed hard. That bridge would be waiting.

I slipped my shoes off and stepped onto the bed. The bottom of the window was barred with a steel grate, held shut with a padlock. The key was in it, and I twisted the lock off and pushed the grate out. It swung on hinges like a door. The bars of the fire escape were cold on my feet.

The stairs led to a ladder that led down to the roof of another building. I walked slowly, holding the narrow rail. My steps made a faint, hollow bong. At the bottom of the last flight, I paused. Listened. Heard the nighthawks and a siren and the whine of a mosquito.

It took a minute to find the ladder from the roof to the ground. I kicked something metallic and it skidded on the gravel. I crouched and listened. Heard nothing. Moved around a brick chimney and found the ladder. Swung around and started down.

On the ground, something scurried and then was gone. A cat? A rat? I waited and then walked down a pathway between the buildings toward a dim black arch. Under the arch was a door. It was steel. The bolts were big and heavy and felt medieval. I pulled a bolt across and opened it and stepped out onto the street.

I was around the corner from the elevator entrance, standing by a windowless brick wall. One streetlight glowed dimly two blocks up. In the faint orange light, nothing moved.

I walked away from the front of Christina's building to the next corner, crossed the street, which was cobblestone with asphalt patches and railroad tracks that shone like scars. Broken glass ground under my shoes.

At the next corner, I turned left again. There was one car on the street, but it had been stripped of its wheels and sat on the pavement like a legless beetle. I walked faster, broke into a trot as I crossed the next street. The bridge lights were straight ahead, the East River somewhere in the darkness to my left. I came to the next corner and stopped.

Poked my head around. Waited.

This was the end of the building closest to the window where the man was watching. Had he been dropped off? Had he walked here from somewhere else? Was he alone or was someone waiting for him?

I eased my way along the wall. Walked slowly, paused every few steps to listen. A hundred feet from the corner, I heard it.

A voice in the darkness.

A radio.

It was ahead of me, close to the wall. There was an entryway, a single opening, one truck wide. I inched along like a man on a ledge and the radio noise grew louder. It was a talk show. I heard the words "Yankees" and "Cleveland." I slowed. And the radio went off.

I froze.

"Yeah," a man's voice said. "Right . . . Police stuff . . .'Cause he could see them . . . Yeah, through the scope. They're great. Use 'em for bird watching or some goddamn thing. . . . You could see the stamp . . . Uh-huh . . . I don't know . . . He's upstairs. Still sitting on him . . . Yeah, shacked up with some babe. A goddamn fox, I wouldn't kick her out of bed . . . Yeah, from the hotel . . . That's her name? Never heard of her. No, nobody else. . . . This neighborhood? You kidding? It's like a graveyard . . . Yeah. Okay. Just say the word and we'll get it done."

I pressed against the wall. The voice stopped. The radio came back on.

He's never gonna recover from surgery and the Yankees knew it and the Red Sox knew it and the Mariners knew it, so why is it the Baltimore front office, in their infinite wisdom . . .

I moved toward the corner of the opening. Got my foot within a foot of it. Within six inches. Eased my shoulders along the bricks. And then I heard something else.

Car springs heaving. A grunt. Shoes scuffing on the pavement.

And then a sigh.

A trickling sound.

And a rivulet of urine running across the pavement and into the gutter.

I waited for the trickling to slow and then stop. The flow of urine subsided gradually. I heard the shoes scuff again, and then a gritty sound, close. Closer. He was coming out of the driveway. He was walking this way.

Looking around, I hesitated, then stepped gingerly backward. There was a doorway, but it was thirty feet away. I moved slowly, watching the opening.

And then froze.

He came out onto the street on the far side of the opening, a stocky figure in dark clothing. I pressed like a spider against the bricks. He turned. Looked up the street. Stood there for a moment as lights appeared in the distance. He had his hands on his hips. The car drew closer until I could see headlights, hear the sputter of a rough-idling motor. He still was at the corner of the building. As the car approached, he stepped back into the garage bay, but still peered out.

The car stopped fifty yards away. I saw the guy reach behind him and take out a gun. He held it close to his leg. The car didn't move.

He waited. I waited. The lights fell away as the car turned left and headed in the direction of the bridges.

"Goddamn mutts," the man said.

And wheeled completely around. Stopped and looked down the dark street toward me. Past me. I held my breath as the Boxer turned and walked back into the alley.

Seventeen.

I eased past Christina like she was a ticking bomb. Made it to Philippe's room, carrying my shoes. Then I took one of the cards out of my pocket, read it by the glow of a clock. Took the cell phone from the charger and punched in the number.

It rang once.

"Yeah," a woman's voice said.

"I'm trying to reach Detective Donatelli or—"

"Jesus, where the hell are you?"

"Who's this?"

"Ramirez."

Away from the phone, I heard her muffled voice say, "It's McMorrow." I eased myself up the wall until I was standing by the window.

"Where are you?" I said.

"Where am I? I'm at Midtown South," she barked. "Where are you?"

"I'm with a friend. Staying with a friend. Where's Donatelli?"

"On the road. Looking for you. What happened to SoHo?"

"I don't know. What happened to it?"

"You were supposed to be going there."

"Who told you that?"

"Nobody," Martinez said.

"The *Times*," I said.

"Whatever."

"Yeah, well, I changed my mind."

"No kidding," Ramirez said.

"And you've been looking for me?"

"You might say that. I mean, don't get a swelled head but you're kind of important to this case we're working on."

"So you don't know where I am?"

"What is this? Some kind of game?"

"No," I said. "It's not."

"So where are you? In case we need to reach you."

"I'm in New York," I said. "I'm not leaving. I'll call you."

"McMorrow, you're gonna get some people—"

I hung up. Then I walked to the window and looked across at the dark windows, where someone was looking back across at me. I pressed against the wall.

The DA's investigator had found me but the homicide cops hadn't. But why?

I mulled it as I stared.

The DA's office employed its own investigators, apart from the police. Police brought cases to the DA for prosecution, but it was the DA's investigators who did pretrial snooping, investigated witnesses, political rivals, anyone else the district attorney needed checked out.

In my time, the DA's office investigators had been ex-cops, private investigators, even ex-military. They were civilians employed at the whim of the district attorney. Cops thought of them as a loose bunch, bound not by any obligation to enforce the law, but by an obligation to their employer.

The Boxer was employed by the DA, Baldwin. Baldwin was employed by Fiore. Fiore was dead, so higher up the chain, that left—

Who?

. . .

I bought newspapers in Brooklyn Heights at a cafe/newsstand where the man behind the counter looked at my sunglasses and Statue of Liberty hat and said, "You making a delivery?"

I said no and bought the newspapers, one of each, and read them in the front seat of Christina's "four-wheel drive thing," a new black Range Rover. The lot attendant had picked me up, backing into the shadows of the garage bay. Christina introduced me only as her friend Jack. She'd left off the McMorrow, which now was strewn across the seat.

It wasn't in the lead headlines, all screaming banners, but in sidebars that began like the story in the *Times*, which ran in a single column starting above the fold. D. Robert got the byline.

The man who spent much of Saturday night with accused assassin Patrick "Butch" Casey said Sunday that in the hours before the slaying, the former New York City homicide detective gave no indication that he planned to murder Mayor John Fiore.

But Jack McMorrow, a former New York Times reporter now living in Maine, said Casey had harbored a grudge against Fiore since, as Manhattan district attorney, he had released a man accused of killing the detective's wife, Leslie Moore, in a 1988 carjacking.

"Of course he was bitter," McMorrow told the New York Times *today. "He blamed Fiore for releasing the man arrested for killing his wife."*

But McMorrow, 40, who has known Casey since they both were children growing up in Manhattan, said the ex-detective gave no indication that he expected to encounter Fiore at the Algonquin Saturday night.

"He said he was going to meet someone. He said he'd be talking to me in a couple of days," McMorrow said. "There was no sign of anything really out of the ordinary. He was working on a long-term project and we made plans to discuss it later."

McMorrow declined to say what the project involved.

Sitting at the curb in the car, I frowned and read, hurtling through the story. It recounted my evening with Butch, his wife's murder, the controversy over the alleged coaching of the key witness. The *Times* had talked to the waitress at the Bull and Thistle, who said Butch had been in before but had never caused any trouble. She said Butch seemed glad to see me, and that at one point we "leaned close together and talked sort of quietly."

The implication was left hanging.

There was a reference to the single stab wound. To Butch's long career in homicide, with a quote from an unnamed police source who said homicide detectives are versed in methods of killing, and Casey had been a particularly astute student of the criminal mind.

Big deal, I thought.

I read on. And gasped.

Authorities have said that Fiore was killed by a single stab wound from a long, narrow blade that penetrated his torso under the left arm and punctured his heart. This method of killing is taught to U.S. military commandos, including the elite Navy Seals and specialized reconnaissance units in the U.S. Army and Marines.

McMorrow left the Times *after a dispute with management over coverage of the Leslie Moore murder. He moved to Waldo County, Maine, a sparsely settled region that extends inland from the mid-coast near Belfast.*

In the small town of Prosperity, Maine, residents said McMorrow's closest friend is Clair Varney, a highly decorated retired Marine with extensive combat duty in the Vietnam War.

Varney was a member of an elite "Force Recon" Marine Corps unit, according to military sources. The sources said Varney's unit and others like it typically were dropped far behind enemy lines, where they observed enemy troop movements, often remaining concealed just yards from jungle trails. Marines who served in these units were taught to kill with knives, garrotes and other silent weapons that would not reveal their presence to the enemy.

According to one resident of Prosperity, McMorrow and Varney are neighbors, close friends, and share an interest in firearms. They often are partners in small logging operations in rural Waldo County.

Contacted at his home in Prosperity Sunday, Varney said he had no comment.

"Well, screw you, D. Robert," I said. "You son of a bitch."

It was all true, or close enough. The seam of innuendo was carefully stitched, precisely written.

As the motor idled and the air-conditioning roared, I picked up the car phone. Dialed the *Times* newsroom, waited while somebody summoned Ellen.

"What's this?" I said.

"What's what, Jack?"

"My friend's military record? Silent weapons? Clair Varney doesn't know Butch Casey. I've never talked to Clair about how to kill people. Clair's got absolutely nothing to do with this. Zip. Nothing."

"Jack," Ellen said. "Put yourself in our place."

"I have. This is a hatchet job."

"It isn't. We have a hugely important story. We have a man accused of killing the mayor of New York City. We have another man who knew him, perhaps better than anyone else, at least anyone else we can find, and was with him up to an hour before the murder."

"I hadn't seen Butch in years. Talk to cops if you want to know him."

"Cops haven't seen him either. We tried."

"So you latch on to me."

"You were there. You were with him that night. You have knowledge that could shed light on this terrible thing."

"But Clair?"

"Clair helps to define you for the reader."

"Oh, give me a break, Ellen. A guy who fought in a war thirty years ago?"

"He wasn't just a soldier. He has unusual skills."

"What?"

"Skills that were needed to commit this murder. How many people know how to stab someone in the heart, first try?"

"In New York? Probably more than you think."

"I don't think so. I think you've lost perspective on this, Jack. I'm sorry, but you're a big part of this story. And we haven't even gotten into the issue of your coverage of Casey's case, his wife's death. Yet."

"Yet?"

"Jack, I'm sorry. But my first responsibility is to the readers. And our job is to provide them with as complete a picture of this event as possible."

"Yeah?"

"So we're going to do a story on the Fiore-Casey connection. His wife's murder. And a sidebar on your disagreement with the *Times*."

"When?"

"Jack, the *News* is already working on it. We can't remain silent on this just because we were a party to it."

I considered it. Butch's run-in with DA Fiore was a big piece of this story. I was part of that piece.

"Will you talk to us?"

"I'll think about it."

"And there will be more," Ellen said.

There was something hesitant in her voice.

"On what?"

"A full-blown profile of Butch Casey. We've got four reporters working it today."

"Yeah?"

"And a story about you."

"What?"

"The long and meandering path that led childhood friends to this terrible parting."

The motor idled. The air blew cool. I closed my eyes for a moment. I felt stripped. Naked. Exposed.

"Well, Jack. Will you talk to us?"

I waited. Shook my head.

"Who else are you talking to? My first-grade teacher?"

"No. But former colleagues here. The ranking editors back then. Tom Wellington, about your work for the *Globe*. Anybody we can get in your town up there. Your—"

Ellen paused.

"We'll try Christina. And your longtime companion in Maine. Roxanne."

"Oh, come on. She doesn't know Butch. She doesn't even know much about me from back then."

"She knows you now."

"Ellen, you're reaching."

"I don't think so. This story is so big you can't possibly reach too far."

"Leave Roxanne out of it."

"The Boston bureau already has people on their way to Portland. Jack, please. Try to look at this as a journalist."

"But she has her own life. She doesn't need this. Why can't you just leave her alone?"

There was silence on the other end of the phone.

"All right," I said. "You want a story. I'll give you a story."

I slammed the phone down. Shoved the newspapers aside. Picked up the envelope and shook out the pages.

Carmine Street. A couple of blocks from Houston, off Bleeker.

I put the Rover in gear and drove.

Eighteen.

The house was a three-story brownstone. There was a tree in front surrounded by a cast-iron grating, like an arboreal holding cell. The door of the brownstone had been red but it was faded toward pink. The railing on the front steps and the gratings on the ground-floor windows had been painted black but were peeling. The place was respectable in a worn sort of way, like an old Burberry raincoat, a twenty-year-old Brooks Brothers suit.

I made one slow pass, then double-parked, took off the hat and glasses and walked up the steps. The brass knocker was tarnished. I rapped with it three times. Waited. Rapped again.

Tilbury could be teaching, I thought, one of those professors who die in the classroom. He could be visiting his wife, one of those dutiful husbands who show up at the nursing home every day at the same time, like clockwork. Or he could be—

Hiding.

People in New York don't open their doors to strangers. A man whose wife has been brutally mugged would be leerier than most. I turned and went back to the Rover, got Tilbury's phone number from directory assistance. I dialed. It rang. I waited. It rang some more.

And then it stopped.

A voice whispered, ''Hello.''

''Mr. Tilbury?'' I said.

''Who's this?''

Still a whisper.

''I'm a reporter,'' I said. ''My name is McMorrow. I'm—''

I slurred my name. Now I hesitated.

''I'm looking into a possible story involving City Hall. And the late mayor. And I was hoping to speak with you.''

''About what?''

''About your wife, Mr. Tilbury. About the attack on her and the way it was handled by authorities.''

He didn't answer. I thought I'd lost him.

''How'd you get my name?'' he said more sharply.

''From records at the police department. Your inquiries are public documents.''

''Well, that's all over with. And I can't talk right now. There was someone at the door. This is the time they do their burglaries, you know. Middle of the day.''

''No, that was me, sir. I was at your door. I knocked but I thought you might not hear me. I'm in my car, outside.''

''I don't—''

I didn't let him finish.

''I'll be right there,'' I said and I started walking and watching the house. On the second floor, a curtain moved. I smiled and waved, went up the steps and waited. I heard the sound of many locks unbolting. And then the door opened slowly, releasing a waft of cool, stale air.

Tilbury was tall, even with a stoop, his hair white and wild, his eyes a startling deep blue. He was wearing rumpled khakis, a wrinkled pink Oxford-cloth shirt and brown loafers. His uniform probably hadn't changed since prep school. His clothes hadn't been ironed since his wife had been mugged. He carried with him the unmistakable odor of an old man.

"I'm very sorry about Mrs. Tilbury," I said. "And I hope I'm not disturbing you."

He looked at me uneasily, so I smiled and held out my hand.

"It's Mr. Murrow?" Tilbury said.

"I won't take too much of your time."

"No, that's all right. I'm retired."

"You taught?"

"At NYU. Mathematics."

"I went to NYU. English literature."

"You look familiar. Ever take mathematics?"

I shook my head.

"What class?"

"Eighty."

"Oh, yes," Tilbury said, as though the year were a good wine and he remembered it well.

We stood there. I smiled again, peeked through the door. I could see a vase of dusty dry flowers, above the vase a photograph on the wall in the hallway. It was black and white. A woman.

"Is that Mrs. Tilbury?" I asked, and when he turned, I stepped past him. He had no choice but to follow.

I stared at the photograph. The woman was in the foreground, hawk-nosed and intense. In the background were bare, eroded hills.

"A dig?" I said, leaning closer.

"Yes. East Africa. Hominids."

"She did a lot of fieldwork?"

"Yes. In the early years," Tilbury said, and then he shook off the doddering dust. "Now what is it, exactly, that I can do for you?"

I turned toward him. The door still was open. He didn't ask me to sit or invite me deeper into the musty tomb of a house.

"I saw your inquiries about the investigation of the attack," I said.

"Yes, well—"

"And I know you had serious concerns about the investigation. You even hired your own private investigator to locate the suspect, after he'd jumped bail."

Tilbury looked at me, his eyes narrowing.

"So what is it that you want?"

"There were several cases during that time period that were similar. They all involved alleged prosecutorial—how can I put this?—sloppiness. Suspects who made bail and skipped. Suspects who were given sentences that, on the face of it, seem way too light."

He didn't answer.

"You went to considerable lengths to stay with your wife's case, Mr. Tilbury. You located, what was his name?"

"Lester John," Tilbury said slowly, as if pronouncing the name of the devil in church.

I slid a notebook out of my back pocket. Like a stalking cat, I kept my eyes on his as I opened it and started to write.

"And two weeks ago, you asked that police pick him up and—"

"They did."

"They arrested him?"

"Yes. He was taken into custody. By detectives."

"Really. So all your work paid off."

He looked at me oddly.

"My wife still is in a nursing home. She's in what they call a permanent vegetative state."

"I'm very sorry."

He nodded, once.

"So are you awaiting Mr. John's trial?"

"No."

I was surprised.

"I understand he pleaded guilty," Tilbury said.

"Really. Did he get a deal?"

"I'm told he admitted to the attack."

"When is his sentencing?"

"Well, first he has to go to another state and stand trial.

He was wanted for something else, a homicide, I believe. In the South. Alabama or Mississippi.''

"So he's going to stand trial there?''

"I think he's going to admit that, too. They said he was tired of hiding.''

Beats an Alabama prison, I thought.

"Was this in the paper?'' I asked him.

"I don't know. I get the *Times*, but they don't always cover that sort of thing. You said you were with the *Times*?''

I considered the question and its tense.

"Yes,'' I said.

"Well, then I'll look for your story, sir.''

It was a dismissal, or the beginning of one.

"But Mr. Tilbury, I think there's a bigger story here. You had to find the suspect yourself, before he was arrested. Others who were victims around the same time had similar experiences. Can you tell me who you dealt with at the police department?''

"No. I don't want to open it all up again. It's over, as much as it can be. This animal is behind bars. He will no longer prey on the innocent and helpless.''

Tilbury stopped talking, then said: "Is that good enough for you?''

"Well, I'd like to talk to you about Mrs. Tilbury, about what you've gone through over the last ten years. Hiring the investigator. Maybe talk to him about how he located this John fellow, how you feel finally having this behind—''

"I don't think so.''

I paused, my notebook in front of me.

"In fact, I don't want to even be in your story.''

"But—''

He put his hand on my shoulder and started to guide me toward the still-open door. I balked, stood my ground.

"I really think there's more to this, Mr. Tilbury, and I can understand why—''

"No, you can't,'' he said. "It's been ten years of hell.

Like a dead person who still breathes. It costs a fortune, and I was nearly out of money when—''

He caught himself.

''I appreciate your interest, Mr. Murrow, but I really don't want to be in your story.''

''But Mr. Tilbury, you already are.''

He stopped.

''Sir, is that a threat?''

''Not at all. It's a fact. Your letters are public documents.''

''I know people at the *Times*. I'll call them.''

''They'll tell you the same thing. Call the journalism professors at NYU. They'll tell you, too.''

''Then I'll take legal action. I'll—''

I looked at him with pity and it must have shown through.

''Goddamn it,'' David Tilbury exploded, white spittle on his lips. ''Don't you understand? He can change his mind.''

''Who?'' I said.

''John. He can change his mind. They told me. If it's a big deal, all over the newspapers, the lawyers read those newspapers. They'll be calling him up, writing to him. Saying, 'Don't take that deal. I can get you off.' ''

''So the police didn't want this arrest publicized?''

He didn't answer.

''Who told you that, Mr. Tilbury? Because in my experience, cops want nothing more than to have their arrests in the paper. And this one, yeah, the guy jumped bail, but wanted for homicide out of state? Nearly a homicide here, with a prominent victim? It just doesn't make sense for them to—''

''It doesn't have to make sense to you, sir,'' Tilbury said. ''And besides, Mr. Murrow, I see no constructive reason to throw dirt at a dead man.''

''Who, Fiore?''

''Good day, Mr. Murrow.''

''Who told you all this?''

''I'm afraid you're going to have to leave.''

"With all due respect, Mr. Tilbury, I think you're get-ting some bad advice here. Publicity doesn't make it less likely a guy will get hammered in court. It makes it more likely. It puts pressure on—"

But then I was out in the heat and glare and Tilbury said, "Good day" one last time and closed the door. As I stood there, I heard the locks sliding home.

Nineteen.

So I knew a couple of things. David Tilbury didn't want to kick the mayor's corpse. And he was getting advice from someone who didn't know the first thing about the press or New York.

You want to scare people? Have Tilbury in the newspaper talking about how this mugging exhausted his 401K. The whole city would be screaming for a piece of Lester John, for a judge to put his head on a plate, for the cops to lock up scum like this before they cost the law-abiding citizens of New York their tax-deferred mutual funds.

But Tilbury had been told to keep it quiet. An arrest for aggravated assault, extradition for a homicide—even in New York, that was news.

Back in the car, I fished out Donatelli's card and called and got a beeper. I punched in the cell phone number and started down the street. A minute later the phone rang.

"Yeah," I said.

"McMorrow?" Donatelli said.

"Right here."

"Right where?"

"Deep in the heart of lower Manhattan."

"In your girlfriend's Range Rover?"

"She's not my girlfriend."

"Okay, she's your sister. Christina Mansell. Lives in a loft in Brooklyn. Where's an artist get the dough for a car like that?"

"She made it the old-fashioned way. She inherited it."

"Must be nice. I'm gonna inherit a funeral bill and one-eighth of four rooms of used furniture. Now where can we get together, McMorrow? I'd like to get a look at you."

"DA's people beat you by twelve hours."

For a moment, Donatelli didn't answer.

"Says who?"

"Says me. They were there all night."

"No shit."

"You guys ought to talk more."

"What can I say? They're assholes."

"Here's another one. You know of the arrest of a guy named Lester John?"

"No."

"Would have been in Brooklyn. He's in his late twenties."

"A lot of people get arrested in Brooklyn."

"This one was arrested here for an old aggravated assault, but he's wanted for homicide in Alabama. They're taking him first."

"Right now?"

"Last week or so."

"What do you care? They got you writing the police blotter now?"

"Something like that. This Lester John mugged an NYU professor in 1988. Practically killed her. Then skipped."

"Outside the subway, right? I think I remember that one. Press jumped on it 'cause of who the victim was. But the guy, I don't know, seems to me he was supposed to have gone south and gotten himself killed or something."

"I heard he was picked up in the Red Hook project."

"Huh."

"Could you check?"

"Yeah, maybe. I'll put my entire staff on it. Now when can we meet?"

"Call me back about this guy. We'll talk about it then."

"Hey, McMorrow, who's in charge here?" Donatelli said.

"Good question," I said. "If I find out, I'll let you know."

I called Conroy's office from a pay phone, told the man who answered that I'd meet Mr. Conroy in fifteen minutes at the coffee shop on Broadway, across from the end of City Hall Park. The man said Mr. Conroy had meetings all day. I told the man my name and said I was sure Mr. Conroy would fit me in.

He did.

I waited against a building just down the street from the shop. Conroy crossed the park in a hurried walk, dashed across the street, peered in the shop window briefly. When he went in, I followed.

"David," I said behind him, and he started, then recovered and turned and smiled.

"Reporters. Always blindsiding you."

"That's right. Sneaky little devils. But in our case it was the other way around, don't you think?"

"Jack, I've always been sorry about that. I was only the messenger. You realize that."

"Sure, David. I know you were just following orders. And it was a long time ago. And now there's nobody left to be mad at, really."

"No," he said, suddenly somber. "It's truly unbelievable."

We got coffee and sat at a table in the back. The table was small and it stood between us like a chessboard in the park. We looked at our cups but neither of us made a move to drink. Conroy's fingers were slender, his nails manicured. His suit was tasteful, always pinstripes, as unvarying as a Yankees uniform. His shirt was white and his hair was thinning. As far as I knew, he had no interests, no sex life with either gender. Just City Hall and Johnny Fiore.

"So this must be hard on you," I said. "You and Fiore were together for a long time."

"It's—"

He searched for the words.

"—beyond comprehension. He was such a great man. Truly a great leader."

"You think he was headed for the White House?"

"No doubt in my mind. Every pinnacle in front of him, he climbed. He was going to address the Democratic National Convention this year. I think he was destined to be one of the greatest presidents this country has ever seen."

"Or not," I said. "Destined, I mean. Because—"

"Because that fool, that pathetic loser of a—"

He caught himself.

"I'm sorry. I know you were friendly with Casey."

"Yes, we established that, didn't we?"

"Like I said, that was business. Nothing personal."

"Of course not."

Conroy looked at me to see if I was being facetious. I wasn't sure myself.

"So you called," I said. "Said it was imperative."

"Yeah, Jack. I mean—"

He lifted the coffee to his mouth but put it down without drinking.

"I know you've talked to the detectives and all. But I just had to talk to you myself. To ask you why."

"Why what?"

"Why he did such a thing."

"We don't know that he did," I said. "That's why we have courts and juries."

"Oh, come off it, Jack. They didn't arrest him for no reason. They have his goddamn fingerprints. His fingerprints in the mayor's blood. He did it."

"That hasn't been established. There's a process."

"Well, I can't wait for the process, McMorrow," he snapped. "I gave fifteen years of my life to this man. I need to know why. Why now? Casey's wife was killed? Too bad. I mean, it's terrible. But—"

"But get over it?"

"Why not?"

"He really loved her."

"I loved working for Mayor Fiore."

He paused.

"Everybody loves somebody, Jack."

"Sometime," I said.

"This isn't the time for humor."

"Sorry. It just popped out. Word association."

"Oh, I know," Conroy said. "We're all under tremendous stress. The grieving process takes its toll. Anyway, I just wanted to talk to you. Privately. Off the record. I won't repeat it to a soul. I just need to know if he said anything. If he gave any indication . . ."

"That he intended to harm Fiore? No."

"Well, what did he talk about? What was he thinking? I mean, was he talking about baseball or something, and then just went out and—allegedly, I mean."

"We chatted," I said.

Conroy's grief seemed to clear and his gaze hardened. He leaned forward as though to snap up the words as they flew from my mouth.

"We talked about old times," I said. "I hadn't seen him in several years. Got a Christmas card every year. A note once in a great while."

"And what did he say he'd been doing?"

"Not too much. I think he sort of puttered around. Took in some culture. He'd toyed with the idea of writing a book."

"About what?"

"About all the murderers he helped convict over the years. He wanted to study them and come up with some sort of pattern."

Conroy looked relieved.

"Sounds academic, almost."

"He hadn't found a publisher. Probably could now, though."

"Oh, God, yes. It's a sick country."

"In some ways."

I waited. Looked at my coffee.

"But didn't he do any investigative work? It seems these ex-detectives all try to be Magnum P.I., at least for a while."

"No."

"Really?" Conroy said.

"You remember he went out on stress disability. Stress and alcohol."

"Oh, yes. I knew that."

"I'll bet you did."

Conroy paused, as though he were going to say something but had reconsidered. When he did speak, he said, "So Casey wasn't working? Just taking walks in the park and feeding the pigeons?"

I looked at him for a moment, considered how to answer that. Conroy was looking into his coffee, but then he looked up, unblinking. I watched him as I spoke.

"He was working on something," I said slowly. "He said it was very big, it would be a big story for the *Times*."

Conroy smiled. Suddenly it was all very amusing.

"Oh, and what was that about?"

"He said it was huge," I said.

"That was all? Nothing else."

"Oh, we talked about it a little. We were going to talk about it some more. But then . . ."

I shrugged.

"Then this happened," Conroy said.

"And the story goes on the back burner, I guess," I said.

"What was it about?"

"It's kind of hard to explain."

"His murder cases? The mob?"

I stood and Conroy stood with me, eyes following mine.

"More like corruption in high places," I said.

Conroy gave a little laugh, his face frozen in a half-smile.

"The usual stuff, then," he said.

"No," I said. "Not really the usual stuff at all."

And with that, I said I had to go, and I did, getting up and walking straight out the door, sticking Conroy with the bill for old times' sake. Up the block, I turned and saw him loping across the park to City Hall, like a lookout running for the village with very bad news.

July 1988

The uniform cop didn't know Butch Casey and she held up her hand and said, "Hey, you," as he stepped over the crime-scene tape and continued toward her.

"Homicide," he said, showing his shield. "I was going by. Whatcha got?"

"Carjacking. Victim dead or close to it. Looks like the shooter got her out, don't know how, got in the car and shot her in the face."

"In and out?"

"Yup."

"No slug."

"Not yet."

Casey looked at the blood that had spilled onto the sidewalk and trickled over the curb into the gutter. It was dark, like chocolate syrup.

"Got a plate on the car?" he said.

"Yeah," the cop said. "We ran her name, got the reg. She worked here. Must've just got off her shift and was pulling out."

"Where was security?"

"Other end of the lot, car broken into."

"Took all of 'em to do that?"

The cop shrugged.

"You got people here?"

"Yeah. They're inside now."

Casey looked at the blood again.

"No shells?"

"Just the victim. A bunch of people around her wigging out."

She shook her head.

"That's why I drive a shit box," the cop said.

"Yeah, well, then it breaks down and you're in trouble anyway. Stuck out in the bush country somewheres."

The cop was black and Casey caught himself, but she didn't seem to be offended.

"You can't win," she said.

"Nope," Casey said. "Well, I'm off. I gotta meet my wife inside. She works here, too. In the E.R. I'll ask her if she knows the victim."

"That's where she worked," the cop said. "E.R. people came out here. They were going nuts."

"Is that right?" Casey said, thinking of Leslie, worried she'd be upset, and then thinking, if she was working on this lady, she wouldn't be mad about him being late. A weird silver lining.

"I better get in there," he said.

The cop nodded. Casey turned toward the lighted walkway that led to the emergency entrance. Took a couple of steps, and then turned back.

"Good luck," he said.

"Yeah, we'll hope the car gets spotted quick, before they chop it."

"Kill somebody for a goddamn car," Casey said. "Goddamn pigs."

"Yeah, even if it was a Lexus."

Casey froze. He started to shake his head. He said, "No."

"Yeah, it was," the cop said, misunderstanding. She took out her notebook. "A Lexus, model ES 300. Dark green."

"No," Casey gasped. "Oh, my God, no."

"What's the matter?" the cop said, looking at her notebook.

"Not Leslie. Please, God, not Leslie."

"You okay?" the cop said softly.

Casey gasped, "Oh, God, no." He stood there for a moment, the life draining out of him just as Leslie's had, and he said it again, softly. "Oh, God." And then he bellowed, clamped his hands to his head. Started up the walkway, running but rigid, and he stumbled, then lurched on, wailing, "No, God, no, oh please, God," because, as he'd always said, at that moment even the worst dirtbag in the world starts talking to Jesus.

Twenty.

The block around the Criminal Courts Building looked like Tower Hill on execution day, but without the glee.

There were satellite trucks in the streets, which were blocked off by police barriers and orange cones. In the courtyard between the buildings people milled in somber clumps, like mourners stalling outside a wake. TV reporters were doing advance spots outside the south entrance hall, where the CRIMINAL COURTS BUILDING inscription, coldly chiseled in the stone, implied that justice always was inevitable, harsh and swift.

It wasn't, but this case might be the exception.

Glasses on, hat pulled low, I stood in line at the building's south entrance. The usual security was a cop with one eye on the job, the other on the clock. On this day there were six cops, two running a metal detector, four just staring. There was no banter between lawyers, no kidding among the clerks. The cops didn't smile. The defendants looked confused.

Fiore's death hung over the place like a grim haze.

My turn came. Christina's car keys went in a bowl, my wallet, too, like an offering at church. I stepped through and the woman cop passed the wand over me, front and back, between my legs. Her partner looked at me and then looked at her.

"Okay?" he said doubtfully.

She nodded, but he looked at me again, like he knew me from somewhere.

"Where you gotta go?" he said.

"Arraignment. AR 1," I said.

"When they gonna . . ." he murmured to the woman.

"Not for another hour," she said.

"You know where it is?" the guy asked me.

"Yeah," I said. "Been there before."

More than once, for the *Times*, but the courtroom had never looked quite like this.

I pushed through the swinging wooden doors and a cop stopped me.

"You," he said.

I froze.

"Take off your hat."

I did, but left the glasses on. Moved to find a seat.

The room was full, not with the usual unfortunates, but with reporters, who sat with notebooks in hand and every few moments checked their watches. I squeezed in next to a young preppie-looking guy who looked away from me with distaste. I figured there must be a reporting pool for something as big as this, and the courtroom would be cleared before Butch was brought in. This guy was getting the scene down. I did the same.

The defendants up front were mostly black and Hispanic. The lawyers were not. Tommy Hilfiger was the uniform of choice and the favored crime was selling drugs. Each case ended with the bailiff's chant:

"Take a step back, turn around, and walk directly to the rear of the room."

I watched for a half-hour, lulled by the sea chantey of the bailiff, by the defendants moving through, resigned and expressionless, as though they were in line to get their driver's licenses renewed.

And then I saw him.

It was through the open door at the front of the courtroom, to the left. Dave Conroy peeked into the courtroom, glancing out at the assembled like the minister ready to start the service. He poked his head in three or four times, then didn't reappear. I waited five minutes, then got up and went out into the hallway. There were cops, people in suits, defendants and reporters. I was about to go back into the courtroom when an unmarked door swung open.

And the Boxer came out.

He was wearing a suit and he stood for a moment and pushed at his tie. Then the door opened again and Conroy emerged. He started down the long corridor toward the atrium. The Boxer followed, thirty feet behind. I brought up the rear.

Conroy walked down the corridor and took a right at the atrium. The Boxer turned, too, and I followed, down a hallway with office doors. A cop stopped and asked where I was going. I said I was looking for the men's room. She said there was one at the end of the hall, and pointed the other direction. I walked slowly back the way I had come, until the cop turned off. I turned back in time to see the Boxer at the end of the hall.

I broke into a trot and followed. When I turned at the end of the corridor, he was stepping into an office. The door closed behind him. I pressed close to the wall and listened.

"We got a problem."

The Boxer's voice.

"What?" Conroy snapped.

"That professor called."

"Jesus."

"Said he told McMorrow all about our man being arrested."

"Goddamn it. What is that son of a bitch doing?"

"I don't know, but the professor told him the arrest was in Brooklyn."

"Which McMorrow can check."

"He was worried it might sour things if it got in the paper."

"Shit."

"So I was right," the Boxer said.

Conroy didn't answer.

"What did I tell you? He's handed it off to Mc-Morrow."

"I know that. I just saw him across the street."

"He was here?"

"Of course he was, Sherlock-fucking-Holmes. I'm glad to see you're on top of things."

"I didn't lose him, Derek did. Got caught in traffic and lost the car. McMorrow must've been hiding in the back. But he'll report in. I mean, the homicide guys told him that. Unless he decides to run home to Maine."

"No, he'll stick around," Conroy said. "The man's a loose cannon. Not a typical reporter. He's . . . he takes things too far. That was his problem before. He gets tangled up in things."

"He's tangled up good now."

"And you're just going to have to untangle him."

"Got to locate him, first."

"You're a professional. Figure it out. He's talked to the professor. Where might he go next?"

"Depends."

"That's brilliant. Is that deductive reasoning or inductive?"

"Don't ride my ass," the Boxer said. "We'll pick him up. Casey said anything about it yet?"

"Nothing. Says he doesn't know anything about any killing, never touched Fiore, the thing with his wife is all in the past. And then he just sits there, almost smug, like everything's going according to plan."

"Well, we're gonna have to have a plan. We got cases scattered all over New York."

"So watch all of them."

"I'll need more people."

"Get them, for Christ's sake. Sometimes I think you forget what's at stake here."

"A lot."

"Everything, that's what," Conroy hissed. "This is history, and you're a part of it, believe it or not. So don't screw it up. Come on. We're late for the inquisition."

The Boxer's response was muffled.

And the door opened.

I whirled away, started walking.

"Where's the bathroom?" I mumbled, still walking. "That guy said there was a bathroom."

I grabbed my crotch. Kept walking, with a limp.

"God almighty," I heard the Boxer say. "The shitbums that come crawling in here."

And then they turned and were gone. I let go of my groin, wondered what Butch had stumbled onto. I wished I could ask him, talk to him, even for ten seconds.

So minutes later, I stood on the back side of the courthouse, across from a little paved park with a beat-up Chinese pavilion. There were pretzel guys in the park and the sidewalks near the entrance were blocked off by barricades and cops.

The media waited.

There were twenty or more TV crews, twice as many reporters. People primped, smoked, talked on cell phones. Helicopters, some news and some police, hovered high overhead, their woofing clatter echoing off the buildings. I stood by two TV cameramen who were wondering whether Bill Clinton would come to Fiore's service or the White House would just send Al Gore.

"You think they'll make this cop do the walk?" one cameraman said to the other. "Interesting situation. He's a detective and they stick together like glue."

"You kidding? He killed the mayor. They'll tar and feather the bastard, bring him in on a rail, but I could be wrong. Hey, you hear who he's got for a lawyer? Lemme tell you, it's gonna be a heavyweight. You can't buy this kind of publicity. I was talking to some guys from France here this morning, and the Japanese are all over it. Right up their alley. They eat this—"

He looked to his right, past me. Grabbed his camera off the ground and broke into a run. The other cameramen followed, sweeping by me in a clattering herd.

There was a blue and white radio car turning the corner.

Behind it was a big NYPD van, and they both slowed and stopped opposite a single unmarked door. Motorcycle cops appeared from the rear, veered around the two marked vehicles and stopped. A police truck swung out from behind the procession and two guys in blue jumpsuits got out and started unloading more barricades.

The park was emptying. The street was full of people. I started to move with the crowd and then I thought, what was all this cop stuff? Wouldn't he be in the custody of Corrections? What color were their—

A car slipped in behind me, from the opposite direction.

I turned. It was black, a big Mercury with tinted windows. There was a second car behind it, identical to the first. The doors popped open, and men and women in suits tumbled out. Ramirez was there. Donatelli, too. Some stood in a phalanx. It was Ramirez who turned back to the second car, the back seat. Leaned in.

And helped Butch out.

His first step was almost a stumble, and with his wrists cuffed in front of him, it looked like he was going to drop to his knees and pray. But then he stood straight, put his shoulders back and looked around, as if to commit the scene to memory.

His jail suit was medium blue and the trousers were too long. He was wearing brown shoes and his legs were shackled.

I moved toward him, ten steps.

"The envelope," I called. "What is it?"

Butch turned and looked and his gaze fastened on me. His eyes widened and he stopped, Ramirez still holding him by the upper arm.

"It was all arranged," he called to me. "There was a plan. Fiore had a—"

Ramirez turned, saw me and pointed. Said, "Hey, he can't be—"

"It's all there," Butch called. "Just put it together. You'll see—"

And the mob descended.

They were jostling for position. Rattling equipment.

Cursing and shoving. A camera hit me in the back and I was elbowed aside and I held my hands up to protect my face. As I spun away, Butch disappeared through the courthouse door.

"Son of a bitch," someone said, and then there was a cacophony of curses and catcalls.

"When's he coming out?"

"You bringing him out here?"

"What kind of bullshit is this?"

"Who you guys trying to protect, anyway?"

The two uniform cops guarding the door stood their ground but said nothing. But now I knew the answer was out there, like the prize in a giant scavenger hunt. Conroy and the Boxer knew, too. The race was on.

Twenty-one.

The Red Hook housing project was near the piers, and that afternoon it teemed with life, like a brick coral reef.

There were kids on the playground, boys tossing basketballs at chain-link hoops. Women sat on benches, strollers parked in front of them. Young guys hunched at the curbs, leaning into the windows of cars. A Monte Carlo. A Lincoln. A Porsche Carrera. When the Range Rover rolled through—heavily tinted windows, steel brush bars front and rear—the young guys raised up and stared.

It was a little after one o'clock. Butch probably was just leaving court to go back to Riker's. I'd come here first, knowing it was on the list, hoping I was a step ahead of the Boxer.

Preferably two.

Lorraine Street ran through the center of the project and 123 to 131 was the second building in. I circled the block and parked in front of the Project Food Store. When I locked the Rover, its lights flashed once, like a lighthouse beacon. The men leaning against the wall by the store looked at me without any expression at all. When I walked up the street, two of them followed.

There were bars on the windows but not on the doors, and the entrance numbers were posted on bright-blue signs. I turned down the walkway at 123, saw a metal door with a small window in the center. I stopped and leaned on the black steel fence.

Little kids walked by and stared. Two teenage boys— big pants, blue bandanna headbands—glared as they shuffled by. A woman watched me from a fourth-floor window. The two men from the store stood by the street and waited.

I took out my reporter's notebook, my Red Cross flag of neutrality. Opened it and scribbled. The boys came back across the courtyard but there were four of them now, all showing the same colors. My polo shirt was dark green.

I hoped green was not significant.

And then an older woman came down the sidewalk, pulling a wire grocery cart. She passed the men, said hello to one of the boys. It embarrassed him, made him seem a little less lethal. She looked me in the eye, said "Good afternoon" and went to the door. Opened it with a key. As she wrestled the cart inside, I slipped in behind her.

We got in the elevator together. She said wasn't it hot, and I said, yes, it was. She asked if I was "from the city," and I said, no, the newspaper. The elevator stopped and I got out and she called after me, "You take care of yourself."

The doors closed.

There had once been numbers on all the doors, I supposed, but no more. I found 203 and started counting up. Nine doors down the hall, I knocked, and in the silent hallway, it sounded like a sledgehammer.

I waited. A man's voice said, "What?" I heard more voices down the hall, from the direction of the elevator.

"Is this 212?" I said.

"What? Who's that?"

The voices down the hall were louder.

"Is this apartment 212? Mrs. Stephens?"

"You got 217. Even numbers, across the hall."

I turned, started back toward the elevator. The four boys came around the corner, two by two. When they saw me, they slowed but kept on coming. They had their hands in their pockets, a spring in their steps.

Ten feet away, I stopped.

"Hey," I said.

They didn't answer.

"I'm looking for Lester John. You know him?"

They looked at me.

"Who are you?"

It was the smallest kid, light-skinned, handsome as a dancer.

"A reporter. From the *New York Times*. I need to talk to Lester John."

"What for you want to talk to Lester?"

"For a story. About something he was arrested for, but he may not have done it."

"So you gonna help Lester with your story?"

"I don't know."

They moved closer.

"You pay for people to talk to you? Like on TV?"

"No."

"Then we don't gotta tell you shit."

The others were smiling.

"You got a hundred dollars, I tell you everything I know about Lester."

"Sorry. No money."

They snickered. The kid looked at them, then at me.

"You got a fuckin' downtown job, you going around with no money? You fuckin' crazy, telling me that? You think we're fuckin' stupid?"

The others laughed. He moved closer.

"Come on, man. Fifty bucks, I tell you about Lester. I'll take you to him. You can take his picture for the *New York* mother-fuckin' *Times*."

The others grinned.

"Sorry."

"You don't think Lester's worth fifty? My friend Lester. That's a crazy-ass thing to do, here in my block. You understand? You coming in here, fucking with me? Fucking with my friend Lester? Pay me the money, reporter fucker.''

He took a step closer. A knife came out of his pocket. He gave it a shake and the blade swung out. I started to back away. The kid moved with me.

His eyes were fixed on mine. He smiled.

''You ain't scared, are ya? You ain't scared a dyin'? Happens to everybody, my man. Just happens to some sooner than others.''

He jabbed. I jumped. The men from the street came around the corner. The older woman was behind them, minus the cart.

''Hey,'' one of the men called. The kids turned.

''Let him outta here.''

''He's interviewing me. 'Cause I'm a friend of Lester.''

The knife went back in the pocket. I brushed by him, stepped through the others and one of them shoved me from behind. I kept going and brushed by the men, too.

''Look at that reporter run,'' the kid called.

I slowed, walked to the elevator. Pushed the button. The men came and stood behind me. The door opened, graffiti sliding into the wall.

''You better get in there and keep on going,'' the older man, the talker, said. He was fortyish and big and solemn. His hands were in the pocket of his sweatshirt. The pocket showed the shape of a handgun.

''Thanks,'' I said.

'' 'Cause we don't want white cops here,'' he said. ''Ugly-ass white apartheid cops.''

''Did white cops come and take away Lester John?'' I said.

''Just go,'' he said, and the door rolled shut.

I closed my eyes and exhaled slowly. The elevator rumbled down and ejected me on the first floor. I went out the door and down the walk, hurried along the street. When I looked back, the men were on the sidewalk watching me. When I turned back toward the Range Rover, I

saw a brown Taurus parked beyond it on the other side
of the street.

There were two men in it, white men, and they were
watching me, too.

The Taurus pulled out. I kept walking. It drove slowly
toward me and I walked faster, broke into a jog.

And then the Rover was between me and their car. It
sped up and passed, and I got only a glimpse of the driver,
the back of his head. Hair shorn on the sides, long in back.
The Taurus drove between the buildings, drew stares from
the loiterers. I watched it as I circled the car and got in,
watched it in the mirror. It turned around in a tree-lined
circle on the other side of the project, started back.

I started the Rover, put it in gear.

Jumped as someone banged the window.

She was fiftyish, young skin and tired eyes and a hand
balled into a fist.

"You the reporter?" she said through the glass.

I buzzed the window down.

"Yeah."

"You asking for Lester?"

"Yeah, I was."

"They took him," she said. "And I can't find out
where he's at. You find him for me, I'll pay you for your
time."

I looked in the mirror, saw the Taurus waiting in the
distance. I unlocked the door.

"Get in," I said. "We can talk about it."

She did, arranged herself in the seat. She was wearing
black bicycle shorts and a red T-shirt that read "Red
Hook Tenants Assoc."

"Mrs. Stephens," I said. "I'm Jack McMorrow."

Lynette Stephens glanced at me knowingly.

"You looking for somebody and somebody else is
looking for you?" she said.

I paused. Looked in the mirror at the Taurus, still sitting.

"Something like that."

"I saw you on the TV but I know better than to believe most of what I see on there. I read the story in the paper, too."

"You still want to talk to me?"

"I'll talk to you if it'll help me find Lester."

"When did he leave?"

"He didn't leave. They took him."

"Who?"

"Police. Detectives."

"When?"

"Two weeks ago tomorrow. Came at night. Said, 'Unlock the door, ma'am. We need to speak to you. We have bad news about your brother.' "

"You have a brother?"

"In Detroit. But there wasn't news about him. I unlock the door and they knock me down on the floor and Lester, he's in bed. They got guns and they kick the door in and they scream at him, put those guns on him and drag him right out of bed in his shorts. He tried to talk and one of 'em hit him in the mouth with his gun and there's blood all over his face and he's saying, 'Call the cops.' And I'm saying, 'They are the cops.' "

"Did they show badges?"

"Hell, no. Just guns. I said, 'You got a warrant? You got I.D.?' They say, 'Shut up, you dirty whore. We'll take you, too, you bitch.' I say, 'Well, just a minute. Who you think you're talking to?' I work for the Transit Authority and I know the Transit cops and I know what's what."

"So then what?"

"Then they were gone. They took him. I went running after them but they got the elevator first, and by the time I got down the stairs, they're putting Lester in a car."

"What sort of car?"

"A black car. That's all I saw. By the time I got out there, it was going down the street."

"And Lester didn't say anything else?"

She pulled the legs of her shorts down. There was a pale surgical scar on her knee.

"He's saying, 'Call the cops.' Then he says, 'Call the mayor.' "

I looked at her.

"I know. The mayor. Then Lester says—his legs are kicking and they got him around the neck and they're jamming his arm—and he says, 'He was the DA. Call Fiore.' "

"He was, wasn't he?"

"Back then?"

"Yeah. When Lester got arrested," I said.

"So? We never saw him. In court it was some skinny little guy."

"Conroy?"

"Maybe. That sounds right. We thought he was going to stick him good, the woman being hurt and all, but it turned out they didn't. I think they musta realized Lester didn't mean it."

"I'm sure he didn't. And Lester got bailed. Where'd he get the money?"

Lynnette Stevens shrugged.

"I don't know. I could have taken two thousand out of the credit union, but I didn't."

"What'd Lester say?"

"He said it was a friend of his."

I looked at her.

"Hey, Lester, he was no Boy Scout. Not my fault. I didn't get him until he was thirteen and by that time, he is what he is. But I gave him a place to live, my sister in jail and on drugs when she was out. Couldn't take care of a cat, never mind a kid. And I tried to get him to go to school. He went sometimes, too. Smart, when he wanted to be."

"Where'd he go after he bailed?"

"Detroit."

"You knew he jumped?"

"Hey, I figured they'd go get him. He was at my brother's."

"And then he came back?"

"Yeah, he came back. I said, 'Lester, they're surely

gonna find you now. Why don't you just go down to the police station and march up and down?' He says, 'Lynnie, don't worry about it. That business is all taken care of.' "

I looked back. The car was moving closer.

"And nothing happened? He didn't get picked up?"

"Not for almost a year. Until this Puerto Rican kid comes. I figured it out later. He comes up to the booth, talks right through the speaker. Says, 'Hey, Lynette.' Like he knows me. 'Hey, Lynette, Lester home today?'

"I look at him. He looks like somebody Lester would hang with. Doesn't look like a cop."

"He probably wasn't," I said. "He probably got a hundred bucks to go up and ask you that question."

"From who?"

"From a private investigator. What'd you say?"

"I said, 'He was when I left. He was sleeping.' And the kid smiles, and says thank you and walks away."

"And nothing happens?"

"Not for two weeks. Then Lester's dragged out of bed and gone."

"And you've tried looking for him?"

"Hey, I'm not ignorant. I called the courts. I called the DA's office. I called the cops, every precinct in Brooklyn, everything in Manhattan. One of the Transit cops, she checked for me, too. She said there's no record of Lester being arrested for anything."

She ran her hands back and forth over her knees.

"So I don't know if you can find him, but maybe if the newspaper was asking and not me, then maybe they'll find that he was . . ."

The words trailed off.

"This isn't Guatemala or Brazil or someplace, you know what I'm saying?" Lynette Stephens said, new anger in her voice. "This is New York. There's bad cops, sure. There's Louima. There's Amadou. Shot forty-one times 'cause he reached for his wallet. But still, police don't just take you out and shoot you."

I looked in the mirror, saw the Taurus, closer now.

"Have you considered," I said, "that maybe they weren't police at all?"

And I slammed the Rover in gear, stomped the accelerator to the floor.

Twenty-two.

"Holy Jesus," Stephens said.

She fell against me as I turned the corner. Fell back and then against me as I turned again. I circled, sped through the project. Kids gawked. The men stared as the Rover roared by, the Taurus in pursuit.

I took a right, floored it and flashed down side streets, wide-eyed faces slipping past. The Taurus still in the mirror, I slammed on the brakes, slid the Rover to the right between parked cars and jumped the curb. I clung to the wheel as we pointed straight up and the tires clawed up an embankment and we jumped another curb. The Rover bounced, scattering pigeons.

"Oh, my God," Stephens said, covering her eyes. I threaded down walkways between the buildings, drove over a hedge. Crashed through a low metal fence. A section of it sailed into the air, clanged to the ground.

I heard shouts from somewhere but the Taurus wasn't in sight.

I jumped the Rover back onto the street on the far side of the project. Threaded my way through the tenemented streets, one eye on the mirror. Nothing showed and I slipped under the expressway, keeping it in sight as I drove north, running red lights, threading between cars and trucks. When I hit a main drag, I looked in the mirror again, then pulled over.

The motor murmured. The air-conditioning was cool.

Lynette Stephens smoothed her shirt. Gave her knees another rub.

"What the hell kind of reporter are you?" she said.

"It's called a stringer," I said.

She looked at me skeptically.

"I'll call for a car."

"You need money?"

"No. I got money."

She paused. Didn't get out.

"So," she said. "They weren't cops who took Lester, were they?"

"I don't think so."

"So Lester's probably dead."

I didn't reply, but she already knew the answer.

"You know why?"

"No, I don't," I said.

"You gonna try to find out?"

"Yeah," I said.

"You're not writing a story, are you?"

"Probably not. But someone else might. With what I find out."

"What do you do, the research part?"

"Something like that."

"Were you in on killing the mayor?"

"No," I said. "I wasn't."

"But this has to do with that, doesn't it? I mean, you don't care about Lester John. Not for his sake."

I looked at her, a good-seeming woman with a mugger in the family. I shook my head.

"No," I said. "Not for his sake."

At the curb at Amsterdam and 83rd, I called Donatelli's pager. After a minute or two, the car phone rang. It was him. He said we had to talk, face to face. I said there was a coffee place on the corner and I'd wait inside. He said he'd be there in fifteen minutes.

In eleven, he rolled up in a dirty blue Caprice, Ramirez in the passenger seat. From my seat in the window, I could see her scowl.

"Hey," I said, as they came in the door. They walked over. Donatelli said, "Hey yourself." Ramirez looked at me sternly, like I'd left the yard without permission.

"You have kids?" I asked her.

She flinched.

"Why?"

"Just wondered," I said.

"I haven't seen my kids in three days," Donatelli said quickly. "Missed two farm league games and one T-ball. This sucks."

"Yup," I said.

"But it would suck a little bit less if I could just see your mug once in a while."

"Feast your eyes," I said.

"I am. DA wants to feast his eyes, too. Go over some things from your initial interview. Times and stuff."

"Should have brought him," I said, sipping a tea. "How'd the arraignment go?"

"You were there," Ramirez said. "What was that about?"

"Just wanted to get a look at him. See if we were talking about the same Butch Casey."

"No, I mean what he said to you."

"I told you about that."

"The conspiracy stuff?"

"Yeah."

"If he's trying to say somebody else stuck Fiore, he's kidding himself," Ramirez said.

"Oh?"

"Prints in the stall," she said.

"Maybe he used it first."

"And then held the door for the mayor? 'Here, use this one. I warmed up the seat for you. By the way, I've always hated your guts.' "

"Reasonable doubt," I said. "How many stalls are there? Four? Three? That means he had a thirty percent chance of getting the same one."

"Yeah, right," Ramirez said.

The woman came out from behind the counter and walked over with my order, a scone. She was meek, with purplish hair and black shoes as big as satchels. She eyed the detectives' guns nervously, as though they might go off at any moment.

"Would you—"

"No, thanks," Donatelli said.

The woman looked toward Ramirez, who gave her the stare. The woman left.

"Sit," I said.

Donatelli did. Ramirez stood over us like a cafeteria monitor.

"What about Lester John?" I said.

"Fugitive from justice," Donatelli said. "Wanted for aggravated assault, back in 1988."

"He was picked up a couple of weeks ago."

"Not by us."

"By somebody. Feds?"

"No record of it. There'd be a record," Donatelli said. "Maybe he crossed the wrong dirtbags."

"Aunt says they were detectives and they were all white. In Red Hook this kind of detail stands out."

"Maybe they were Russians. Light-skinned Colombians."

"No, she meant white-bread white. Like you."

"Maybe she's feeding you a line of crap," Ramirez said. "People like blaming the cops for everything."

"No record of it," Donatelli said.

"Well, he's gone."

"He broke some poor lady's skull open," Ramirez said. "What goes around, comes around."

I sipped. Donatelli stretched his legs out.

"What do you do to relax?" I asked Ramirez.

"What's it to you?" she said.

"I can picture you hunting sharks or something."

"She target-shoots," Donatelli said. "Has a rumpus room full of trophies. Tell him about it, Rambo."

"Rambo?" I said.

"Can we get back to business?" Ramirez said.

I put my tea on the table.

"Sure," I said. "Victim's husband thinks he was arrested, too."

"Who told him that?" Donatelli said.

"I don't know. He'd been writing to Fiore about it."

"So some college-intern politician's kid gets to mail back the form letters," he said. "Who the hell knows what was said?"

"Or misunderstood," Ramirez said.

I took a bite of half the scone, and held up the plate to Ramirez to offer the other half. She shook her head. Donatelli took the scone, looked at it once and chomped off half of it.

"How closely do you work with the DA's investigators?" I said. "Like that guy who sat in when you talked to me."

"Not very," Donatelli said, chewing. "They got their own agenda. But I asked them about finding you first. They said it was just a mix-up. Somebody was supposed to call but they went off and didn't, and so we weren't notified. Happens."

"You talk to them in the last hour?"

He shook his head.

"Tell anyone there you were going to meet me here?"

Donatelli shook his head again. Ramirez watched me closely. I sipped the tea and tried to decide. Would Ramirez run to the Boxer? Were they all in this together? Ramirez clearly disliked me but Donatelli didn't seem to. Or was it just the role he'd been assigned? Was anyone in this city what they seemed, or were they all disguised?

The words formed in my mind. I could hear them, in my voice.

You know, the Boxer guy and Dave Conroy know about Lester John. As soon as I left the professor's house, he

*called the Boxer. He called the DA's office. They know
all about it. And they're worried.*

I choked them back.

"I've got a question for you, McMorrow," Ramirez
said, edging closer. "What did Butch Casey say to you
this morning? What did he mean? 'It was all arranged.
There was a plan.' "

She looked down at me and waited. Donatelli, about to
take a bite, paused and looked at me, too. I looked up at
Ramirez, and her irritated scowl had been replaced by an
expression that was neutral, a carefully made-up mask.

"Yeah, what is this, McMorrow? Is this more about
this conspiracy Butch was telling you about? And what
did you say to him this morning?"

"Did you say something about an envelope?" Ramirez
said.

She tried to smile but came up short.

"We just need to know what's going on in his head,"
she said.

I looked at her and made my decision.

"You do?" I said. "Why?"

Twenty-three.

Just up the block from Maria Yolimar's apartment, I parked. Opened the envelope and reviewed my notes.

She calls the mayor's office. Claims her husband is missing. He was taken into police custody and disappeared.

Maria Yolimar says the mayor knows where he is. Calling every year on the anniversary of his disappearance, she's dismissed as a crank.

I stuffed the envelope under the seat and looked out.

The street was wide and the buildings had at one time been handsome, if not grand. The doorway at 486 West 165th Street was stripped like a plundered Mayan ruin, but still was framed by a delicate cement filigree. There were buzzers in a battered panel beside the open door. The hallway inside the door was dark, even in the afternoon. A rusted sign on the wall said there was a $25 fine for littering.

I didn't think so.

Just up the block, three men were bent over the open hood of a dented Honda. They watched me, their expressions hostile and cold. I went to the door of 486 and peered at the buzzer plate.

There were twenty buttons, half as many names. Most of the tags were faded, covered with grime. Of those that were legible, one was M. Yolimar.

Sometimes you got lucky.

I pressed the button. Glanced back at the men, who were still staring. I didn't know if the button worked or had been broken for five years. I'd stepped into the hallway when a woman's voice crackled something.

I pressed again.

She spoke again. In Spanish.

"Maria Yolimar."

"Who is that?" in English.

"Jack McMorrow. I want to talk about your husband and the city."

"She's not here," the woman said.

I pressed again.

"She's not here. She's gone to work."

"What apartment? I'll come back."

There was no answer. I looked at the list of names, tried to discern a pattern to the numbers. There was none. I stepped back to the curb and looked up. Saw a child peering down at me from an open window on the third floor. An arm reached through the curtains and pulled the child back.

I took off my glasses and went inside.

The hall was dark and smelled of cooking. Murmurs came through the doors. Music in Spanish. A game show in English. A baby crying, in no language at all.

At the second floor landing, I heard someone coming down. Three teenage girls, red-lipped, shoulders tattooed. They glared at me as they approached.

"Do you know Maria Yolimar?" I said.

As though I hadn't spoken, they continued on.

I kept going, up to the third floor, where the fire door was propped open. I stepped into the hallway. It was like dusk, lighted by a single bulb at the far end. The carpet was threadbare, with patches of floor showing through. I walked slowly down the hall and tried to orient myself.

At the second door on the left I stopped. It was unmarked, except for the peephole.

I stood and listened for a moment. From the other side of the door, I heard Grover, from *Sesame Street*. A child's voice laughing. I knocked. Grover shut up.

A woman's voice came through the door. "Who's that?"

"This is Jack McMorrow. To see Maria Yolimar about her husband and City Hall."

"I told you. She's working."

"Sorry to bother you, but it's important."

"You police?"

"No, a reporter."

That silenced her for a moment, and then I heard another woman's voice, and the first one answering. They spoke in rapid Spanish. I caught "journalista" and "Maria" and "viejo." Waited. The kids were whining, saying they wanted Grover back. I knocked again. The door opened slowly. A woman in a flowered bathrobe looked out, hair mussed, eyes close set and narrowed.

"Maria Yolimar?"

"No. I'm her sister."

"I'm Jack McMorrow," I said. "I'm a reporter. I need to talk to her about her husband."

Her eyes opened wide. I could smell her sleepy breath. "They found him?"

"No," I said gently. "But I need to talk to her about how he disappeared. Or to you."

She hesitated.

"You know what happened to him?"

"No," I said. "I'm sorry, I don't. But I want to know what you know."

"For the newspaper?"

"It's still important," I said.

"You think so?" Maria Yolimar's sister said.

I sat on a plastic patio chair with my notebook out. Maria Yolimar's sister sat across from me on the black vinyl couch, her long hair unbrushed, her robe pulled protectively around her, bare feet set squarely on the carpet. An older woman sat at the other end of the couch and watched the children, three of them under five. They watched *Sesame Street* again.

Maria Yolimar's sister apologized for not being dressed. She worked at a laundry, she said. She worked all night. I nodded, noting that there was something childlike about her, that she was one of those people who, when asked a question, felt obligated to answer.

But then, before I'd even asked a question, she turned gray.

"You're the man who—"

"Who knows the other man. That's right. And that other man, the one they say killed the mayor, was investigating Julio's case. He asked me to look into it. He thinks there's an important story about something that happened."

The older woman looked at me and leaped off the couch toward the children. Maria Yolimar's sister stood and her feet thumped on the floor. She looked toward the phone, then back at me.

"I'm not here to hurt you or frighten you. I haven't done anything to anyone."

"But you . . . on the TV—"

Maria Yolimar's sister looked at me and took a step back. The older woman herded the children into the bedroom and closed the door.

"Please, don't be afraid," I said, holding my hands up, still clutching the notebook. "I didn't do anything. I just know him, the other guy. I'm just a reporter. I know him because I'm a reporter."

She looked bewildered.

"I want to find out what happened to Julio Yolimar."

The sister didn't sit down, but she didn't run or call the police. She stood and I stood, too, and she answered my questions, perfunctorily at first, then more completely. The older woman stayed in the bedroom with the door shut.

"He didn't stab nobody," the sister said.

"The French doctor?"

"He said it was a mistake. He told Maria, when he got out of jail, everything would be OK. He said to her what the police said was lying. He said he'd get out in a few weeks."

"What? On bail?"

"I think so. I'm not sure. Julio said to her, 'Don't sweat it.' That was his saying, you know? 'Don't sweat it.' He said it all the time. He'd say, 'Don't sweat it. Everything gonna be great. We're gonna move to a big apartment.' I didn't believe him."

I wrote in the notebook. Looked up.

"But he was right. Julio was telling the truth. He came home and he said, 'They let me go. They got the wrong guy.'"

"Was that true?"

"I don't know."

"But he was released?"

"I don't know. He was home. Maria said he had money. He said they gave it to him for saying bad things about him that weren't true."

"For damaging his reputation?"

"Right."

I looked doubtful.

"Did police come looking for him?"

"No. Nobody came. But Julio, he liked people."

"Really," I said.

"He liked to talk a lot," she said.

"Uh-huh."

"And he had this money. So Maria and him, they went out one night. Stayed out late, went dancing. And she said they were walking home and this car pulls up, and it's a police car."

"A blue and white one?"

"No. All black, but you know it's a police car."

"Where was this?"

"End of the street. Right here. 'Cause she told me, they

stop in the park and—. They're like newlyweds, you know?''

She broke off.

"Could you leave that part out?'' she said.

I nodded.

"Well, she's putting her clothes back on and Julio is already dressed and he walks up onto the sidewalk and this car pulls up and this guy says, 'Hey, Julio. Hey, Yolimar.' And he goes over and they talk for a minute. There's two guys in the car. Two cops. Detectives. Maria said she saw them. From over in the dark.''

"Right.''

"And then Julio comes back and he says to Maria, 'I'll see you a little later.' ''

She acted it out, with different voices.

"She say, 'Everything okay?' 'Cause she's still thinking a little that he escaped. He says, 'Fine. I just need to do something for these guys.' ''

"And he left?'' I said, still taking notes, trying to get all of it.

"Got in the car. That was it.''

"What was it?''

"He never came back,'' Maria Yolimar's sister said, arms folded under her breasts. "Nobody ever saw him again.''

"What day was that?''

"A Friday.''

"No, I mean, what was the date?''

"Oh. I don't know. Summer. I was working in the laundry. My first year, so I was fifteen.''

"How old are you now?''

"Twenty-five.''

"These your children?''

"Yeah.''

I scrawled the date in my notebook. Paused. The bedroom door opened a crack and the older woman peeked out.

"But Maria called City Hall?''

"Yeah, on the anniversary. It was her feeling of duty. She's like that."

"But why the mayor's office? One of the reports said she said she knew Johnny Fiore would know about it. Just because he's district attorney doesn't mean he knows everything about everything that happens with the police."

"He was in charge. He had to know."

"Why?"

"You have to ask Maria."

"If I ask her, what will she say?"

She didn't answer. I smiled gently.

"Just give me a clue. So I know whether this is worth pursuing."

She brushed at her hair. Picked at her eye. Then took a deep breath and wrapped her arms around herself tighter. She wanted to tell me. She would tell me. She just wanted to be asked again.

"Just a hint?" I said.

"Well, she will tell you, like she told me, she kissed Julio good-bye and she said, 'Julio, why you working for the cops? After they lied.' And he said, 'Those aren't just regular cops. They're special cops. They work for Johnny Fiore.' "

"The district attorney."

"That's what he said. When's this going to be in the paper?"

"I'm not sure. Soon."

"What paper?"

"The *Times*."

"You going to put my name in the paper?"

"I'd like to. Do you mind?"

She looked away, stroking her hair, suddenly self-conscious.

"How do you spell it?" I said. "Is it M-A-R-I-A?"

She pursed her lips. Wouldn't meet my gaze.

"You're Maria, aren't you?" I said. "You're not her sister."

Maria Yolimar stared at me and after a moment, slowly nodded.

There was a thump from the bedroom and then crying. She started for the door. I stepped to the window and looked down.

The Range Rover still was there. The guys were under the hood of the Honda, their buttocks and legs showing. From the direction of Amsterdam, a blue car appeared. It was a Ford, a Crown Victoria. It pulled up to the Honda and stopped.

One of the men from the Honda walked over to the big sedan. He leaned down and then back. The man stuck something in his shirt pocket and pointed toward 486. The car pulled away and beside the Range Rover it slowed, then continued up the street and stopped.

A man got out. He was smallish and slim, wearing a baggy floral shirt and jeans. The car pulled away and turned at the end of the street, then stopped a hundred yards up the block, to my left. The first man was out of sight. As I watched, a second man got out of the car and crossed the street. He had hair cut short on the sides, long in the back. He was walking toward the building.

It hadn't taken them long.

I turned back. Maria Yolimar was at my elbow.

"You really think you can find out what happened to him?"

"I don't know," I said, still looking out.

"Hard on everybody. His family, too. Not knowing. 'Cause they been through this twice. You don't know if the person is dead or alive. It's like those guys who never come back from Vietnam, you know what I'm saying?"

I said I did.

"Julio's mother, she has Julio and she has her nephew, who she raised like a son 'cause his mother died in Santo Domingo. He got arrested, too. Police said he killed this lady, but he didn't do it. They let him out, but he never came home at all."

I listened, half turned toward the window.

"So could you ask about him, too?" Maria Yolimar said.

"Sure," I said.

"His name's Ortiz. Georgie Ortiz. But when they arrested him, they got it all wrong. They called him Muriqi."

Twenty-four.

A chill ran through me, and when I spoke, the words came out in a raspy whisper.

"Who did he kill?"

"He didn't kill nobody. The police lied."

"Who did they say he killed?"

"Some lady from the hospital," she said. "They said Georgie stole her car and shot her. Right in the face. He wouldn't do that."

"I'm sure. You don't remember her name?"

"No. But they said Georgie had the car and he brought it to the junkyard, but he didn't."

"He didn't have the car?"

"Oh, he had the car. But he bought the car. They arrested him and said he killed her, and lied and said he was at the hospital. That's where it happened."

"Why did they do that?" I asked, knowing the answer.

"'Cause the lady who died?" Maria Yolimar said. "She was married to a cop."

"Oh," I mustered. "You know which cop?"

"I don't remember."

"Have you been reading all the stories in the paper?"

"No. I don't read the paper. I watch the TV, but usually it's kids' shows. *Sesame*."

"Right," I said.

I smiled, let the thread that connected me to Butch to Julio to Georgie just drift away. Maria Yolimar stopped talking and looked at me and then looked toward the bedroom. A child began to cry. She said, "I gotta go," and walked to the door, pushed it open and closed it behind her.

I let myself out.

Walking down the hall, I sorted through it.

Yolimar and Ortiz were cousins. Both men were charged with murders that same summer but were released. Both men had some contact, at least indirect, with Johnny Fiore, then Manhattan district attorney. Both men were missing.

Had Butch made this connection? Had he gotten this far?

I didn't think so. If he had, Maria would have said so. If she'd realized that my friend, the same cop who was in the news for killing the mayor, had been involved in Georgie's case, she wouldn't have opened the door to me at all. So I was making progress, moving—

Up the stairs, to the roof.

It was flat and black and hot, strewn with stones and broken glass. I wound my way around chimneys, a water tank, flushed a nighthawk from its daytime roost. Keeping to the center of the roof, out of sight of the street, I walked to the end of the building.

Between the buildings was a ten-foot gap, a yawning chasm. Close to the edge was a long plank, on which someone had sprayed The Bridge.

"No thanks," I said.

I swallowed hard and turned to the rear of the building to look for the fire escape. At the edge of the roof, I dropped to my knees. Peeked over. The rusted steel grating was ten feet below. If I hung by my hands, it would be a four-foot drop and then I'd be on my way to the ground. Circle around, jump in the car and go.

Simple enough.

The simmering tar was soft under my knees. I crawled along the edge until I was centered over the landing. I turned around and eased my legs off the roof, into the air.

My feet waggled in space. I looked back. My knees were on the lip of the roof. I looked for something to grip, but there was nothing, just tar and gravel. I reached back and cupped my fingers over the edge. Inched my way off. Lowered myself onto my belly and looked back again, back and down—

Saw the man from the car round the corner and look up, then duck back.

I squirmed back onto the roof and rolled away from the edge. A back alley? What better place for me to be found, dead after a drug buy, dead after a mugging, dead because somebody wanted my fancy car?

It happened.

They knew I was on the roof now. Probably were coming up the stairs. One shove, no more problem. I scrambled up and, in a crouch, trotted toward the hatchway. Eased the door open and listened.

Heard nothing. Then steps. More than one person. Deliberate and steady, climbing closer.

I closed the door. Looked around. Saw nothing. Heard voices.

Christ.

I circled the roof and found a flattened beer can, ran back to the door and wedged it underneath. Then I trotted to the far end of the roof and stood, three feet from the edge.

Two feet.

I looked down five stories to a trash-filled alley and backed away.

The plank was twelve feet long; it said so in faded lumber-yard marker on the butt end. Eleven inches wide and an inch and a half thick. Probably stolen from a scaffold.

I bent and picked it up. It was sun-bleached but solid. I stood and lifted it and gravel came with it as I swung it in the air, stagger-stepped toward the edge and let it go.

It came down with a bang. I knelt and shoved it farther across, until there was a foot of plank on each roof. I adjusted it so it was square.

There was a bang on the door. Then another.

I swallowed. Started across and the plank flexed under my weight and my foot caught the edge and I started to stagger, fell to a crouch, dived forward and landed.

One knee on the roof.

Hands clawing at the tar and rocks.

And then I was on.

I turned.

Both men were running across the other roof toward me. One had a gun against his leg. On my knees, I shoved the plank back.

I heard it clatter on the ground as I scrambled backward, rolled to my feet, ran and dodged, behind one chimney, then another, heard a smack but no crack, no shot. Just a *splock* sound, then another, shots from a silenced gun, and then I was behind the shack that led to the stairway.

The knob on the door didn't turn.

It was locked.

But it opened when I yanked and I tumbled down the stairs, three steps at a time, then four, leaping with one hand on the rail, bursting into a hall where the doors leaned open and the ceilings had fallen.

I leaped over trash, bolted in a door and ran for the window. I looked out and there was a fire escape. I tried to open the window, but it was nailed shut, sprayed with graffiti. I took a step back and kicked through the glass, punching it out in chunks.

I sliced my ankle but kept kicking until the hole was big enough. I crouched, kicked the bottom pieces free of the frame and glazing, and squeezed through, the glass slicing at my crotch.

But then I was out and I half-dived, half-ran down each flight, the steps ringing like gongs, all the way to the second floor, where the ladder that had once dropped to the ground was gone.

I fell to my knees, grabbed the bars and swung. Let myself hang and dropped. Fell into garbage bags and wood and broken toys, lurched to my feet and ran along the chain fence until I came to a place where it had been ripped open.

I squeezed through, ran down another alley, and came out on the next street, where I slowed and walked up the block toward Broadway, blood seeping into my shoe.

I was standing in front of a liquor store at Broadway and 169th Street, next to some guys who were hanging out. Two of them were drinking beer from cans in paper bags, talking and laughing. A third was using the pay phone to return incoming calls to his pager. They wondered what I was doing there and I wondered, too.

Donatelli and Ramirez pulled up to the curb and the man at the pay phone hung up and started up the block. The other men lowered their bags. I walked to the car and got in the back.

"Nice neighborhood," Donatelli said. "Whatcha got, a death wish?"

"Nobody bothered me but white guys," I said.

Ramirez turned and looked at me.

"Now what is this story you're trying to tell us?"

I stared back.

"Is it me or do you seem skeptical?"

"Chased you onto a roof and shot at you?" she said. "In the middle of the day? Even around here . . ."

"And the gun had a silencer," I said.

"And you were helicoptered off the roof in the nick of time."

"I walked across a plank to the next building."

Ramirez turned and snorted.

"Hey, I can show you. Amsterdam and 165th. Halfway down the block. It's number 486. It was on the list."

"What list, McMorrow?" Ramirez said.

"The list of people. People in the cases Butch was looking into. Cases that didn't get prosecuted in the summer of 1988."

Donatelli pulled into traffic. Neither of them said anything.

"He was working on this," I said.

Donatelli yawned.

"Sorry," he said.

Ramirez looked out the window.

"And Dave Conroy knows about it. I heard him talking about it at the courthouse with that guy from the DA's office."

No reaction.

"They said they'd stake out the places I'd be going. They knew about it before, but the college professor, the one whose wife was almost killed by Lester John, he called them."

"This is a case from ten years ago?" Donatelli said, turning off Broadway onto a cross street. "Why's he calling them now?"

"Because I went to talk to him."

"Yeah, well, you show up at my door asking off-the-wall questions about my wife's ten-year-old murder, I might call somebody, too," Ramirez said.

"She wasn't murdered. She's in a vegetative state."

I could feel Ramirez roll her eyes.

"Yeah, well, that's about how I feel," Donatelli said. "Two hours' sleep in two days."

"You getting much sleep, McMorrow?" Ramirez said.

I looked at her, the taut lines of her perpetually angry face.

"Yeah. Why?"

"I don't know. I thought maybe you were up all night with that artist woman."

She paused.

"Talking," she said, and I could see her smile.

I didn't answer. We were barreling down St. Nicholas, past the park. Donatelli hit the brakes and swung hard onto 165th. I looked between them. The blue car was gone. The Honda was there, but the hood was down and the men working on it had left. The Range Rover was where I had left it.

"It gets dark, that car is history," Donatelli said. "Tomorrow morning, it's in Jersey someplace in pieces."

He pulled up to it.

"That's the building," I said. "And next door is where I went down the fire escape."

They looked at 486. It was quiet. Tranquil.

"Want to see it?"

They looked at each other and shrugged.

"Hey, why not?" Donatelli said. "I need to stretch my legs."

We got out. I looked around warily. Donatelli stretched and groaned loudly. We walked across the street, Ramirez reluctantly bringing up the rear.

"Used to be crack city up here," Donatelli said. " 'Til Fiore got in and we kicked the scum out. And you know who thanked him the most? People who live in places like this. They could walk down the street for a change."

I didn't say anything. Led the way up to the third floor, went to the Yolimars' door and knocked.

"What are we doing here?" Ramirez said.

"I just want you to meet these people," I said. "They've got two people missing. Got picked up, then released, then disappeared."

"Happens, McMorrow," Ramirez said. "It's called being a fugitive from justice."

"I know that. But this is different. There's—"

The door opened a crack, the chain still on. It was the older woman. Behind her, the apartment was quiet.

"Hi," I said. "It's me again."

She showed no recognition.

"I wanted to see if Maria would talk to these detectives. About Julio. And Georgie."

A blank stare.

"Is she home?" I said.

"She go to work," she finally whispered. "She gotta work all night."

"Hey, listen, McMorrow," Ramirez said, behind me. "We've got stuff to do. We can't—"

"Shhhh," the woman said. "The babies. They're sleeping."

She repeated it in Spanish.

"Hey, senora, we'll vamoose," Donatelli said.

She closed the door. He smirked at me.

"So that's your Deep Throat?"

"She's not there. But come on."

I led the way, walking quickly to give them no chance to negotiate. They followed, Ramirez muttering "Christ" behind me. I went to the stairs and made my way up. The door still was open, the flattened can was on the gravel. I led the way to the end of the building, scanning the ground for spent shell casings. I couldn't find any.

"They fired from here," I said, at the edge of the roof. "I was on the other side. The board fell down."

I peered over. There it was, in the rubble. Donatelli and Ramirez peered over, too.

"Yeah, there's a board all right," Ramirez said, looking down. "And there's the busted tricycle you rode across on."

"You think I'm making all this up?"

"No," she said. "But I'm beginning to wonder about everything else you've told us."

"Well, screw you, then."

"Easy," Donatelli said, backing away.

"I kicked out a window and went down the fire escape over there," I said. "You want to see the cut?"

I bent and pulled my pants leg up, yanked my sock down. The blood was dried, the slice long and thin.

"Oh, please, McMorrow. Keep your clothes on," Ramirez said.

"There's something here, I'm telling you," I said, standing up. "Julio Yolimar was a cousin of Georgie Ortiz. He's the guy who killed Butch's wife."

Donatelli looked at me, suddenly interested.

Ramirez shook her head.

"Well, that fits, doesn't it?" she said. "The man's obsessed. On a vendetta. Butch pulls the files on the guy's family? Ten years later? What's he saying, these people helped kill his wife?"

"No."

"Face it, McMorrow. Butch cracked up. It isn't his fault. Maybe I would've, too. Maybe not. Butch Casey isn't the only one who life's handed a crappy deal. But he's chasing around with all these bullshit theories and then he goes and kills the mayor of New York City in a bathroom. He's whacked out."

She started across the roof. I looked at Donatelli.

"Hey," he said. "I mean, it's mildly interesting, if you've got nothing else to do. But we got a dead mayor, McMorrow. What can I say?"

"What deal was she handed?" I said.

Donatelli glanced at me.

"Ramirez?"

"Yeah."

He hesitated.

"She don't talk about it, so don't say I told you."

"I won't."

"She had a kid. He was two. Got sick and died, just like that. Some weird infection. Husband couldn't take it and walked. Moved in with his secretary or something. Now she's got no kid and no husband. Works like eighty hours a week."

"And every bust is a little bit of payback?"

Donatelli shrugged.

"Whatever gets you by," he said, and started across the roof.

I followed, down the stairs, out to the street. Standing on the sidewalk, Donatelli paused. He asked me when I'd be coming in to go over things again. I said maybe in the morning. He asked if I was staying at the artist's place and I said I didn't know.

"Be careful in this neighborhood," he said.

"What for?" I said. "It's my imagination, right?"

I walked to the Rover, got in and watched them drive

to the end of the block and stop. They waited. I waited. We sat there, the three of us, like stubborn children. I started the motor and turned the air on high. Sat some more. Finally, they pulled out, took a left.

I put the Rover in gear and was wheeling it around—when the phone rang.

"Yeah," I said.

"Jack McMorrow?" a man's voice said.

He sounded young. New York.

"Yeah, who's this?"

"That don't matter. What matters is this lady by the name of Roxanne Masterson. She lives at 43 Ocean View, South Portland, Maine, which is a condo right on the harbor there. She drives a dark green Explorer, Maine registration 9871Y. Her unlisted phone number is 799-3121. Her car phone number is 877-9989. Her office is on Forest Avenue in Portland, Maine, and she starts work most days about eight in the morning. She's thirty-one, five-seven, 130. Roxanne has a very nice body, a real pretty face, too. Thick dark hair, big eyes. I can personally think of any number of guys who would be glad to tie her to her bed, rip her clothes off, and put the boots to her. Maybe they could take her right out of her car and bring her to some hick motel. Let me tell you how that works. You still there, bucko?"

Twenty-five.

I didn't answer. He was talking about renting a motel room, closing the blinds. Said it could happen because there were no cops in Maine.

"But most of all it could happen because her boyfriend is in New York fucking around with shit of which he knows nothing about."

He paused. I waited.

"So you been warned, pally. You go back to goddamn Maine and you find your little lady and you lock the doors and you stay there with her. Or we'll find her. You got that, Jack?"

I didn't answer.

"I said, you got that, Jack?"

"Yeah," I said.

"Too bad," he said. "I was kinda looking forward to it. That Roxanne, she's a babe. You know what she wore to work today? This black skirt, pretty short. A white T-shirt and a vest. And you know, when she climbs in that Explorer, the skirt goes way up. Outstanding legs, Jack. And I'm a leg man, myself."

There was a click and the phone hissed. I hit the button and dialed Roxanne's number at home. A robot voice came on, asked for my mobile authorization code. I slammed the phone down, pressed for the operator. Another robot answered, said operators were busy and calls would be answered in the order in which they were received.

I threw the phone on the seat and drove.

At Broadway I took a right, floored the Rover, weaved around a livery cab. I saw crowds. Stores for tortillas and sneakers, soda and beer. I ran the lights, and saw the discount liquors, the same one. I pulled over, hit the flashers. Cars honked behind me as I climbed out, and there was the same guy, back on the phone.

I tapped him on the shoulder and he turned. Remembered me and the cops. He dropped the receiver, started to put his hands up, looked past me for my backup.

"Hey, who you roustin, man? I didn't do nothin'."

"The phone," I said. "Police emergency."

I grabbed the swinging receiver, dialed as he backed away. Punched in my card number. The phone played a bit of music, then clicked a few times.

"Come on," I said.

Finally, a ring. Another. A hiss and Roxanne's voice: "I can't come to the phone right now. . . ."

I called her office, got another machine. Called back to the condo and, a finger in my ear, shouting over the traffic, left a message for her to call me. I called her car phone, got "the mobile mail box." Left a message there, too. Told her to call me in the car and at Christina's. I said I'd keep trying. Told her to go to a friend's, to go to a restaurant, not to be home alone.

I'd explain.

And I did, to Clair, who answered the phone in the shop in his barn.

"Slow down," he said.

"But he knew what she wore to work today," I said.

"He acted like he knew. You don't know what she's wearing. Maybe he made it up."

"Yeah, but he talked about her climbing in her car, and—"

"Jack, she's okay."

"But Clair, this guy was serious. I had somebody take a shot at me today."

"Well," Clair said.

"They missed."

"Glad to hear it."

"But this guy, he sounded—"

"Jack, Roxanne's okay. I think she might be on her way up here."

I stopped talking.

"I tried her in the car, couldn't get through."

"Maybe she was talking to somebody else, Jack."

"Why's she coming up there?"

"Needed a break, I guess. Things have been a little hectic."

"Reporters?"

"Oh, yeah," Clair said. "And you're a pushy bunch, you know that? This one fella, he flew up from Boston or some goddamn place, drove all the way up from Portland. He came flying in the dooryard in this little purple car last night. Started asking all kinds of questions. I didn't say much. Just got in the truck and told him I was going up to the shooting range."

"Clair," I said, "this is serious."

"I know, but let me finish my story. So we go rattling up across the ridge, reasonable pace, but you know, that old tote road's still a little rough in places, and around West Montville, his little car is losing some spare parts from underneath, starting to sound a little rough, seemed to me."

"Clair."

"And we come out on Mountain Road, and you know the skidders got that road all tore up. Ruts two feet deep. Almost got stuck other side of Hogback, 'fore I crossed Halfmoon Stream and popped out on 220. Quite a little bit of water still flowing through there, for this time of year. 'Course, we have had some rain."

"Clair."

"Don't you want to know what happened to the reporter in the little car?"

"No."

"I couldn't tell you, because I never saw him again."

"Uh-huh."

"So you over the panic stage now?"

"Yeah, I think so."

"Because you're no good to anybody when you're panicking. I've seen too many guys get brainlock at just the wrong time. Now's the time to think straight. Be deliberate. Be rational."

"But you know this is no joke."

"With Roxanne? Yes."

"You know what they're saying in these stories about you?"

"Oh, yeah. They found my file at the Pentagon or wherever the hell they keep it," Clair said. "But you know, they never 'say' anything. It's all innuendo and implication, little sneaky jabs. Tripping over each other, shoveling the garbage, looking for the next scandal. Oh, well. This, too, shall pass."

I heard a tool clink in the background.

"So, Jack. Now somebody's taken a shot at you. I told you not to wear those gold chains."

"You got a minute? I'll tell you what's happened."

"Tractor's running, so just give me the high points," Clair said.

But he didn't mean it. I had his ear.

I started with the Boxer watching the loft. Tilbury the professor. What I heard at the courthouse, what the woman said about Lester John. Julio and Georgie and their connection to Butch, to each other. The guys on the roof, the guy on the phone.

"Huh," Clair said. From the barn, I could hear Mozart. On Broadway, it was merengue and blaring horns. I looked up the street, saw a blue car but it was a livery cab.

"You think these cases were fixed?" Clair said.

"By who? I mean, these aren't high rollers. Lester John

was snatching pocketbooks. Julio and Georgie I picture as a couple of smash and grabbers. They go to jail, who cares?"

"You ought to find out who bailed that guy."

"I can try."

"Who the judge was. Who the prosecutor was."

I remembered the clips.

"Fiore himself, at least for Julio and Georgie. I'm not sure about Lester."

"These DA's investigative people. They operate independently?"

"Very. It's like New York's CIA."

"Maybe one of Fiore's guys was taking payoffs," Clair said. "Maybe Fiore, too."

"Why? He doesn't need money from some two-bit thief. He chewed these people up. Stepped on them like they were bugs. That's how he got elected."

"But he didn't step on these two."

"Maybe somebody else did," I said. "Because where are they?"

I looked around. The guy with the beeper was fifty feet up the block, glaring at me and slowly moving closer.

"I'm going to call Roxanne again," I said.

"She said she might come up, have dinner," Clair said.

"Clair, don't let her stay in our house alone. And try to get her to stay with you for a couple of days, until I can get back."

"She'll be in good hands up here. What about you? You can't just jump in the truck and leave?"

"Cops have my truck. And they want me to stay within reach for a little while, anyway. And—"

"And you're into this and you don't want to walk away from it."

"Now I don't know. I think Butch was onto something. I think he found the scab, and I've started picking it off. But is it worth it?"

"Why didn't he pick it off himself?" Clair said.

"I think he was going to. He said he wanted me to write about what he found."

"Then why'd he do what he did, or at least what they say he did?"

"I don't know," I said. "Maybe he didn't."

"I've half a mind to come down there and keep you from screwing things up," Clair said.

"No. Just ask Roxanne to call me right away. And keep an eye on her."

"Jack, she said she might come up," Clair said. "She didn't say for sure."

Twenty-six.

On the way downtown, I called Donatelli's pager. He didn't call back. I called Midtown South but he wasn't there. I asked for Ramirez, and the woman said they'd left together. I called the pager number again, and drove.

Just above the Village, the phone finally rang and I grabbed it.

"Hey, McMorrow," Christina said. "Where are you?"

"Just above Broadway and Fifth. Headed back."

"You eat red meat?"

Meat?

"I guess. Why?"

"I'm thinking take-out. There's this place in Williamsburg, they do porterhouse for two. It's really fantastic."

"Oh?"

"For tonight. I don't think we can go out, not the two of us."

"No?"

"Oh, lots has happened," Christina said, her voice bright over the cellular hiss. "The police have called. That was before lunch. Somebody named Ramirez. She was in a real snit. Bit of a bitch. Said she wants to talk to you and the district attorney does, too. At his office. And, let's

see, there's been a black car on the corner since ten
o'clock, before that it was a white one. The *Times* has
called over and over. You're supposed to call Ellen and
Robert something.''

''I'll call them.''

Christina hesitated.

''Well, Jack, they weren't just calling for you. They
wanted to talk to me. They say they have to disclose who
you were with at the hotel and where you've been staying.''

''Why?''

''Ellen says it's a conflict of interest for the newspaper
to withhold this information from the readers.''

''That's a crock.''

''But she said she won't give the specific address.''

''But you're in the phone book, aren't you?''

''It just says Brooklyn.''

''It still stinks. Ellen is the reason I met up with you
here in the first place. Now she's using that.''

''Well, whatever,'' Christina said.

Whatever? It seemed oddly philosophical.

''Oh, and Roxanne called. I just talked to her on the
phone.''

''She did?'' I barked.

''Don't worry, McMorrow. I didn't get you in trouble.''

''That's not what I'm worried about.''

''She was worried about you.''

''Where is she?''

''She didn't say specifically. Maine, I guess.''

''Portland?''

''I don't know, Jack. I didn't grill her. Anyway, she
said the media has really been after her. Some Maine TV
guys got her leaving her office, she said. Chased her to
her car. She was thinking she'd talk to the *Times* this
afternoon. She wanted to talk to you first. Mostly I think
she just wanted to talk to you.''

''I'll call her,'' I said, then paused. ''I don't know if I
should stay another night with you.''

"Jack, I talked to Roxanne. She was fine. We made plans to get together sometime."

Oh, great, I thought.

"This story with you in it. When's it running?"

"I don't know. Tomorrow? This is a big deal, you know, McMorrow. I don't think they're going to sit on anything, especially if it's an exclusive. They'll want to splash it."

Christina, suddenly media savvy?

"Ellen said she wanted to talk to you about it today."

"Okay," I said. The light changed. The taxi behind me honked and swerved to pass.

"You know, some serious things are happening with all of this, Christina," I said. "Very serious stuff. I think you should know—"

The phone got fuzzy, Christina's voice was faint.

"We'll talk, Jack. I'll call the parking man and tell him you're on your way. Just pull up and he'll drive you over and drop you. Call from the car at the lot and I'll come down. I've got another call, Jack. 'Bye."

And Christina hung up. I didn't.

I called all of Roxanne's numbers, left more messages. I called Donatelli's pager and punched in the car phone number, called again and punched in the number at the loft. I dialed until there was nothing more I could do.

Sagging in the seat, I crossed the Manhattan Bridge, the elegant web of the Brooklyn Bridge to my right.

I barely noticed.

So you been warned, pally. You go back to goddamn Maine and you find your little lady and you lock the doors and you stay there with her. Or we'll find her.

I could do that. I could leave tonight, catch a flight or a bus. But the DA. What would they think if I took off? Could they come and get me? Invent some sort of charge to hold me in jail? And then where would Roxanne be? With Clair, I hoped, but hell, I didn't know where she was now.

She'd be okay for tonight. The warning had been received. I'd stay and talk to the cops in the morning, tell

them I had to get back to my life. I'd come back for a
grand jury or a trial or whatever. They could call me anytime. If I wasn't home, I'd be out cutting wood. They
could leave a message.

I turned off the bridge, wound my way back toward the
river. This time I approached the parking lot from the
Navy Yard side, driving slowly between the darkened factories. A block away, I turned off the lights, hoping the
Rover would blend into the shadows.

But then I was out in the open, and the car seemed as
conspicuous as a parade float. The parking attendant that
night was a plump white-haired man who popped out of
his little building and gave me a big wave. I stopped at
the razor-wire gates and he closed them, locking them
with a chain and padlock. I called and Christina answered.
I said we were on our way and then I got out and climbed
into the backseat. If the man thought this strange, he
didn't show it.

He even made small talk, until I flopped down on the
seat.

When I raised myself up, a car was approaching. A
small red car. I crouched. It passed. A woman was driving
but she didn't look at me. I hadn't seen her before.

We waited. Where was she? The parking guy whistled
and I dug a five-dollar bill out of my pocket and handed
it to him over his shoulder. He said thank you and called
me sir. I heard a motor behind us and half-turned.

It was a minivan with fake wood sides. It was coming
toward us, driving slowly on the cobblestones. And then
it slowed more, eased over a pothole and I could see the
sliding door pop out and start to open.

"Get down," I said, and I did but the driver just turned
and looked at me, half-smiling, like I was joking.

And the bay door clattered open.

I shouted this time, "Get down." Kicked the door open
and threw myself out. Christina was standing there, one
arm stretched above her. I grabbed her and pushed her
inside, pressed her hard against the wall.

"Jack," she said.

She laughed, put her arms around me.

"Glad to see you, too," she said.

I looked back, saw the driver grinning and shaking his head, and the minivan moving slowly up the street. The door was shut.

The driver said, "You all set now?" and winked. Christina straightened her tank top and her shorts, went to the door and reached up for the handle. She gave him a wave and pulled the door down, plunging us into darkness.

"Hold that thought," she said, "until we get upstairs."

In the loft I went right to the studio window and looked out. The van was gone. There was a black car at the corner to the right, a vague shape in the darkening dusk. Christina came into the room and came up behind me, putting her hands on my shoulders and leaning against me.

"Paranoia becomes you," she said, her mouth close to my ear.

"Somebody shot at me today."

She tensed, interested. Kept her hands on my shoulders.

"Really? Where was that?"

"Washington Heights."

"Well, they probably thought you were a rival drug dealer."

"They chased me up onto a roof."

"So?"

"So, it had to do with Butch and things he was looking into."

"Things?"

"Irregularities, you could call it. Cases from the eighties."

Christina didn't answer for a moment. Her fingers gently kneaded my shoulders.

"So they killed the mayor and framed Butch for it to get rid of him?"

I shook my head. Her fingers pressed.

"Seems unlikely, doesn't it?" I said.

"A bit over the top, even for New York. Why kill the mayor?"

"I don't know. Maybe he was in on it."

"Well, he's not going to tell anybody that. Why would he?"

"I don't know."

"So there's no need to kill the mayor. Why not just kill Butch and be done with it?"

"I don't know."

"Framing him doesn't do any good. He can still talk in jail. He can get somebody else to look into—"

"He did," I said.

"Oh," Christina said.

"And they told me to stop."

"Today?"

"Yeah. That's why I don't think I should stay here."

"Because you're not going to stop?"

"I'm not sure yet."

Christina kneaded deeper and bent close to me.

"Same old McMorrow," she whispered. "Same old Jack."

Twenty-seven.

At eight o'clock the phone rang. I was watching the news on the big screen, where Butch, coming out of court this time, still looked small. I picked up the phone and answered hesitantly. It was a man's voice. He said he was a nurse at Maine Medical Center in Portland.

"What?" I blurted.

"Is this Mr. McMorrow?"

"Yes."

"I'm calling for Roxanne Masterson."

"Oh, God," I said. "Is she okay?"

"Oh, yeah. Fine. She just wanted me to tell you that she hadn't had time to return your calls because of an emergency. A DHS emergency."

I sagged back into the chair.

"She's been here since this afternoon. The police were here, too."

"What happened?" I asked.

"Well, I can't really say because it's all confidential. But it's, well, it's a pretty sad case. An abuse case. Sex abuse. The little girl has been here all afternoon. Roxanne came in with the mom, and right now I believe she's out trying to place the other four children. She asked me to call you and tell you she'll call as soon as she can, but it could be a while.''

"If you see her, tell her to be careful," I said.

He didn't answer.

"Could you do that? Tell her what's going on down here may spread up there.''

"Um, okay, I guess. What's going on . . . what was that again?''

I repeated it and he said he'd try. I called Roxanne's car again, her office. Talked to the machines. Hung up and stared at the TV. Well, at least she was with other people. Foster parents, kids, Portland cops.

In the throes of domestic strife, she'd be safe.

I turned the channel and watched Butch exit the courthouse yet again. The route of the state funeral procession, still two days away, was flashed on the screen. Reserve your balcony now.

Christina came out of her room in a short shift sort of thing. She was still buttoning it up as she crossed the room.

"You ready?'' she said.

I turned off Bill Clinton in mid-condolence. Christina arranged the sixty-dollar take-out meal at the table: steak, creamed spinach, French fries and onion rolls. She opened a bottle of cabernet sauvignon. It was from a vineyard in California I'd never heard of. Christina lighted candles and poured the wine into crystal wineglasses.

"I just can't drink out of paper cups,'' she said. "I'm sorry. My mother always said 'The glass should be commensurate with the quality of the wine.' Those sorts of things are very important to Mum. Ah, yes. The ritual of alcoholism.''

On that note, we sat. Christina raised her glass for a toast. To what, I thought.

"To an escape from all our problems,'' she said. "No matter how fleeting. The escape, I mean.''

She looked at me, her eyes reflecting the flickering candles. Our glasses touched.

Christina was oddly animated at dinner. She talked

about her show, her plans for a larger installation that would expand its scope. She went on about Christophe and his Australian "woman-child," then delivered an inside account of how Ellen's marriage had ended.

"Again, she's twenty-four," Christina said. "He's old enough to be her father. What is with men and their absolute dread of mortality and aging? I mean, look at Mick Jagger."

She sipped her wine, took a bite of steak.

"Not you, Jack. You always had the long view of things. That's why I think you questioned your work as a journalist so much. I always thought that. You were very good at what you did here, a very good writer, but I think you were after a more timeless sort of expression."

I tried to smile.

"I'm surprised you gave it that much thought," I said.

She smiled slyly. Took a long swallow of wine and reached for the bottle.

"Oh, I did. One time—oh, God, I shouldn't tell you this. It's the wine, probably. But one time I, well, I said your name."

I looked at her.

"While we were, you know. Doing it."

I felt myself blush.

"Now don't get embarrassed. Oh, I shouldn't have told you."

"It's okay."

"But you know what was really funny? I thought Christophe would get all mad. You know, get up and stomp out of the room. But he didn't."

I didn't know what to say.

"He wanted to hear more. Isn't that bizarre?"

I shrugged. Didn't answer.

"Pathetic, really, I thought. I don't know what I was thinking with him sometimes. I mean, he could be great. Fun and dashing and very smart. Very quick conceptually. Ideas just came to him. An idea a minute. But then he had these weird little nooks and crannies. In his character, I mean."

So we ate and Christina talked. Dessert was chocolate mousse cake, which I skipped and she picked at. At eleven, she asked if I wanted to watch the news. I wanted to say no. It had been a long day.

Through windows. Across planks. Down hallways where kids waited with knives.

But I was a player in this game now. I needed to know as much as possible. I needed to know what they knew.

On WNYC, it was my friend Stephanie Cooper, still hard at it. This time she was at the Museum of Natural History, on the sidewalk out front, where she'd persuaded a relic of a custodian to talk about Butch as a kid following his dad around the halls. There was a still shot of Butch's father when he was a New York cop. I looked at him, felt the doors of memory pried open. I remembered Mr. Casey, as my father called him, picking me up and holding me high over his head. I felt his big hands under my arms.

Stephanie must have felt something, too.

"It was here that the young Butch Casey began what would be a decades-long friendship with Jack McMorrow, son of a museum entomologist."

Then the custodian, a white-haired woman I vaguely remembered.

"They were little buddies. Butch was the one with the devil in him, roaming the back halls. The McMorrow boy was the one Butch recruited for his little adventures."

She said it the Irish way, "divil." Then she smiled. The camera switched to Stephanie.

"It was a fateful connection," she said, staring soulfully with the museum turrets behind her. "And it continued until minutes before Butch Casey allegedly took a knife and plunged it into the heart of the mayor of New York. Accompanying him on this night, the night of the most devilish adventure of his life, was his childhood buddy, Jack McMorrow."

Stephanie paused triumphantly.

"This is Stephanie Cooper. At the Museum of Natural History in New York."

The anchor thanked her, said there was more to come. "WNYC revisits the murder that may have pushed this homicide detective over the edge. We talk to residents of the West Village, where Butch Casey lived quietly after leaving the police department. Meanwhile, Casey's closest friend, Jack McMorrow, remains in New York in the company of Brooklyn artist Christina Mansell, with whom he was staying in a Midtown hotel. More from WNYC's Rick Greene."

"What?" Christina said.

"Shhhh," I said.

Rick was in front of Police Headquarters, but the tape switched to a press conference. Police Commissioner Kiley stood at a podium while motor drives whirred.

He said the investigation was proceeding, but much remained to be done.

"Is Casey cooperating?" someone called out.

"I can't comment on that at this time."

"Are you convinced that he acted alone, or could there be other arrests?"

"As I said, we continue to investigate. We are following up all possible leads to determine whether any conspiracy took place. You can be assured the investigation will proceed on all fronts until we are absolutely one-hundred percent certain Mr. Casey acted alone or he didn't."

"Mr. Commissioner, are you investigating Jack McMorrow, Casey's friend at the pub that night?"

"No comment."

"What about the woman McMorrow was with at the Meridien? WNYC has identified her as Christina Mansell. Will you be talking to her about a possible wider plot that ended with the assassination?"

"Oh, my God," Christina said.

"We will continue to talk to anyone and everyone connected with Mr. Casey," the commissioner said.

The phone rang. Staring at the screen, Christina answered it.

"Oh, I know. It's outrageous . . . I don't know. I have

a lawyer but he just does the loft stuff . . . You think I should? . . . Talia, get real . . . I just stopped by . . . No, he's not dangerous . . . We're sitting here right now. We just finished dinner and turned it on. We're both absolutely flabbergasted . . . Do you really think so? I never thought of that. . . .''

Christina talked, her bare feet up on the chest in front of the couch. I watched the segment on Butch in the Village but it didn't say much. A few neighbors saying he was quiet and polite. They missed the lesbian bar. The segment on Leslie Casey's murder was better, with footage of Fiore at the time, of Georgie Ortiz, except the caption said his name was Muriqi. There were rapid-fire shots of newspaper headlines: *Homicide Hits Home . . . Fiore Says Cops Overstepped . . .*

And then a *Times* headline:

Police Say D.A. Let Murderer Walk.

By Jack McMorrow.

I leaned forward and there was Stephanie Cooper, now in front of the *Times* building. Did the woman ever sleep?

"It was this story, sources say, that got McMorrow in hot water with his editors at the *Times*. The story outlined the police investigation and quoted Casey himself defending homicide detectives' procedures and blasting John Fiore for his decision not to seek a grand jury indictment of Georgie Ortiz. But sources say the problem for McMorrow was that he did not tell his editors that Casey was not only one of his best sources on the police department, but one of his oldest and closest friends. This is Stephanie Cooper, reporting for WNYC at the *New York Times* in Manhattan."

I took a deep breath. Shook my head. Felt like I was caught in a wave and it had torn off my clothes, tossed me naked on the beach. Sources at the *Times*. Sources at the museum. On the television, in the newspapers. And where the media left off, the man on the phone, the guys on the roof, in the cars outside, took over.

It was relentless and it showed no sign of letting up.

Christina said good-bye, started to put the phone down. It rang again. She answered.

"Fantastic? No, I don't think it's fantastic . . . Yeah, I've heard of him . . . He does? . . . You called him already? . . ."

I got up from the couch, left the television on. Christina, still talking, was reaching for her wineglass. At the door to her bedroom I paused and peered in. The window to the fire escape was open, the bars unlocked. I walked in, knelt on the bed and swung the bars closed. Easing off the bed, I crossed to Philippe's room. I could hear Christina talking, the excitement in her voice.

"He said that? Get out!"

I went into the darkened room and slowly closed the door. Stood motionless for a moment and then eased my way to the windows, where I stood against the wall and looked out.

The black car had moved from one corner to the other and was parked in the shadows, just the hood and windshield showing. I peered at the windows across the street but saw only darkness. I waited. Remained still and silent, like a bird-watcher who knows that you learn more from what you hear in the woods than from what you see.

In this blackened canopy, the sounds were distant. Horns. The rattle of traffic on the bridge.

The creak of a chair.

A barely audible yawn.

It was the sound of someone leaning back. Stretching after hours in the same position.

I pressed myself against the wall. Was it a spotting scope this time? Or was it a scope on a rifle?

Wait for McMorrow to go to bed, put a bullet in his pale, glowing image. If he gets in the sack with the artist babe, shoot 'em both.

I waited. Heard another yawn, then the creak of a chair again, as though whoever it was had settled back in to watch and wait.

But they wanted me to leave, didn't they? It was the police who wanted me to stay? Did they want to know what I was doing, as long as I still was here? Which of them was it, watching my window in the dark?

From the other room I could hear the television. Christina's voice, then a pause, and the phone ringing again. For me? And then, ''I know. I can't believe it. I was just saying to Jack . . .''

I stood there against the wall and felt myself start to sag. Forced myself straight. Listened. Looked out and saw the black car, still there. I watched it but nothing moved. I waited, felt myself start to waver again, eased my way back to shelves that ran along the wall. On the top was Philippe's stuff; on the bottom, in this closetless space, were blankets and towels.

I felt for a blanket, pulled it from the stack. Staying against the wall, I unfolded it and went to the window. Climbed up on the steam radiator and reached as high as I could, feeling for a nail or a hook. I found one and poked it through the corner of the blanket. Grabbed the other corner and, sliding along the floor, crossed to the other side of the window, and stood up again. Hung that corner up, too. The room went even darker. The sounds of the New York night were muffled.

Still crouching, I went to the side of the bed and undressed. In my shorts, I stretched out on top of the sheets. Heard Christina's voice in the other room. A murmur from the TV. As I felt myself drifting off, I hoped Roxanne was safe. I wished I had brought my rifle.

And then my eyes opened, like a switch clicking on. I was awake. The room was black and I started to panic. Remembered the blanket. Remembered the news. Remembered all of it.

Heard a step behind me. Heard the door creak faintly.

Twenty-eight.

I stayed still. Listened. Another step. I pictured the fire escape. The bars pushed open. There was another step, then weight on the bed and I was ready to lash backward. An elbow and a fist, and then—

I smelled her perfume.

I felt Christina settle in behind me. Her breath warmed my back. Her hand touched my hip. Her lips grazed the back of my neck. Her bare breasts pressed against me. She sighed very softly and said, "Oh, I missed you."

She kissed me, very gently. My neck. My shoulder. My neck again. She sighed and I felt her lips, her cheek. I didn't move, not sure what the first move should be.

Turn over and tell her to go away? Turn over and take her in my arms, melt into her, feel her against me?

She stroked my hip. Ran her hand down my leg and back up. I closed my eyes.

"You don't have to decide, Jack," Christina whispered. "Just lie there. Don't decide anything."

She pressed against me, all of her, and she felt bigger than Roxanne, longer and stronger. I could feel her hips, her hair, the hardness of her and then one leg rode up on mine, and I felt her begin to slowly grind against me.

Her hand reached over me, ran down my chest. Her tongue flicked across my ear, and she said, "Oh, Jack." Her hand was on my belly, her fingers sliding under the waistband of my shorts. I could feel myself start to harden, felt her fingers slide under the shorts and touch me. Take hold of me. I reached down, felt her hand, took it in mine—

And gently pulled it away.

"I can't do this, Christina," I said.

She stopped. Hovered there for a moment, against me, all around me. And then she gave my cheek a kiss, but a very different one, like a kiss good-bye, and settled back down beside me.

"Hey, it was worth a try," she said, and I heard the wine in her voice.

"I'm sorry," I said. "I just can't. It wouldn't be—"

"It wouldn't be right?"

"No, it wouldn't."

"You always do the right thing now, Jack?"

"No, but I have to this time."

She rolled onto her back.

"When you left me, I didn't think that was right."

"It wasn't."

"But you know what I told myself? I said, 'Christina, it isn't you he's running away from. He's running away from himself.' "

I thought about that.

"Yeah," I said. "Maybe."

"So that way I could say it wasn't anything personal. You didn't leave me, Jack. You just left."

"I'm sorry."

"It's okay."

She sighed.

"So you must really love your little social worker."

"Yeah. I do."

"That's fine. Hey, I don't really need anybody. I can stand on my own. Hell, I've been doing it since I was a little kid. You know when I started? Standing on my own, I mean?"

I did, but I said no.

"When I was nine, my mother put me on a plane all by myself and sent me off to school in goddamn Switzerland. You know what? I thought I'd come home for the weekend. Nobody told me you just stayed there. Oh, God, I was pathetic. Did I tell you I'm the kid in my brick-wall show? The kid in the painting?"

"No," I said. "But I guessed."

Christina put her arm around me and took my hand in hers.

"Oh, McMorrow. You know what I get tired of?"

"No. What?"

"Starting over. Convincing myself that this is the guy, this is the one. 'Cause I can't admit it isn't. You know what Christophe told me? He told me when he got back from the Caribbean, we'd have a baby. Instead, he ran off with one. Ha, ha. That's a joke, Jack. You're supposed to laugh."

"I'm sorry."

She got up on one elbow, her breasts against my back. She leaned close to my ear.

"You want to have a baby, Jack? Just screw me right now. Inseminate me. It'll be our little secret."

I didn't answer. She dropped back down.

"Just kidding," Christina said. "Or maybe not. I really do. Want a kid, I mean. Maybe it was having Philippe, even though he was somebody else's. But my own baby. You know, I'm thirty-eight. How old is Roxanne?"

"Thirty-one."

"Oh, so she's got time. I don't have a lot of time. Tick, tick, tick, you know? I mean, starting from scratch with some new guy? In New York? Christ, I'll be fifty before he decides whether he's ready to consider 'commitment to a relationship.' Whatever happened to love at first sight?"

She gave a sad little laugh.

"So when you showed up, it was like it was meant to be. I mean, I always loved you, Jack. I didn't know that then but I do now. Funny how you get things too late. So with you, it wouldn't be starting from scratch. I could just start up where I left off, and you could—well, I thought maybe you would, too. We had a very good thing there, didn't we?''

''Yeah,'' I said.

''Remember?''

''Yeah, I do.''

''And we had a lot of fun, didn't we?''

''Yeah, we did.''

''But now you found somebody better.''

''Not better. Different.''

''And a social worker. I should have known. Mr. Harsh Reality couldn't settle down with somebody who just paints silly little pictures.''

''I don't know about that, Christina. Things just happen in funny ways.''

''But now you're really in love with this woman, aren't you?''

''Yeah, I am,'' I said. It seemed an odd thing to say with another woman naked in my bed.

''That's nice, Jack. Nice for you.'' She squeezed my hand. Her fingers were very long. ''I mean that.''

''Thanks.''

''But you know what, Jack? Sometimes I feel like everything I've been given in life—you know, I'm attractive.''

''Very.''

''I've got more money than most people.''

I thought of Prosperity, where there was very little.

''More than you know,'' I said.

''I'm talented, I guess. I mean, the *Voice* called last week. They want to do a piece. They don't do that for just anybody.''

''You're very talented, Christina,'' I assured her.

''And I can't have what everybody else has. Which is somebody else, somebody I love who loves me back.''

''Christophe didn't?''

"He loved the package. He loved the idea of me. He didn't love me."

"He didn't deserve you."

"Right. So here I am. Naked, in all my glory. What are you waiting for, McMorrow? Don't you deserve me either?"

She laughed again. I didn't say anything. She still was holding my hand.

"And I can't even get laid, McMorrow. I can't even get laid."

She chuckled and then was quiet. And then she spoke again.

"You know, Jack, I have a bad feeling about all this."

"About this?"

"About all of it. I feel like doing this, coming in here to be with you, it went all wrong. It just went all wrong, and when things go wrong with me, they usually go wrong in bunches."

"Maybe you're wrong about that."

"I don't think so. I have a bad feeling about Fiore and your friend and all of this mess. A funny feeling. You know today, I was here working. Usually, I feel really safe and secure in here. Hidden in my aerie, you know?"

"But not today?"

"No, today for the first time I can remember, I really felt kind of nervous."

"But you're locked in, Christina," I said.

"That's just it, Jack," she said. "It was weird. After a while it went away, but for a moment I felt really trapped."

She held my hand tighter.

"I know the feeling," I said.

And then Christina was quiet. And after a moment, her breath slowed and lapsed into an easy rhythm and she was asleep. When I turned, her eyes were closed, the lids shadowed and translucent like a baby bird's.

I remembered that about her. She would be talking in bed, usually after wine, and she'd be telling me some long, involved story and the story would end. Ten seconds later, Christina would be sound asleep and I would still be wide awake, alone with my own thoughts.

Well, here we were again.

So with Christina sprawled next to me, I thought about Roxanne, told her I was sorry. I listened to the sound of the night, muffled behind the blanket, to the sounds of the loft. The whir of appliances, the buzz of a fly, the creak of old wood. And then I fell asleep, until I dreamed of Roxanne and she was there, in that room, and I was trying to say that it wasn't anything, Christina was just lonely. And Roxanne said over and over, "But Jack, you love her," and I tried to say that wasn't true but no words would come out.

And I awoke.

It was black in the room, with faint lines framing the window. I remembered the blanket. Felt someone and tensed. Christina. I remembered her, too, and she gave a woozy sigh as I slipped down and around her and got to my feet.

In the paling darkness, I went to the window. I listened to Christina's even breathing, then took the blanket and eased it open a crack. The window was dark and silent. The black car wasn't in sight. The neighborhood was still and the city sounds were distant and faint. The sky to the west still was blue black.

I turned back to the shelves, felt my way along the blankets, the shoes, the sweaters, the stuff Philippe didn't need in the Caribbean. I pulled the sweaters out one by one until I found a sweatshirt. It was dark with a hood. I yanked it on, then padded the floor with my hands to locate my pants. Found them, then my shoes. Leaned down to the bed and touched Christina on her bare shoulder.

She awoke slowly.

"Hmmm."

"Christina, I need the car," I said.

"Hmmm."

"I need to go for a ride."

"Hmmm."

"Could you call the guy?"

"Uh-huh."

I got the phone and she said it was speed dial 5 and I pressed it and she sat up, bare-chested, and opened her eyes and slurred, "Zwee, it's Christina. Did I wake you? Oh, I know. My friend Jack is going for a ride. Jack McMorrow."

"I'll come get it."

"No, he'll walk over, hon."

And I did, in the silent early morning. Dew dripped from the rails of the fire escape and the rungs of the ladder were slick. I dropped to the ground, made my way to the steel door. Putting the hood up, I tucked the envelope deeper under my belt and eased the door open. Stepped out and started up the street.

The lot attendant asked my name. I told him and he held out the key. He held the gate open, and when I drove through, the black car from the corner was waiting.

Twenty-nine.

The black car was small and nondescript and it followed as I wound my way through the factory streets, the darkened projects where only occasional lights showed. When I jumped on the BQE, the car was fifty yards back. When I eased into the left lane and pressed the throttle, it stayed with me. When I wove between tractor-trailer rigs, it wove, too.

On the highway, I got the Rover up over ninety and gained some distance, then swung between trucks into the right lane. Screened by trailers, I floored it again and the Rover's V-8 surged. When I hit the toll plaza for the Verrazano Bridge, the black car was three trucks back. When I swerved through a line of orange cones and made a U-turn back into Brooklyn, the driver of the black car was paying at the booth.

I saw a bare arm. A man with dark hair. And then I was gone.

Fifteen minutes later, I was parked in front of a fruit stand in Brighton Beach, just over from Coney Island. It was 4:40 and the dawn was coming slowly, a slate gray sky pressing upward against the darkness. In the Russian enclave, a few people were out and about. They came from a place where you queued up for butter at three in the morning, for bread at five. The least they could do, in this country where stuff was so routinely and obscenely plentiful, was to get up early and walk the dog.

So I sat in the car and watched them, stolid men and women in nylon windbreakers. But I watched the street ahead, the mirrors, too. After twenty minutes, the black car hadn't appeared. I stuffed the envelope under the seat, pulled my hood up, got out and started walking.

The clip said Vladimir Mihailov lived on Brighton 4th Street. The cross streets were all numbered off Brighton Beach Avenue, the main commercial drag. I crossed the avenue at Brighton 1st Street and walked up. It was me and the old people and the dogs sniffing the light poles in front of shops where the signs were in Cyrillic. A gray-haired guy wearing a white apron threw up the screen in front of a deli. A refrigerator truck idled in front of a produce stand. It was almost quaint but this was New York. There had to be a stained underbelly.

In Brighton Beach, it was the Russian mob, rapacious killers and thieves. I wondered if Mihailov had been connected, if he had been stealing BMWs as more than a solo act.

At Brighton 4th Street, I turned off, pulled my hood lower, and started up the sidewalk to try to find out.

The houses were small, shabby bungalows with fenced front yards the size of a parking space. They were drab except for brightly painted front doors, which might have been a Russian thing. But one house was even more distinctive. From a distance I could see the yellow tape wound like ribbon across the front steps. As I approached, I counted the numbers. Sure enough, it was 1283 that the New York Police Department had decorated. An NYPD radio car was posted out front.

One of the cops was a black man and the other was white. They were drinking from paper cups, talking and smiling, and they turned to one another as I approached. I looked at the house.

The tape said Do Not Cross. It barred the way to the

front door, which was robin's egg blue. The glass in the storm door was broken, with jagged shards still in the frame. There was a TV satellite dish screwed to the roof of the front porch, its antenna pointed toward the street like a weapon. The car parked out front was a new Cadillac Seville.

I passed on the other side of the street, glancing over and continuing on. At the end of the block I crossed the street and stood for a moment and looked back. I looked at my watch, as though I were expecting to meet someone. Stood at the curb. After counting to fifty, I checked my watch again, then slowly started back.

Halfway up the block, a man came out of the front door of a house and trotted down the stairs, carrying a shopping bag. When he turned, I sped up and fell in beside him.

In small-town Maine, this would have been expected. In New York City, it was like grabbing a stranger's crotch.

The man with the bag was fiftyish, balding and big, with long arms, a barrel chest and a black mustache. He was wearing Nike sneakers. He looked at me and scowled. I smiled out from under the hood.

"Feels like rain," I said.

He looked away.

"So what happened up the street here? The place with the police tape?"

He walked a little faster and didn't answer.

"I'm looking for a guy named Vladimir Mihailov. You wouldn't happen to know him, would you?"

Still walking, the guy turned and stared, suddenly frightened. He glanced at my hands, which were in the sweatshirt pockets. He looked like he might start to run.

"I don't know those people," he blurted.

"What people?" I said, but he whirled around, and with a half-skip, hurried away in the other direction.

I looked after him, then turned and kept walking. The guy's abrupt about-face had caught the attention of the cops in front of 1283, and as I approached, they watched me. I saw them murmur to one another and I knew they were trying to peg me.

Somebody collecting money? A guy who had picked a very weird place to go cruising? Somebody checking out the scene of whatever had happened at 1283? The perp at 1283?

The passenger window rolled down.

"Hey, buddy."

I looked.

"Yeah, you. Come here."

I stopped. The cop was young, with a military haircut and silver-rimmed glasses. He opened the door and got out, showing short sleeves, black fingerless gloves and muscle-builder's forearms. The driver, who was smaller, got out, too.

They approached. The muscular guy pointed a forefinger at me.

"Hands outta the pockets. Where I can see 'em."

I took them out.

"Now some I.D."

He was in front of me, the driver behind me, to my right.

I reached for my wallet.

"Slow," the muscleman said.

"I got him," the black man said, circling to my side.

"Hey, I'm just walking down the street," I said, smiling. "Don't you need some sort of probable cause?"

The muscular guy smiled and showed his teeth.

"You want probable cause? This is a homicide scene, chump. You're lingering in a suspicious manner."

"I'm lingering because you told me to stop."

"Did I ask for any lip? Who was that you were talking to, the guy who ran when he saw us?"

"I don't know."

"You're talking to him walking down the street but you don't know him? Hey, what do you think I am? Stupid?"

"I was just asking him what was going on here. With the police tape and everything."

"Why you want to know?"

I held out my driver's license.

"Maine," the muscular cop said, peering at the license as though it needed decoding. "What the hell you doing here, Mr. McMorrow?"

I hesitated.

"Working."

"Working? Working how?"

"I'm a reporter. I work for the *Times*."

"That right? Must be a hell of a commute—"

He looked at the license again.

"—from Prosperity, Maine."

"What's the name again?" the black cop said.

"McMorrow. Given name Jack."

"Hey, you know who—"

He stepped closer.

"You mind taking off the hood, sir?" the black cop said.

I glanced up the street toward Brighton Beach Avenue.

"I'd rather not," I said.

"Jesus Christ," the muscular cop said, and he stepped toward me, grabbed the hood and yanked it backward.

"Whatcha hiding under there?"

"Easy," the black cop said. "You know who this is?"

"Some shithead who wants to play games."

"No, this is McMorrow. The McMorrow who's Butch Casey's friend. You know. The guy he was drinking with?"

Even in the muscular cop's head, it clicked.

"You're in the paper," he said, staring at me with new fascination.

"Not by choice," I said.

"What are you doing here, Mr. McMorrow?" the black cop said.

"I was about to ask you that."

"We're securing the scene of a homicide," he said.

"When did it happen?"

"Early this morning. Around 2:30."

"Who's the deceased?"

"Who's asking the questions?" the muscular cop said.

''You can watch it on the news like everybody else. So what I want to know—''

''Was it a guy named Vladimir Mihailov?''

They stared at me. The muscular cop moved closer, his eyes fixed on mine.

''How'd you know that name?'' the black cop said.

Thirty.

"Mihailov was four names ago," Ramirez said. "There was Michalek and Ivandek and he was living as Ivanov when he came back here."

From under my hood, I looked out at the bleak, narrow street two blocks from Mihailov's. We had driven over at my insistence. I did not want to be seen.

"His mother died," Donatelli said. "He'd been living in different places, all in Brooklyn. Borough Park. Flatbush. He changed his appearance. Dyed his hair. Grew a beard. Shaved it off."

"So he was sort of in hiding?" I asked.

"Ah. Sort of halfhearted hiding. I mean, he didn't go to Moscow or anything. He still was working for a guy named Iwanow. The *W* is a *V*. Guy was a fairly big-time loan shark. Mihailov was his muscle. One of 'em."

"The one who comes knocking?"

"Right."

"So how did a guy like that get turned loose so easy after he hit the rich kid on the head and took his BMW?" I said.

"These Russians are no dopes," Ramirez said. "Maybe they had something going with the judge. Maybe they knew somebody who knew somebody. Shit happens. Let's not kid each other.''

"It stuck out in Butch's mind. Fiore was quoted in the story when they picked him up. Mihailov, I mean. Talking about the need to clean up the scum, take the city back for law-abiding New Yorkers. He was campaigning.''

"Guy never stopped campaigning,'' Donatelli said.

"But listen, if Fiore was in on it directly, the guy should have been gone, right? Instead, he gets some Mickey Mouse bail and he's out.''

"So Fiore missed one, McMorrow,'' Ramirez said. "Probably was just looking for an audience. Went on to the next tragedy and got all worked up all over again.''

"If it was routine, why did Butch pull it out?''

Ramirez snorted.

"Hey, you want me to tell you how Casey's mind works? This is a guy who killed the mayor. Are we forgetting that here?''

"He's just charged with it.''

"Give me a break, McMorrow. He's guilty. And he's a squirrel.''

"But Mihailov was on his list,'' Donatelli told her. "And Mihailov gets whacked. Somebody knocks on the door. He answers. *Pop, pop, pop.* Three hours later, McMorrow walks up. What's wrong with this picture?''

"Hey, where were you at 2:35?'' Ramirez said.

"Asleep,'' I said.

"You got witnesses?''

I pictured Christina, naked against me.

"Yeah,'' I said.

"I'll bet you do,'' Ramirez said. "Was it good for her?''

"Oh, come on,'' Donatelli said. "McMorrow didn't kill Mihailov. The guy was just in a business where that happens. He was a punk. These guys don't die of old age.''

"Thank God for small favors,'' Ramirez said.

"But why now?'' I said. "After ten years? The day I

come looking for him? The day after somebody takes a shot at me—"

"You say. 'Cause you've heard silencers on TV," Ramirez said.

"And I'm warned off. And threatened."

"You say you were threatened."

"You think I'm making all this stuff up?"

"No," Donatelli said. "I don't."

"Because you can check me out. I'm not some kook. I'm a reporter, for God's sake. Reporters don't make things up."

"Hah," Ramirez said.

"You know what I mean," I said. "This is real. Lester John's gone. Who hauled him off?"

"His drug-dealing buddies," Ramirez said. "And pardon me if I don't get all upset over the idea of him floating in the East River. I save my sympathy for people who deserve it. And there are plenty of them, McMorrow."

I thought of her son.

"Then why does Tilbury think John was arrested?"

"Christ! 'Cause he's senile, McMorrow. I don't know."

"That guy didn't call me yesterday because Butch was imagining things," I said.

"Maybe not," Donatelli said.

"Hey, I've got my assignment," Ramirez said to him. "Look out for McMorrow here so he can tell his story to a grand jury and tell it in court. Which I'm trying to do. But he's off on some crazy wild-goose chase and you're gonna go with him? What do you think you're gonna find out, McMorrow? That your buddy didn't do it?"

I didn't answer.

" 'Cause forget that, if that's what you're thinking. He's a goner. Gonna go down as the dirtiest cop in history, I'm sorry to say. Got the mayor's blood on his hands, literally."

"Then why is the DA's man after me?"

"He's got the same job as us," she said, turning to me.

"He's trying not to lose you. And you're making things pretty goddamn difficult."

"Somebody's making things pretty difficult for me," I said.

I paused.

"I want protection for my friend."

"In Maine?" Donatelli said.

"Yeah. Roxanne Masterson."

"Then you should talk to the Maine cops."

"I want you to talk to the Maine cops," I said. "Portland. South Portland. State Police."

They didn't answer.

"Hey, you want my help, don't you? Well, so far it's been all one way."

They looked straight ahead.

"Or I start forgetting things," I said.

"We don't need you," Ramirez said. "I mean, we can get a conviction without you."

"Without me, you're going to have a hard time proving long-term intent, or whatever you call it. That's why you need me. Without me, maybe you've got a bitter cop who flew into a rage or something. A guy whose wife was murdered. He's a crime victim. I'm the one who can tell you that he was talking about the mayor that night. Or not."

"You are a ballsy son of a bitch," Ramirez said.

"You talk to the Maine cops. They watch TV. I call them, they'll just hang up."

They didn't answer. Ramirez shook her head in disgust.

"Now we gotta baby-sit his whole family?"

But Donatelli got out his notebook and started asking questions.

Roxanne's name and address, her address at work. Her telephone numbers, both places and in the car. The car registration, type of vehicle. The time she got to the office, the number where she could be reached that morning.

And I gave it to him, with an ominous sense of déjà vu. Everything Donatelli asked for, the man on the phone had already known, and had recited to me in about the same order.

"Is this routine for you?" I said.

"We get a lot of this stuff. People are always threatening to pop witnesses, especially if you're working with people you've flipped. If you're gonna try to guard somebody who isn't in custody, these are the things you ask."

"If you're a cop," I said.

"Yeah," Donatelli said. "I suppose."

They dropped me two blocks over, at the end of another street of miniature houses with Easter-egg doors. I pulled my hood forward and walked back up to the main drag, where more Brighton Beachers were out and about.

So I fell in with them, young guys in baggy shorts, old men in slacks and straw fedoras, women who stood at the produce stands and squeezed the peaches, one by one. The heat was rising from the damp pavement and the hood felt like a hot towel on my head. I considered taking it off, then stopped at a newsstand, where a dozen Butches were splattered like a Warhol painting.

And thought again.

The *News* had a photo of Butch played huge, over half the front page. He was in the background at a press conference, in a sweatshirt and Yankees hat, listening as the brass took credit for some major bust. They'd cropped the picture to center him, smirking as he leaned over.

I was bent toward him. I looked like I was about to laugh.

The lead story was about the killing of Leslie Moore, with her head shot set into the text. The headline said, "Wife's murder left Casey a broken man." But in the lower right was another, smaller headline: "Casey and McMorrow: Partners in Crime," it said, and then below it, "Detective and Reporter Worked NYC Mean Streets in 80s."

I kept the hood on.

The *Post* had Butch on the cover, too, but with a knife

in his hand. I looked closer. It was a murder scene in 1986, the caption said; Butch had taken the knife away from a killer. The effect was jarring, and grossly misleading.

The *Times* had this story, top left, three columns: "Starcrossed Friends: History Turned on Fateful Last Drink." And "A Funeral Like No Other: Fiore Service Could Rival JFK's."

I bought all three papers, keeping my face turned away from the woman behind the counter. And then I walked up the block, past another newsstand where Butch Casey peered out from amid porn magazines. I turned away, crossed under the elevated tracks and continued on. On the other side of Brighton Beach Avenue, I looked around the corner and saw the Rover in front of the fruit stand.

There were cars in front of and behind it, all the way up the street, but they were empty. There was a dark-haired man just this side of the Rover, watching a little dog poop. When the dog had finished, the man took out a tissue and bent over to wipe its behind.

I walked quickly down the street, on the side away from the car. Nothing unusual showed. The man with the dog was putting its droppings in a plastic bag. I strolled down the block, turned in a driveway and walked between two houses. I waited, then eased my way back to the corner of one of the buildings. I looked up the block, then crossed the street, and started up, my hood still up.

People were looking at fruit. They were meandering up and down with grocery bags, coffee in paper cups. The man with the dog was still picking at the ground. I felt in my pocket for the car keys. Got my fingers on the door opener. Took a last glance behind me. There were no cars coming up the block, nobody in the cars that were parked.

I turned back. The man with the dog was still crouched at the curb. And as I watched, he put the Baggie of droppings in the pocket of his windbreaker. Took something else out.

And put it under the Rover's windshield wiper.

I started to yell, "Hey," but caught myself. He'd turned

away from me and was walking up the block. The dog
trotted jauntily and the man hurried him along. I looked
at the car, then followed.

They turned the corner, wove through the crowd. Then
the man reached down and picked the dog up. I wanted
to see his face, but his back was toward me and he was
hurrying. He stepped out into traffic, crossed between the
passing cars and broke into a trot. I waited as the cars
rushed past, and when the traffic broke, he was gone.

I turned back.

Eyed the car from a distance, the white paper still on
its windshield. I walked to the fruit stand, felt the peaches.
Looked up and down the block, then bought two apples.
The man dropped them in a sack. I turned and unlocked
the Rover's doors. Snatched the paper and jumped in the
driver's seat.

I backed up, jockeyed out of the space. Hit the gas and
rounded the corner, floored it through a yellow light,
turned at the next block and unfolded the paper as I drove.

It was Roxanne.

A blurry likeness. A fax of a fax. A head shot from a
newspaper, with a fragment of a story.

The note was typed. Two lines.

LEAVE N.Y. A.M. TODAY WED. NO MORE CALLS.
NO MORE TALKS. OR SHE'S DEAD. YOU'LL GET
HER IN MAIL. HEAD FIRST. LAST CHANCE.

I put the paper down on the seat. Felt my mouth go
dry. I looked down at Roxanne's face again, and punched
the throttle.

I had to leave. I believed them now. The man with the
dog. The man on the phone. The men on the roof. How
many of them were there? How had they found me? After
they'd killed Mihailov, had they waited? Had they known
I'd show up? Where had they been?

I drove fast and hard, cutting off cars, passing on the
right, on the left. The Rover roared as I caught a parkway,
put the pedal to the floor and hung on to the wheel.

And the phone rang.

"Go to hell," I shouted, but it kept ringing and I reached for it.

"Yeah," I barked.

There was a roaring sound, like a jet engine.

"Yeah," I said again.

"Jack?"

It was Roxanne. Her voice was faint, fading in a crackle of static.

"Hello," I said.

"Jack?"

"Rox," I shouted.

"Jack, I can barely . . . you. Can you hear me? Jack?"

"Yeah. I can. A little."

The phone hissed and crackled, the signal ricocheting off satellites. The motor roared.

"Jack, this damn phone. There's something wrong with it," she said. "But if you can hear me, I wanted . . . you to know I love you. I wanted to tell you and I'm on my way to a client's home and I won't be able to call for a while and . . . I don't want anything to change. It hasn't changed, has it, Jack?"

"Roxanne," I said.

"Oh, you must think I'm being silly, but I have a bad feeling. I'm worried about what's going to happen . . ."

"Roxanne."

". . . to us. To me. Am I still, I don't know . . ."

"Roxanne, where are you?"

"Am I still yours? Or would you rather . . . this glamorous person. Maybe that's what you want? Maybe I was just a phase. I don't know."

"Roxanne?"

"Jack, can you hear me?"

"Yeah," I shouted.

"Good, Jack. Tell me. Am I wrong to be worried? Are you worried, too?"

"Yes," I shouted. "But not—"

"Oh, Jack," Roxanne cried, and then her voice slipped away.

That much she had heard.

Thirty-one.

I tried calling back. A robot voice said Roxanne was out of range. I tried Christina's and she answered brightly.

"Yeah, she called. Good thing she didn't arrive in the middle of the night, huh? Sorry about all that, Jack. It was the wine. I shouldn't have—"

"It's okay. Did Roxanne say where she was going?"

"No, she just said she was working. Going to see a client, I think."

"She didn't say when she'd be back?"

"No. We didn't talk that long. Jack, I know there's no real reason, not on your part anyway, but it was a little awkward. Women just can sense these things."

"Oh?"

"Not that it wasn't cordial. She's very nice. She thanked me for helping you and I think she meant it. Well, there was a little edge to it but that's to be expected. I invited her to come down if you're stuck here much longer. She sounded like she might."

"She did?"

"Hey, I can't have you back as a lover, I can at least have your lover as a guest. God, it would be like a movie, wouldn't it? We should only speak French. Hold up cards. With English subtitles.''

She laughed. I didn't.

"No, really, I'd like to meet your friends. It would be like getting a look at your new life, Jack. Hey, listen. How much have you told her about what's been going on? With Fiore, I mean. Because I didn't think it was my place to—"

"I'll fill her in," I said. "Is that black car still out there?"

"No," Christina said. "But the van with the wood sides is."

"God, I wonder who that one is?"

"I don't know. You want me to go ask them?"

"No," I said.

"Jack, I was only kidding. Have you seen the papers?"

"Seen 'em. Haven't read 'em."

"We're in the *Times*. And Ellen called already, looking for you. And the reporter, Robert. Stephanie Cooper. *Dateline*. *20:20*. The phone's been ringing since five-thirty. Let's see. I kept a list. I've got it right here. A woman from National Public Radio. She sounded Irish. Another woman, said she writes a column in *Newsday*. A guy from the BBC. A guy from some German newspaper. The *Voice* again, but that was for me. *Time Out New York*, that's mine, too. And the same guy from the *Times* who called before and I gave him the car number. He said he was a photographer.''

"Young? New Yorky?"

"Yeah," Christina said. "He said his editor told him to get in touch with you to arrange a fresh photo. About time, I thought. They can't keep using that one of you with the blood on your shirt. I mean, it makes you look like some kind of—"

"He wasn't a photographer, Christina."

"No?"

"He told me to back off, to leave New York or he'd have Roxanne killed."

"Oh, no. Oh, I'm sorry. Does she know?"

"No. She couldn't hear me."

"Maybe that's better," Christina said. "It would just scare her."

"She's scared already," I said and I put the phone down.

I was skimming north along the shore, with the Verrazano Bridge ahead of me and barges and tugs plodding the gray-watered bay to my left. I glanced once, then hit the gas and soon was going too fast to look. Swinging onto the expressway, I cut across Bay Ridge, with its endless gritty rooftops, and thought, well, maybe this would be better for Roxanne, the anonymity of New York, the crowds in which to get lost.

In Portland, with its dollhouse housing projects, its finite boundaries, its goldfish-bowl downtown, Roxanne couldn't hide. In New York she could just disappear.

Couldn't she?

But they'd found me easily enough, as though there were a beeping tracking device on the Rover. Racing north, I glanced around. Caught myself. Was I cracking up, imagining a James Bond movie come true?

I glanced at the note, still on the seat. I wasn't imagining that. And if they found Roxanne, if they followed her out into the country, got her on some lonely road . . .

I picked up the phone and dialed Roxanne's car. Got the robot voice again. Roxanne was out of range. But not out of reach.

Zwee, the parking lot guy, took a circuitous route between the black-brick blocks, skirting the Navy Yard, coming in from the water side. But there was only so much you could do, and when the Rover swung around the corner, the men in the red car looked up. I saw two of them. White. Middle-aged. Nobody I knew. Then Christina's door rolled open. Butch's envelope tucked in my pants, I rolled out. Zwee kept going and Christina snapped the padlocks shut.

In the darkness she brushed against me and I felt her shudder, and it wasn't with fear.

"Sorry, McMorrow. It's an involuntary reaction. I'm jumping out of my skin these days, for some reason. Probably hormones."

In the elevator, the light came on. Christina's doubts of the previous night had vanished and she chattered about the phone calls that had come in since we'd talked.

"You got a call from a producer for Dan Rather," she said.

"Uh-huh," I said.

Her face was alive, her eyes sparkling with an almost coked-out glitter.

"Well, don't you want to talk to him?"

I shrugged.

"Jack, it's Dan Rather."

Christ, I thought. Some hood was threatening to kill Roxanne and the thought of talking to Dan Rather was supposed to get me all weak in the knees?

"So?"

The elevator stopped.

"You could tell him about Butch. The woman said they're doing a full-blown profile."

"Them and everybody else."

She pulled the door open and turned to me.

"You could tell them about this thing that Butch was working on."

"That would help matters."

She started into the dim passage. I followed.

"Maybe the threat of it would help matters," Christina said.

She unlocked the door.

"I don't know enough," I said.

"Do they know that? Maybe it would help to go on the offensive a bit. Say to them, 'Listen. Leave us alone or I put this whole thing on the national news.' "

Christina swung the door open and light spilled out.

"I don't know," I said. "Sometimes threats keep somebody at bay. Sometimes they backfire."

"Well, maybe they should get the idea that their threats might backfire."

Christina stepped into the loft, cocked her hip and looked back.

"Just a thought," she said.

And not a bad one.

Christina had that quality. Just when you'd sized her up as a dreamy artist, she revealed her conniving side, her competitive edge. She'd fought her loft landlord to a standstill, maneuvered her way into galleries and shows. When I'd first met her, she'd deftly nudged out a rival for my affections, just as she'd tried to do the previous night.

So her instincts were sound. But was this the time?

I thought about it as I stood at Philippe's window and looked out at the red car, still parked at the corner. Could I tell this cop whatever the hell he was to back off or I'd take my story to the press? I'd have their ear, but how much of a story did I actually have?

At this point, it was a collection of odd coincidences, old Fiore cases gone astray. Missing criminals in a city where criminals weren't missed. A comatose victim and her doddering husband. I still hadn't talked to the woman who was raped. I hadn't tried to find Drague, the rapist. I hadn't talked to Digham, the kid whose skull was broken. In terms of a real reportable story, I wasn't there yet.

So what did I have that really said something was seriously wrong?

I had a guy who was worried enough about me and my questions to threaten to kill an innocent woman, put her in the mail in pieces. That much I had.

So I called Roxanne every five minutes, or maybe it was two or three. In between, I tried the Digham Foundation on East 64th Street. A snooty-sounding woman said there was no one in the office but I could leave a message.

I said I'd like to leave a message for Mr. Digham.

"Mr Digham the third or Mr. Digham the fourth?" she said.

"Both," I said, and I left my name and number. If she recognized it, she didn't show it. Snooty people are good at that.

I tried Clair, too, to enlist him, to ask him again to watch out for Roxanne. But there was no answer. I dialed the detectives' pagers. Roxanne again and the robot voice answered. The red van still was on the corner and the black car was back. Like foes in opposing trenches, they sat and watched. I did, too.

Christina made tea and toast and we sat with the newspapers like the cozy couple she had wanted us to be, at least the night before. I scanned the *Times* story about me and Butch, which started with our childhood friendship and ended at the Algonquin. It described Leslie Casey's death and quoted police department sources as saying Butch blamed Fiore for botching his wife's case and letting Georgie Ortiz go. My nemesis editor at the *Times* said my pursuit of that story was overzealous, that I was a talented reporter and a good writer, but I had turned the Butch Casey story into a cause.

"The *Times* does not tolerate that," he said. "No credible newspaper does."

"Screw you, you pompous ass," I said.

Christina looked up from the *Times* arts page. I dialed again. And again. And again. Until finally, at 9:40, the phone rang back.

"Jack."

"Yeah."

"It's Robert."

I sagged. Felt like hanging up but couldn't.

"You read today's story?"

"Yeah."

"Well?"

"I thought it was thorough and accurate," I said. "Thanks, I guess."

"Don't thank me. That gets around this place, I'll be up in Maine with you, writing about the selectmen."

"You could do worse."

"I don't think so. But listen, Jack. I'm calling on official business."

"Okay."

"I'm doing a story for tomorrow's paper. I don't think anybody else has it."

"Oh?" I said.

"It was a tip. Guy owed me one and he delivered. Anyway, this woman, she was scared, you know, afraid she'd get in trouble because she didn't go to the cops right away. So she went to them today. And I got a tip and I got her on the phone and she talked."

Sanders paused. Wary, I waited.

"So Jack, this is what I've got."

He cleared his throat. He was nervous. I braced myself.

"Jack, I talked to an employee at the Meridien today."

"Yup."

"Jack."

He cleared his throat again. I waited.

"Jack, the employee said Casey dropped a large envelope for you at the hotel at six o'clock Monday morning. Jack? You still there, Jack?"

October 1988

He looked the part. Silver hair. Half-glasses. Sleeves on his custom-tailored shirts carefully rolled up. He went to parties with Henry Kissinger and Barbara Walters. Had been ballooning with Malcolm Forbes. There was a photo on his office wall to prove it.

If the editor liked you, you were golden. If he didn't, you were done. It was just a matter of time.

In the beginning he'd been impressed by the new guy, McMorrow. He'd even stopped and chatted with him in the newsroom. He'd told him he thought his perspective was a little like Murray Kempton's, but his stuff was a lot more readable. Other reporters overheard the compliment and ground their teeth. McMorrow just smiled.

But there was something about McMorrow, a vaguely irritating aloofness. All reporters had an independent streak, the editor knew, some more than others. But when he told McMorrow he liked his stuff, McMorrow said thanks but not like he really cared. When the editor offered to edit one of his stories, to go through it himself, McMorrow had acted like he could take it or leave it. Did McMorrow know to whom he was speaking? Did he know the editor of the New York Times *didn't talk to just anybody in the newsroom? What was the man's problem?*

So when Dave Conroy called from City Hall that morning and said he wanted to come over to talk about McMorrow, the editor said, "All right. Come ahead." When Conroy laid it all out, that McMorrow and the cop whose wife was murdered were childhood chums, lifelong friends, the editor listened.

When Conroy said McMorrow's reporting couldn't be trusted, he didn't disagree. When Conroy said McMorrow had joined up with Casey on this mission to find Casey's wife's killer, the editor didn't say anything. When Conroy said McMorrow was a liability for the Times *just as Casey was a liability for the police department, he didn't argue. When Conroy asked if McMorrow had disclosed his relationship with Casey, the editor said he didn't know.*

Conroy left. That afternoon, the editor called McMorrow. He told him they needed to talk. He told McMorrow to bring a union representative.

McMorrow didn't. He walked in the door alone, nodded to the metro editor, Ellen Jones. Sitting in a chair in front of the big desk, McMorrow had that same infuriatingly cocky look on his face and the editor had to check his temper.

"Jack," he said, leaning on his desk, "we've got a problem. David Conroy was here from the mayor's office. He talked to me about the Casey story."

"What did he do? Try to put a positive spin on letting a killer go?" McMorrow said.

"Not really."

"Losing his touch, then. Guy could do P.R. for the devil himself."

"Jack, I know you're close to this story."

"Casey didn't coach anybody. The witness is solid. It was so obvious, when you talked to her, that she really saw what she said she saw. You read the story."

"I believe I did."

"It speaks for itself. She was just afraid. Needed to be reassured that if she told police what she saw, Yolimar wouldn't just get turned loose. Which is what happened. I guess she had good reason to be scared."

The editor looked at Ellen Jones. She shifted uncomfortably in her chair.

"Jack," the editor said, getting up from his chair, leaning across the desk, "why didn't you tell us you knew Casey when you were a kid?"

McMorrow didn't answer right away. The editor picked up a legal pad and read from notes.

"That your fathers worked together at the Museum of Natural History."

"It's a big place. And they didn't work together. Butch's dad was in security. I mean, my dad was in entomology. So what?"

"Or that you were close personal friends as kids. That you've kept in contact with Casey for all these years. That you had dinner with his wife at least twice in the six months before she died."

"So I send him a Christmas card. So what? We had dinner once. Once we were supposed to have drinks and I was late. Saw him for fifteen minutes."

"You've put this newspaper in a terrible position."

"No, I haven't. I was the only one willing to tackle this story. And she said nobody coached her. Nobody influenced her. You think I made that up? Hell, get her in here. She'll tell you. She was a good witness and Fiore tossed her. That's the story. Why did he dump a key witness in a high-profile homicide? That's the—"

"This newspaper's integrity is the story," the editor

exploded. "This newspaper's integrity stands above everything else. We don't write about our personal friends."

"Baloney. Read the op-ed page."

"That's opinion. I'm talking about the news pages."

"You think reporters don't know cops? You think reporters here don't have drinks with flacks and assistant commissioners and staffers and everybody else?"

"That's different, Jack, and you know it."

"No, I don't. I covered this issue just like I would for any other cop in the New York Police Department."

"For any other cop? We don't do stories for people."

"You know what I mean."

"I thought I did, Jack, but I'm not sure anymore. You should have recused yourself and you didn't. You should have told Ellen and you didn't. Your stories are tainted by the appearance of bias."

"My stories are straight down the middle."

"I said, 'appearance.' "

"I'm not biased. I'm interested."

"Who gave you the name of the witness?"

"A cop."

"Casey?"

"No. Another detective, one who's working the case."

"Gave it to you because you're a pal of Casey's."

"Gave it to me because it was an injustice and he knew I'd write about it."

"Oh, come on."

"No, I won't come on. This is a damn good story and it isn't done."

"It is for you, Jack."

"What's that mean?"

"I want you to take a couple of weeks off and think this over."

"I'm suspended?"

"Yeah, you're suspended. You've given me no choice. Go home."

"Just like that? Some two-bit flack from the mayor's office comes in and feeds you a line and I'm gone?"

"Jack," Ellen said.

"This is ridiculous."

"What's ridiculous is you covering this story, Mr. McMorrow," the editor said.

"What was wrong with my coverage?"

"I don't know. Now I don't know."

"What about all the people you know socially? All these New York movers and shakers. You going to turn down the next black-tie invitation?"

"You goddamn disrespectful son of a bitch! Who the hell do you think you're talking to?"

"I know exactly who I'm talking to. And when Ortiz kills somebody else, I'll send you the clip. From the News *or the* Post, *'cause I'm sure we won't cover it."*

"You're gone, McMorrow. Get out of here."

"Let's cool off," Ellen said. *"Let's just take a break and get ourselves together."*

"Am I fired?" McMorrow asked.

"No, Jack," Ellen said, stepping between them.

" 'Cause I'll go," McMorrow said. *"You just say the word. I'll do this someplace else. I didn't sell my soul when I came here. I'll find a paper with some balls."*

"Go then, McMorrow. Go find some crusading rag."

"Come on, guys," Ellen said, moving Jack toward the door. *"This isn't constructive."*

She got McMorrow into the newsroom, where all work had stopped and all eyes were on them.

"See, Ellen?" McMorrow said. *"This is what happens when you have these social climbers in the newsroom. Goddamn ass-kissing sycophant. Sucking up to all the goddamn celebrities. It's pathetic."*

"You should have told us, Jack. I think you know that. You should have told us and you know it."

But McMorrow was on his way to his desk and he wasn't listening. He grabbed his jacket and strode to the elevator, punched the button with his fist and left.

And for the next two weeks, there were no McMorrow bylines in the *Times.* This was duly noted in the mayor's office, and acknowledged privately by Conroy and Fiore.

Every morning, Conroy scanned the Times *and then went to Fiore's private office and put the newspaper on the mayor's desk.*

"Nothing," he said.

"Good," Fiore said. "Because it really bordered on harassment, didn't it?"

"Yes," Conroy said. "It was almost actionable."

But no action was taken by City Hall. After two weeks, Fiore stopped asking about McMorrow. The mayor was focused. Confident. He joked at his press conferences, called the reporters by name. He launched a new initiative, which he called "New York City: It's no longer a dream."

In an editorial, the Times *praised Fiore's vision for the future. "By returning basic moral principles to policy making, the mayor has helped us all remember why we came to New York, why we stay here, why we have chosen this city to pursue our dreams, which, after all, are our common bond."*

That day, at the 11 A.M. news meeting, Ellen Jones reported that Jack McMorrow had returned to work. But he would be taking a break from metro reporting. McMorrow would be doing news features. His first assignment was a story he'd had on his list for months, Jones said. It was about a tiny weekly newspaper for sale in a mill town in Maine.

Thirty-two.

On the other end of the phone, Sanders waited.

I didn't say anything.

"This envelope would have been dropped off about two hours before Casey was arrested," he said.

I still didn't reply.

"I asked the cops about this and they said they weren't aware of any such envelope until this morning."

He waited. I took a deep breath. I let it out slowly. Christina turned a page in the newspaper and it made a loud crackle.

"Is that true?" Sanders said. "Did Casey deliver an envelope to you Monday morning?"

My mind tripped over possible answers. If I said yes, the police would want the envelope—and a chunk of my hide. Could I end up in jail with Butch for withholding evidence? Hindering the investigation?

Roxanne would be left dangling in the wind.

The cops would want the envelope anyway. They could be on their way over. Was I ready to turn everything over to them? Was I ready for them to know what I knew? Was I ready to show them what I didn't know?

Donatelli, yes; Ramirez, maybe. Conroy and the Boxer, no. How could I keep them separate?

"No comment," I said.

"Jack, this woman was very specific. A white envelope. She said a man she later identified as Butch Casey walked in a little after six and left it at the desk. Very calm and polite. Casey, I mean. Said it was a nice morning for a walk. She said she gave it to you later in the day. I'm assuming that was after you were questioned by police. Of course, she didn't know you were connected to Butch Casey at that time. I guess she hadn't watched the TV. She said she'd felt sick and had been in the ladys' room or something. Is this true?"

"No comment."

I spat the words. Christina looked at me.

"Jack," Sanders said, the newsroom hum in the background, "I've got to go with this. You know that. You understand, don't you? I mean, you've been in my shoes a hundred times."

I didn't answer. I knew what he wanted. He wanted me to start talking, about anything or nothing, and every syllable would be scribbled in his notebook and before I knew it, he'd have his comment and then some.

"Jack. I'm sorry, but this is a big story. I mean, what's in the envelope? The knife? Bloody gloves? You don't comment and it leaves it up to the readers to fill in the holes. And they aren't going to be thinking it's Butch Casey's favorite recipes."

I swallowed.

"Okay, Jack. Here we go. One more time. Did Butch Casey leave you an envelope or some sort of package at the Parker-Meridien Monday morning?"

"No comment."

"If so, were investigators told about this potential evidence?"

"No comment."

I heard paper rustle.

"Did a Parker-Meridien desk clerk hand you this envelope later Monday?"

"No comment."

"Did you receive anything from Butch Casey after you left him that night outside the Algonquin?"

"No comment."

I waited. Christina stared. I started to formulate some sort of apology, some way of telling Sanders I wasn't angry with him, that I knew he was just doing his job. I thought of asking him what time the hotel person had called the cops. I pieced the words together in my mind, rearranged them over and over.

And said nothing.

"Well, good-bye, Jack," Sanders said. "We'll talk again, I hope. No hard feelings. And if you change your mind, call me back. But not too late."

It already is, I thought, but I didn't answer and he hung up.

"What was that all about?" Christina said.

Before I could answer, the phone rang again.

D. Robert, I thought. Giving it one more try.

"Yeah," I said.

"Is this Jack McMorrow?" a woman's voice said cautiously.

"Yes."

I waited. There was a hiss. I listened. I heard someone breathing. A click and then more hiss. And then a voice. A man's voice.

"Jackie. I hope you're doing okay, my friend. Is this a fucking mess or what?"

"Butch?" I said, but he kept talking.

I said his name again. Butch didn't answer, and then I realized why.

His voice was on tape.

"I'm in here, and Jesus Christ, all I did was go in there to take a crap. Really, Jackie. You gotta believe me. And Jack, you gotta help me. I got this lawyer, but I'm gonna shitcan her. She's saying, 'Cop a plea. Maybe I can keep you outta the chair.' I say to her, 'You want to see a death sentence? Leave me in here with all these shitbums I put away.' Jackie, everybody wants to fucking kill me. Jackie, you gotta help me. Please.''

He paused. I heard him breathing over the hiss. There was a rustle, as though someone had bumped the tape player against the phone.

"Hello," I said.

"Jackie, the answer has to be in that envelope. I was close to something. You know how I knew? I was digging around and I got a call. 'Back off, mother-fucker, or they'll be doing your homicide.' Those exact words. That's when I knew.

"Now, all those people got just as much motive as me. They should all be on the list. Where were they? Guy, his wife's skull is smashed. Banker lady raped. Some rich kid put in a goddamn coma. Hey, there's people who could afford to order up a hit, even on a mayor. I mean, there's guys out there will do anything for ten grand. And some lady's husband missing, probably got whacked. All from the same time, all blaming the mayor for screwing up when he was DA. That's no coincidence, Jackie. Writing him letters, calling him on the phone. I didn't even do that, Jackie. I didn't do any of that. So help me God. But when I start looking, I get warned off.''

The tape hissed.

"Look into this for me, please. Get it to the *Times*. As a friend. Do anything you can, Jackie. I don't know who else to ask. Jackie, I got nobody. I mean, I never felt so alone in my whole goddamn life. Please, believe me. And don't tell anybody you heard from me. Somebody's going way out on a limb to let me do this. So this is off the record. Thanks, buddy. I'm saying that 'cause I know you and I know you won't let me down. Now take care of yourself. Watch your back, my friend.''

There was a click. A clatter.

"Hello," I said.

The dial tone buzzed.

"Who was that?" Christina said.

"Butch," I said.

"Oh," she said. "Was that his one phone call?"

My guess was somebody who worked at Riker's. A guard or a social worker. Or maybe somebody with the lawyer's office. Probably cost Butch some serious money to have his message relayed. But he was in so deep. How did he think my digging into these other cases would get him out?

I put the phone down and sat there on the couch. Christina got up and walked over and put a hand on my shoulder.

"You okay?" she said.

"Yeah."

She gave me a squeeze and walked away. I sat stone still, my mind whirling.

Butch seemed upset but not desperate. It was as though he still thought he could extract himself from this predicament. Or I could. But how?

Was Maria Yolimar at the Algonquin that night? I didn't think so. She probably was working in the laundry, up to her elbows in dirty sheets. And did she want the mayor killed, after all these years? No, she wanted to know what happened to her husband. And she thought Fiore held the answer.

No more.

Nor did Tilbury want Fiore dead. He'd gotten what he wanted, or so he thought. Tilbury thought Lester John finally was in custody, that he finally would see some justice. When I came knocking, Tilbury had called somebody, probably the DA's office, to make sure things were still on track.

That sent the Boxer and Conroy scrambling, but why? Because they were afraid one of these cases would clear Butch Casey? And if not Butch, then who? Had they killed their own mayor? Conroy, who worshiped Fiore, had spent years of his life in dutiful service.

Conroy couldn't have known Butch was going to be at the Algonquin that night, because I didn't know Butch would be there. And even if Conroy were some demon child, if his veneration of the mayor had for some reason twisted into hate, how could he have set Butch up for this? Could he have seen Butch going into the bathroom and just seized the opportunity?

Hey, there's that jerkoff detective. Haven't seen him in years. I guess I'll stick the mayor now.

With what? The knife the mayor's aide carried to all black-tie fund-raisers? The bicycle spoke in his sleeve? The ice pick he carried in the lining of his Armani suit?

There was a gap, a connection I couldn't make. Something had brought out the hounds. And with Butch stuck in a cell and the case against him apparently rock solid, someone still was desperate enough to chase me to Brooklyn, up to Washington Heights, across a roof with a silenced pistol.

And desperate enough to threaten Roxanne.

I couldn't walk away not knowing why, not knowing whether I'd walked far enough. And I knew I wasn't going to run away from New York. Not again.

I went to the bedroom and took the envelope from my bag. Scanned the papers and separated the two clips and a memo, all about Drague, the guy who'd raped the young woman on the East Side. I put those in my bag, under my clothes.

"Jackie. The answer has to be in that envelope."

Perhaps about that much, Butch was right.

Thirty-three.

Ramirez didn't think so.

"You mean this is it?" she said, flipping through the clips and memos.

"Yeah."

"There was nothing else? Just these old newspaper stories? A couple of piddley complaints?"

"This is what Butch was working on. I told you that."

"He kills the mayor of New York City, then walks the streets, arrives at your hotel at six in the morning to give you this? This is bullshit."

"It was 6:48," I said.

She'd called from her car, parked in front of Christina's door. She was alone. Donatelli had gone home for a few hours, she said.

"He wanted to see his kid play baseball," she'd said, pretending that made no sense at all.

"Good for him," I said.

She looked at me, trying to figure out whether I was serious.

"The fact is, this is serious business," Ramirez said. "You withheld evidence in the biggest homicide case in the history of New York City."

"Okay, so what are you going to do with it? I've been trying to tell you about this stuff, and you made it sound like I was nuts."

"That's not the point," Ramirez said. "The point is this material was handled by the prime suspect in a killing, after the killing took place. He gave it to you. You had a responsibility to give it to us. We asked you. Somebody asked you. I remember specifically somebody asking if—"

"The DA's boy there," I said. "I call him the Boxer."

"Dannigan?"

"Is that his name? I never caught it. Well, he wanted to know if there were papers or documents. It was the only question he asked in that interview. The only time he spoke. And he and Conroy were talking about it. About getting a call from the professor."

"Well, who else is he going to call about prosecution of a crime in New York? The president?" Ramirez said.

Christina came from the kitchen with coffee and biscotti. Ramirez looked at her like she was some sort of slutty gun moll, but took a cookie anyway, holding it in her manicured claws. She chewed, then picked up a black coffee and sipped it. Putting the cup down, she jerked a thumb at Christina, who had sat down on the arm of the couch, crossed her legs in black culottes.

"Can I talk in front of her?"

"Sure," I said.

Ramirez leaned toward me, so close that I could see the pores in her nose, the clumps of mascara on her lashes. I could see a mole on her chest where her collared blouse was open.

"I think this is a goddamn smokescreen," she said.

I stared back.

"To cover up what?" I said.

"I don't know," she said. "You tell me. But what I see here is a bunch of old stories. Some scraps of paper somebody fished out of a wastebasket at City Hall. Christ, you were a reporter. What if somebody walked into the

Times and dumped this stuff on your desk? What would you do?''

She didn't let me answer.

''I'll tell you what you'd do. You'd stick it in the bottom drawer with the rest of the crackpot stuff. You'd say, 'I got real stories to write.' ''

''If there's nothing to it, then what's this?'' I said.

And I tossed the windshield note onto the table.

Ramirez scowled and picked it up and unfolded it. I took a sip of coffee and watched her face for reaction. There wasn't any. She scanned the note, put it back on the table. Roxanne stared up at the three of us.

''So you're involved in a relationship with this woman in Maine?'' Ramirez said.

''Yes.''

She looked at Christina.

''Oh,'' Ramirez said. ''How nice.''

''We're old friends,'' Christina said.

''I'm sure you are,'' Ramirez said.

''So doesn't that tell you something?'' I asked her.

''It tells me somebody typed up this note and put your friend's picture on it. That's all.''

''A guy left it on my windshield in Brighton Beach this morning.''

''What guy?''

''A guy walking a dog. An older guy. The dog was small, like a little poodle.''

Ramirez finished the cookie, wiped a crumb from her mouth.

''When we get stuff like this, you know who we look at first? The person who's supposed to be the target. You know who we look at second? The person who found the note. Or got the call. Or whatever.''

''I didn't write this. I wouldn't write this.''

Christina huffed.

''You think Jack wrote this note? That's the most ridiculous thing I ever heard. I saw him when he got back. I saw him after they called before. He was upset. To think he fabricated this whole thing, that he used those words, that's . . . that's ludicrous.''

Ramirez didn't even look at Christina, much less reply. When Ramirez spoke, it was to me.

''Who?''

''I don't know. More than one person has this place staked out. When I went to Brighton Beach this morning, somebody tried to follow me.''

''Why?''

''They don't want me to dig into these cases.''

''Why not?''

''I don't know. I'm finding that the perpetrators are all missing.''

''This is New York,'' Ramirez said. ''Dirtbags don't usually live happily ever after.''

''Yeah, but if you had warrants for five people, and you went hunting, wouldn't you come up with at least one or two?''

She considered it.

''Probably. If I got lucky. If they didn't know I was coming.''

''They didn't know I was coming. And they're gone. I've got zip.''

''Who?''

''Lester John. Julio Yolimar. Georgie Ortiz.''

''The guy who killed Casey's wife? He's not in here.''

''Well, I include him because I know Butch does. And there's Vladimir Mihailov.''

''I can introduce you to Mihailov. Kind of a quiet guy now.''

''He's gone, too.''

''Jeez, McMorrow. If you want to write about dirtbags who jump bail or get blown away, I'll give you a room full of stuff like this.''

Ramirez picked up the clips and papers and stuck them back in the envelope. She stood and I did, too.

''I'll talk to Donatelli today. He takes you more seriously than I do. We'll get back to you about that threat, and the DA wants to talk to you. I'll show Donatelli this note. Where's your girlfriend now?''

She looked at Christina and smiled.

''The one from Maine, I mean.''

Christina glared.

''She's—she's there,'' I said.

''She been informed about this?''

''I've been trying to call her all morning. I haven't been able to reach her.''

Ramirez paused.

''If somebody really intended what they said there—and the vast majority don't—she should know.''

''I'm going to tell her. And have a friend stay with her.''

''You got lots of friends, huh, McMorrow?'' Ramirez said.

She didn't look at Christina. She didn't have to.

Ramirez put the envelope under her arm and started across the loft toward the door. We got up and followed, to let her out, lock ourselves back in. In the elevator there was a cool silence against the backdrop of rattles and bangs. The door opened and Christina went to the overhead door. Unlocked it and rolled it up. Ramirez started across the garage bay and then stopped.

''McMorrow.''

''Yeah.''

''You said what if I had warrants for five people. But you named four. Is there another one I'm supposed to know about?''

I hesitated, pictured the papers in the bag. Ramirez talking to the Boxer.

''Not that I know of,'' I said.

She looked at me closely, this woman who had made a career of ferreting out liars, and now did it with a vengeance.

''I think you're full of shit, McMorrow,'' Ramirez said, and she dipped under the door and was gone.

• • •

I went back to the phone. It kept on ringing.

I told Stephanie Cooper that I had no comment. I told the CBS producer that I did not want to be interviewed at this time, not even by Dan Rather. I told the woman from L.A. that I didn't need a "deal maker," thank you very much. I told two SoHo gallery owners, a reporter from the *Voice* and a writer from the magazine *Elle* that Christina Mansell couldn't come to the phone.

She was in the shower. And then she was in the bathroom for a long time. And when she came out she looked, as Ellen Jones had put it, "quite smashing."

Christina had changed to a short khaki skirt and a black scoop-necked sleeveless blouse. She was wearing earrings that dangled, and she was carefully made up, with lipstick that glistened and smoky shadow around her eyes. Her rouge was so pale as to be unnoticeable. Almost.

"Do you like this shirt, Jack?" she said, doing a quick model's whirl.

"Sure," I said.

"It's Fendi."

I looked at her blankly.

"The designer?"

I shrugged.

"They have very nice things."

"I'm sure. Are you going out?"

"No," Christina said. "But we're having lunch. If we're going to be stuck in here, we can still have fun, right?"

But she wasn't dressed to cook. Christina was dressed for comparison's sake, and I felt a twinge of sympathy for Roxanne. I pictured her, driving some potholed road, still working after being up half the previous night trying to find homes for beat-up kids. I felt a vicarious pang of jealousy. If Roxanne had nothing better to do than primp, if she could spend the morning taking calls from her admiring public—

And then I regretted thinking that at all.

Christina got on the phone and made her calls. She started with *Elle*, and I saw the excitement in her face, the attempt to sound blasé when she finally reached the writer. "Well, I suppose. Of course, we could talk. Let me check my calendar."

I took the cell phone and went into Philippe's room. Dialed Roxanne's car and got beeps, tones and finally the digital voice. I hit the button and went to the window and looked across. The factory window was dark.

Looking down, I saw the red van parked just beyond the corner, up the street to my left. I saw the black car roll by at the corner to my right. Had that guy said he'd kill Roxanne? Was he right there?

With the cell phone in my pocket, I walked out to the big room. Christina was still talking. I picked up her keys and showed them to her, and she nodded and I left the loft and walked to the elevator.

I punched the button. Nothing happened. I hit it again. Still nothing. I went to the stairwell, which was dark even at midday. How many steps had there been? Eighty-something?

I started down, my shoes scraping on the concrete. I kept one hand on the wall and it was cold. At the third floor, something skittered away. On the second-floor landing, I thought I heard a door bang somewhere in the building. Another tenant? But they were away, Christina had said. The owner?

I continued on, slowly. At the first floor I saw light under the door and I pushed it open and stepped through. I was standing in the garage bay, with the overhead door to my left. I waited a moment and listened, heard a bang, but then a truck motor outside. I stepped to the door, leaned down and felt around, ran my hand along the base of the door until I felt the lock, the cold metal, a jagged edge.

Where the hasp had been cut.

Thirty-four.

I froze, crouched low. Listened. Looked behind me in the darkness.

Saw nothing.

Heard nothing.

Raised myself up, very slowly.

The lock had been cut on the inside. Someone had entered the building some other way and then cut the lock. But they'd left it in the hasp. That meant they still were inside. That they probably intended to come back to this door.

I looked around. Listened hard, straining to glean every creak and tick. The bay was silent at first and then there were noises.

A rustling in the Dumpster. The brief buzz of a fly. I took a step and the rustling stopped. I waited. Listened. Watched. Heard a clank. Muffled, somewhere to my left.

It was the factory floor, sprawling and dark and filled with metal and machines, barrels and boxes. Was it a thief looking for copper? A homeless person? They usually didn't lug bolt cutters. Someone who had been watching from outside, deciding it was time to get in?

To do what?

In the dim light, I walked very slowly to the swinging factory doors. They had been chained shut, but when I felt for the chain, it was gone. And then I stepped and there was a clink and I felt the chain, coiled on the floor.

I stood at the door and listened. The Dumpster rustled again. I counted to ten but heard nothing from the other side of the door. I touched it with my fingertips and pushed gently.

It swung open, silently at first. Then a creak. I stopped. Waited. Listened. Squeezed through.

The room was lighter than the garage bay, with grime-blackened windows at the far end. I stood and watched, saw the vague shapes of machines, smelled oil and dust. I listened. Heard a motor but it was outside. Something buzzed by my head, something big like a bee. I looked and saw it briefly, flying away from me toward the windows.

Where a figure stood.

It was silhouetted against the gray of the glass. For a moment, it didn't move, and then it did. The head turned. I saw a profile. A man?

He was looking out the windows. I watched and then started to edge closer.

I slid my feet along, inches at a time, placing them carefully, like a hunter walking a leafy forest floor. After ten feet, I stopped. He half-turned and froze. I did, too. He listened. I breathed slowly and silently. He turned back toward the windows. I moved again.

After twenty feet, I could see his hands, black hands on the glass. But then the face turned and it was pale. He was white, looking down, taking off a pair of latex gloves.

After each step, I froze. As I got closer, my footsteps seemed louder, a gritty sandpaper sound with each footfall. I was a hundred feet away. Eighty feet. Seventy-five. I stopped. Felt the top of a machine very gently. Ran my fingers over some sort of metal bar.

I picked it up. I heard him sniff. He cleared his throat. Not like the man from the window across the street.

"Oh, come on," he said softly, his voice strangely high and girlish. "What are you waiting for?"

He wasn't talking to me. He was turned away, peering through a crack in one of the windows. I held the bar in both hands and started toward him.

A step. Stop. Another step. Stop.

He checked his watch and then reached down to the floor. He came up with a pair of bolt cutters, pliers with three-foot arms. I stopped. I still could rush him from here, hit him before he could get the bolt cutters around. Hit him in the shoulder, in the arm.

"Come on, will ya?" he said.

I gripped the bar. Took another step. And another. I was forty feet away. Closer. Closer.

And the phone rang.

He started and turned. I ran toward him, the phone still ringing in my pocket, and he dropped the bolt cutters and jumped up on the casing, pushed the window open. I saw his face as the light spilled in. It was one of them from the roof, the one with the flowered shirt. He jumped through the window, and as I reached it, slammed it shut. I started to shove it open, saw a flash of shadow and, dropping the bar, covered my face.

The glass shattered, showered me with shards. I staggered backward, felt a stinging on my arms, on the backs of my hands.

I held them out in front of me, saw the glint of glass splinters in my skin. I went to the window, looked out. There was no one in sight. The phone in my pocket still was ringing.

I brushed at my hand. Eased it into my pocket and took out the phone. Hit the button.

"Yeah," I said, breathless.

"Hey, Jack," the youngish voice said. "You been out?"

"Uh-huh."

"How safe you feeling now, buddy?"

I hesitated, caught my breath.

"I'm feeling just fine," I said. "How 'bout you?"

He didn't answer for a moment. A shard of glass fell from the window frame and shattered on the cement floor.

"What's that?" he said.

"Nothing," I said.

"So when you leaving? Or do I gotta start packing for my trip to Maine? Be kinda nice, you know? Haven't had any in a while."

"I'll bet."

"Watch your mouth."

"And you be careful up in Maine," I said. "Up where I'm from, they eat skinny little gold-chained wimps like you. They eat 'em for breakfast."

"What?"

"There's a lot of woods up there. They'd never even find you."

"Who the hell—"

"And the cops know. I didn't even have to tell 'em. They've got a whole envelope full of Butch's stuff. The stuff he was working on. And the cops have been following me. And if they're following me, they're probably following you."

"You're blowing smoke, McMorrow. You can blow it up your—"

"And I got a nice long look at your man there with the tweezers. Tell him he was about two seconds away from getting his head caved in. And I've got the bolt cutters. And I'll bet there's a good print on them somewhere. And I'll bet that print is in the system. I'll bet you're on there, just like a mug shot."

"Kiss my ass, McMorrow."

"And the homicide guys will be here any minute. And maybe they'll yank all of you out of your cars."

"You're fulla—"

"Unless you back off right now and I don't give 'em these things. Unless you leave me alone and don't go anywhere near me or Roxanne or Christina or anyone else I know. And I'll do what I have to do with the police here and then I'll go home. And you won't see me again and we'll all live happily ever after."

"What envelope?" the youngish voice said. "You're fulla shit."

"Nope. They have it. But I don't think they can make much of it. And they're sort of busy right now. But the more you push, the more they're gonna think there's something in there. The more you push, the more inclined I'm gonna be to talk. And I'll get a name off the prints and I'll give it to the *Times* and the other newspapers and TV and I'll put all of those hounds on your trail. Like the cops times a hundred. The more you push, the more they'll all know I'm not just blowing smoke. Don't you get it? You're the only real thing they've got. So just fade away."

He didn't answer. I stood in the light of the broken window, felt the heat streaming in from the street, felt the balance tipping with each moment of silence.

"When you leaving?"

"I think I have one more session with the cops and DA's people. Then I think I can go."

"Cops coming there now?"

"Yeah. They were here earlier but they had to leave. Said they'd be right back."

"You gonna give 'em those snips?"

"That's up to you. You gonna clear out of here?"

I could feel him thinking.

"How do I know you won't just spill your guts?"

"You don't, for now," I said. "So you'd better back off and wait and see. Nobody comes looking for you in the next couple of days, you'll know I didn't."

"Who's squeezing who here, McMorrow? I think you're forgetting."

"No, I know. And if I think you're still on me, if I think even for a minute you're near anyone I know, I'll squeeze harder than you've ever known."

"Who the fuck do you think you are? You're running with the big dogs now, you fucking newspaper wimp asshole."

"I'm going to hang up now."

"Dangerous game you're playing, McMorrow."

"Dangerous for you, too," I said. "And you and your boss have a lot to lose, don't you?"

He didn't answer and I pressed the button. A single bead of sweat rolled down the side of my face.

"It could have been the landlord," Christina said. "He's always pulling stuff like this. That's why I bought a whole box of locks. Cutting them off. Turning off the heat. Putting barrels of rotten smelly stuff in the stairwell. One time—"

"It's not the landlord, Christina."

"Who is it?"

"The black car. Same people who followed me to Washington Heights. I caught one on the first floor, but he got out the window."

"Not the red van?"

"I don't think so. That's the cops. The regular homicide cops. This is somebody else who's afraid of what's in that envelope."

"How do they know what's in it?"

"They don't, exactly. That's what has them so rattled, I think."

"What are they trying to hide? Why are they so interested in watching you?"

"I'm still working on that."

"Even after what they said about Roxanne?"

I hesitated.

"We'll see," I said, but even at that moment, Butch's voice echoed inside my head.

I don't know who else to ask. Jackie, I got nobody.

I put the bolt cutters under a shelf in Philippe's room, then stepped near the window, saw the red van on the corner. The black car was gone.

I went to take a shower. Afterward, I shaved and stared at myself in the mirror. And then I caught myself. Who was I primping for? Did Roxanne have reason to be worried?

I shook it off. Of course not, I told myself. I still was the same old Jack.

Wasn't I?

Dressed again, in shorts and a polo shirt Christina had washed and dried and folded, I sat back down at the phone. I dialed Roxanne's car number over and over, pausing while Christina ordered lunch. Lobster salad and crab cakes, split pea soup and a salad of arugula, pear and blue cheese. The restaurant in Brooklyn Heights delivered.

"How's that sound?" Christina said cheerily.

"Fine," I said. "You know, you don't have to just wait on me. You can work or make your calls or do whatever you need to do."

"No, that's okay," she said. "We'll have a nice lunch."

She paused.

"But at some point I do have to call the *Voice*," she said, and then she hurried off.

I watched her from across the big room as she went to the bathroom and freshened her makeup, then took lotion and rubbed it onto her long, bare legs. It was strange. Christina seemed almost oblivious to everything else that was going on. Oddly exhilarated. I wasn't any of those things. I was worried. Wary. Weary.

I got up and went to Philippe's window and looked down. The black car wasn't in sight. The red van had changed corners. I watched for a moment, and when I came back into the living room, I heard the door close. Christina's footsteps in the hall.

Back at the window, I heard the street door roll up. Christina stepped out, like a model posing against a red-brick backdrop.

As I watched, the red van turned the corner to my right. A white minivan rounded the corner to my left and sped down the street toward Christina.

"Look out," I called.

The van approached. There were two men in the front,

I could see the guy in the passenger seat reach down and then the driver braked hard.

"Look out," I shouted.

The passenger door flew open and the guy was out, the driver, too. The driver was trotting, coming around the back of the van. The other guy was moving toward Christina, carrying a paper sack. He was opening it.

"No," I called.

The guy looked up. The other man rounded the back of the van. He looked up, too.

"Christina," I yelled, and she looked up at me. "Get back."

"Jack," she called out. "It's lunch."

Thirty-five.

At the table, Christina picked at her crab cakes and chattered on about the neighborhood, how SoHo and Williamsburg had been gentrified, and SoHo had H. Stern and Yves St. Laurent, and how sad that had been to watch, and I remembered it in the old days, didn't I?

I nodded. Sipped the soup and drank a Corona. Christina talked as though we were on a first date, and it occurred to me that she had started all over with me, started from scratch. She'd backed off but she hadn't surrendered

"So tell me," Christina said, having let the subject of SoHo coast to a halt. "What is it that Roxanne does with these children she finds?"

I didn't answer and Christina waited.

"Foster homes," I said finally.

Still she waited.

"You know, you don't have to do all this," I said.

"What?"

"The fancy food. It's really not—"

"Just because we're stuck here doesn't mean we have to live like refugees, Jack."

"I know," I conceded. "But this New York food thing. I don't know. Maybe I've just had it."

"Maybe the problem is that you haven't had it."

I looked at her.

"Just kidding," Christina said, leaning toward me. "I'm trying to cheer you up, McMorrow."

"I know. But I may be beyond cheering."

"Why?"

"I don't know. Because I'm helping one friend and hurting another."

"No, you're not," Christina said.

I felt a surge of anger, like something coughed up. I choked it back down.

"What do you mean?"

"Well, I'm sorry but it's true. I mean, really. You haven't done either of those things. You haven't helped Butch. You haven't hurt Roxanne."

"Yet," I said.

"Yet," Christina said.

"I told them to back off. Or I'd really go to the cops and the TV and the papers."

"This man today?"

"His boss. On the phone."

"Were you just bluffing?" Christina said.

"I don't know," I said.

"Does he believe you?"

"I don't know. It's so hard when they could be anywhere. This place. You don't know."

"Where they are?"

"Or who. Or which ones. Is somebody a cop or some goddamn killer? Are they the same thing? They switch cars, switch people and I'm back to square one."

We stared at our plates and at each other. No one spoke. It was Christina who broke the silence, saying, "I don't know how to help you. But I know I'm enjoying your company."

"Even with this?"

"Even with this."

"I don't want it to end up hurting you, too, Christina. Maybe you should leave the city."

"I'm not going anywhere, McMorrow. I'll do what I always do. I just replace the lock."

We ate in silence for a few minutes, but the meal, the pretty delicacies, seemed silly. Lobster salad while Rome burned, I thought. And then I pictured someone torching this building at night. The factory floors and timbers, soaked with a century of grease. It would go up with a roar. I flinched.

"You okay?" Christina said.

"Yeah."

"So?"

"So what?"

"What happens next? If you had to guess."

"I guess they have to decide whether they can live with this stalemate. How long they can have me out here loose, with this damaging information."

"Damaging to whom?"

"I don't know. The guy on the phone. Conroy and the Boxer guy. The guys across the street maybe. The cops? I don't know, really. I don't know what I know."

"And they don't, either," Christina said.

"But I know there's something there."

"Or why would they do all this?"

"Right."

Christina finished her wine and put her glass down.

"So the way I see it, you're right on the edge. You know enough to be a problem, but not enough to really go anywhere with it."

I felt a rush of déjà vu. Another of Christina's bursts of perception.

"So the question," she said, "is how well do they know Jack McMorrow? Because if they know you, Jack, if they know what you're like, they know you won't be able to walk away. Not with Butch, your friend, asking for your help."

I remembered Conroy's words to the Boxer in the courthouse. *A loose cannon . . . not a typical reporter . . . he takes things too far . . . he'll stick around.*

"They know me," I said.

"Well, then," Christina said. "That's not good."

We agreed to stay put because at least the cops were watching the loft. Sneaking in downstairs and cutting a lock was one thing, but a serious assault while police watched was another. Wasn't it?

But stay put and do what? Field calls from reporters? Order out for more delicacies? Help Christina paint? Watch Butch be dissected on television? Read more about Johnny Fiore's legacy?

The question hung there at the table. Christina made a pot of black tea. I poured. It felt very English. Inside we sipped; outside the natives were circling.

"I need to go out," I said.

"Where?"

"Butch's neighborhood in the Village, for a start. He had a friend there who runs a bar. And—"

I hesitated. Christina looked at me expectantly, leaning forward and showing the curve of her breasts.

"And there are other people I can visit. Victims—"

I hesitated again. It was Christina's presence but why would that matter? What was holding me back? Weren't we in this together? Look what this had done to her—

The phone rang.

"A.M. news cycle is beginning," I said.

Christina got up and answered it.

"Oh, hi," she said. "No, it's fine . . . No, really. I appreciate your interest . . . I'm a big fan of your writing . . . No, of course I'm not just saying that, Richard. . . ."

She headed for her bedroom.

"Is this my big breakthrough?" Christina said, as she disappeared from sight. "I don't know. You tell me . . . Oh, I know. It's been just the craziest time. . . ."

I sat there for a minute and then I got up and went to Philippe's room and got my money, my papers, the cell phone, and a notebook. I knocked on Christina's door and she covered the phone and I pointed to the fire escape and she said, "Take care, Jack," but then she was talking again.

"And catharsis is expressed in art. Yes, that's it exactly, Richard. . . ."

I started down the stairs, thinking Christina had a remarkable ability to take things in stride. I thought about it all the way to the parking lot, where I told the attendant I needed a car for a day or two. He looked at me, eyes narrowed, until I took out the cash and then he said he had one that might be available. I asked if it was stolen and he shrugged.

"Guy leave it, he don't come back. I don't know why. Maybe he got deported. Maybe he got killed."

"Happens," I said.

"Anybody asks, I say it got stolen."

We agreed on a hundred dollars, because I was a friend of Miss Mansell. The car, parked against the sumac-lined back fence, was an old Camaro, white with one of those black brassiere things on the front and New Jersey plates. The interior smelled like cigarettes and there was a cardboard picture of a naked woman hanging from the mirror. For another twenty dollars, the guy drove it out of the lot with me crouched in the back.

No questions asked. After all, this was New York.

He got out a block away and started walking. I took the papers out of my pocket, spread them on the seat next to me, like a list of Saturday errands.

Talk to the rape victim.

Find the rapist.

Go to Butch's neighborhood and nose around.

Figure out where it all fit into this horrific mess.

Thirty-six.

The cell phone was dying, a faint red light telling me to go home and put it in a charger. I spotted a pay phone outside a cafe on Atlantic Avenue, a Cuban place. There was change in the car's ashtray. I was on a roll.

My hand over my ear to shield out the noise of the traffic, I called the number on the East Side rape clip. A woman answered with what sounded like "Brown, Brian and Alder." I asked for Kim Albert and the woman said, "You mean Kimberly Bromberg," and before I could disagree, she clicked off.

I waited. Watched the traffic for a black car. A white car. Anyone who seemed to be watching me. There were lots of black cars. White ones, too.

And then a young woman's voice: "Ms. Bromberg's office."

"This is Jack McMorrow. I'm a reporter. I write for the *New York Times*."

A white lie. Pale gray.

"Oh, hi. We have someone here who deals with the press and gives comment on the market. Let me connect you. His name is—"

"No, I'm not calling about the stock market. I'm calling to talk to Ms. Bromberg, if she's the former Kim Albert.''

"She is, but she's very busy right now, and we really like our press inquiries to go through that office. So let me—''

"This isn't really a press inquiry," I said. "It's personal.''

"Oh. Does Ms. Bromberg know you?''

"No, but—''

"Then I'll take a message, but she's not available at this time. If you'll tell me—''

"I know she'll want to speak to me right now. Just tell her I'm calling about George Drague.''

I heard her sigh. Give a little tick with her tongue. And then I was on hold again, and then Kim Albert, now Bromberg, was on the phone.

"Yes," she said briskly.

I introduced myself. Asked her if she was the Kim Albert who was the victim of a violent crime in 1988.

"Who is this?''

I identified myself again, trying to sound reassuring. And then I repeated my question, and there was nothing reassuring about it.

"Yes," she said warily. "What do you want?''

"Ms. Bromberg, I'm looking into several criminal cases from about ten years ago that may have been mishandled by prosecutors. Your case is one of them.''

For a moment, she didn't answer. I could almost hear her swallow.

"You aren't going to use my name, are you?" she said softly.

"Well," I said. "It is a matter of public record.''

"Please. I know it's probably on some court document someplace, but please don't put my name in the paper.''

"Well, we can talk about that.''

"Is it money?''

"No. God, no. I'm a reporter. Really.''

"Well, I just got married and it would just be—''

I steeled myself.

"I'd like to accommodate you," I said. "Probably I can. First, what I really need is for you to just tell me a few things about your case."

Confidentiality dangled in front of her like a carrot.

"Well," she said, "I'm not sure what I can tell you. You won't use my name?"

"We can talk about that. Would you rather we met in person? Because I can come over to—"

"No, no. I mean, this is fine. But I have only a couple of minutes. I have to run a meeting."

I took out my notebook and pen. I'd prevailed, but at a price. Always at a price.

"I'll make this quick, and I hope my bringing this all up again isn't too painful for you."

"No. Not if my name isn't in the paper. Or anything that could identify me. Because they kept it all out of the papers before. My part, I mean."

"They said you were a stockbroker. Is that still true?"

"More or less. It's like calling a cardiovascular surgeon a doctor, but close enough."

"And you were assaulted on the East Side. The circumstances were as described in the *Times*?"

"Yes," she said softly.

"And they arrested the man?"

"Yes, they did. Four days later."

A car horn blared and I covered the receiver.

"Where are you?"

"A pay phone. I apologize. I forgot to charge my cell phone, so here I am. I've been interviewing people in Brooklyn."

"For this story?"

"Yes. It could be."

"And who's your editor at the *Times*?"

"Ellen Jones. I work with her on the national desk."

I pictured her writing that down.

"So I understand you called the mayor's office about this. This was—"

"I called several times. I suppose there's a record of that, too?"

"Yeah," I said. "Why did you call? Was there a problem?"

"Well, yes."

"Could you tell me a little about it?"

She hesitated. Another line to cross.

"Just the basics," I prodded. "Really. Just bare bones."

"Well, okay. At first the problem was that I was told he was going to go to prison for a long time and then all he got was three years."

"Who told you he was going to get a longer sentence?"

"The district attorney, Mr. Fiore. He was very kind. I mean, I thought he was. He took quite a personal interest in my case. He said it symbolized what was wrong with this city, and on and on. He said he was going to lock the man up for a long time. It was in the paper. All his promises."

"This was when he was running for mayor?"

"Yeah," Kim Bromberg said. "I didn't quite get that then. That part. You know, you're the victim of something like this, it's like the whole world should feel the way you do. I mean, it should be so obvious. But you know they can't possibly. It's very strange. Very isolating."

More traffic. I covered the phone. Uncovered it.

"But Fiore didn't lock him up?"

"Well, he pleaded guilty. I went to the sentencing. And the judge, he said he was going to follow the prosecutor's recommendation. And he said up to three years. And I was sitting there and I almost fell over. I mean, three years. For what he did?"

"I'm sorry," I said. "So did they explain to you what happened?"

"Oh, yes. Mr. Fiore and his assistant there, this skinny little guy, afterward they were falling all over themselves to be nice. They said there were sentencing guidelines and they were limited as to what they could do. And there was all this, I don't know, specific stuff about what he actually did. How . . . how far he went. I guess that was true. It just wasn't what I was led to believe at all. And my parents. My father, he's passed away since then, he was just wild. I mean, he was sick, he had cancer, but he came down from Upstate and he threatened to go to his congressman and go to the press and make this huge stink. And Mr. Fiore said he could do that, but it wouldn't make things easier for the victim.''

"You?"

"Right. But you'd have to know my dad. He was used to getting his way, being in charge.''

"So what happened?''

"Well, the dad in him edged out the CEO, I guess. But then, it was just seven months later, the man got out completely.''

"Out of jail?''

"Not even a year. They let him out on probation. And the district attorney's office didn't oppose it in court or anything. I was supposed to be notified, as the victim, but they sent the notice to my old apartment. I got it, like, three days after the hearing. I called up and asked what happened and they said, 'Oh, that's all done. He's been released.' ''

"Was Fiore involved?''

"No. It was somebody else. He was mayor by then.''

"And he was getting tough on crime and all that?''

"I know. That's what was so strange. But by then my father was really sick, he had cancer and it had spread to his liver. He died in 1989, about two weeks later. I didn't even tell him.''

The operator came on, asked for more money. I pumped in two quarters.

"Hello?"

"Sorry," I said. "You said your father—''

"He was dying. Nice way to go, you know? I almost wish he'd never known about any of it. I mean, it just killed him to think this happened to me. You can't imagine what that does—''

"No, I can't imagine," I said. "So was he too weak to complain?''

"He was," Kim Albert Bromberg said, with a hint of pride creeping into her voice. "But I wasn't."

There was a noise away from the phone.

"Oh, they're calling for my meeting. Listen, I really have to—"

"So what did you do?"

"I told them I was going to go public. Put my name in the paper and everything. God, looking back at it now, I can't believe I did it. I mean, I was twenty-three years old. Fiore was the mayor and he was already like God. But this animal was loose, he was back in the Bronx or wherever he came from and I was still going to a counselor, still couldn't—well, I had physical problems from the head injury and from the . . . the rest of it. And he was probably just out there laughing."

I scribbled, the pad pressed against the phone.

"I'll be right there," she said, to someone else.

"So what happened?"

"You're not going to use my name?"

"No."

"Well, we had this meeting. He took me out to lunch, believe it or not. This steak house below Times Square. Very nice."

"The mayor?"

"No. His aide or whatever. Conway. Conroy. Little guy, kept talking about history and the mayor's accomplishments and all this. I felt like saying, 'Listen, you little twerp, I'm not here to hear a testimonial.' But he said I could do more damage to women's causes than good. I could scare women so they wouldn't come forward. I said maybe they shouldn't come forward, if this was the way the system was going to treat them. I didn't back down. I was through backing down."

"But you didn't do it? I don't remember anything like that in the *Times*."

"Well, we went around and around. I was ready to walk out and call the *Times*. I mean, I was about to call them right from the restaurant. Say, 'This is my story. Come take my picture.' "

"Why didn't you?"

"Well, I was about to leave when he said he had a proposal. I suppose it's okay to say this, now that Fiore's gone."

"I'm sure it is."

"He said, the Conroy guy, I mean, he said the mayor understood what I'd been through, and he regretted the way it had turned out. And so because of that he would make a donation to this organization for rape victims and battered women in the city. He'd donate a hundred thousand dollars to increase awareness of these kinds of issues."

"If you went away quietly?"

I waited for the answer. She was thinking but then she spoke.

"He said if my story went public, and then the mayor made the donation, it would look like he was trying to buy his way out of it or something. I can't remember how he put it. But he said it would spoil the whole thing, and politically they might not even be able to do it. But I could do all this good for women, for other rape victims. Maybe the money would be used to toughen the laws, lobbying and whatever. I might save somebody else."

"So you agreed?"

"Yeah. What else could I do? And about a month later, there was this story about this group of Fiore's backers giving a hundred thousand to this rape awareness group. I got a copy of it in the mail. Nothing else. Just a clipping. So he came through. I'll give him that."

She covered the phone, and I heard muffled words.

"Listen, I do have to go. Now, no names, right? Nothing that would identify me?"

"Nothing. I promise."

"Now, what was your name again? Morrow?"

"Jack McMorrow," I said.

"Wait," Kim Albert Bromberg said. "Jack McMorrow. That's the reporter who—"

"I'm sorry for everything that happened to you," I said. "Thanks for your time."

I hung up and walked to the car, the notebook clenched in front of me.

Another screwed-up case. Another disgruntled victim. But was the hundred thousand a payoff? Had they really planned to make this donation? Where had the money come from? It didn't matter. It was Fiore money. It was Conroy money. It kept a crime victim from squawking, this time a victim whose father had clout. But a hundred thousand? All to prevent a little bad P.R.?

"Uh-uh," I said aloud. And I closed the notebook and allowed myself a smile.

And the phone rang. I picked it up. Hit the button.

"Yeah."

"You just don't get it, do you?" the youngish voice said.

Thirty-seven.

The voice was fuzzy, the static drifting in and out.

"Get what?" I said gingerly.

"Get that this ain't no fucking game."

"I understand that."

"I don't think so. You're playing with fire, McMorrow."

"How's that? I thought we had a deal."

"You don't make deals with me, McMorrow. I give the orders and you follow 'em."

"What? You talked to the Boxer and he didn't go for it?"

"The Boxer?"

"The DA's guy."

"You only got me, McMorrow. And here's the only deal you're gonna get. I want you to go back to that fucking dump and pack your shit and go back to Maine and stay there."

I didn't answer.

"You think I'm joking?"

Still I didn't answer.

"You fucking chump. You think I'm joking, you go look for your little girlfriend. She's in that fucking Range

Rover, two blocks over, by the river. Look for a big white truck with a fish on the door. If you get there quick, maybe she won't suffocate. But then again, you know how dogs die when people leave them in a hot car? Last warning. Go see what you did to her, McMorrow. 'Cause you did it.''

The phone hissed. I threw it down. Started the car and screeched into traffic. Down the hill, through lights, swerving left and right. The car bounced and skidded, and near the river I tried to call the cops, looked away for a moment and scraped the side of a truck. Horns blared and I stomped the gas and the phone fell somewhere under my feet and I kicked it aside. Slowed on the last block. Turned. Looked left. Looked right.

A fish, I thought. A fish truck. A refrigerator truck. A single truck in New York.

"Oh, Jesus," I said.

There were alleys between the factories, lots ringed with barbed wire and filled with rusting trucks and cars and junk. I saw a white cab on a silver trailer. No fish. No Rover. A cream-colored van with broken windows.

What did he mean by white? Pure white? All white?

"Hang on, Christina," I said. "Hang on."

The road ended under the bridge at a riverfront park, a place where people took walks and drugs. I backed up and smoked the tires and turned around. I had the riverside on my left, the factories on my right. Both had jogs and nooks and crannies, trash-filled alcoves where a car could be hidden.

"If she's in the sun," I said, the words trailing off.

I made another pass, then swung right, away from the river, and looped back. Now it was all factory blocks, barred windows and graffiti. I passed a deep alley, glimpsed something white. I backed up. Looked and leaped out.

The truck's nose poked out from behind the corner of a building. The front tires were flat. The rear end was backed up against a loading dock. There was a fish painted on the door and it was smiling.

The Rover was around the corner, against a chain-link fence.

"Oh, no," I said. "Oh, God, no."

I could see her arms, white and pale, held high like Jesus' arms on the cross. The top of her head was against the window. Her breasts were bare. Her fingers had been closed in the top of the door.

I yanked hard on the door and Christina stirred. Her eyes opened and then closed. Her mouth was covered with duct tape and her face was a terrible blend of flush and pallor.

I tried the back door. The tailgate. The other side of the car was against the building. I found a broken block of concrete in the rubble and smashed the back window. The alarm blared but the shattered glass hung. I kicked it out, catching my shoe and hopping on one foot.

"Son of a bitch," I hissed and yanked my foot loose and reached through and found the handle and opened the door. The alarm blared. I climbed in and reached through and said, "It's okay, Christina," and pulled that handle, too.

The door popped open. Christina was kneeling and she started to fall forward and I caught her, turned her gently and sat her on the seat. She swayed and closed her eyes, then opened them, then started to make a gagging sound like she might vomit. I picked at the edge of the tape and she whimpered and I tore the tape aside, and it sounded like Christina's face was being torn. She shrieked, then sobbed, her hands cradled in her lap like injured birds.

I held her. All of her fingers were blood-red and crimped, the ends swollen like sausages. Christina looked at them like they belonged to someone else but then suddenly reached up to pull her shirt and bra back up. She couldn't grip them and I did it for her, slipping the straps over her scratched shoulders, the fabric over her breasts.

Her Fendi top was torn.

"It's okay," I said, and she closed her eyes and opened

them and sobbed again and nodded, and then started to talk.

"They were in a van," she said weakly. "It was blue. I was just going to go up to get a movie, a movie for us, so we wouldn't just have to watch the news all the time. So we could just watch a movie."

She cried and rocked.

"And oh, God, they stopped behind me and I saw the masks and there was another car in front of me, and I couldn't move and I thought the doors were unlocked and I reached for the button. And I hit it and it unlocked them, 'cause they were locked already, I got it wrong. And they opened the door and they—"

She gave a dry sob.

"They said—"

"It's okay," I said. "You don't have to talk."

"They said this was for you. For Jack McMorrow. And next time they'd—"

"Don't," I said.

Christina looked down at her hands, which were laid on her lap. Her thighs were scratched and she was wearing one sandal.

"They said they'd do awful things," she said. "They said the things right out loud, Jack. They did. They said they'd do these things to me and Roxanne. They'd go to Maine and do these things."

Her eyes closed.

"Oh. I feel like I'm going to be sick. Oh, Jack, I don't want to be sick in front of you."

She bent her head and I held her, my arm around her shoulders. I rubbed her arm and said it was okay, the words rasping because my jaw was clenched. Still rubbing Christina's arm, I looked up at the building above us, turned and scanned the walls and roofs behind.

Gulls slipped past overhead. There was no one in sight.

"I think we'd better get you to a hospital, Christina," I said, and then hesitated. "Is it just the fingers?"

She knew what I was thinking.

"Yeah," Christina said, looking at the ground, her one

bare foot. "They said they were doing my fingers because I was a painter. They said I was lucky I wasn't a hooker. But they . . . they looked at me. And Jack—"

She paused. Swallowed and tried to wet her lips.

"They cut me, Jack," she said.

I swallowed.

"Where?"

"On my stomach. I couldn't see, but it was like . . . it was like they were writing."

She looked down. Tried to pull the top up but couldn't with her swollen fingers. I took the fabric and lifted it and there was blood on the waistband of her skirt, but not a lot. I pulled the blouse higher.

Below her navel they had scratched her. The skin was red and swollen. The blood was smeared. The letters were scrawled, like initials carved in a tree.

MCMORROW

Broken fingers and surface cuts weren't a priority that day at the Brooklyn Hospital Center, so we sat in a waiting room that, with its crying babies and feverish mothers, was like the hold of some disease-ridden ship.

The uniform cops, two hard young men with boot-camp haircuts, came and went, reports in hand for what they called an assault/attempted sexual assault. They said a detective would be calling Christina, but I'd already called our detectives. It was a little after nine when they came in, spotted me and sidestepped their way through the babbling, coughing throng.

They nodded and Ramirez crouched in front of Christina and patted her arm.

"Can you tell us about it?" Ramirez said, a new gentleness in her voice.

"Yes," Christina said. "I can."

She told them what had happened, what had been said to her, about me, about Roxanne. She said she wasn't raped but one of the men had fondled her breasts and lifted her skirt. A loud truck had gone by and one of the others said they had to go.

"And the cuts?" Donatelli said.

"They said they're not deep," Christina said.

"More like scratches," I said. "My name. My warning."

And then Christina's name was called and a nurse came out and touched Christina's arm as she led the way to an examination room.

"Still think it's a smokescreen?" I said to Ramirez.

She ran a hand through her lacquered hair and looked away, then back.

"And where were you when all this happened?" she said.

I told her about the pay phone, the cell phone in the car.

"Like I told the other cops. A young voice. New York, New Jersey accent. Knows who comes and goes at Christina's building."

Donatelli looked at Ramirez, then back at me.

"Believe me now?" I said.

"They told Christina they'd go to Maine to carry out these threats on this Roxanne person?" Donatelli said.

"Yeah."

"If you didn't leave?"

"Right."

"You staying or going?"

"That's partly up to you."

"We'd rather you stayed a few more days," Ramirez said.

"But we can get you protection," Donatelli said.

"No thanks," I said. "But I'd appreciate it if you could do something for Christina. If she stays in the city."

"What about your friend in Maine? Roxanne?"

"She doesn't know about this. I haven't been able to reach her."

"I'll call Portland P.D."

"Like I asked you to do already."

Donatelli shrugged.

"We were getting to it."

"They know her there. Some of the detectives."

"She'll probably be all set, them being down here."

"For now," I said.

"So?" Ramirez said.

"So what?"

"So what's it all about?"

"I've been trying to tell you."

I looked to Donatelli.

"She show you the stuff from Butch?"

"Yeah, I saw it. But it looks like kind of a long-term project, you know what I'm saying? We're talking ancient history."

"And somebody doesn't want any of it dug up," I said. "I was telling you that. Now you've got this."

"We're doing our best," Donatelli said.

"And look where it got us. She could have been killed. Tossed in the river. I thought you were watching the loft."

They looked at each other.

"It was the afternoon. And from what I'm told, the officers on duty attempted to follow a white Camaro but lost it."

"They didn't come right back? What'd they do? Stop for a sandwich?"

"No doughnut jokes, McMorrow," Donatelli said.

"So you staying or going?" Ramirez said. "What's the deal?"

I thought of Conroy and the Boxer and these cops, too, all of them sitting at that table together at Police Head-quarters. All of them, together.

And I sat there in the midst of the sick and suffering and didn't say another word.

By a roundabout route I took Christina to Ellen Jones's apartment in SoHo. Ellen arrived by cab as we pulled up in the Camaro. She ran to Christina as she got out of the car, put her arms around her shoulders and said, "Oh, you poor dear."

The doorman came running, too, and took Christina's bag, which I had packed while she was being treated, having her hands X-rayed, getting a tetanus shot.

"For God's sake, I'm not an invalid," Christina said. But her walk was tentative and the snap was gone from her hips. They helped her up the stairs. I followed her and at the door she turned to me, her mummy-wrapped hands in front of her.

"I'm sorry," I said.

"Hey," Christina said gamely, "Monet did some of his best work when he had cataracts. Maybe this will be a new Mansell period. Take care, McMorrow."

I hugged her with one arm and kissed her cheek.

"Now you get all hot to trot," she whispered, mustering a weak smile. And she went through the door, the doorman following her. I stood there for a moment and then walked back to the car. Ellen came back to the sidewalk as I slung myself into the seat. The motor roared and smoked, an embarrassment in this neighborhood.

Ellen peered into the car.

"We have to talk."

"Yes, we do," I said. "In a day or so."

"A day or so? Why not now? If this is even remotely connected to you and Casey and Fiore—"

"Ellen," I said. "Off the record, there's nothing remote about it. And when I have a little more information, I'll talk to you. Tell Sanders he's finally going to get his precious Pulitzer."

And I put the car in gear and pulled away, driving south to Brooklyn, where the bridge was lighted, the sunset was fading and Christina's neighborhood was still. Her building was dark and silent, like the home of someone who has died. I rolled past at the end of the block but there were no cars in sight. Were they staying away? Were they still in the window?

Looking up at the brick cliff walls, I circled. Parked the car around the block in an empty lot, behind a van that was filled with trash. I walked around the block slowly, slipped through the gate and climbed the fire escape. The window still was open and I crawled inside, like a cave dweller coming home.

The loft was still, the rooms silent. I checked them one by one, then went to the door. I listened, my ear against the cold wood, then eased the door open and listened again. The hallway was quiet, the elevator was down. I heard sirens but they were in the distance.

Back inside, I closed the door and bolted it. Then I went to the kitchen and opened the refrigerator. Light spilled out and I reached in and unscrewed the bulb. I wolfed the leftover crab cakes and lobster salad, drank a Corona in three gulps.

And then I sorted through the knives in the drawers, on the rack on the counter. There were butcher knives, filet knives, long thin knives like something made in prison. I took one or two of each and went first to Christina's room, and then to Philippe's room. On the beds, I arranged the knives like surgeon's instruments, then covered them with the sheets.

One knife I kept with me, a small, wood-handled one, on the chance that in this sprawling, black-roomed building, I wasn't alone.

Thirty-eight.

Like eyes in the dark, my ears slowly adjusted.

First silence. Then my own breathing. Then the distant noises of the city: the rattle of trucks on the bridge. The sound of horns, faint as migrating geese flying high overhead.

I was in Philippe's room, sitting in a straight chair against the wall, next to the window. The knife was on my lap. Butch's papers, too. In the dark, I strained to listen. Heard the refrigerator humming. A tire screech, not so distant.

The phone, jarring me upright like the jab of a blade.

It jabbed again. Again. The machine clicked and whirred and Christina answered, in absentia. Then another beep.

"Jack, just checking in. I'm on the road. I'll call later. I love you. I'm thinking about you, Jack McMorrow."

I came off the chair, lunged for the phone, grabbed it as Roxanne hung up.

The machine clicked and rewound. With the light flashing in the dark like a winking red eye, I called Roxanne's home. Another machine answered and I told her to be careful. Told her she'd been threatened. I said she probably should stay with a friend. Call Clair and tell him what had happened. I called her office and said it all again. I called her car phone, but another machine said it wasn't in service.

I cursed it. And then the loft was silent again. But just for a moment.

I heard voices outside. I edged to the window. Three figures were lurching down the middle of street. One tripped and staggered. Another threw something and it smashed. A bottle. One of them cackled. A woman. They reeled on their way. I watched until they were out of sight and then I went to my chair. With the knife in my hand, I tried to think.

I had victims, but no perpetrators. Ortiz was gone. Mihailov. Lester John, too. But Drague, the rapist, where was he? Prison? The Bronx? Maybe he was out there. Somebody or something had to be, or I wouldn't be pinned in here. I'd find Drague. I'd ask him why he got off. I thought of all the jailhouse interviews I'd done, guys in jumpsuits and slippers who had looked me in the eye and said they were the real victims.

Would Drague pull that one if I found him? How brazen was he? Would he tell me anything? Why should he? I supposed I could just play to his sense of civic duty, tell him he could be an important source in the investigation of possible corruption in the Fiore administration. Or had someone else already figured that out?

I had to hurry. But I had to sleep. Just rest up for a little while, then leave before dawn. A nap, then get my stuff. Maybe I wouldn't come back here, call Roxanne from wherever I ended up. A hotel. Someplace small. Wear the hat and the glasses to check in and—

The ringing again. Christina's voice, talking to me in a dream. Saying she couldn't come to the phone until she got the writing off her. They would grind it off with big machines.

A beep. I woke up. It was very dark. I was in the chair. I lurched upright, staggered to the living room, heard a familiar hiss. Then a man's voice.

"Jackie," Butch said.

I felt a chill, like I'd heard a ghost.

"Sorry to bug you again. But listen, buddy. I left you the stuff at the hotel. But if you didn't get it or something, I left another one. And I found some more stuff. I was gonna tell you before but then I thought I'd wait to see how secure this manner of communication is, you know? Girl's taking a hell of a chance but she believes I'm innocent. Nobody else does, so I guess I'll live dangerously and try again. What do I have to lose, right? So Jack, there's another package for you. I put it in the mail to this old guy in my building, used to work for the Post Office. In case something happened to me in connection with this investigation. Well, it did, but not quite what I had in mind. Hey, life sucks and then you die, right? Anyway, his name's McLaughlin. It's an envelope. You say to him, County Slago. That's the password. Guy reads Tom Clancy, what can I say? 'Course he may be a little jumpy now, with all that's happened. But he's a good shit. I told him it was for a friend of mine, which is what you are, Jackie. A friend like no other, to do this for me. Hey, thanks, buddy. Thank God for you, 'cause it's friggin' hell in here, Jackie. It's hell on earth. I wouldn't kid you."

The tape clattered. The phone clicked. The machine beeped. I played the messages back, hearing Christina's friends, reporters, a Frenchman who called Christina "darling." Christophe? And Butch, like the voice of the dead.

And then the room was still again. I looked at my watch. It was 1:20. I'd leave by five, hit this McLaughlin guy before he turned the whole thing over to the cops, if he hadn't already. I'd call Roxanne before she left. Or maybe she'd call. Maybe she'd driven back from way up north, placing a kid. But I couldn't answer. I couldn't answer because if it wasn't her, then they'd know where I was. I'd wait by the phone. When it rang, I'd hear her voice and answer.

Ten minutes later, it did.

I sat in the dark with my hand on the receiver. Listened.

Counted off Christina's message, word by word. Got ready to pick up. And froze as the young voice came out of the dark.

"McMorrow. Heard you had some problems. New York can be a rough place. But so can South Portland, Maine. I heard of a lot worse. People getting hurt and killed. Sometimes they never find 'em at all, ever. Wouldn't that be a bitch? For the rest of your life, not ever knowing what happened to somebody? Are they alive? Are they dead? How'd they die? Was it quick? Was it slow? Did they call out your name at the end? There's no safe place for a woman alone anymore. It's a sad commentation on the state of our society, isn't it, J.M.?"

The machine clicked. I swallowed. I sat on the couch and waited for the night to pass.

I didn't sleep. I didn't doze. I held the knife. Watched the hands on my watch slowly circle. At quarter to three, I got up and went to Philippe's room and got my duffel bag, put the papers in it and then went to the bed and pulled back the sheet.

I put the knives in my bag, too. And then I went to the window, where the black sky would soon begin its slide toward gray dawn. I looked out. Watched. Waited. At a minute to three, I picked up my bag and gave the window a last look and listen.

From across the way, I heard someone's watch beep the hour. If they were watching the front, would they be watching the back?

A third route: the factory window, like my friend.

I backed out of the room and went to the door. I listened. Slipped the bolt out and eased the door open.

The hallway was dark. The building ticked once and was silent. I took a step out and stopped. Listened. Held the knife in front of me. I took another step and another, all the way to the elevator. It was down. I went to the top of the stairs and stopped.

Somewhere below me, someone sniffed.

I backed away. Felt the wall with my hand until I came to the door. I went in and closed it with a single, barely perceptible click. The bolt slid across. I crossed the loft and slipped out Christina's window and down the fire escape, carrying my bag and my shoes.

It was 5:45, the sun still below the brick horizon. I'd parked on Broome Street, where a woman had just unlocked the doors of a cafe. I got out of the car and went in. From behind the counter, the woman looked at me like she had her hand on the holdup alarm. I asked for tea to go and went to the pay phone.

I dialed. Charged the call. Waited for Roxanne to answer. Her phone rang four times and there was a click and a hiss and I sagged. Roxanne said hello on tape, and then there was a clatter and she sleepily said, "Jack?"

"Baby," I said. "You okay?"

"Mmmm."

"Where were you?"

"Bucksport. A foster home. I got home at two-thirty. But are you okay? I've been trying to call. I've been so worried. I thought something happened."

"No, nothing . . . well, something happened."

"What?"

Her voice was sharp now.

"Something happened to Christina. She was attacked."

"Oh, my God. Is she—"

"She's okay. Well, she's hurt, but she's all right. They broke her fingers."

"God, Jack."

"Yeah, they stopped her car and roughed her up and shut her fingers in the door."

"Oh, no."

"Yeah."

I hesitated. The woman put my tea on the counter. I turned away from her and covered the phone.

"It wasn't good. They—"

"Did they catch them?"

"No."

"What did they—"

"It was a warning. They want me to leave New York. They want me to stop looking into this Butch thing."

"Why?"

"Because there's something going on. Butch was onto something. He called it 'corruption in high places.' "

"Did you tell the police?"

"I tried, but they didn't really believe me. I think they're starting to now."

"Well, can't they catch them? They must have cops all over the place."

"You'd think so. But that's part of the problem. It's hard to tell who's who."

"God, Jack, just get out of there. Come home."

"I'd like to but—Listen, where are you going to be today?"

"I've got to work. This mother wants her kids back and she's trying to get a hearing and the lawyers are going back and forth and this foster home is just temporary."

"You're going back up to Bucksport?"

"Yeah."

"Can't somebody else do it?"

"Well, no. It's my case. So unless I'm deathly ill . . ."

I winced.

"Roxanne, they threatened to come after you."

"What?"

"They told Christina you'd be next."

"They'd come to Maine?"

"I doubt it. I think they're just saying that. But I want you to go to Clair's. Stay there for a couple of days. Not at our house. At Clair's."

"I can't, Jack. I have things I have to do. I can't just not show up."

"What if you were sick?"

"But I'm not."

"Rox, this is serious."

"I thought you said they were just bluffing."

"They probably are."

"Who are they?"

"I don't know. A voice on the phone."

"Will they hurt you?"

"They haven't been able to find me. It's a big city."

"Why don't you just come home?"

I hesitated. The woman put my tea in a bag and then placed the bag on the counter. She tapped at the register keys and looked over at me.

"I don't know if that's the answer."

"Why not?"

"I don't know. I'd be so conspicuous there. The reporters will be swarming. I mean, where do I hide in Prosperity? Or in Portland?"

"You could go somewhere else," Roxanne said.

"And stay there all by myself? In hiding? I can't do that."

"Why not?"

"Because—"

I paused, considered the words.

"—because there's something here. I'm getting closer to it."

"A story?"

"It could be an unbelievable story."

"You would write it?"

"No. I couldn't. I'm in it."

"Story about what?"

"I'm not sure. About criminal cases. There's a string of them where something's not right."

"And Butch's wife is in the string?"

"That's right," I said.

"God, Jack."

"I know. That's why I want you to go stay with Clair and Mary. I've talked to Clair. I told him some of it. You'll be safe there."

"Jack, I can't. I've got a three-year-old in temporary care, an eleven-year-old in a shelter for teenagers. I'm responsible for these kids. I can't just disappear."

I winced again. "Please, Roxanne," I said.

"Jack, I can't."

"Then how 'bout if Clair stays with you? He can drive you around to your appointments."

"Like a bodyguard?"

"Yeah."

Roxanne didn't say anything.

"So I'll call him," I said.

"I don't know. I'm really not supposed to—"

"Come on, Rox."

"Let me think about it. I'll call you."

"You can't."

"You're not at Christina's?"

"No. It wasn't safe."

"My God. So where are you now?"

"A pay phone in SoHo."

"Where are you going?"

"The Village. I need to talk to some people. Will you call Clair?"

"I'll think about it."

"Roxanne, come on."

"You're the one who needs a bodyguard, Jack."

"I'm okay," I said.

"I don't think so," she said.

"Well, Jesus, Rox. We only have one, right? And he's in Maine."

"Where you should be."

"I will be."

"When?"

"Very soon."

"I'm worried, Jack."

"I want you to be," I said. "That's what I'm telling you."

"I'm worried about you."

I almost told her there was no reason to worry about me. Almost.

Thirty-nine.

Butch's place in the Village was a plain four-story brick building where the press had been camped but had finally moved on. There was a tree out front to which the remnants of a mountain bike were chained, and in front of the tree, a parking space. I wedged the Camaro in, ignoring the hydrant, and put on my Yankees hat and sunglasses. A woman walked by the car and looked at me like I'd just put on a ski mask.

I got out anyway. Went to the doorway, where there were more buzzers than names. One of them was McLaughlin. Apartment 215.

I pushed the button.

"Yeah," a tinny voice said from the metal box. "What do you want?"

"I'm here for that package," I said, leaning close to the speaker. "Butch sent me."

"Who's this?"

"Jack. Butch's friend. Here for the package. You know, County Slago?"

He didn't answer.

I waited and then scowled and turned around. A jogger thudded by. A kid with a dog was standing by the curb, plastic bag in hand. I walked up the street to the main drag, turned and walked until I found trash cans, with garbage strewn around them. They'd been pawed through, but I found a cardboard box, folded it shut and walked back to Butch's door, where I buzzed the next name on the wall.

A girl answered, saying "Yeah."

"UPS," I said. "I've got a package."

"For Feinstein?"

"Yes, ma'am."

I looked at the name on the wall.

"R. Feinstein."

"That's my mom."

"For R. Feinstein. It's from Victoria's Secret."

"It is?"

The door buzzed and I popped it open. I left the empty box in the foyer, and passed the girl as she hurried off the elevator. I got in and went to the second floor, where the doors were plain and the air was stale. Under number 215 was a small shamrock.

I knocked on it. Heard steps. Felt someone peering through the peephole.

"Yeah?"

"I'm Butch's friend," I said softly. "We were cut off."

"What?" the old man said.

"County Slago," I said.

The door swung open.

McLaughlin was tiny, unshaven, wearing plaid shorts and slippers with black socks. His undershirt was gray and his flesh hung like cobwebs from his bones. The apartment was dark on a sunny summer morning and smelled like a nursing home, that faint odor of antiseptic and waste.

I smiled and apologized for coming so early.

"It's okay," he said, his face taut. "I'm up."

"Butch said you have something for me."

He looked at me.

"That was before," he said.

"Before . . . ?"

"Before Casey put this place on the map. For a couple of days there, I couldn't even walk down the street without somebody sticking a camera in my face."

"It's terrible," I said.

"Then they went away."

"Television," I said. "Short attention span."

"They were a pain in the arse."

He looked at me carefully, as though trying to decipher my face.

"Casey really did it this time, didn't he?"

"I don't know," I said. "I just know what they say he did."

"I just know what I heard on the news, read in the paper. God, they were swarming all over me there for a while. I just said, 'What can I tell you about Casey? He was a good neighbor. Didn't talk too much. Didn't have anybody over, really. Had a bit of a fondness for the whiskey, if you know what I mean.' "

He paused, savoring the memory of all the attention.

"But a nice man. Always said hello to me. 'How you doin', Mr. McLaughlin? How are you today, sir?' Even when he was in his cups, he was always polite to me."

"Was he in his cups often?" I said.

"Well," the old man said, "I don't like to tell tales out of school, seeing as I had a bit of a fondness for a pint, in my time. Still take one on occasion. Good for the ticker."

He touched his mottled white skin.

"But Butchie did like his whiskey," he said, still reliving his moment under the lights. "Not so much lately. He told me two drinks a day was his limit. More than that, he said, you can get into big problems. Liver and all that. He drank down at the corner at the girls' bar there. You should talk to them."

"Why?"

"I mean, that's what I told them."

"Oh."

"Not you."

"I just need the package."

Reminded to be wary, he closed the door an inch or two.

"Well, I don't know."

"Didn't it get here?"

"Well, yeah. It came yesterday. You know, he mailed it third class. For another fifty cents, you can have first class. I worked in the Post Office forty-three years. Penny wise, pound foolish, you ask me. Third-class stuff gets third-class treatment, I always said."

I grinned.

"You still have it?"

"Maybe. You a cop, too?"

He looked at me warily, getting a kick out of having some power.

"An investigator," I said.

"Got a fancy name for everything now, don't they?"

"Yeah, they do."

"You undercover?"

I remembered the hat and glasses.

"Yeah."

"I suppose you still have to keep working, even after what happened."

"That's right."

"Terrible thing. I liked Fiore. Kicked some of these bums in the ass. About time, too."

"I suppose."

An odd reaction from a cop. McLaughlin didn't seem to notice.

"I know Butch is supposed to have done a terrible thing, but maybe he didn't, you know? I was watching on the TV the other day, how many people been put in prison for these murders, twenty years later somebody else says they did it. They let the first guy out, if they haven't stuck him with that needle or he hasn't been killed by these animals in the jail."

I nodded.

"So maybe it's a mistake. I'm going to wait and see before I go condemning the man. I'm going to wait, see if Butch comes back. And when he does, I'm gonna give him his mail."

He turned slightly and looked to his left.

"It's for me," I said. "I was working with Butch."

McLaughlin shook his head.

"I don't know. Something funny about it, though. Why didn't Butch just give you the stuff?"

"He couldn't. I was working undercover. I had a C.I., and if I got blown, they'd have killed him."

"A C.I.?"

"Confidential informant."

"A snitch?"

"Yeah."

"Like I said. Fancy name for everything."

"Right."

He looked at me closely again.

"You look familiar. You been on TV for busts or something?"

"Maybe."

"Wait a minute. I know who—"

There was a scurrying noise behind him, then something whipped past his feet. A white cat scurried down the hall.

"Oh, Jesus," the old man said. "You get back here."

I stepped aside. He hobbled down the hall on his bowed legs, shorts flapping. The cat turned the corner and I walked into the apartment. Trotted through the living room and into the kitchen. On the counter there was a stack of papers: bills, flyers. No envelope.

I ran back to the living room, leaned into the bedroom. The bed was unmade, the room was dank. There were toilet articles on top of a bureau, dirty clothes in a mound on the floor. I stepped in. Stepped out. Turned and saw a manila envelope. But I could hear the man coming, scolding the cat.

I ran to to the table, picked up the envelope. It was behind my back when he reappeared, the cat squirming in his arms. I was standing just inside the door.

"They'll eat 'em, you know, these goddamn Orientals," he said.

He walked past me to the bedroom, slung the cat in and closed the door. He turned and looked at the table where the envelope had been. When he looked up, I was going out the door.

"Hey, you son of a bitch," McLaughlin said. "What the hell you think you're doing?"

I took the stairs at a trot, down and out onto the sidewalk and up the block, away from the car. At the corner I turned and kept walking, looking for a place to stop.

And there was a storefront with blacked-out windows. The stenciled sign on the metal door, SISTERS. The door was propped open by a plastic pail. I stood in the doorway and tore the envelope open, and inside it was another envelope, slightly smaller. I slid it out and opened that one, too.

The papers seemed to be identical to the documents in the package at the hotel. Same memos. Same clips. Until I reached the bottom of the stack.

There was an extra page. It was from the New York City Department of Corrections. A petition for the parole of George Drague, 26 Manida St., Bronx, N.Y. Drague was to be released May 15, 1989. His contact was Marie Drague (Mother). In tiny handwriting at the bottom of the page were the words: *No objection. D. Conroy.*

I stuffed the papers back in the envelope and stepped inside.

It was an oversized cafe, with a bar on the left and a dance floor at the rear. There was a bulletin board inside the door with notices and names and gay leaflets. The place was empty and the chairs were upside down on the tables and there was music playing—a woman singing and playing acoustic guitar. I called out, "Hello," and a woman appeared, way in the back. She said, "We're closed."

I didn't leave. She started toward me.

She was a stocky woman with small, round glasses, a

bead in her nose and a T-shirt that read, "Duke Tennis."
She was holding a broom, and as she got closer, she
clenched it with both hands like a weapon.

"Are you Linda?" I said.

She hung on to the broom, looked at my face, waited
to answer.

"Yeah."

"I'm Jack McMorrow. I'm a friend of—"

"I know who you are. His buddy from Maine."

"The TV?"

"Yeah. And the newspapers."

"I imagine you've been following this."

Linda didn't answer.

"Because Butch said you were a good friend of his."

"It's all relative," she said. "But I guess I was fond
of him."

"Was?"

She looked at me more closely.

"Kind of hard to like someone who does that, don't
you think?"

"Maybe he didn't."

She didn't answer but her eyebrows raised skeptically.

"Do you have a minute?"

"Is this for some story?"

"No. For my own edification."

She frowned and then looked down at the floor.

"Hey, if you don't mind a little dirt. But you're used
to it. You're a reporter."

She turned her back to me and started sweeping the
floor along the wall, herding cigarette butts and clots of
dirt in front of her. I followed.

"So Butch came in here quite a bit?"

"I guess."

"Every day."

"Not every. Most days. Early, around five."

"Did he know people?"

"Some. I mean, the regulars. He kind of stood out."

"An older man. . . ."

"In a lesbian bar, yeah. First time he came here it was

early, and he was the only one here, you know, and then the place slowly filled up.''

I smiled. She kept sweeping.

''It took him a while to get it, but when he did, he was funny about it. He was pretty funny, sometimes.''

''Did he talk much?'

''Some. I mean, he didn't get on a soapbox or anything. He'd watch the TV. Usually we have sports on early. He'd drink his Irish whiskey. We have nachos and light food, microwave kind of stuff, and usually he'd eat something.''

''Did he talk about the city?''

''What, like war stories? Cop stuff?''

''Yeah.''

Linda looked at me and didn't answer. And then her expression changed, as though she had made some sort of decision.

''Okay,'' she said. ''At first, not at all.''

''And after that?''

The long pause again.

''I don't know why I should talk to you,'' she said.

''I don't know why you shouldn't.''

I waited. She considered me a few moments more. And then started in.

''Okay, but I don't want to be in the newspaper.''

''I couldn't put you there if I wanted to.''

''I suppose. So what was the question?''

''Did he talk about his job. City Hall?''

''Uh, not really. I mean, if we were watching the news and there was some crime thing on, sometimes he'd say, like, 'Hey, there's old Joe Smith. I worked with him.' Or he'd tell you about some murder case he'd worked on. One time these moron guys walked in and thought they were gonna give people a hard time and old Butch got right in their faces with his police I.D. and told them to take off and they did. It was nice of him. I mean, he didn't have a gun or anything and there were four of them. We called him 'Columbo.' ''

She swept, working her way toward the bar. I followed.

''But he didn't talk about his wife?''

Linda stopped sweeping and turned to me.

"To me he did. Not to the general public."

"Did he seem very bitter about it?"

She turned to me, broom in hand, and stared.

"You're his friend, right?"

"Since we were little kids."

" 'Cause I don't know if I should be talking about Butch's personal life like this to just anybody."

"I'm not just anybody. Not to Butch."

She turned back to the floor.

"Well, wouldn't you be bitter? If they let the guy go who killed your wife? And you being a cop? And some people saying it was your fault?"

"Yeah. I would."

"So Butch, he was angry. And he was bitter. And he was sad and lonely. Hey, this is New York, right? Join the club."

She swept the dust and butts into a pile and left that pile and started to sweep again.

"How angry did he seem?"

"You mean did he threaten to kill Johnny Fiore? No. Did I think something was wrong inside him? Yeah."

"Why?"

She stopped.

"Hey, I'll tell you just what I told the detectives. Something was simmering inside the man. I could see it when he was quiet, when he wasn't telling a story or whatever. He'd just sit there and you could see the wheels turning."

"Did you ask him what he was thinking?"

"You mean did I ask him if he was homicidal? No. Did I ask him if he was okay? Yeah. He always would snap out of it and put on his happy face. Make some joke. But I knew."

We were near the rest room. Linda continued in. I hesitated, then followed. She pushed open the door of the first stall.

"So were you surprised, shocked to hear what he'd been arrested for?"

Linda swept around the toilet. She snapped an empty

roll out of the toilet paper dispenser and then looked back at me.

"No," she said.

"No?"

"Hey, I wasn't. I mean, a guy in his situation, mad at the system, he isn't gonna kill just anybody. If he's going to do it, it's going to be somebody big."

"Like Fiore?"

"Or somebody else high up. The mayor wouldn't have been my first choice."

"Why not?"

Linda didn't answer. Instead, she stepped out of the stall, left the rest room and strode away. She went behind the bar and bent down, and when she came up, she was holding a white paper napkin. She put it on top of the bar. I looked at it and then back up at her.

"So?"

"Look."

I leaned closer, then looked back at her.

"No. Closer. Really look."

She reached behind her and turned on lights that illuminated the wooden surface of the bar. I picked up the napkin. I could make out letters.

"With a spoon or a fork or a toothpick or whatever," Linda said, "he'd sit there and sort of doodle."

I read the napkin and handed it back to her. Suddenly I felt very tired, a little sick, like I'd rummaged through someone's drawers and found something dirty.

"Did you give this to the police?"

"Not that one, a different one," Linda said. "But I saved a bunch of 'em over the past couple of months and they all say the same thing."

She held the napkin up to the light, but I'd already seen it. At a certain angle, you could see the words plainly:
Kill/Sully

"I figured it would be somebody named Sullivan," Linda said. "Maybe some cop."

Forty.

"Sure there's Sullivans," Donatelli said. "There's even a bunch of Officer O'Malleys. We talked to all the Sullivans and nobody had a beef with Casey. We can't find any Sullivans in his life anywhere else, either. We looked."

He spoke away from the phone and I waited. The naked woman on the mirror swung in the breeze. Donatelli came back.

"McMorrow, no offense, but this is just more peripheral bullshit. I don't need bar napkins. I got a guy with the deceased's blood on his hands. It's over. I know you guys gotta fill space, but that's the way it is. Short and sweet."

I shook my head.

"No, it isn't. You've got Christina Mansell."

"Maybe she pissed off some dope dealer."

"You've got all these threats."

"Alleged threats."

"Don't give me that 'alleged' crap. You're taking the easy way out."

"Come here and say that. A bunch of very tired police

officers will tear you limb from limb. Hey, I've been home six hours in three days.''

"I haven't been home at all.''

"So don't fraternize with assassins.''

"It's too late," I said.

"You got that right, McMorrow. You're finally gettin' real.''

"No, I'm not," I said.

"Casey did it, McMorrow. Accept it and move on.''

I thought about that.

Butch did it. I knew him. Leave him to rot and go home? Leave the questions unanswered? Leave all of it behind? Run back to Roxanne with this always haunting me?

Right there in the car, I shook my head. The naked woman on the mirror did, too, swinging back and forth.

If I ran, I couldn't ever really get away from it. Not in Prosperity. Not in Portland. Not for a waking moment, or a sleeping one, either.

"Make your life a lot easier," Donatelli said.

"No, it won't," I said and I hung up, checked the mirror and cut across traffic.

Hunt's Point was a jut of land just below where the Bronx and East rivers mixed, like blood spilled into a tub. Ships came here with produce that was unloaded, packed into trailers and trucked to supermarkets near you. The trailers were kept in sprawling lots ringed with razor wire strung with windblown trash, like ragged wash hung on a jagged clothesline.

It was a little after one and the day seemed years long. My conversation with McLaughlin in the Village that morning was buried under Linda in the bar, Donatelli on the phone, hours of mulling it all over.

But the time for mulling was over.

So I drove down Hunt's Point Avenue, where everything was still under the pale gray sky. I remembered coming here at night with a photographer. The story was about the prostitutes who serviced the truckers. The women were desperate, drug-addicted ghouls who, when they weren't plying their trade in sleeper cabs, stood in clusters in the rubble-strewn lots. Now the prostitutes were gone, probably moved along in a Fiore sweep. The lots were fenced off.

The point seemed even more desolate, like a village after a massacre.

I drove in a circle and turned off the main drag into the warren of narrow streets behind the asphalt plain. I was searching for Manida, but there were no street signs. Finally I pulled over at a little one-aisle bodega and the man behind the counter directed me. I got back in the Camaro and took two lefts and a right, like a coursing hound on the track of George Drague.

On both sides of Manida there were respectable Victorian-style tenements. Several of them had windows and doors fortified by ornate steel gratings. The bars were painted white and red and made the houses look like gingerbread jails.

Number 26 was one of those.

Its bars were white turning to rust. The patch of grass was shaggy and brown. There was a dented black Monte Carlo parked out front but the shades in the windows of the house were drawn. The treeless street baked in the heat and nothing stirred.

I drove by once, then turned onto the next block and drove slower, locating the rear of number 26 through the fences. There were bars on the back windows, too. I circled back and parked out front.

Took a notebook off the seat. Turned it so the reporter's label showed. Took a deep breath and then paused. And then I got out and, like someone seeking asylum, stood and banged on the steel grate.

No one answered.

I tried the next house. Nothing. The one after that. Still nothing. Three houses down, a curtain stirred behind the bars, but nobody came to the door. At the fourth I knocked and waited, sweating in the midday sun.

And the door opened.

It was a woman, short and stout, wearing what used to be called a housecoat.

"I already found the Lord, if that's what you're selling," she said.

"Well, not exactly. I'm looking for a man named George Drague."

She fell back a step.

"I'm a reporter," I said quickly.

That stopped her retreat. She looked at me curiously and I waited for the moment of recognition. It didn't come. Perhaps she got her news from the radio.

"What'd Georgie do now?"

"What'd he do?"

"Yeah. He kill somebody or something?"

I smiled.

"I hope not. Would he?"

"I don't know. I don't know what Georgie would do now. I haven't talked to him since he was a little boy."

"You've lived here a long time?"

"Fifty-two years."

"That's a long time."

"Went by quick. What'd Georgie do?"

"I don't know. That's why I need to talk to him."

"What paper?"

"The *Times*."

Her eyes widened. She brushed at her thin white hair, as though I might suddenly take her picture.

"So he musta done something terrible, bring the *New York Times* all the way up here."

"Has he done things like that before?"

"I don't know. He goes to jail. He comes back. It was his mother's house and then his sister lived there."

"Does she still?"

"No, she left. She couldn't stand him either."

"Georgie still around?"

"If he is, he's hiding in the cellar. Some guys come looking for him last night. They come back this morning, four o'clock. I saw the car. Tough guys. Or maybe cops, but they didn't act like cops. I figure Georgie got the wrong people mad this time. Pushed it too far.''

"But you haven't seen him?"

"Not for a couple days. Georgie's scum but he ain't stupid. Probably hiding.''

"Where's he go when he isn't hiding?"

"When he ain't hiding?"

"Yeah. Where's he hang out?"

"I guess you don't know Georgie. If you did, you'd know.''

I waited. She savored her moment.

"Hootchie-kootchie joints. Been that way since he was a kid.''

The woman leaned forward confidentially.

"Thinks with his thingie, you know what I'm saying? Sad for his mother. She was a very religious person. We prayed together, you know.''

"Really," I said. "That's interesting. Now, any hootchie-kootchie joints in particular?"

"How do I know? You think I know one from another?''

"No. I just thought you might have heard.''

"Booze and drugs and loose women. You find a place that has those things, you find Georgie. You know he was raised Catholic? Drague's French. Grandparents from Canada. His father stayed here after the war, worked the docks. Now, he was a son of a bitch. Name was Albert but they called him Bert. Meanest—''

"So is there any place around here he might hang out?''

"You're asking me? I don't know. I stay here. My niece does my shopping, takes me to the doctor. I got my Bible. I got my radio. I mind my own business. I can't keep track of Georgie Drague and his running around.''

"Of course you can't," I said.

"But I've seen him in the car place. Talking to the other good-for-nothings. My husband, he worked his whole life on the docks. Never missed a day, forty-eight years. Not like these lazy bums.''

"Is the car place around here?"

"End of the street. You find bums, you find Georgie. You know, his mother, she'd turn over in her grave. She tried with him. Not her fault. Just a bad seed. I told her that. 'Nothing you can do,' I said. 'Some people are just like that.' "

"You're right," I said. "Some people are."

"And you can't tell when they're babies," the woman said. "They all look cute. I always say, you don't want to know what the future brings. Because—"

"What kind of car was it?"

"What car?"

"The one with the tough guys."

"You're not putting this in the paper, are you?"

"No. I'm just trying to find him so I can talk to him."

" 'Cause I don't want anything to do with any of 'em."

"This is between us."

"Okay. It wasn't a car. It was one of those little vans you see now. Like them, whatcha call it, the soccer moms drive. They got out, two of 'em, and they went up and stood beside the door for a minute and then they fiddled with something, the locks, I guess, and they went in. And then they came out after a few minutes and I could see one of them, he shook his head to the guy in the van. And they left."

"Was the van blue?"

"Yeah. Saw it under the light when it went by."

"You get the plate number?"

"No. Like I said, I mind my own business."

"Good idea."

"You got that right. Now what's this story about, any-way?"

"I'm not sure," I said as I turned away.

"When's it gonna be in?"

"I'm not sure of that, either."

"Kind of a loose operation, that *New York Times*, ain't it?"

"Sometimes," I said. When I got in the car and looked

back, her door had closed. The curtain in one of the windows was moving.

The car place was a junkyard ringed by a falling palisade fence. In the front there was a twisted house trailer on which the words "car parts" had been sprayed in black paint. There were men in the door of the trailer and more men outside the dark hole of the garage door. I parked in front, opened the notebook and scrawled the cell-phone number on a dozen pages. I tore them out and stuffed them in my shirt pocket. I left the notebook on the seat. The knife, too. Glanced out and gathered myself up.

As I walked toward the garage, the men turned toward me and stared impassively. They were white, black, Hispanic, but the look was the same. It was the impregnable stare they used for cops, for Immigration, for strangers whose motives were unknown.

When I reached them, I said, "Hey."

They stared. Barely blinked. Nobody made a sound.

"I'm looking for a guy named George Drague," I said.

Nobody moved. Nobody spoke.

"Lady down the street says he stops in here sometimes. I just need to talk to him."

They seemed to have stopped breathing.

"I'll tell you why I want to talk to him," I said. "And this is the truth. A friend of mine, a woman friend, was beat up yesterday in Brooklyn. Ripped her clothes off and broke her fingers. George didn't do it. In fact, I'm told he's going to be next. On the receiving end from the same people. And I want to find him so I can find them. Anybody else been looking for him?"

They didn't answer, but their eyes said yes.

"So I figured I could either go to the cops or I could find George myself."

I reached for my pocket and they flinched. I took out the pieces of paper and they stared at them. I tried to pass the papers around, but the first two guys put their hands in their pockets and looked me hard in the eye. Same for

the third and fourth. Finally, the fifth guy, an older man
with graying stubble, reached out a grease-stained hand
and took one. I kept going around the circle and two other
men took the papers.

"My name's Jack," I said. "I'll be in the area for an
hour. Anybody gets an idea where I might find George,
call this number."

The older man nodded. They stood there, holding the
papers like they were tickets for a door prize.

"You have wives, girlfriends, daughters? There were
three or four of these guys. They wrote something on her
stomach with a knife. Closed her hands in her car door
and left her there."

I saw eyes narrow. A couple of them turned the papers
to read the number.

"I'll tell you," I said, "I'm pretty nervous doing this.
I'm a little off my turf. But a man's gotta do what a man's
gotta do, right?"

It was corny, but they didn't disagree. I didn't think
they would.

So with nothing else to say, I walked to the car and got
in and very deliberately arranged myself. And then I
started the motor and revved it, and waved as I started
off. One man shook his head. Another spat. A couple of
papers fluttered to the ground. But not all of them.

At the same bodega, I bought a coffee in a paper cup
and a bag of pretzels. I paid the same man and he carefully put the coffee and pretzels in a bag, like I was in
first grade and he was packing my lunch.

I started to turn away and then I turned back.

"If you were looking for girls around here, where
would you go?" I said.

His face clouded over and he shook his head.

"I don't care about that. I'm trying to find a guy who
does."

The man started rearranging things on the counter.
Then he took a rag and started wiping.

"You're not police," he said, still looking down.

"Nope."

"What?"

"Reporter. From a newspaper."

He kept wiping.

The man said something in Spanish. Then, "Bad places."

"One nearby?"

He was scraping a grill.

"When you leave here, you going north?"

"I can."

"You go out to the boulevard. You take a right. You drive that way and you look to the right. See the sign. XXX, all that trashy stuff. But alone, you be careful, sir. Very tough place."

"That's why I didn't wear a tie," I said and I smiled. He glanced at me, then turned away as though he couldn't bear to watch.

I took the right and started up Southern Boulevard, underneath the highway, driving slowly, clenching the wheel. My heart started to pound and my breath came quickly. I tried to tell myself it was anticipation, but it wasn't. It was the stomach rumble of fear, and when the phone rang, I jumped.

"Yeah," I said.

"Beaver's," a man's voice croaked. "On Southern."

And then he was gone. The car was quiet. I drove on, slowing to look at the dingy buildings. Warehouses. Stores. A tire shop that was closed. And then there it was.

I pulled over and parked. Opened the bag and took out the coffee. Took out the pretzels and opened them, too. Sipped and watched and procrastinated. Picked up the knife and considered it, then tossed it aside. Bring a weapon, you'd better be damn quick to use it, my friend Clair always said. Or it would be used on you.

I'd ask my questions and leave. In and out.

But the doubts crept in. These people wouldn't talk. I'd be better off just telling the cops. Take a chance that Drague wouldn't be silenced. Maybe it would come out, whatever it was. Maybe it would come out without me.

But then I pictured Christina, pinned to the window. I

felt the relish in the young guy's voice as he talked about Roxanne. I heard Butch's voice, asking for help. And I swallowed some coffee and a little of my fear, and went in.

Forty-one.

It was like walking into a sideshow tent at a grotesque sort of carnival.

There was a narrow entranceway that smelled of beer and urine, and then a door that opened to a dark room with a plywood bar. Next to the bar there were a few metal patio tables at which a half-dozen men sat drinking. A waitress came from behind the bar and threaded her way between the tables, a round tray carried below her bare, jiggling breasts.

That was the topless part.

The men and the waitress turned in unison, staring at me with sullen disinterest. And then they turned away. I didn't wait to be shown to my table.

I sat on one of the three metal stools at the bar. The other two were unoccupied. There was a basin on the floor behind the bar and it was filled with Budweiser bottles and ice. There was nothing on tap. No liquor in sight. The thick half of a pool cue leaned against the wall.

Someone's cigarette was burning in the ashtray in front of me.

The waitress came back with her tray, walked behind

the bar, and picked up the cigarette and took a drag. I smiled. She blew smoke in my face.

She was white blonde, olive-skinned. There was a burn scar on the side of her neck, another scar, long and white, across her breastbone. She had a rose tattooed on her left shoulder and it was the flesh-pink color of a birth mark. Her breasts hung from her chest like clinging children and her expression said she could be neither insulted nor flattered.

"Could I have a Budweiser, please?" I said.

She turned to the basin and bent over. Her spike heels were white and wobbly, and her skirt was short and red. Her underpants were black lace with a tear at one of the seams and her legs were thin and bare. She swung back and her breasts swung a moment longer.

She put the bottle in front of me and stubbed out the cigarette.

"Four," the waitress said.

"Four dollars?"

"No, pesos," she said.

"I thought this was happy hour," I said.

"It is," she said.

I smiled. She didn't. I handed her a ten. She pulled the front of her skirt away from her sagging belly and took out a small roll of bills. Pulling off two, she dropped them on the bar, where they lay like fallen leaves.

Like my mother always said: Don't put money in your mouth. You don't know where it's been.

The waitress started loading more bottles in the tub, her underpants in my face. I took a sip of beer and a man came through the curtain and stared at me. He was short and solid, with a barrel chest and dark hair swept straight back. I nodded. He did, too, but he turned and said something to the waitress. Without looking at him, she shrugged.

I drank the beer and turned toward the tables. A couple of the men turned to look at me, then turned away. I saw tattoos and tank tops. Two other men turned to stare at me, like they were standing watch on a ship. The waitress turned back and took a pack of cigarettes from under the bar. She lit one and inhaled.

"Place fill up at night?" I said.

"Oh, yeah," she said. "When the girls get here."

"There's more?"

She looked at me, her eyes narrowed.

"You trying to pull my chain?"

"No. Not at all. Place just seems small. Where's the stage?"

She jerked her head toward the far end of the room, which wasn't very far away.

"You know most of the people who come in?"

The waitress half-smiled, and gave a little snort.

"Why you asking, detective?"

"I'm not a cop."

"Oh, yeah? What are you, lost?"

"A reporter. Want to see my press pass?"

"That a come-on?"

"Nope. I just thought you might want to see it."

"Keep it. I got no comment."

I could feel the men watching.

"I'm not working," I said.

"Slumming?"

"Looking for somebody."

"You and everybody else."

She stubbed out her cigarette.

"I mean a guy."

"You're in the wrong bar."

"No, I mean I need to talk to him. This guy."

"And you think he comes here?"

"That's what they told me down the street. In the Point."

The waitress shrugged, then bent down to get something. I could see the freckles on her back, the snake of her backbone. And then she came up with a pail of ice and dumped it in the tub.

"George Drague," I said. "That's his name."

The waitress dumped another pail.

"What's your name?" she said, not looking at me.

"Jack. Jack McMorrow."

"I think I heard of you somewheres."

"No kidding."

"Yeah. What paper?"

"The *Times*."

"Don't read it. Musta been someplace else."

"So what's yours?"

"My what?"

"Your name."

"Mercedes."

"Really?"

"No, but close enough. What you looking for this guy for?"

"His name came up in a story I'm doing. You know him?"

"Never heard of him."

"Would you tell me if you had?"

"Probably not."

I smiled and took a sip of beer.

"Think those guys over there might talk to me?"

"You shittin' me? They wouldn't tell you if you was on fire."

"Can't hurt to try," I said, and I started to swing off the stool.

"No," the waitress said.

I swung back.

"Hey, I don't want you to get hurt," she whispered. "Not here. 'Cause I'll get stuck cleaning up your blood."

"I'm tougher than I look."

"You got a gun?"

I shook my head.

"Then you're not tough enough. I don't think you get it. This isn't—"

The big man came through the curtain and stood with his hands on his hips. He looked at the waitress and jerked his chin upward.

"No, not a cop," the woman said. "A reporter."

I smiled.

"You got questions for me?" he said, his accent Greek or something like it.

"Nah, he's looking for somebody named Joe Green," the waitress put in. "I told him we never heard of him."

The man scowled at me.

"Don't bother the help," he said. "This is a place of business."

I held up my beer.

"And I'm a paying customer."

I held his gaze until he turned to the waitress, gave her his boss look and stepped through the curtain.

"The *Times* could put this place on the map," I said.

"Yeah, right. We'll put that plastic stuff on your story and put it in the window."

"Laminate it," I said.

"Right."

"You can't buy that kind of publicity."

"Sometimes publicity is a bad thing."

"I suppose," I said.

She put another beer in front of me. I took a long swallow and finished the first one. She took the bottle and the bills from the bar.

"Keep it," I said.

She did.

"You find this guy, it gonna be a good thing or what?"

"Better than if other people find him first."

"What's that mean?"

"They might kill him, if they can find him."

"And if you find him?"

"I might keep him from getting killed. Then again, he may be beyond help."

"What'd he do?"

"Raped a woman. Beat her up."

The waitress looked at me and for a moment she looked troubled. But only for a moment.

"The one I know about was a few years ago," I said. "Nice girl, worked downtown. This guy grabbed her and pulled her into an alley on the East Side. Near where she lived."

"Did he kill her?" the waitress said softly.

"No. Just made her life hell."

"He's a pig," she said. "For doing that, I mean."

"You know him, don't you?" I said.

She turned around and dumped another bucket of ice.

"Nope. Never heard of him."

"Know what happened to another woman?" I said.

I told her about Christina, and she closed her eyes, put her arms across her breasts.

"I hate these guys, think they can do that," she said.

"You mean Georgie?"

She frowned and shook her head, her nipples against her forearms. I heard a chair scrape the floor.

I turned and she did, too. Three of the men at the tables were walking toward me. The others were getting up, too. I swiveled toward them but stayed on the stool. The first guy, a fat balding man with big arms and hair on his shoulders, stood in front of me.

"You're bothering the lady," he said.

She shook her head.

"Ray-Ray, it's okay," the waitress said. "We was just talking."

"Talk's over," Ray-Ray said. "Hit the fucking road."

"It's okay. He wasn't bothering me."

"Hit the road," he said, his friends crowding closer.

"Ray-Ray," the waitress said, "chill."

The curtain whirled and the big guy appeared.

Ray-Ray didn't seem to notice.

"I'm gonna count to three," he said.

"If you get stuck, we'll chime in," I said.

He lunged for me and got my shirt and pushed me back off the stool and onto the floor, and he was on me and I could smell him, hear shouting, the waitress screaming, "Stop it."

I came up on my side and I got to my knees and someone shoved me from behind, onto Ray-Ray, who wrapped his big arms around my neck and squeezed.

The screaming was louder and I swung at his face with both arms, felt teeth and his wet mouth and he started to bite me. I couldn't breathe and I clawed at his arms, his face, his eyes. She was screaming, "You're killing him," and I could hear myself gurgling. Somebody kicked me in the back, in the legs, and his grip tightened. We both stopped thrashing but he didn't let go. I couldn't get a breath. I kicked. I couldn't get loose.

The breath wouldn't come.

I screamed but no sound came out, and I tried to say "Stop," but it came out a cough. I felt weaker and something hard hit my shoulder, over and over, a club, and a man's voice was saying, "Let go, let go," but it was too late. Everything was gray and black and I was going limp, couldn't see, heard a scream but it was faint, like a dream.

And then everything was quiet.

And cold.

"Come on," the voice said, from very far away. "Come on."

I heard her, felt something wet. I opened my eyes and there she was, staring down at me so that her white hair hung down, her breasts, too.

"Oh, thank God," the waitress said. "You all right? You gonna be okay? Jesus Christ, what a day."

I looked at her. Tried to swallow, but it hurt and I grimaced.

"Hey," she said, "just take it easy for a minute."

She swabbed my face with a rag. It smelled like old beer and I pushed it away. I looked around. Saw my stool. Cigarette butts. Dead cockroaches. A peanut.

"Christ, you passed out for a minute there. Good thing you didn't die or something."

"Yeah," I said.

I looked around.

"Where is he?" I rasped.

"Ray-Ray? He left. Chico kicked him out. He was pissed."

"Oh," I said.

"He doesn't want any more trouble here. Just got his license back after somebody got shot. They'll shut us down, they keep getting calls. You okay now?"

I raised myself on one elbow and looked around.

"How long was I out?"

"Just for a couple minutes. I think your windpipe got squeezed."

"It's called being strangled."

"He just gets carried away. 'Cause you insulted him."

"I did?"

"About the counting."

I sat up.

"Good thing I didn't start in on his mother."

"Ah, Chico whacked him pretty good. Got him off you."

I turned my neck in a slow rotation.

"Where's Chico now?"

"He went out. "

"What? Move the drugs in case the cops come?"

She shrugged, moving the rose up and down.

"No cops?"

"No. Nobody called 'em."

I sat there and thought for a minute. Felt my face and my neck. The waitress was on her knees in front of me, peering into my eyes as though she were looking for clues.

"What if I call them now?" I said.

"Who?"

"The cops."

"For what?"

"Report an assault that took place inside Beaver's. Big guy tried to strangle me. Another guy hit me with a pool cue or something."

"He was saving your ass."

"I don't know that."

"I just told you."

"Then you could tell them."

"The cops? No way."

"You're a witness," I said slowly. "You give a statement. I sign a complaint. They round up everybody else. Poke around the place a little, run everybody's name through the cop computer."

I paused.

"Your name, too."

I stood up slowly and stretched, feeling the bruises in my back, my legs. The waitress stood, too. Pulled down her skirt, an odd gesture of modesty. She looked at me coldly.

"Or else," I said.

"Or else what?"

"Or else you can tell me where Drague is."

"How the hell should I know?"

"You know him. Where's he shack up when people are looking for him?"

"I don't know."

"Then I call the cops. I'll just dial 911."

"You can't use the phone."

"I'll call from the car."

"I thought you were a nice guy."

"I am. That's why I'm here."

"Drague would kill me."

"He won't know."

"Sure he will. He'll find out."

"I've been talking to people all day. Maybe it was one of them."

She teetered on her heels.

"I shoulda let 'em beat the shit out of you."

"Too late."

"Maybe not," she said.

"Suit yourself," I said. "I'll go call."

The waitress looked at me and then her shoulders sagged and she shook her head, then leaned close.

"Down the street," she whispered, her cigarette breath warm and moist. "There's a mattress store but it's closed. There's a house attached to the store part. In the back. Second floor. But let me tell you, Jack whatever your name is, you already pushed your luck. I don't know what this story is, but you oughta quit before you get killed."

"Thanks for your concern," I said.

"You think I'm kidding?" the waitress said.

"No," I said.

"You think it can't happen to you?"

"No," I said. "I don't think that, either."

"You don't get nine lives around here, let me tell you."

"How many do you get?" I said.

"Not as many as you're gonna need, you start screwing with these people."

"What people?"

She didn't answer.

"How 'bout a bathroom? You have one of those?"

The waitress motioned toward the hallway with her chin. I walked out, saw a door on the right with a gouge in it. I pushed it open and stepped in, hooking the door shut behind me. My kidneys hurt and I felt like my bladder might burst. There was one bowl and I urinated into it, watching for blood. I didn't see any and I was zipping my shorts when there were footsteps in the hall, then voices.

"Whaddaya mean 'guys'? I had a guy in here a little while ago. Said he was a reporter. Now we got more guys?"

It was Chico's voice.

"White guys," another man said. "First I thought they was fucking cops, but then they started offering cash for the son of a bitch."

"How much?"

"Two."

"Two hundred?"

"Two thousand."

"For Drague?"

"For his 'location,' they said."

"Jesus. What's that piece of shit gotten into now?"

"I don't know. But two thousand bucks. You know where he is?"

"He's around. Saw him last night. He was cranked, eyes popping out of his head. He said he was going under for a while, but he left with a coupla the girls."

"He better keep his mind on business, he wants to stay alive," the other man said. "This kid, he talks like he's in a movie, but he's got a big gun and he's itching to ram it down somebody's throat and pull the trigger.''

"The other guy?''

"Two more. One I could see was older. Mean-looking. Might be a cop, but if he is, he's on his own. I mean, I seen the cash. So what do you think?''

"About what?''

"The money. Two grand for Drague.''

Chico said something I couldn't hear.

"You don't want it?''

"No. That's garbage. Their first offer. Don't you know shit about business?''

"They got cash. Kid showed me a buncha money.''

"We ask for ten.''

"For Georgie Drague?''

"We go low as five. But we work 'em for a while. Walk away and make 'em sweat if we have to. We got what they want.''

"What do I get?''

"You get a grand.''

"You cheap mother. I brought you the deal.''

"I know where he is.''

"Two.''

"Fifteen hundred.''

"All right, but that's on five. I want three if we get ten.''

"We get ten, I'll kiss you on your junkie mouth. Where are these guys?''

"Up the block, in a van. I told 'em to wait.''

"Let's go. But let me do the deal.''

"May need a gun, get the money loose from that little punky bastard. Probably thinks we're dumb shits.''

"He'll learn,'' Chico said. "You drive.''

I heard the jingle of keys.

"They're gonna kill Georgie, you know,'' the other guy said.

"Uh-huh,'' Chico said.

"You think they'll kill the girls, too?''

"I don't know,'' Chico said.

''They're big girls. They know what they're gettin'
into.''

''Or they don't,'' Chico said. ''Sometimes it's better
that way.''

Forty-two.

Did I know what I was getting into? No, and maybe that was better, too.

The mattress store was a quarter-mile south of the bar, where the boulevard bends away from the elevated highway. The building was a house with a store stuck on the front, and a faded sign, FUTONS. The windows were covered with plywood, the plywood covered with graffiti. I drove by once, circled back and drove by again. Down the side street, I parked and watched the mirror for a blue van. Three of them drove by. One was full of kids. The others, I couldn't tell.

So I drove for ten minutes, winding through the tenement streets, and finally parked a half-block back from the mattress place. I shut the car off and looked around.

The houses were close-set and run down and kids, mostly of color, were clustered on the stoops like seagulls. They looked at me and called out something and laughed. I nodded and then I looked up the street to the rear of the building. There was a beat-up Toyota parked near a wooden stairway. The stairs led to a door on the second floor. The door had a window. The window had bars.

I got out of the car, notebook in hand. The kids said,

"Hey, mister," and I smiled at them and tried to hold that pose as I walked toward the building, climbing the stairs like steps to a gallows, still deciding what to say.

Drague was holed up. He had drugs and girls and probably a gun. At least one. I climbed the last stair and stood in front of the door. Pad in hand, I smiled at myself in the window glass and knocked on the metal door.

I waited, knocked again. Smiled blissfully, like someone selling religion. I looked at my pad and made a notation. I'd raised my hand to knock again when the shade moved aside.

I peered in and kept smiling.

"George there?" I said.

The shade moved aside and a woman's face appeared behind the bars. Or was it a child? She saw me and jerked back, out of sight.

"I gotta talk to George. It's an emergency."

I knocked again. Dropped the smile. A different face appeared. A haggard woman, gray-skinned, her hair greenish blonde. She peered at me and then waved me off and shook her head.

I held up my pad.

"I'm a reporter. I have to talk to George."

The women looked at me blankly. I put my face next to the glass.

"Really," I said. "They're coming to kill him. They'll kill you, too, if you don't get out of here."

That must have made more sense in her world, because the door opened a crack. I pushed it and the woman pushed back, but I pushed harder and it fell open. The woman backed away from me, a kitchen knife held in front of her.

She was hollow-eyed and gaunt, dressed in a black slip. Her legs and feet were bare. The slip had a stain on the front. The knife was dirty, too, like it had been used to cut cheese.

"Get the fuck outta here," she hissed.

"Where is he?"

"I don't know nothin' about it."

"That won't help you. Who's he with?"

"She don't know nothin' about it, either. She don't know nothin'."

Her eyes searched me, like she was trying to place me. But her look was glassy. There were pipes and bags on the table, beer cans and cigarette packs.

"This is fucked up," the woman said. "This is so fucked up."

"Where is he?"

She pointed the knife toward a hallway.

"Just him and your friend?"

She nodded.

"What are they doing?" I asked, but then I listened and heard the rhythmic squeak of bedsprings.

The woman looked at me, taut and tense and confused.

"You gonna kill him?"

"No."

"Don't kill her."

"I won't kill anybody."

"You're gonna kill him, ain't you? You're here to kill him."

"No," I said. "I'm going to interview him."

She looked at me blankly again.

"Can I leave?"

"Go," I said, and she took keys from the table and circled me slowly, the knife still in front of her, her bare feet making a shuffling noise on the filthy floor. And then she was out the door, tripping down the stairs like a tawdry Cinderella.

"Hurry up," George Drague called from deeper in the apartment. "I want both of yuz. And bring me some beers."

I quietly crossed the kitchen to the refrigerator. Inside, there was a torn cardboard twelve-pack of Heineken cans. I took two and started down the hall.

There was a door on the right. It was open a crack and light spilled out into a dark room opposite. I could see a couch. I could hear the bedsprings squeaking.

I walked slowly until I was standing at the door. I

paused. Took a deep breath. Clenched my notebook. Gripped the cold cans.

"Hurry up," Drague called. "And don't forget the beers."

The squeaks quickened and a woman moaned.

"Come on, you can make more noise than that," he said.

She moaned more loudly. I knocked.

"What the hell you doing?" he said. "Get in here."

I pushed the door and it opened slowly. Drague was naked on the bed and the girl was on top of him. She was naked, too. There was a red garment beside her and when she saw me, she grabbed for it.

Drague looked at me, his mouth gaping open.

"What the—"

The girl slid off him, holding the red cloth against her chest. Drague rolled away from me, fell to the floor and came back up. He had a pistol and he pointed it at my face.

"Don't," I shouted. "It's not me. I'm not the one looking for you. I'm a reporter."

"Don't move," Drague screamed. "Keep your hands up."

"I'm from the *Times*," I said. "The *New York Times*."

"Shut up. Hands out. Drop the paper."

I let the pad fall to the floor, and the beers, too. They rolled under the bed.

"I'm here to help you."

"Shut up. Shut up or I'll fucking kill you."

Drague stood slowly. His gut hung loosely, and his penis had gone flaccid. He had tattoos on his shoulders. One was a red devil. The other was the dragon Kim Albert had described.

"They're gonna kill you," I said.

"Shut up or you're dead."

The gun was on me. He had it by both hands.

"On the floor," he screamed.

"I'm not armed," I said, but I fell to my knees.

"Down."

I dropped to my belly, my chin on the carpet. He came around the bed and stood over me. I could see his feet. His toenails were gnarled and ragged.

"Search him," Drague yelled.

The woman padded toward me. Her toenails were painted red. They passed my face and she paused and then sprang for the door.

"You bitch," he shouted. "Get back here."

She kept running. He stood over me for a moment, and then I felt the gun barrel against the back of my head.

"Don't move."

I didn't. He felt my waist at my back, slid his hand around to the front. Switched hands and did the other side. I could hear him breathing heavily. Cursing to himself.

"They're coming to kill you," I said.

"Shut up."

The gun barrel pressed hard against the back of my head and I grimaced and then I felt him dig my wallet from the back pocket of my shorts. I heard him sorting through it, felt cards drop onto my back like playing cards from a dealer.

"Jack McMorrow? Who the hell is Jack McMorrow?"

"That's me. I'm a reporter."

"I hearda you. Why've I hearda you?"

"Butch Casey. The mayor."

"You been on TV. What is this? What the hell is this?"

"I need to talk to you."

"You need to shut up. What do you need to talk to me for?"

"Kim Albert."

He paused.

"I don't need to talk to you about anything. A newspaper reporter? What the hell kinda newspaper reporter comes in here—I need to blow a fucking hole in the back of your head is what I need to do."

"They're gonna kill you for Kim Albert. That's why they're looking for you."

"Nobody's looking for me."

"Sure they are. That's why you came here."

"How'd you find me?"

"Somebody told me. But somebody's gonna tell those other guys, too. Chico at the bar was trying to sell you for five-thousand bucks."

"What?"

"He's doing the deal right now."

His feet shifted and I saw him reach for clothes. He put on underwear, big blue bikinis.

"Don't move. Don't even think of it."

Shorts went on next, baggy black ones. Then running shoes, Nikes. He scuffed them on, stumbling once, and didn't lace them. The shoes came around me and Drague stood by the door.

"Up. Sit on the bed. Hands on top of your head."

I moved slowly to my feet. Turned to face him. He was wearing a white T-shirt with the words RALPH LAUREN on the front in big block letters, like it was the name of a college. He was wild-eyed over his black goatee. His gun hand was trembling.

"Talk. But you friggin' move, I'll blow your head off."

I nodded. Swallowed but my throat was dry.

"I ain't kidding."

I nodded again.

"They're going to kill you for Kim Albert."

"Who?"

"I'm not exactly sure. I think the mayor's guys."

"The mayor's killed. You mean the dead mayor?"

"Yeah. But his friends are alive."

"What are they looking for me for?"

"Kim Albert."

"That's all over."

"It's only over when you're dead," I said.

"It was ten years ago. I did the time. Nobody cares about that now."

"Yeah, they do. They don't want you around at all."

"Why not?"

"I'm not sure."

"Whaddaya mean you're not sure? You come in here

and you're not sure? I think this whole thing is bullshit.''

"It isn't. They're coming. They offered two and Chico wanted five. Him and another guy he called a junkie.''

"Marcel? That snake! I'm gonna kill him! And I'm gonna kill Chico. They're dead. I mean, they are dead.''

"You're the one they want dead.''

"Why me? I kept my mouth shut. I kept my end. It's over. I never said a word.''

"About what?''

"About—''

He stopped.

He raised the gun.

"You're a cop. You're wired.''

He reached out and tore my shirt open. Ripped it open at the belly, too. Turned me around and squatted and yanked my shorts down to my ankles.

"I'm not a cop, George,'' I said. "And telling me is the only thing that'll keep you alive.''

"I gotta get outta here. That bitch take the car? Shit, the bitch took the car.''

"Tell me first. Then I'll drive you.''

"Nothing to tell. The job got done. It was business.''

"What kind of business?''

"Business, for God's sake. I did a job. I got paid. Who besides Chico and Marcel?''

"I don't know. So you were paid to attack Kim Albert?''

"What the hell,'' Drague said. "You think I did it outta the goodness of my heart?''

We were in the kitchen. He had paused to guzzle a beer.

"Let's go,'' Drague said, turning me and shoving me toward the door.

"I'm telling you, George, the best protection you have is to talk,'' I said. "Talk to the cops. Talk to the newspaper. Talk to TV.''

"You're nuts,'' he said. "This is nuts.''

"You go back on the street and they'll hunt you

down," I said, hands still on my head. "You know they will. But once you go public, it's like insurance. Once it's out, it's too late. Something happens to you, it just proves everything you say is true. So there's no reason to shut you up, except maybe revenge, and they'll be scrambling too much to save themselves to think about that."

"It is true."

"I believe you, George."

"You could put this in the *New York Times* or some goddamn place?"

"Yeah," I said. "I could."

"But they'll put me back inside."

"They can't. You can't be tried twice for the same crime."

"Don't lie to me."

"I'm not. I swear. It's the law."

"TV, too?"

"They'll be knocking your door down."

He considered it, then tossed back the rest of the beer.

"So what do I get?" he said, flinging the can off the wall. "For talking?"

"You get to live," I said. "You'll save your skin and then you can walk."

"I don't get money?"

"Maybe you can sell your story to the tabloids. Go on the talk shows."

He considered that, sorting through his drug-addled brain.

"You mean like *Oprah*? Sally fucking Jesse?"

"Sure," I said.

"She pays, doesn't she?"

I didn't know.

"Hell, yes. Big bucks. Tabloids, too. They'll pay big bucks. If the story's what I think it is."

"What do you think it is?" Drague said.

"I think you got paid to be part of a crime wave."

"I didn't kill anybody."

"I know."

"I just put some rich bitch in the hospital."

"Why rich?" I asked.

"What are you, stupid? 'Cause I jump some Raggedy Ann coming home from some factory, who gives a shit? I grab some rich guy's wife or daughter, that's news."

"And that's what they wanted?"

He finished the beer. Went to the window and looked out, then came back to the table. He stuck the gun in the pocket of his shorts and it pulled them down on the right side. I dropped my hands from my head and he started gathering up the crystalline chunks and bags of powder from the table. Some powder spilled, and he put it to his nose and sniffed, like it was snuff.

" 'Make headlines,' they said. That's why I picked her. Little chick with a briefcase. I figured I'd bang some Yuppie. Hey, it worked."

"So you didn't know Kim Albert?"

"Hell, no. I had to hang out in these little candy-ass coffee places looking for somebody. She caught my eye 'cause she had a nice little butt. I mean, I needed somebody halfway good-looking, you know what I'm saying? I can't just turn it on and off like a light switch. I ain't some animal."

"Where'd they find you?"

"Where do you think? Riker's. I'm sitting out there awaiting fucking trial and they all of a sudden spring me on P.R. bail. I go home, I'm living with my mom. She's riding me, saying I sit home all day and she goes to work. She was a cook. Made macaroni for the fruitcakes at the hospital up at Morris Park. I'm like, 'Give me a break. I been in jail for six weeks.' Like an hour later, I get this call. Guy says he's got a job for me."

He was leaning over the table, crumbling dark crystalline stuff into a small glass pipe.

"One for the road," Drague said. "Anyway, so I said, 'Who is this?' He said, 'I'm a friend of a friend.' I said, 'What kinda work?' He said, 'I need somebody taught a lesson. A lady.' I figured this is his ex or something. I say, 'I don't go around whacking people, pal.' He says,

'I'm not talking about whacking somebody. I'm talking about giving 'em a serious spanking.' "

"Who?"

"Anybody. It didn't matter. I mean, it had to be a kind of person. One of those snotty bitches who look right through you on the street, noses in the air. I'm thinking, Jeez, this guy holds a grudge or what? Some rich bitch stands him up and he wants to get even?"

"How much?"

"I ain't telling you."

"You don't tell the story, you're still worth killing."

"Five before. Five after. If I get caught, I do short time and get another five grand when I get out, if I keep my mouth shut."

He lighted the pipe and drew the white smoke into his lungs, his eyes narrowing.

"How'd they know you'd do short time? Rape is serious."

"That's what I said. My record, I could get ten years. I hang up. Couple nights later a different guy calls. Little faggoty voice but smart-sounding, you know? He says he'll guarantee I don't do more than a year. I say, 'for a Class A sexual assault? Who you kidding?' He says, 'Leave it to us.' I say, 'Bullshit, I will.' "

Drague put the pipe down and looked at me. There was a new sparkle in his eyes as he took the gun from his pocket, gestured with it as he spoke.

"So then he says, 'You know that little girl you popped?' This is the young one I was in jail for. Hey, she was working as a dancer. I mean, come on. I'm supposed to get her birth certificate? And he describes her, right down to the underwear she was wearing. He says, 'Her memory is getting better.' I say, 'How do you know so much about that?' He says, 'Who do you think got you out? And if we can get you out, we can put you back in.' "

"And you believed him?"

"Yeah."

"Why?"

"Because I recognized the voice. I think he wanted me to know. I think he knew if it was some *jaloni* calling saying these things, I'd tell him to kiss off. But I knew who it was."

"Who was it?" I said.

I waited. Drague opened the refrigerator and took out another Heineken. Opened it and tipped it up. His Adam's apple jerked as he gulped it down. He wiped his mouth with his forearm and pointed the gun at my head.

"Maybe I should just kill you."

I breathed slowly, in and out. He lowered the gun and smiled.

"Just dickin' with ya."

He laughed. Killed the beer instead. Banged that can off the wall.

"So who was it?"

"Who was it?"

"Who offered you the job?"

"Oh, yeah. I was tellin' my life story, wasn't I? Well, here's the good part. The punch line."

He paused, and his expression darkened.

"I don't get bucks for this, you're dead. I'll hunt you down."

"It's a deal," I said.

"I can do it."

"I know you can."

Drague seemed reassured.

"It was the prosecutor. The skinny little asshole who did my case."

"Conroy?" I said.

"Yeah. You know him?"

"Yeah," I said.

"What do think of the story so far?"

"Very good."

"You don't believe me, you can listen to the tape."

"You taped Conroy?"

"A little insurance. Until now, I didn't think I'd need it."

Forty-three.

We walked down the sidewalk toward the Camaro, Drague just behind me, the gun in the front of his shorts. The kids weren't in the street. They weren't on the stoop. The block was hot and silent, and I could hear the scuff of Drague's running shoes on the pavement.

"We'll go get the tape first?" I asked him.

"Yeah, sure, I got it hid."

"And then to the *Times*?"

"Sure. They'll pay me money?"

"No, but they'll make you legit. Being in the *Times* will up your value for the people who do pay."

"How 'bout a hotel?"

"They'll do that much."

"A four-star place. And a case. I'm cranked right up. I'm gonna need a case to ease back down. I want a case of Stella Artois. It's Belgian. And a real high-class hooker."

"How 'bout we settle for the beer? For now."

"Okay. We gotta get this story out there first, anyway," Drague said, like it was his idea. "That's my insurance."

We were at the car. I had the keys out. The street was oddly quiet, with nobody outside. I looked around, then opened the car door. Drague went to the other side. I glanced up and down the block and then I peered up.

From the second-floor windows, children were watching. Why were they inside? What were they waiting for?

"Car's kinda beat," Drague was saying. "Don't they pay down at the *New York Times*? TV guys, some of them got nice rides. I saw this chick once, she's on one of the shows, reads the news, this hot little blonde. Hey, wouldn't I like to—"

We both looked back.

The blue van had come out from between the houses, bouncing over the curb. Tires squealed and it was coming toward us. I started to get in the car but there was no time. Drague was crouched against the fender, eyes wide, gun out. I got clear of the car door, started to run, heard, "Freeze! Police!"

I turned. It was the guy from Christina's, the one with the bolt cutters. He'd come from the doorway on Drague's side.

"He's not," I shouted, but Drague had half-turned and was starting to put up his hands. The guy had a handgun and he ran at Drague and swung and hit him with it, and I heard Drague say, "Hey, what are you—"

I turned back and the van was on me, the door sliding open, a man leaping from it as it skidded to a stop.

He had a gun, too, and as I turned to run he started with, "Police officers! Stop right there."

But I didn't stop, just kept running, and I could hear his footsteps behind me, a roar and then the van was on me, squeezing me against the cars and I was grabbed from behind, slammed down, my cheek scraping the pavement. I lashed back with my feet, kicked the guy as he swung at me with the pistol, hitting me in the arms, the forehead, shouting, "You're under arrest. You're under arrest."

I tried to roll under a car but he caught my ankle and pulled, got a handcuff around my wrist. I punched him with my free hand, tore at his hair, screamed, "They're not police, call the police!" and then I heard the spray, felt it on my face, in my eyes, and it burned.

I couldn't see, but I felt the other cuff go on, felt myself hoisted to my feet by the handcuff chain.

"Watch your head," the voice said, as he pushed me toward the van door and then inside.

It was a youngish voice, the voice from the phone.

"Get help," I screamed. "Call the police."

"I told you, McMorrow," he said, his mouth close to my ear. "Runnin' with the big dogs now."

He shoved me into the van, onto the floor, where the middle seat should have been. The Boxer was at the wheel, his head turned away, but even through the Mace I knew it was him. The factory guy sat on the backseat and the young guy was somewhere behind me.

Drague was beside me, and as the van pulled away, he started right in.

"I don't even know this asshole. I mean, he barges into this place, I'm in the sack with this chick and there he is. I ain't told him jack shit, but you wanna take him out, fine. I'll just disappear. I'll just—"

There was a thud. I heard Drague gasp and I braced myself. Waited. Said, "Oh," as the kick hit my ribs.

"Shut up," the young guy said.

"This is stupid," I said. "It's too late. If I were you, I'd—"

I saw it coming, braced again.

"Uh."

It was the bolt-cutter guy kicking. The young guy talking.

"—I'd be headed for Mexico or Europe or Canada or someplace. When this comes apart, you don't want to be—"

"Shut him up," the Boxer said. "I don't need a lecture."

"I'll pop him now," the young guy said.

"No, wait," the Boxer said. "Not in the middle of traffic."

"Hey, it was over," Drague said. "I did it. I didn't talk. What the hell you doing this for?"

"McMorrow dug it back up," the Boxer said.

The van swayed, then leaned to one side, leveled off. I heard horns, trucks. The boulevard.

"I didn't talk all this time. I ain't talking now."

"Shut your mouth," the young guy said.

"You gotta believe me. What'd I do?"

I heard a siren approaching, then passing and fading.

"Somebody back there called it in," the young guy said.

"Leave us and take off," I said. "Two murders, you'll get the death penalty."

"You're thinking of Casey," the Boxer said.

"That's where I hearda you," Drague said.

"Jeez," the factory guy said, "Are these guys annoying or what?"

"It was his gun," Drague said. "I took it off him. I was gonna bring him to you."

"Shut up, you pathetic piece of human shit," the young guy said.

"Well, Jesus, let me through, you goddamn idiot."

It was the Boxer, shouting at traffic.

"Don't kill me," Drague screamed. "Don't kill me."

Oh, God, I thought. Oh, God, help me. Please help me.

"Mace the asshole," the factory guy said.

Please, God.

"Will you let me in this fucking lane?" the Boxer said.

The van had slowed. Suddenly it accelerated, shuddering like a jet, and I saw the factory guy brace himself, his eyes wide.

"Jesus, you're gonna kill us," he said.

"Let me go," Drague said. "I got friends, man. They'll fuckin' hunt you down."

"Shut up," the young guy shouted.

"Slow down," the bolt-cutter guy said. "Ten minutes, it'll be over."

"You don't know these guys," Drague was saying. "They're Hell's Angels and they'll—"

"Shut up," the young guy screamed.

"He's got a tape," I said. "He taped everything. When you were making the deal back then."

There was a moment when nobody said anything. The van swerved and slowed.

"What?" the Boxer said.

Drague paused, probably trying to decide whether having a tape was good or bad.

"Every word," he said. "I got you, numb nuts. I got that little bastard, Conroy. You think I'm stupid?"

"Where is it, shit for brains?" the young guy said.

"It's safe. And if I ain't back by tonight, it goes to Geraldo. I left orders."

"Oh, Jesus, this guy is full of shit," the young guy said.

"You'll find out," Drague said. "You'll find out the hard way, you fucking, two-bit, pretty-boy lackey."

There was a thud and I heard Drague's breath gush out and then the young guy, hair slicked back, smelling like magazine cologne, was on Drague's back, the gun pressed against the base of Drague's skull.

"I'm gonna kill you, you mother—"

But Drague was strong and he writhed under the young guy, tried to roll him off.

"Hey," the Boxer said.

I turned onto my hip, facing the bolt-cutter guy. He was starting to his feet, the gun in his right hand. I squirmed and lashed out with my feet, kicking his shins, once, twice. He swung the gun and there was a flash but no pain, and I kept kicking and the van turned and the bolt-cutter guy fell sideways against the door.

I was on my knees, then my feet caught and I half-fell, half-lunged on top of the young guy and I bit his shoulder hard, getting bone. There was a muffled scream and the gun was waving and it went off, so loud you felt it, and he rolled me off, but toward the Boxer, and I fell between the front seats. I writhed and kicked and the Boxer was slamming my head with his fist as he drove, his other hand on the wheel.

And I wriggled down, wrists cuffed behind me, my face gashed by buttons and knobs. I slid lower, the knobs against my shoulder now, twisted again and squeezed my head against metal, my shoulder against the Boxer's leg, his shoe, his foot on the gas pedal.

I rammed his foot. The motor roared. I held the foot and pedal down.

The Boxer hollered, "No!" I braced myself with my feet against the seat. He twisted his foot but I had it pinned. The motor was whining, the van shaking and the others screaming now, and then the van was turning, the tires starting to squeal, louder and louder and then no squeal at all.

And it was turning over and there was an explosion near my head and then a crash and everything was whirling and whipping, tearing and grinding and shouting and screaming, and something was on my legs.

The van was still. I couldn't move.

Forty-four.

"I thought I was gonna talk to the newspaper," Drague said, sitting in the back of Donatelli's unmarked car, next to the wreck, the ambulances, the radio cars. Children ringed the scene, eyes bright, nerve ends electrified by sirens, lights, guns and blood.

"You will," I said. "I called them. They're on their way."

They'd pulled me free after an eternity, using a tool that pried the dashboard off my shoulder. The Boxer was gone by then, taken to the hospital for treatment of a few broken bones. A cop rode with him in the ambulance. Another rode with the bolt-cutter guy, who had been thrown from the wreck. They called it massive head injuries. They didn't think he'd live.

But I was okay. The young guy, the one on the phone, was okay, too.

The Boxer had told the radio-car cops that his name was Dannigan and he was a police officer, but he didn't have ID. The guns that had rattled around inside the van had burned-off numbers, and so did the Ruger nine millimeter they found stuck in the Boxer's belt.

I said Dannigan and the others were taking us to be

executed. And yes, I knew Dannigan was an investigator with the office of the Manhattan district attorney.

The radio cops had looked at each other.

"What a cluster," one of them said.

I asked them to call Donatelli and Ramirez, and they did.

And I learned later that in the back of Donatelli's car, right there in the lot, Drague started talking, pouring the story out as fast as he could, because after all, I had said it was his insurance, his ticket to the big time. He talked about the payments, the hunt for the rich girl, the words gushing out like there was a bilge pump inside him. Ramirez and Donatelli listened and then Donatelli got out of the car and walked to the radio car where I was telling a Bronx precinct detective the story for the third time.

"He says he's gonna make Sammy the Bull look like a fifty-dollar snitch," Donatelli said to me. "You think he's for real?"

"Yeah," I said. "It all adds up."

It was another day turned into a blur of endless questions and cold, bad coffee. We finally emerged in the late afternoon at Police Headquarters. Donatelli said he'd been interrogating the young guy, who turned out to be from Newark and was wanted on a warrant out of Las Vegas, where he'd shot a man in the knee while working as an enforcer for a loan shark.

This time, he said, he'd been hired by the Boxer to shut somebody up. The Boxer's lawyer had arrived and told him not to say another word.

And then, after one last question, glances around the table, it was over. When I left Police Headquarters, Donatelli and Ramirez walked me down to the foyer. We were talked out, exhausted. Donatelli shook my hand, and said he'd like to bring his wife and boys to Maine sometime, maybe see a moose. I told him to save my number. Ramirez shook my hand, too, her grip more firm than her partner's. She said she wouldn't apologize because it was her job to be skeptical.

"But I'm glad I was wrong," Ramirez said.

"Jeez," Donatelli said. "I can't believe what I'm hearing. Let me get that on tape."

As we stood there, we heard a rush of voices behind us. It was George Drague being escorted out the front door by two detectives, past a couple of camera crews and a print photographer. Drague waved the cameras off as he was escorted to the Lincoln, the door of which was held open by Gerard, the *Times* security guard. D. Robert Sanders got out and helped Drague in.

A very bad man, he was, for that day, maybe for a few more, worth his weight in gold.

Forty-five.

I left the police station and walked through the park, where a woman was feeding pigeons, a guy in a suit was working at a laptop and tourists were admiring historic City Hall.

I walked past them and started up the steps.

The detective inside the door was talking to a pretty woman in a suit. He distractedly asked me where I was from. Turning away from him, I said Maine but probably could have said Mars. What's to guard in the henhouse when the chickens have been killed?

He looked at me for a moment, then ran a metal detector up and down and I was in. I glanced down the hall, past the graceful gates that barred the public from what had been Johnny Fiore's offices. There was a woman behind a counter, and another security guard, but they looked more somber than watchful.

I walked past the press office, saw the reporters at their computers, continued on to the pay phone in the alcove, where it always had been. There was a city directory and I looked up the number and dialed.

A young woman answered and I asked for Dave Conroy. She said he was in conference, could she take a message? I said, "Tell him Jack McMorrow called. I'll be in the Governor's Room, upstairs. I'll wait."

So I did, in the second-floor room with the big chandeliers and the walls lined with oil paintings of people who had made their mark. John Jay. George Washington. Alexander Hamilton. All dutifully portrayed for posterity by John Trumbull.

And then I turned and there he was.

I was standing at the end of the room, in front of one of the marble fireplaces. There was a security guard at the far end of the room, a woman who was yawning and checking her watch. When she saw Conroy, she straightened up. When I saw him, I smiled, gave a little wave.

He walked toward me, in his navy suit, his little tasseled shoes. He tried to appear composed but I could see it in his eyes. The wildness of panic.

"Hello, Jack," Conroy said, as though he still could make things right.

"David," I said.

We shook hands.

"I was looking at the luminaries," I said. "A real who's who, isn't it?"

Conroy looked around at the paintings.

"Yes. The best and the brightest," he said. "Some truly amazing men."

I looked at him.

"This is what you wanted, wasn't it?"

He looked puzzled.

"Not for you," I said. "For Fiore. You wanted him to be the kind of person who gets his painting on the wall. You wanted him to do great things."

"He did," Conroy said.

"I don't know," I said. "A hundred years from now will they care that he locked up a bunch of street-corner drug dealers?"

"Johnny Fiore did more than that, McMorrow. He was a great man. If he'd had more time, he would have been president. He would have been a great president."

"But he had to get there one step at a time, didn't he?"

"I don't know what you mean, McMorrow."

Conroy gazed at the paintings, a smile pasted on his pale face.

"He had to make the next rung on the ladder. From DA to mayor. Mayor to Senate. Senate to the White House."

"So? Listen, McMorrow, I've got a meeting."

"I'll bet you do. Got a lawyer yet?"

"Listen, I thought you had something important to—"

"I do, David. I want to tell you I understand how much you did for Fiore. You haven't gotten enough credit for what you did for him."

"I didn't do it for credit," he said. "That's not my role."

"Oh, I know. You're the behind-the-scenes guy, the worshipful acolyte. The guy who saw the crime numbers coming down in '88. Remember that?"

He shook his head.

"McMorrow, spare me your conspiracist fantasies."

"And you knew some people wouldn't vote for Johnny Fiore if they weren't afraid. I mean, the guy was a Democrat, but he still needed to pull those Republican votes in to put him over the top. He needed crossovers. He needed minorities. He needed everybody to be scared to go outside."

"McMorrow, I'm sorry, but I don't really have time—"

"And crime waves are funny things. Unpredictable. And damn, if things didn't calm down that summer. Who could have predicted? What, all the criminals go to the Hamptons? And the election a few months away? So you ordered up a crime wave, didn't you? Kind of like you order Chinese. What did it cost you? Fifty grand? A hundred? You can buy a lot of crime for a hundred grand."

"Oh, this is fantasy, McMorrow."

"I don't think so. I don't think the police think so. They've got George Drague over there. But you knew that, right?"

"They don't tell me about every petty criminal they arrest."

"And Dannigan. They got him at the same time."

"So he's a crooked cop. I'm not his boss. I had little to do with the man."

"He's got a lawyer, still trying to save himself, but he'll take a deal. He'll flip. And Drague is absolutely spilling his guts. And you know, he says he's got you on tape. Smarter than he looks, I guess."

Conroy went white. He tried to swallow but couldn't.

"So if you wanted to make a deal with me to keep things quiet, I can't help you. It's too late."

We stood there, not speaking. The security guard woman approached and tapped her watch. He waved her off.

"And Drague, he's not just talking to the cops," I said. "He going to the *Times* today, then tabloids, TV. I think he's got some idea he can sell the movie rights. 'A Rapist for Hire.' You know, these days it might happen. It's a perverse time we live in, don't you think? Good guys turn out to be bad guys and sickos are turned into celebrities."

Conroy didn't answer. His breath was coming in short little huffs.

"So it won't leak out in dribs and drabs, David. It's going to come out in one big splash. The *Times* tomorrow. Everybody else piling on after that. Did you get the call yet? Did you know what it was about? I figure they'll have to bring the U.S. attorney in because of Dannigan and you working for the city. What an indictment this'll be. God, the conspiracy charges alone. And then they'll want to know what happened to Lester John and Ortiz. That bastard who broke Christina Mansell's fingers, he'll flip for sure. He'll be a regular gymnast."

Conroy was gray. Sweat had broken out on his upper lip like a string of transparent pearls.

"I suppose you could try to dump it all on Fiore," I said. "I mean, he can't defend himself now, can he? Or was that the idea, David? Was he in on it from the beginning? What was it, the small sacrifice for the greater good? Or did he find out later and threaten to hang you and everybody else? Is that why you stuck him in the bathroom there?''

"I didn't," Conroy hissed, his little white teeth showing. "I wouldn't. Everything I did was for him. For the last ten years. Everything. And we did great things. We transformed this city. We made it a place you can live in again. We made it great again. Don't you forget it.''

"But it's all gone to hell, hasn't it? Even the timing. This'll come out, and I bet even the second-day story will be right up there beside Fiore's funeral. Right there in the *Times*, the newspaper of record. Forever and ever.''

I looked around at the paintings.

"No portrait for your boy, David.''

"You goddamn bastard, McMorrow,'' Conroy exploded, and he kept saying it over and over, his white fists clenched at his side, until the words petered out into a gasp and a sob.

"You know, Dave, if a cop were in this situation, he might eat his gun, as they say. I wonder what somebody like you does. Choke yourself on a memo?''

And I stepped around him and, with his eyes closed, Conroy said, "It's all ruined. It's all ruined.''

And he was right. Johnny Fiore would be remembered for nothing else but this, for as long as he would be remembered at all. His accomplishments, his contribution, his years of public service, all forgotten. He would forever be the New York mayor who bought a crime wave.

And as I was leaving the room, I almost stopped right there.

It was all ruined. Wrecked. Smeared.

Sullied.

When I got to the Bull and Thistle that night, the regulars were trickling in, patting each other on the back, hoisting their beers, treating themselves to the fleeting comfort of camaraderie.

I sat at the same table where I had sat with Butch. The

same guy was behind the bar and the same waitress was working the back of the room. I ordered a pint of Guinness, and when the waitress served it, she gave me a second look.

"That's right," I said. "I'm the same guy."

She went back to the bar and said something to the bartender. He glanced over and then quickly turned away. I sipped and ran through it again.

It couldn't have been Conroy who killed Fiore, I thought. But it could have been Dannigan, if something had happened. Maybe Fiore hadn't been in on the whole thing. Maybe he had threatened to blow the whistle. But then why Butch? Why was he there? Why were his bloody prints in the bathroom stall?

Maybe he found Fiore and ran away. Maybe he was stalking Fiore, going to tell him off again. And he walked in on the mayor's dead body. And he was drunk, so he fled.

Except he didn't.

I pictured Butch, hurrying up the sidewalk after he'd said good-bye to me. His quick, short strides. His call that he'd get me the stuff. I saw him backing away. Something in his eyes. A sharpness. A purpose.

The waitress passed and I waved her over.

"That night," I said, "did you—"

"I'm not allowed to talk about it," she said.

"What about the bartender? Can he talk about it?"

"He's not supposed to talk about it either."

"Says who?" I said, but she already was walking away.

I looked over at him. He was making some sort of drink in a shaker. The bartender had known Butch, I was sure of it that night. But when I'd said something, Butch had brushed it off and launched right into that story about somebody shooting somebody else. Was the bartender somebody Butch had put away? God, Butch was lucky the guy hadn't put something in his whiskey. He was lucky—

Or was he?

I got up from the table and walked to the end of the bar. The bartender waited as long as he could and then walked over.

"Another Guinness?"

"No, thanks. I just want to talk to you for a minute."

"Kind of busy."

"It's kind of important."

"Yeah, well, what I do here is kind of important, too," he said, pouring the shaken drink into a glass.

"I'll bet," I said. "I'll bet you're glad to have a job like this. Get to meet all kinds of different people. Actors. Students. Cops."

He looked at me.

"He arrested you once, didn't he?"

"What?"

"Butch Casey arrested you."

"Nah. You got the wrong guy."

"I don't think so. Were you the guy who shot the other guy having an affair with his wife? Or was it some other homicide he worked?"

"Hey, buddy. I don't know what you're talking about, but in about two seconds you're gonna be out on the sidewalk."

"Why don't you just call the cops? I know a couple of detectives. Talk to them twice a day. I think they'd be glad to check your ID, run your prints."

"Hey, I'm not doing anything wrong. I'm not bothering nobody."

"Did your time, and now you're keeping a low profile? But I wonder. The people who own this place know where you really were all those years? They know why?"

He stepped quickly to me.

"Shut up."

"I guess not," I said.

"It's old news," the thin man said.

"I suppose. But what'd you think when Butch Casey came in?"

"He came in here a lot."

"Never blew your cover?"

He shook his head, almost imperceptibly.

"Did he want free drinks?"

"No."

"Cops on the mayor thing know you knew Butch? How you knew him?"

He looked away.

"I didn't think so," I said. "What, you change your name? Come in here with a fake identity?"

The thin man looked around the bar. The waitress came back with her tray and he looked at me and smiled.

"Is that right?" he said loudly.

"Three Sam Adams," the waitress said.

He opened the bottles and handed them over. The waitress motored off.

"So," I said, "you and Butch had this little secret."

"He was a good guy," the thin man said, looking into the beer cooler. "He wasn't out to screw anybody. What do you want?"

"I want to know what happened that night."

"I was right here. Got nothing to do with me. I saw it on TV like everybody else."

"That's right. You were right here, serving drinks to the guy who once arrested you, and now they say he went directly from here to killing the mayor."

He gave me a hard look.

"Get lost," he said.

I reached over the bar and picked up the shaker.

"Fine. I'll take this and have them run the prints on it. See who you really are."

He snatched the shaker back. I smiled.

"Okay, I'll take my glass. I'll send somebody else in here and have them get served. Or maybe I won't. Maybe I'll leave tonight and never come back, never say a word."

The guy half-turned, his pale blue eyes narrowed to slits.

"What do you want? Money? 'Cause I don't have any."

"I don't, either. Don't need it. I want something else."

He looked at me.

"I want you to make me the same drink you made Butch that night."

He stared.

"You can send it over with the waitress," I said. "And then I've got to go. The cops want to talk to me some more. Two detectives. Ramirez and Donatelli. I'm sure they'd be glad to talk to you. Or not."

I walked back to the table and sat down. I took a swallow of Guinness. I waited. And in a couple of minutes, the waitress delivered my drink.

It was whiskey, a double shot in a rocks glass. I held it up and sniffed. Felt the blood drain from my face, then a heavy, pressing sadness.

I took a sip.

"Oh, well," I said aloud and pushed the glass away.

Butch hadn't been drinking. He'd been sober. He'd been ready.

He had been drinking tea.

So they gave Drague good play in the *Times* the next day, right side above the fold, in a package with two other stories: an advance on the route of the funeral procession, and a political analysis on maneuvering within the Democratic Party as a result of Fiore's death. There was a refer line to a Lifestyle story about how the city already was dressed for mourning because everyone wore black.

But Drague was the lead.

In the story, written by Sanders, Drague called himself "a terrorist for hire." He said he was paid by high-level officials in the office of Manhattan District Attorney John Fiore to commit a crime that would strike fear in the hearts of law-abiding New Yorkers. The police commissioner said Drague's claims were being investigated, as would any charges of police or prosecutorial corruption.

When asked if there appeared to be any basis to the

accusations, the commissioner said only that Drague's claims were being taken "very seriously."

And then it unfolded, a mushroom cloud of scandal.

The morning the story broke, David Conroy was found dead in his SoHo co-op. He'd taken an entire bottle of Secanol, washed down with Absolut. The *Daily News* was the only paper to report the flavor of the vodka as citron. According to a police source, Conroy had served it to himself ice cold.

He left a note apologizing for his actions and the disgrace he brought on the city. He said Fiore knew of the crime-wave plan in concept, but was kept insulated from the particulars. The mayor left it to Conroy to keep the secret, which is what he had been trying to do, right up until the end. He said he didn't expect anyone to be killed but the criminals got carried away.

Leslie Casey was just in the wrong place at the wrong time.

And who could have known the woman would be a policeman's wife? Conroy wrote. *What were the odds?*

That was reported Friday in all the dailies. On Friday night, my friend Stephanie Cooper broke a story that said the Boxer, Matthew Dannigan, and the young guy from Vegas were negotiating a plea bargain. The young guy was fingering the Boxer. The Boxer was laying the whole thing at the feet of Conroy and Fiore.

The Boxer said he was ordered by Conroy to orchestrate the crime wave in 1988 in order to "bump" the numbers. The general plan was approved by Fiore himself, the Boxer understood. Conroy later ordered the murders of Ortiz and Yolimar because they wanted more money. Lester John made the mistake of coming back to New York; he was buried at sea in a bale of garbage. Mihailov was killed because he was a loose end and I was asking questions; Drague would have been dead if I hadn't found him first.

And that night the guy thrown from the van died of his injuries.

And it went from there, story after story, news spot

after news spot. And of course, none of it could be denied, not by dead men. Not by Johnny Fiore.

That, after all, was the plan. I knew because Butch told me.

After he'd pleaded guilty.

Forty-six.

Butch took the plea in exchange for life without possibility of parole.

The killing of his wife was the mitigating factor, but still this caused a couple of days of uproar in the city, where many people thought Butch should be executed. His plea also caused much disappointment in the media, which had to scrap big plans for coverage of his trial.

Having denied the press and public those small pleasures, Butch went quietly.

We met at Riker's in November. I came down from Maine with Roxanne to spend that promised weekend at the Meridien and to attend Christina's opening at a gallery on Broome Street. The paintings were part of a series called "Scars: New York City." They showed minutely detailed sections of pavement, each with a bloodstain and a flower or a blade of grass.

The *Times* covered the show. Christina was there with her new beau, her orthopedic surgeon, who did knee replacements for heads of state. He looked like Warren Beatty; Christina looked lovely, in a short black sheath and red splints on her surgically repaired fingers.

She kissed me, hugged Roxanne.

"You doing all right?" I said.

"Sometimes," Christina said, and then she turned away to her newfound public.

For them, she was charming. Many of the people there were apparently celebrities, the kind who get their pictures on the *Times* party page. As we were leaving, she was telling the *Times* critic that the attack had forced her not only to learn how to paint again, but to learn how to see.

He nodded seriously and took notes. Three weeks later, Christina would make the cover of *New York* magazine. In the photo, she stared unsmiling, a palette knife between her splinted fingers.

"Out of the Ashes," the headline said. "Painter Christina Mansell Ushers in the Post-Fiore Era."

At the hotel that night, I turned off the light and opened the drapes and Roxanne stood naked by the bed in the city glow and then slipped in beside me.

"Hey, darlin'," I said, as she nestled against me.

"You're sure you wouldn't rather have a glamorous big-city blonde?"

"No," I said. "I wouldn't rather."

"What would you rather?" Roxanne asked, and then she kissed me and touched me in the place Christina had touched, in the city where Christina had wanted me and part of me had wanted Christina. And Roxanne's touch was like absolution.

After we made love, she slept. I got up early and caught a cab to Riker's Island. It was raining and there was something very solemn about the long bridge and the river, with its dull gray chop. The penitentiary was gray and dull, too.

So I sat in the little visiting booth, with the Plexiglas wall and the speaking grill, and the obscenities carved in the counter. And then I heard that universal prison clank and clunk, and there he was, dressed in pale blue like a hospital intern.

We couldn't shake hands so we held them up, like an

Indian greeting in an old movie. We picked up the phones.

Butch smiled and asked me how my trip was. I said it was fine. I asked him how he was and he said he was okay. He asked me how Roxanne was and I said she was good.

"And your buddy there? Clair?"

"He's fine. Back in Maine, getting wood in."

"That's right. Gotta keep the farmhouse warm."

"Right."

"You can have the cold. I can't stand it. Guess I don't have to worry now, huh?"

He smiled. Looked down at his hand. I thought of us as kids, all the times he'd given me a hand up, a pat on the back. Butch scratched at something on his finger and then looked up at me.

"So, Jackie."

"So."

"It got a little rougher than I thought it would. Sorry about that."

I shrugged but didn't answer.

"But I had to bring you in. You were the only one I knew who could pull it off. Get it out there. And Jesus, we brought down the whole house of cards, didn't we?"

He grinned.

"Yeah. I guess."

"You see, I didn't know anybody else who could do the reporting part. I knew they couldn't just blow you off."

I didn't answer.

"I mean, I coulda just gone to the press first, but you know what would've happened. They would've said, 'Ah, he's just some ex-cop with an ax to grind.' "

"Maybe."

"And even if they tried to check it out, you know what Fiore would have done. He'd have all the answers. An explanation for everything. And who are they gonna believe? Butch Casey or Johnny Fiore? You know what I'm saying? He would've laughed them out of his goddamn office. They'd all have a good laugh on old Butch. A good laugh after they killed his wife.''

He drifted away for a moment, then came back.

''Well, I guess we know who had the last laugh, don't we?''

I looked at him.

''So that was the plan? 'Kill. Sully.' ''

''Yeah. Did I tell you about that?''

''No, I read it on a napkin at that Sisters place.''

''No kidding? Huh. Well, it worked, didn't it? He's gone. And there ain't gonna be any statue for Fiore now, is there? And kids won't read good things about him in the history books. I mean, he'll be right in there with CIA traitors and all the other goddamn cowards.''

''Maybe.''

''And you know, Jackie, that hits him where it really hurts. The man wanted to be remembered. For good things, I mean.''

''Right.''

''He wanted to get his name on some building, on plaques and all this shit. Ha.''

Butch leaned forward, his eyes bright, his mouth fixed in a toothy, voracious smile.

''I fixed him. I fixed him forever.''

''You could have gotten me killed, Butch,'' I said.

''Ah, Jack. Those mutts? That punk from Vegas and Dannigan? The guy's a loser. You know, I heard when he was a rookie in California someplace, he ran on his partner and got him shot. And Conroy, that little wimp.''

''That little wimp was calling the shots.''

''And now he's offed himself. Sayonara, sucker.''

''Butch, they killed three people. They could have killed three or four more.''

''Jack.''

''You shouldn't have done it, Butch. You shouldn't have done it to me. You shouldn't have done it to the city.''

He leaned back and his expression hardened.

''Hey, Jackie,'' Butch said. ''The city? They can't

stand the truth, tough. And you, Jackie, you're a pal. We go way back. I mean, right to the beginning. Our dads and all that. I like you a lot. Love you, even. Like a little brother.''

I waited.

''But I loved Leslie more. And I wasn't gonna let her just get forgotten. I had to get them back. For her. And this was the only way to do it. The only way.''

''Was it just that?''

Butch didn't answer.

''How many murders did you investigate over the years, Butch? How many of those people—the survivors, I mean—how many of them got over it?''

He shrugged. His face was somber.

''Most, right? They may not have ever been the same, but they didn't throw their lives away. What was it you told me when we were kids? You suck it up and you keep going. But you didn't.''

Butch looked away. He licked his lips, then turned back to me and smiled.

''Jackie the reporter,'' he said. ''Always got one more question. Well, my friend, maybe that 'Suck it up' advice doesn't apply when it's your wife who got shot in the face. And you don't have a house full of kids to come home to. And you're just alone, I mean, so alone it's like this weight is on you, just crushing you to death, every minute, every second, until you don't know whether you can go on. You don't know if you can take your next breath.''

''Was it just being alone that was crushing you?''

Butch smiled.

''Oh, Jack, I told you I'd tell, didn't I? Tell you why I was late to pick her up.''

''Yeah, you did.''

I waited. Butch took a deep breath.

''It's kinda stupid, really. I wish it was more earth-shaking. I really do. I was supposed to pick her up. She was gonna leave her car in the lot at the hospital and we'd go home together. But I was having a coupla drinks. With this TV reporter. She had questions about a case I was working. Then we got talking about my book idea. I kept saying to myself, 'Just ten more minutes.' But she was cute and was kinda cuddling up to me. Vanity is everything and all that.''

Butch gave an unfunny laugh. Shook his head.

"So you used me,'' I said. "Because you felt guilty.''

He shrugged.

"Yeah, in a way. But it was Fiore who gave the order. Said it was okay to do all this. Pound that lady into a vegetable. Rape that girl. Hammer that kid for his Beemer. And kill my wife.''

Butch leaned forward, looked through the glass at me.

"It was the principle, Jackie. You should understand that. You of all people.''

I looked away, thinking of Christina hung up by the hands, my name on her skin. I remembered being chased across the roofs, the gun on my head. The guy asking, could he kill me now? So they'd deserved what they'd gotten. And Fiore himself?

I remembered a little boy who fought for his father's honor on the school playground. It was the principle.

So no, I didn't condone. Yes, I did understand.

Me, of all people.

"So,'' I said, after a moment. "How did you get at him?''

"Well, I had to be on my toes,'' Butch said, excitement in his voice. "That's why I didn't drink or anything. I'm in the back of the room and he's in there, all the muckymucks kissing his ass, and he says something to Conroy and Conroy comes back, and he doesn't see me but he says to the detective, 'Clear the men's room.' So the detective, he goes in and checks it out. He comes out, somebody calls to him. Fiore's still working his way through the crowd. I slip behind the cop, go in and stand on the toilet, wait for Fiore to come in. But he comes through the door in about two seconds. I had gloves, but I'm trying to get 'em on quick and I poke a hole in one

of the fingers. I guess that's how they got the print. Then
again, it's not like I really cared about getting away with
it. Just so the job gets done, right?''

I nodded.

''Anyway, his pants jingle in the next stall. He's sitting
down. I pop the door open and there he is. His eyes bug
out. And I've got this ice pick, sharpened like a needle.''

I took a deep breath.

''So did you say anything to him before you did it?''

He hesitated.

''Two words,'' Butch said. ''For Leslie.''

''Did he know what you meant?''

''He knew. I could see it in his eyes.''

''And what'd he say?''

''Nothing. For once in his goddamn life, Johnny Fiore
didn't say a word.''

Epilogue

It was November and the roadside was thick with leaves washed from the Prosperity woods by a cold, heavy rain. As we walked, Roxanne leaned against me.

"So what did he say in this letter?" Roxanne said.

"About the same. Said he saw Donatelli and Ramirez on *Larry King*. I guess she had a makeover. Talking about investigating the homicide of the decade or something like that. I guess they have a big book contract or something."

"Huh."

"And Butch asked me if I knew Ramirez had a kid who died. And he wanted to talk about books. He said he's going to read everything by Nathaniel Hawthorne because he heard Hawthorne came up with all these great ideas just sitting in a little room."

"Like being in solitary."

"Right."

"So he acts like nothing happened?"

"Yeah, in a way."

"You going to write back?"

"Yeah, I guess so."

"You really can forgive him?"

"I don't know."

"You don't feel betrayed?"

"Sure, I do. Used. Burned. But mostly I feel like that little circle of people you think you really know and trust has gotten a little smaller. But maybe that's life. The circle gets smaller until you're the only one left. Come in alone. Go out alone."

"Jack," Roxanne said, "don't think that."

"I don't, really. And I don't want to be all angry and bitter forever. We only have so much time here. I don't want to spend my time like that."

"How do you want to spend it?"

"Like this," I said.

Roxanne took my hand and we kept walking. We passed Clair's house and then his barn, where smoke was coming from the chimney above the workshop. Through the window, we could see Clair working. From the road, we could hear Mozart.

And then we were home.

Since Butch and Fiore, we'd stripped it as bare as the trees, our haven from what Clair called the culture of distraction.

The walls were painted white. There was a bed, a desk, a table and a computer. The shelves were full of books, the television gathered dust and the phone line ran directly to an answering machine. I returned calls from Roxanne, from the *Times* Boston bureau, from Ellen Jones, who had included me on a couple of national projects.

I didn't return calls from George Drague's lawyer-turned-agent, from nutcases who read the Fiore assassination web page on the Internet, from talk-radio hosts, newspaper reporters and television producers who still phoned occasionally. One had phoned that afternoon, while we walked.

He was from a television news show. Its name didn't matter, nor did his. But I listened to his breathless pitch as he tried to convey the urgent need to talk that day, that afternoon, that minute.

"I think it's time," the man said, "that we put this Fiore thing in perspective."

Oh, but I've already done that, I thought, as he futilely recited his phone numbers. Fiore and Conroy wanted that painting on the wall. Butch wanted revenge. They wanted all of it too much. There was a lot of good in them, but it was tainted.